By J.S. Cook

Because You Despise Me

KILDEVIL COVE MURDER MYSTERIES
Dark Water
Dark Mire

Published by DSP Publications
www.dsppublications.com

DARK MIRE

J.S. COOK

DSP PUBLICATIONS

Published by

DSP PUBLICATIONS

5032 Capital Circle SW, Suite 2, PMB# 279, Tallahassee, FL 32305-7886 USA
www.dsppublications.com

Dark Mire
© 2021 J.S. Cook

Cover Art
© 2021 L.C. Chase
http://www.lcchase.com
Cover content is for illustrative purposes only and any person depicted on the cover is a model.

Trade Paperback ISBN: 978-1-64405-899-2
Digital ISBN: 978-1-64405-898-5
Trade Paperback published March 2021
v. 1.0

Printed in the United States of America
∞
This paper meets the requirements of
ANSI/NISO Z39.48-1992 (Permanence of Paper).

For Paul.

ACKNOWLEDGEMENTS

A HUGE thank you is due to Elizabeth North, publisher of Dreamspinner Press Publications, and all the editors, artists, designers, and behind-the-scenes administrative staff who put their efforts into seeing this book to publication, especially Andi Byassee, without whom this book would not exist in its present form.

DARK MIRE

J.S. COOK

DSP PUBLICATIONS

PROLOGUE

MUCH TOO early to be out here picking berries, and she wouldn't be anyway. The old woman—Eileen, Azariah's mother—had made sure to fill her head with old wives' tales about the unwary being fairy-led, enticed away to some foreign country not of this world and made to live in slavery. "They'll play you the finest music you ever heard, my dear, and you mightn't want to dance but you will. Oh, you'll dance all right. Dance till ye dies."

She shuddered reflexively, her usual response any time the old woman crossed her mind. Yes, she was Azariah's mother, and it was only right they take on the care and housing of her, especially now she was so feeble. "It's the right thing to do," he'd said. "She brought me up when Dad was down in the lumber woods, working all the time. I owes her that much, and blood is blood."

Yes, blood is blood, she thought now. Blood drove her out here onto the barrens, away from Eileen's incessant complaining, her constant talk and dire warnings. And it was blood that would try to bring her back, the hardening and stinging of her overfull breasts, ready to let down milk the moment young Barry cried for it. But the baby, too, had driven her outdoors. Ever since she brought him home from the hospital, he'd seemed to do nothing but cry, wailing inconsolably, face red and fists clenched. The nurses told her she'd bond with him, but so far the overwhelming love she'd expected to feel was noticeably absent.

She hadn't even wanted children, but Azariah had insisted. Having children was what you did, and his Apostolic Pentecostal faith dictated you have as many as possible. Breeding and raising the Lord's army was the highest calling a woman could aspire to. If only she had known, she might have chosen differently. Her friends, even the psychiatrist she had been seeing in St. John's, had encouraged her to think about it carefully. But she'd been mad in love with him, had willfully closed her eyes to his family's extreme beliefs. When he told her to stop cutting her hair, she'd obeyed; similarly, she'd agreed when he asked her to stop wearing cosmetics, to trade her skintight jeans for more modest ankle-length skirts. It had been worth it in the beginning. She knew Azariah loved her, was utterly devoted to her, and she loved him. She'd spent too long living an ungodly life, ricocheting from man to man, selling herself cheap in the bars and nightclubs of St. John's.

But this latest was the final straw, the one that broke her back.

"We'll get started on the next one as soon as possible," he'd told her. "That's what God wants." Even though she was just out of hospital and still bleeding heavily, he'd forced her legs apart and drove himself inside of her.

"We're supposed to wait six weeks," she protested. "That's what the doctor said." The birth had been a difficult one, and the baby's head had ripped her open. "I'm too sore."

"This is what God wants," he repeated. When he finally rolled off her, the sheets were soaked in her blood. "Mam'll see to ye," he told her.

The old woman had come with fresh cabbage leaves and made a compress for her. It didn't help. Eventually the bleeding stopped of its own accord, but the doctor's stitches had come apart where Azariah's zeal had torn her open again. Eileen gave her something to drink that made her nauseated and eventually sleepy, and she fell into a stupor. When she finally woke, an entire day had passed, and the baby was crying. The baby was always crying. She rose and washed herself, dressed in jeans and rubber boots and a thick wool sweater, layered her raincoat over it. Still only April, and the weather was capricious this time of year. It might rain for days, or it might snow—you never knew. She pulled a knitted cap over her hair and shoved a pair of gloves into her coat pocket. Eileen stopped her at the door.

"Where do you think you're going?" she asked.

"I'm going for a walk."

"And that you're not!" The old woman was furious. "That baby has been in there crying. He wants feeding, and you're going to feed him." She grabbed Deborah's arm between her stick-thin fingers and pinched her cruelly. "You get in that room and feed that youngster."

"Feed him yourself!" Deborah yanked her arm from the old woman's grasp.

Eileen was outraged. "Ye'll burn in hell for this."

Deborah spun away from her and reached for the latch on the outer storm door. It was rusted, in need of replacement or repair, like most things around this place. The house itself was little better than a tilt, a hastily built structure of salvaged wood and stone, a ramshackle dwelling that all but advertised the misery within. "I don't believe in hell!"

"It's shocking, that's what it is. Pure shocking. Ye're his mother—"

Deborah rounded on her. "I never wanted the fucking youngster in the first place." She slapped her palm upwards against the latch, and it finally gave, but not before scraping her fingers painfully. She swore and then put her damaged fingers in her mouth, sucking. With a push the door opened, and she was out.

She was free.

A light but insistent drizzle was falling, the thin stream of water sifting down upon her, wetting her curly dark hair. She set out at a fast pace, moving uphill from the house and striking out across the strip of boggy ground that separated her from the road. She had no clear plan in mind. She'd get out to the high road and hitch-hike into St. John's, get work in one of the clubs down on George Street. Sure, she'd just had a baby, but it would be no time before she got her figure back, and then they'd see something. She hadn't lost her confidence. She could twirl around the pole with the best of them. As for Azariah, she was finished with him. He could do as he liked, and his mother too. No doubt they'd decry her as a fallen woman, an unfit mother who abandoned her days-old infant to his fate. Well, that was too bad. Needs must when the devil drove.

She had just crossed in front of the old United Church when she heard it, a thin sound like a cat's meow. At first she thought the everpresent wind was playing tricks on her, the way there sometimes seemed to be voices in it, hissing and singing. The old woman said the dead were all around, and if you had ears to listen, you could hear them whispering. But Deborah thought that was so much shite. Like most things Eileen said, one'd be well advised to take it with a heavy dose of salt.

"Hello?" She felt like an idiot, standing by herself in the lane and calling out into the darkness, but what if someone was there? What if an animal or child had fallen into the ditch and injured themselves? She'd never forgive herself if she let an animal suffer. She loved animals. "Is someone there?" She heard it again, the same low cry. "Do you need help? Are you hurt or something?"

"Missus, I fell down." The voice came from behind her now, and she whirled around. A small girl stood there, grinning broadly. Her long curly dark hair was pulled back in a yellow ribbon, and she was wearing a party dress, also yellow. She was barefoot and wore no coat or hat. "Can ye help me go home?"

"Go home?"

"It's over there." The girl turned and pointed back in the direction Deborah had come, towards the barrens. "Mam'll be awful worried about me." As if on cue, she started to cry, such a sudden eruption of violent weeping that Deborah took a step back, startled and discomfited.

"She'll smack me," the child wailed. She lunged forward and grabbed Deborah's hand, squeezed so hard it hurt. "I don't want to get smacked. Please, missus."

The drizzle thickened into rain: hard, spattering drops that felt like there was ice in them. Deborah pulled her hood over her head and squinted into the deluge. "Where are we going?"

"Just over here."

The girl tugged on her hand, propelling her forward with preternatural strength. They crossed the high road and continued, passing Driscoll's Road and the outskirts of the town, heading in a southerly direction. Deborah could smell the sea in the distance, but it was growing fainter, and the foliage around them began to thicken, the surrounding trees seeming taller now, almost blotting out the sky. They had long since left the road and were travelling down a narrow, muddy path that wound its way around boulders and tree roots. Several times Deborah stumbled and would have fallen but for the girl's insistent and often painful grip on her hand. It felt like she had been walking for hours, and her feet hurt.

"I can't keep going," she told the girl. "I don't think you're leading me anywhere at all."

"We're almost there," the girl assured her. She turned back, and in the darkness her face seemed lit with an unnatural glow. "You'll love it. Sure, they'll be having a party."

"A party?" Deborah scoffed. "Yes, mind now."

And then she heard the music, accordions and fiddles, and a woman's voice singing something unutterably sweet and beautiful. They emerged into a grassy clearing, roughly circular in shape, with a neat white house at its centre, all the windows lit up with a warm golden glow. There would be people in that house, Deborah thought, and perhaps a cup of tea, and she could get in the warm and rest herself and think about what she wanted to do.

"See?" the girl said. "I told you." She called something Deborah couldn't make out, the door was flung open, and a woman about Deborah's own age was framed there.

"Elena?" the woman called. "Is that you?" She peered into the darkness. "And you're after bringing us a visitor." As Deborah neared the house, the woman held out both hands to her, clasped her wrists, and drew her inside. "We're right glad to see ye," she said. She was beautiful. No, Deborah thought, not merely beautiful but… luminous. She seemed to glow from within the same way the girl had just now. Her eyes were the palest green, and her hair was the burnished red of a blasty bough, and her skin as pale as milk. "Come and warm yourself a while by the fire."

The house was larger inside than it had initially appeared, and a great round table, set with many places, was groaning with food: platters of roasted birds and wild game, grouse and moose meat, whole salmon laid out glistening with salt, and bowls filled with boiled vegetables, potatoes and carrots and fresh turnip greens. It wasn't even the season for greens. That was July or August, and this was April. It was April, wasn't it? It had been April when she left the house. It had definitely been April. The room was full of people, some sitting by the fireplace—enormous, vast, giving off a glorious heat—while others were lined along the walls. Several musicians were playing instruments, and people rose to dance in the centre of the massive—yes, it was massive; the room was absolutely huge—ballroom, whirling each other merrily in a lively reel.

Someone rose from one of the chairs by the fire and pressed a glass into her hand. "Have a drop of stuff, my dear. It'll warm ye to the marrow of your bones."

The brew tasted of honey and lavender. The room was warm. A tall young man with dancing dark eyes whirled her into the reel, and Deborah was laughing as she hadn't laughed in ages, not since marrying Azariah and coming to this awful place. She let the man swing her around, and the room went past at a dizzying rate; she could barely keep her feet. Her legs were aching from the strain, and she'd begun to bleed again.

"I can't keep up," she gasped, her breath coming hard, a sharp pain beginning in her side. "I want to stop!"

Eileen's words were ringing in her ears: "…you mightn't want to dance, but you will. Oh, you'll dance all right."

The music rose and fell, at first deafeningly loud, then falling to little more than a whisper. The walls were going in and out, and she was being made to dance, just as the old woman had promised. She would dance until she died. She was panting, could barely draw breath to protest, and then she was back in the woods, sometimes running, sometimes stumbling, not sure where she was going, and the house, with its lights and music, faded into nothing but a wide dark space filled with the sound of the wind.

CHAPTER ONE

THE WET snow that had been falling all morning continued to fall relentlessly, finding its way down the back of Royal Newfoundland Constabulary Inspector Deiniol "Danny" Quirke's collar. It was April, for Christ's sake, and it should be spring or at least something like it. No bloody hope of that. Newfoundland didn't do spring. What it did was endless months of cold, wet misery, unending rain and drizzle until the end of June when the tiny fish known as capelin made it ashore to spawn and it could finally be summer. He sat back on his haunches, ignoring the creak in his fifty-year-old knees, and frowned at the body. A young woman lay face down in the icy bog, her long dark hair fanning out around her shoulders, a clump of soggy peat moss clutched in her fist. "Who found her?"

The assembled group of uniformed RCMP and RNC constables, four of them in total, looked from one to the other. A tall sandy-haired young man with an apologetic expression flipped through his notebook. "Hunter," he said.

Danny stood up, his knees cracking painfully, and studied his constable. Kevin Carbage was his name, poor bugger.

"Hunter?" Danny encouraged.

"Yes, sir. A hunter found her. Or should I say a poacher. He was out this way looking for rabbits."

Danny glanced around but could see only themselves. "I'm guessing he pissed off out of it."

Two of the constables exchanged glances again. "He was a poacher, sir. Reported the body on his mobile phone." He was a short, burly young man with a rugby player's body type and something of an attitude. "Could be anywhere now."

"Help me turn her over," Danny ordered. Two of the constables moved towards the girl's corpse, one on either side. Danny crouched down, cupped his hands around the nape of her neck. "Slowly, now."

She tumbled gradually through space and landed on her back. Danny examined her features, but he didn't recognise her. "Has anyone been reported missing recently?"

"No, sir," Carbage supplied.

"I want Bobbi Lambert's forensics team out here," Danny said. "Now if not sooner." The forensics chief had been seconded to Kildevil Cove from St. John's after Danny had personally requested her. He'd met a lot of forensics technicians in his time, and she was the very best. He walked a short distance away from the others and fished out his mobile phone. He didn't need to look up the medical examiner's number, since he knew it by heart. The line rang five times before Dr. Regan Lampe picked up.

"What?"

"Good morning to you too," he snapped. The wet snow began to fall harder, aided by a strong northwest wind, a feature of the Newfoundland spring and a harbinger of abject misery. "Got a body for ye."

"Not yours, is it?" she asked.

"No."

"Well, thank Christ for that."

"Don't fucking start with me, Regan." His cheeks flushed hot with anger, despite the cold day. "I've got a young woman lying dead in a bog in New Melbourne. How long until someone from the Carbonear hospital can get over here and collect the body?" The small cottage hospital in Old Perlican was closer, but the area's medical examiner was attached to Carbonear. Regan Lampe wouldn't have been his first choice in any case. She was brash, overconfident, and hated men in general, not him in particular. Her snotty manner hadn't won her any friends.

"I'm sorry," she said, not sounding sorry in the least.

"How long?"

"I'll get someone over immediately."

"Fine." He didn't wait for her to say goodbye. When he'd ended the call, he made his way back to the body. Carbage was bent low, treading a careful path around the girl's corpse. He'd put on a pair of bright purple nitrile gloves and held a plastic evidence bag and a pair of tweezers at the ready. As Danny watched, he plucked a small piece of paper from the ground with the tweezers and dropped it into the bag without touching the sides.

"Nicely done," Danny observed. "Who taught you forensics?"

"Chief Inspector Fraser, sir," Carbage replied. "She's very thorough." He held up the plastic bag so Danny could see. "Looks like a twist of waxed paper, possibly a paper towel or even a tissue. Might have had it in her pocket." He shrugged in a self-deprecating manner. "Could be nothing. Maybe I should have left it for Bobbi?"

"No, you did right to take it." Danny leaned over the young woman. Something about her face wasn't quite right. It was….

Her left eye was missing. He straightened up and walked a few paces away, stopped to stand in a grove of larch trees, steadying himself, breathing deeply through his nose. The empty socket gaped vividly in his memory, wet and red and sticky looking. *Jesus.*

Carbage was at his side in an instant. "Are you okay, sir?"

"I will be." He knew the sight of that raw, ragged hole in her skull would stay with him for a while. Danny dismissed the other constables and waited with Carbage until forensics was done with the body, the ambulance came, and the paramedics loaded the young woman's corpse inside.

"Sin," Carbage observed as the ambulance doors closed. "She was pretty looking."

Danny turned to eye him. "Did you know her?"

"Not really, sir. It's just a general observation." He gazed after the ambulance, his open notebook in his hand and an unreadable expression on his face. "Too bad." He flipped his notebook closed and put it back into his pocket. "Do you want me to follow behind?" he asked.

"No, it's fine," Danny said. The snow had thickened, each fat flake hitting his skin with a wet slap. He shivered and huddled closer into his coat. "No point in getting in Dr. Lampe's way. She'll have a report for me soon enough. We might as well get back. You can ride with me."

"Strange thing to do," Carbage observed once they were both in Danny's car. "Taking out her eyeball like that." Carbage's own eyes were a blue so brilliant they didn't look quite real. "Was it deliberate, or did the killer do it just for devilment?"

"I don't know," Danny said. He turned the key and started the car. Immediately a blast of cold air spewed from the heating vents. "I think T.S. Eliot was right," he observed wryly, with a glance at Carbage.

"About what, sir?"

"April really is the cruellest month."

THE NEW police substation in Kildevil Cove elicited both admiration and annoyance from the local residents. Those who had reason to fear the law were disgruntled, but many of the older people appreciated the added security that a police presence implied. Not that there was any great amount of crime in Kildevil Cove. Apart from the arson of Danny's late grandfather's house the previous autumn and the accidental drowning death of Llewellyn Single thirty years before, there had never been even a burglary in the small town. But Chief Inspector Moira Fraser—Danny's boss and a friend of many years—was wary. The increase in recent years of drug-related activity had alerted her to what was to come. For now the methamphetamine dealers and their cohorts were largely confined to the capital city of St. John's and its environs, but that was about to change. The drug had begun to turn up in even the smallest and most isolated fishing villages, and it wouldn't be long before meth and its concomitant crime found their way to Kildevil Cove. Such was the way of things.

Moira had appointed Danny to the role of supervisor at the Kildevil Cove substation of the Royal Newfoundland Constabulary. He was responsible for policing in not only the village itself but also the surrounding areas, which took in several small communities for some 100 kilometres in either direction—essentially the entire central region of the island's Avalon Peninsula. He was to monitor the area for evidence of crime and establish a cohesive working relationship between the police and local residents. When necessary, he would liaise with the RCMP, but for practical purposes, he *was* the police, along with four rather inexperienced constables ("Too green to burn," as Danny put it) in uniform and a desk sergeant named Marilyn Dobbin, who had already put in twenty years with the RNC and was nearing the end of her career. They had two patrol cars and an unmarked car for Danny's use, or when he or any of his officers needed to go undercover.

Moira had acquired an empty hall that had once belonged to the Loyal Orange Lodge, a massive structure outfitted with all the lavish accoutrements that might be expected, including bright blue interior walls and a gigantic oil painting of William of Orange seated on a rearing horse. Danny remembered the hall in its previous incarnation, a place where the locals gathered for Christmas concerts and autumn fairs, communal meals at huge trestle tables to mark some special occasion. He remembered accompanying his grandmother to the pie- and jam-tasting competitions, seeing the rows of homemade jellies glistening like jewels in their clear glass jars.

All that was gone now. The hall's interior structure had been subdivided, with modern "pods" erected to separate the workers and give some semblance of privacy. Wiring for phones and high-speed internet had been strung along and through the ancient building's rafters, and in places even the venerable ceiling beams had been bored with holes to allow the passage of electrical conduit. Danny's office was at one end, with a ceiling-high partition and a door. It gave the illusion of concealment, but even the slightest whisper could be overheard. Moira Fraser's department had requested interior design bids from all and sundry; the winning bid featured a lot of blond wood, and walls painted in reassuring greys and greens, but Danny wasn't convinced. He knew how slowly the wheels of government could grind. Sure, it would be nice when it was finished. If it was ever finished.

Constable Kevin Carbage's twin sister, June, met them at the door. She and Kevin looked nothing alike. Where he was tall and sandy-haired and slim, she was compact, short, a sturdily built woman with a luxuriant fall of thick dark brown hair. From what Danny could tell—he'd known them but a few weeks—their personalities were vastly different as well. Kevin was calm and easygoing, whereas June was sharp-tongued and quick to anger.

"There's someone here to see you," June said, suddenly and without preamble. Her brother shot her an outraged look, but she ignored him.

"There's someone here to see you, Inspector Quirke," Kevin said reprovingly. Danny waved a hand, dismissing the breach of protocol.

"Who is it?" he asked. Truth be told, he was eager for the distraction. Despite his many years as a police officer, he'd never gotten used to finding corpses, and it always left him badly rattled. Death from old age and its related complications was inevitable, the way of all flesh. But premature death, unnatural death, that he couldn't reconcile.

"It's an old man," June said. She exchanged a look with her brother. "He didn't want to talk to anyone else. Insisted it had to be you."

"Where is he?" Danny asked. Someone in the building was brewing coffee; the smell was making his mouth water.

"In your office," she said sheepishly. "I know what you told me, but that corridor is drafty, and he's really old." This was possibly true, but then again, anyone over fifty must have looked ancient to someone as young as June.

"I'll go see what he wants," Danny said. "And bring me some of that coffee, would you?"

Danny took a moment to hang his coat on the hook by the door before turning to acknowledge the old man sitting on one of the spare chairs in front of his desk. He was at least eighty and looked older, his lank grey hair escaping from under a dirty woollen hat. He wore a padded tartan shirt of the sort favoured by local fishermen, worn thin at the elbows, the front caked with dark stains, the origins of which Danny didn't want to guess at. His jeans had probably once been blue but had faded over time to a dirty off-white.

"You got to do something about it," the man said. He scraped at his stubbled chin with one horny paw. His fingernails were filthy and bitten nearly to the quick.

"What is it?" Danny asked. Just then June appeared in the doorway with a mug of coffee. She sat it down on his desk, shot a look of distaste at the old man, and disappeared back the way she had come.

"You got to get them crowd out." The old man looked hopefully at Danny's coffee and licked his lips. "I've tried tellin' 'em, but they won't go. No, sir, they won't go." The stench of body odour rose from him like a foul miasma.

Danny backed away and sat down. He took out a notebook and pen. This was absolutely ridiculous. Why the old man couldn't have spoken to one of the constables was anybody's guess. He tamped down his annoyance, asked, "Your name, sir?"

"Tommy Power. Sure, you knows me!" the old man barked. "I used to fish on the Labrador with your grandfather, bhoy."

Right. Yes, of course. Danny suddenly remembered him, although it had been many years ago and the years had not been kind to the old fisherman. He'd stop by the house at Christmas time for "a drop o' stuff" with Danny's grandfather. He smoked unfiltered Camels and swore an unending stream of profanity as they sat at the kitchen table playing cards. "How can I help you?"

"I already told ye." The old man closed his eyes, his seamed face contorted with the apparent effort of it. "They're on me land. I wants 'em gone. You got to make 'em go."

"Who's on your land?"

Danny tasted the coffee and recoiled. It was horrible, tasted like boiled aluminium. The new police substation was outfitted with a top-of-the-line Keurig, but obviously no one had bothered to read the instruction booklet.

"That Christian crowd," Mr. Power replied. "Out there all hours singing hymns and banging on them Jesus tambourines." Only in Newfoundland, Danny reflected, was the Son of God's personal nomenclature used as an adjective. "You got to do something. If they're not gone by the weekend, I'm getting me shotgun out, and they'll see something then."

"I'll send someone out to check on it as soon as possible," Danny said. *It just won't be me.* He didn't say this last part aloud.

Mr. Power hauled himself to his feet with some difficulty and settled his knitted cap more tightly on his head. "Bad wind out there today," he remarked. This wasn't saying anything in particular, since the island was known for wind. A day without wind usually heralded an oncoming storm, a nor'easter coming up from the "Boston States" or the remnants of a hurricane. "'Tis not good. Anytime there's a wind like that, my son...." He broke off and shook his head, his expression mournful. "Someone's like to lose their life in a wind like that."

Danny walked with him to the front door. "Be careful going down over the steps, now." He held Mr. Power's elbow until the old man could get hold of the handrail.

"Never you mind me," Mr. Power said. "Just get rid of that crowd. Living on my land, not paying me a cent of money for the privilege. Shitting and pissing all over the place, and the youngsters as saucy as dogs. 'Tis enough to turn your guts."

Danny went back inside and found Kevin in the kitchen, alternately tinkering with the Keurig and frowning over the instruction booklet. "Kevin."

"Sir?" He closed the lid of the machine and pressed a button. At once it started groaning, and after a moment, a thin stream of faintly coffee-coloured liquid dribbled out.

"Tommy Power was just in here. He says there are people camping on his land without permission. Can you go check it out?" It wasn't a request; Danny was being diplomatic.

"Right away, sir." Kevin gave his coffee a reluctant backwards glance.

"Make it first thing tomorrow," Danny said. "I'll need you to write up your report on the dead girl today. That's top priority."

"Yes, sir," Kevin said. "First thing."

KEVIN CARBAGE was smarter than your average cop, but it had taken a great many years and a lot of professional intervention before this was made apparent. As a boy, he'd been seriously dyslexic, unable to read even the simplest text but brilliant at mathematics and science. His inability to decipher the written word held him back, frustrated his native intelligence, and in high school, he'd come dangerously close to dropping out, becoming one of those typical young men who hung around the fish plant and the shops, doing nothing. Luckily a sharp-eyed guidance counsellor had noticed his facility with numbers and had pushed to have him tested. His IQ placed him just inside the genius range. The dyslexia was conquered by a rigorous training program, and he entered university on a full scholarship and graduated with a science degree.

He was thirty-eight years old and unmarried, although he'd been seeing Karen, a nurse in nearby Winterton, for more than ten years. He was sure they would eventually get married or something. He hadn't yet asked her, and she hadn't bothered to press the issue. They'd agreed to remain celibate until marriage, a decision that appealed to her more than him, so intimate encounters were confined to kissing and petting while clothed. Kevin considered himself a patient man, but he was starting to get frustrated with the state of things. Karen was pretty and physically appealing, but there was no longer any spark between them. He wondered if there ever had been. He certainly didn't lie awake at night thinking about her, and she didn't feature in his occasional erotic dreams. She was a nice girl, and she would make a good wife. He could imagine them living together in a house he would build on land he'd inherited from his family, but as for the rest of it? He allowed himself a mental shrug. She didn't excite him in any tangible way. Of course, that was normal when you'd been together for such a long time. Didn't most relationships go that way after a while? There was nothing wrong with him. It was simply natural.

Danny had asked him to visit Tommy Power's place to check out some people who were camping on his land. He suspected they were probably the same group who passed through every spring and summer, a religious sect calling themselves the Harvesters. They were originally from around Deer Lake, harmless enough, a variant of the Apostolic Pentecostal denomination in which Kevin himself had been raised. They travelled around singing and preaching, often knocking on doors to beg a meal or a cup of tea and rarely staying in any one place for more than a week or two. Most people had no problem with them camping out, as long as they cleaned up after themselves. From what June had said, Kevin didn't think this latest group were following the rules. June's route to work each morning took her past Tommy's land, and she said this particular assemblage seemed unruly and disorganised, not at all the quiet, polite Harvesters of summers past. They'd piled up garbage in the middle of the field and set fire to it, and several of the women were stringing wet clothes to dry on Tommy's prized apple trees. Children were running around, some of them barely clothed in the April chill, beating and banging on the doors and windows of Tommy's house. It was no wonder, she'd said, that Tommy was pissed off.

As Kevin parked the car beside Tommy Power's field early the next morning, he noted a group of young men, all neatly dressed in dark trousers, white shirts, and ties, standing huddled near a gatepost smoking cigarettes. The smell assaulted Kevin's nostrils as he walked towards them. They weren't only smoking tobacco either. Not much he could do about it, though. The stuff was legal now, although strictly speaking they weren't supposed to be smoking it in public.

"Good morning," he greeted them. "Grand day again today."

One of the group muttered something, and the others laughed.

Kevin kept his tone deliberately neutral as he said, "So you're stopping here for a while?"

"Spreading the word of the Lord," one of them replied. He was standing near the back. Kevin couldn't make out his features. There had to be at least twelve to fifteen of them in the group. Behind them he could see the fallow expanse of Tommy Power's field, still winter brown, the branches of the apple trees bare and empty. A group of children were taking turns jumping in a mud puddle, while a small tawny dog ran circles around them, barking excitedly. The dog, seeing Kevin's approach, ran to him, and he bent to pet it.

"Her name's Lucy." A young girl of about twelve or thirteen separated herself from the group and came to meet Kevin. "What do you want?"

He gave the dog a final pat and stood up. "I'd like to talk to whomever is in charge."

"That's Malachy," the girl said. "I'll take ye." She led him across the muddy field, past heaps of burning trash and makeshift tents erected over spruce poles. The dwellings seemed to be constructed of whatever materials the Harvesters could find, including bedsheets, rubber tarpaulins, and discarded fishing line. Several young children, all of whom ought to be in school, were kicking around a soccer ball while others watched from a short distance away. Apart from the children, no one seemed to be doing anything much. "Malachy's over this way," the girl said. She led Kevin to a teepee made from stretched canvas pulled over wooden poles. The front entrance was covered with a flap of cloth. "Malachy!"

A middle-aged man with lustrous black hair styled into an elaborate pompadour appeared. At first only his head and shoulders emerged from the tent; then a moment later the rest of him followed. Kevin saw with a shock that his legs were withered and useless, tied together with twine. His upper body, by contrast, was powerfully built, his arms and torso bulging with muscle. He propelled himself forward on his hands.

"Cops to see ye," the girl remarked. "Dis fella here."

Malachy looked up at Kevin and smiled. He had dark eyes the colour of pure obsidian, but with a cold intelligence. He hoisted himself onto a chair in front of his tent and drew his bound and useless legs over to the side. "What can I do for the constab?"

"The man who owns this land wants you to move on," Kevin said. "You don't have his permission to be here."

"His permission?" Malachy laughed, displaying two rows of shiny white teeth. "We're doing the Lord's work," he said.

"I understand," Kevin replied, trying his best to be conciliatory, "but he's asked that you move on. You have to respect his wishes."

"Or what?"

"Or I will have to arrest all of you for trespassing."

"You?" Malachy looked him up and down. "Sure, what's you going to do, ye pup?"

"Mr. Power says you're fouling his land." Kevin glanced behind him. "There are no proper sanitary facilities in place and no clean water supply. These children are old enough to be in school."

"We're trespassing?" Malachy dug a finger into his own chest. "Us. All of us crowd here are trespassing?"

"That's what I said, sir. I must ask you to leave."

Malachy leaned back in the chair, manually shifting his withered legs. "The earth is the Lord's," he said, "and—"

"—the fulness thereof," Kevin quoted, "'the world, and they that dwell therein.' Psalm 24, verse 1." He shifted his weight. "Still and all, you have to leave. I'm sorry. I'm sure you can find some more suitable place to camp elsewhere."

"Listen here, you fucking little piece of shit cop." Malachy was all but spitting with rage. "Me and mine will go where we wants to go, and there's not a fucking thing you can say about it. You think I'm afraid of you?"

"Papa Malachy!" A small girl came running up, red-faced from the cold and out of breath. "Ye got to come and see the dolly that Delilah found."

Malachy's manner changed in an instant. All at once he was the soul of kindness, warm and avuncular. "What's that, my love?"

The girl pointed back the way she'd come. "Delilah found a dolly!"

The piercing scream that followed froze Kevin's blood in his veins. He'd only ever heard a scream like that once before in his life, and he had never forgotten it. It was a sound from his nightmares. He spun on his heel in time to see a young woman of about nineteen or twenty running, holding something in her arms. Her mouth was open in a silent rictus of horror, and tears were streaming down her face. She thrust the bundle at Malachy. "Look!"

He and Kevin both looked. "That's the dolly that Delilah found!" the little girl said.

Only it wasn't a doll. It was a baby, cold and blue and dead, the skin broken and macerated, barely clinging to the tiny, sunken face. Kevin clenched his teeth until his jaws ached, then reached for his mobile phone. So much for clearing the Harvesters off Tommy Power's land.

"This is Carbage," he said to the dispatcher. "I need to secure a murder scene."

CHAPTER TWO

DANNY HAD just pulled into a parking space at Carbonear General Hospital when his mobile phone rang. He reached for it as he got out of the car and squinted at the screen. His partner—Danny couldn't bring himself to call him a boyfriend; it seemed too juvenile—Tadhg was forever saying that Danny needed reading glasses, but he'd be damned if he'd shell out his hard-earned money for something he'd only need to wear every now and then. "You can get cheap ones at the Buck or Two," Tadhg said, "for a couple dollars. Don't be so friggin' tight, bhoy. Ye're straining the shit out of your eyes, sure."

Kevin Carbage was calling, and Danny groaned. He didn't know Carbage well, but he hoped he wasn't the kind of young cop who needed to clear everything with his superior before he so much as picked his nose. If he was then he and Danny were going to have a problem.

"Kevin?"

"Sir, w-we've got—" Carbage's voice temporarily dropped out. Danny winced. The mobile phone coverage here wasn't the best. "—blue, not s-sure how l-long. I mean, what I'm trying to say—" Carbage seemed to be pretty worked up, and Danny wondered why. Kildevil Cove and its surrounding communities were hardly a hotbed of crime. His voice came back on a burst of static. "—dead baby."

Oh God. "A dead baby."

"Yes, sir." Carbage said something else, but the connection wavered and dropped. Danny closed out the call, then pressed redial, but it went straight to voicemail. He paused, wondering if he should reconnect with Regan Lampe later. A dead baby in a place like Kildevil Cove was massively improbable and spawned a million questions Danny would have to answer. Where had it come from? What had happened to the mother? Was it infanticide, or a stillbirth improperly disposed of? How long had the baby been there? And where, exactly, was "there"? He tried Carbage again. The young constable sounded apologetic when he answered.

"Sorry, sir, I'm having trouble with me phone."

"Listen, get up on a hill, find a better signal, and call me back, will you?" Danny said. "I'll keep my phone on."

He rang off and went into the hospital. At this hour, eight thirty in the morning, only a few medical personnel were present. Regan Lampe could have waited to call him, but she knew waking him out of a sound sleep would piss him off, and it had. He'd spent the night with Tadhg at his house on Eigus, the secluded island he owned in Conception Bay. They'd planned to have a lie in the next morning and take Tadhg's boat into St. John's for a leisurely breakfast before Danny made the two-hour drive to Kildevil Cove to start work.

Danny and Tadhg had been best friends in boyhood, until a tragic misunderstanding drove them apart. They had only recently found their way back to each other, and the relationship was still new, still fragile. Private time together was important, and he and Tadhg just weren't getting any. Between Danny's new job at the Kildevil Cove substation and Tadhg working every hour of the day to re-establish his failing business, they barely had time for a couple of quick kisses now and then. Regan's call, coming at six in the morning, had woken him out of a sound sleep.

He found her in the basement of the hospital, sitting behind the desk in her office to one side of the morgue. She was Inuk and ridiculously pretty, with long, shiny black hair to her waist. She wore it loose, sometimes held back from her face with a pair of caribou bone combs that had belonged to her great-grandmother. Danny remembered her wearing them when he was at university with her. She'd come south from Nain to study medicine at Memorial University of Newfoundland in St. John's.

"You got here," she said sourly, not bothering to look up from her laptop. "Sorry if I dragged you out of dreamland."

Danny didn't rise to the bait. He and Regan had never been what anyone would call friends. Her competitive personality drove a wedge between them; she always had to be right, had to be the first, had to be best at everything, even when the stakes were miniscule. He'd attempted friendship with her, but her abrasive nature drove him—and everybody else—away.

"Oh, I was already awake," he said airily. There was a single chair in front of her desk, and he sat down in it, uninvited. "Tell me about the girl in the bog."

"No." She closed the laptop and stood up. "I'll show you instead."

He followed her out of the office and through the autopsy suite to a large brushed-steel door set into a concrete wall. "Cold storage," she said unnecessarily.

"I know what it is," Danny replied, fighting to keep annoyance out of his voice.

"Full marks," Regan retorted. She tugged at the handle, and the heavy door swung back, revealing a concrete room, its cinder-block walls painted white. Inside were two hospital gurneys. One was empty, its shiny surface gleaming like a fresh insult. The other held a shrouded figure. With a wholly superfluous flourish, Regan yanked the sheet back, revealing the head and naked shoulders of the young woman they'd found in New Melbourne. The typical autopsy Y-cut had been neatly and precisely stitched back together. The girl's head was propped up on a plastic brick, not unlike those used by yoga instructors for balancing exercises. Her right eyelid was closed over the intact eyeball, but the left was open, exposing the empty socket.

"She did that herself," Regan informed him, indicating the livid scratch marks around the area. "As far as I can tell, she dug the eye out with her fingernails."

Danny's stomach roiled, and the coffee and toast he'd eaten for breakfast threatened to come back up again. In his long career as a police officer, he'd seen self-injury before, but nothing so extreme, so violent.

Reagan pulled the sheet down to the girl's waist, and Danny had a sudden urge to avert his gaze. This girl wasn't much older than Tadhg's daughter, Lily. "See?" Regan bent the corpse's right arm at the elbow, bringing the hand up. Traces of blood and tissue were evident under the fingernails.

"Why the hell would she gouge out her own eye?" Danny wondered.

"That's your department," Regan said. "I can tell you she'd given birth in the recent past."

Given birth? Danny's thoughts jumped to the dead baby. Could there be a connection there? He started to mention it but stopped. It would be premature until he got more information from Kevin, but it was a strange coincidence. Too strange?

Regan dropped the sheet neatly over the young woman's head and nodded towards the autopsy suite. "Got something else for you."

He followed her over to a gleaming white counter where various tissue samples and internal organs had been sequestered in metal pans. She slipped on a pair of nitrile gloves and, pulling one of the pans towards her, poked at what was inside. It looked like some sort of meat, dark red and speckled with black spots. "Am I right?"

Danny had no idea what she was talking about. "I don't follow."

"It's her liver," Regan said. "Completely necrotic. Dead tissue. The sclera of her remaining eyeball is yellow. This girl was in acute liver failure when she died."

"What would cause that?" he asked.

"Acetaminophen overdose," she replied. She pushed the pan containing the dead girl's liver back into its original position. "Or she could have ingested poisonous mushrooms. I've seen both cases. The end result is similar, so I couldn't tell by looking. I could have wasted the department's money by running a full blood panel and sending frozen sections off to the RCMP lab, but I didn't."

Danny waited.

"The Meixner test," Regan said. "You've heard of it?"

"Express fluids from fresh tissue onto a piece of newsprint, let it dry, and add a drop of hydrochloric acid. If it turns blue, you've got amatoxins," Danny said.

"Pfft. First-year biology with Dr. Carr," Regan said. "Everybody knows that."

"Did it?" Danny asked. "Turn blue, I mean."

"It did." She nodded at the mobile phone in his hand. "I hope you told your team to gather materials from around the body. If I were you, I'd be looking for *Amanita muscaria*."

DANNY MULLED over what Regan Lampe had said while he waited for the elevator. Of course the forensics team had taken samples from the ground around the dead girl's body, so if she had ingested the mushrooms—either on her own or by force—there might have been fragments left behind. Surely to God most people nowadays knew not to pick and eat wild mushrooms unless they were very, very sure what they were eating. People had died from foraging wild plants, some of them quite horribly. A young actor, originally from Carbonear, had gone into septic shock and died after ingesting what he'd thought were harmless chanterelles. It was all over the news.

Or perhaps the girl had been given the mushrooms by someone who'd told her they'd make her high as a kite. Young people were always looking for the next great high, something to take them out of the world for a while, fool their minds into thinking they were flying or some other such shite. Sure, he and Tadhg had smoked their share of marijuana in their teenaged years, long before it ever became legal, but Danny had never really seen the point. At best it made him laugh his arse off for about twenty minutes before the high devolved into a raging headache and a sudden, powerful hunger for junk food. He'd never bothered with any of the hard stuff, cocaine or heroin or methamphetamine, and once he'd started university, his only choice of high was marijuana. He and Tadhg had always bought from the same guy, a fellow named Ford—

"Danny Quirke."

His train of thought halted abruptly, and he turned. A man about his own age approached from the other end of the corridor. His light brown hair was simply cut, falling nearly to his shoulders, and he wore faded jeans with work boots and a plaid lumberjack shirt under a padded puffer vest.

"Danny Quirke," he said again and laughed. "Lord Jesus Christ. What are ye at, my son? I haven't seen you in donkey's years!"

Ford Maddox. His name had always been a bit of a joke, once Danny got to university and had to read Ford Madox Ford's *The Good Soldier* in literature class. "Ford?"

"Sure, you know it's me." He seized Danny in a powerful bear hug, nearly lifting him off his feet. "Look at ye," he said, once he had let go and stepped back. "You're looking good." Ford's American accent had softened over the years, was now overlaid with a patina of Newfoundland English, but he still sounded like the Deep South. Ford's mother, a native of Newfoundland, had married an American and moved to Athens, Georgia, with him. Ford had been born and raised there until the age of nine, when he and his mother came back to Kildevil Cove. Sadly, she had died soon after, leaving Ford alone.

None of Ford's mother's people were able or willing to take him, so he ended up in the foster system. That was when Danny met him; Ford joined his grade four class in elementary school. He was being fostered by Flossie Palmer, a local woman who took in troubled children and tried to love them back to health. Sometimes it worked. She'd done all right with Ford, who not only graduated from high school with Danny and Tadhg but had gone on to study structural engineering at Memorial University.

"I heard you're a cop now," Ford said. He stood back and looked Danny up and down, smiling broadly. Ford had one of the best smiles Danny had ever seen. Once you'd seen it, you immediately wanted to see it again as soon as possible. "I was sorry to hear about your wife."

Danny nodded. "Thank you."

"I heard it was... bad." Ford's whisky-coloured eyes searched Danny's face. "Can't have been easy."

A pang of loss struck Danny in the chest. Yes, he was with Tadhg now, but he would always love Alison, and her death from fatal familial insomnia had been incredibly traumatic. The nature of prion diseases meant they killed slowly and insidiously, from the inside out, replacing healthy brain tissue with clumps of mutated protein. In Alison's case, the disease initially manifested as an inability to sleep, something they both put down to her age and the advent of perimenopause. She developed dementia, eventually losing the ability to think, talk, or feed herself. Two days after being admitted to palliative care, she slipped into an irreversible coma and from there into death.

"It was," Danny replied. He switched the subject quickly, asking, "So what brings you here?"

"Oh, I'm in the area, doing some work on that new bridge span over Veterans Memorial Highway. Normally my guys are on site without me, but I like to drop in now and then, see how they're doing." He gestured at his face. "Having some trouble with my teeth." It was then Danny noticed Ford's left cheek looked a little swollen. "Doc had to take a couple of my molars. Cracked all to hell, they was."

"Ouch," Danny said. He winced in sympathy.

"Yeah. I grind my teeth at night. Doc says I'm supposed to wear one of those mouth guard things, but I can't sleep that way." Danny could relate. He tended to grind his teeth as well. Tadhg had told him he even did it in his sleep. Maybe he needed to do something about that before his molars started going.

The elevator dinged and the doors slid open. "Which way are you headed?" Danny asked. He stepped back and held the door for two hospital porters wheeling a tired-looking woman on a gurney. Her hair was stuck to her face with sweat. She'd probably just come from the case room, he thought, and shuddered. The idea of having to push a full-term baby out of your body gave him the heebie-jeebies.

"Going back to the job site, unless you want to get a coffee or something," Ford replied. "I figure maybe you can spare twenty minutes for an old buddy."

Danny laughed, gestured for Ford to enter the elevator ahead of him. "I think I can pencil you in," he said. They reached the lobby and agreed to meet at a small restaurant on Water Street, just up from the post office. Danny's mobile phone rang the moment he left the hospital. He hadn't heard from Kevin Carbage since the young constable had called to report the dead infant. He wondered what the hell Carbage was up to.

"Sorry, sir." Carbage's apologetic tone failed to mollify Danny. "It's been a bit crazy here trying to keep this Harvester lot together and get statements from everybody."

"Where are you now?" Danny asked. He switched the phone to Bluetooth mode and fitted the earpiece to his ear.

"Still at Tommy Power's field, sir. Been here all morning. I've got June helping me out, but truth be told, we're stretched thin."

Danny started the car and turned on the heat. The wet snow had stopped, and the sun was making a tentative appearance through the clouds, but there was no warmth in it. He shivered, rubbing his hands together while he waited for the blast of cold air from the car's vents to turn warm. "Tell me about the dead baby."

He put the car into gear and pulled out of the hospital parking lot onto High Road South, heading towards Carbonear's modest downtown. The town had been settled in the early 1600s, and, like most of Newfoundland, its inhabitants were descended from the Irish and West Country English fishermen who'd originally arrived as part of the migratory fishery. For hundreds of years it had flourished, the people fishing for Northern cod, but confederation with Canada managed to obliterate in fifty years what five hundred previous years could not, and by 1992, the codfish stocks were completely exhausted, thanks to the foreign fishing fleets.

Like so many other smaller villages around the coast, Carbonear emptied of its people, many of whom went to large Canadian cities like Calgary or Toronto in search of work. Now the town was merely a shell of its former self, many of its vibrant storefronts shuttered, houses abandoned, its streets all but empty. Danny remembered when Carbonear had been a local center of commerce, the place where everybody went to shop for groceries and other sundries. When he and his twin sister, Sandra, were children, a trip to Carbonear with their grandparents was a big deal. If they were lucky, Nan would give them some money from her change purse for an ice cream.

He listened as Kevin relayed in simple terms the discovery of the infant's body. "One of the young women came running up with it, sir, but a little girl found it in the woods, half buried in peat. She said she seen a hand poking up and went to see what it was."

"Infanticide?" Danny wondered aloud. It was the same old story; a young woman found herself in trouble and, rather than confide in the adults who would no doubt shame her, hid the pregnancy, giving birth in secret and either killing the infant if it was born alive, or hiding the corpse in the event of a stillbirth. "Keep them together and get those statements. Don't let anyone leave until you've spoken to them, and don't let them talk to each other. That includes children. Didn't you say it was a little girl who found the body?"

"Yes, sir."

"All right. Get the baby's body to Regan Lampe as soon as possible," Danny said. "Tell her I want a full autopsy. It's vital that we determine cause of death. If this child was recently born, her mother may still be about."

Carbage groaned audibly. "Sir, don't make me talk to her. She'll give me the rough side of her tongue like she always does."

Was Carbage afraid of Regan Lampe, Danny wondered. He fought down a chuckle. "Sorry, Constable, those are my orders."

Kevin sighed. "About the Harvesters, sir. The weather's taken a turn for the worse. Do you think we can get them in out of the cold somewhere?"

Danny ran a mental check of available public or semipublic buildings in the New Melbourne area. "Try one of the churches," he said. "Get them into the United Church there on the high road if you can. The door should be open, but if it's locked, Myrtle Single lives in the mauve-coloured house beside it. She'll have the key."

"There's something else, sir. Like I said, there's just me and June here by ourselves. Judging by a rough head count, there are at least fifty Harvesters. If we're to get their statements, it's going to take hours, possibly through the night. I could use a few more hands."

"I'll call Moira Fraser, see if she can round up some volunteers." He disconnected Carbage and called Moira. She picked up on the first ring.

"What's going on in New Melbourne?" she asked.

"Kevin Carbage said they've found a dead baby in a farmer's field," Danny said.

"Yes, I've heard about the dead baby." Her voice rose in both pitch and tone. "For Christ's sake, Danny, why wasn't I informed? I've just had some reporter from the *Evening Telegram* on the phone asking for a statement. You should have called me as immediately."

"I was at the hospital," Danny explained, "seeing Regan Lampe about the girl in the bog."

"That's no excuse," Moira exploded. "I need to be able to trust you to keep me informed of anything important, day or night."

"I'm sorry," Danny said. He wasn't. Fuck Moira anyway. He couldn't do everything at once.

"You're on your way over there now, right?"

"Of course." He momentarily considered whether he should text Ford and cancel but decided against it. Twenty minutes here or there wasn't going to make a whole lot of difference, and now was as good a time as any to let Kevin Carbage show what he could do. Speaking of which…. "Moira, my constables have about fifty potential witnesses to get statements from, and they're stretched thin. Can you send them some help right away?"

"I will take care of it," she answered shortly. "I can expect regular updates from you, Danny?"

"Yes, Moira." Jesus. Had she always been this much of a ball-buster? "Look, I've got another call coming in. I'll be in touch." He closed the connection before she could say anything else.

THE MAIN Street Restaurant would hardly rate in any large city or even sizeable town anywhere in the rest of the world, but for as long as Danny could remember, they'd had the best fish and chips he'd ever eaten. He pulled into a parking spot in front of the restaurant and shut off the car, clicking the key fob to engage the automatic locks—which was ridiculous, he knew. The entire street was deserted, and even if anyone had been around, the chances of their breaking into his car were minimal at best. But it was an ingrained habit with him. He simply couldn't help himself.

He made fun of Tadhg insisting that the doors be locked before they went to sleep at night when he visited Tadhg's house on Eigus. "It's a friggin' island, bhoy," Danny would say, exasperated at Tadhg's endless checking of the locks. "They'd have to swim a long distance to get to us in the first place." But though he teased Tadhg, he couldn't escape his own worries. Danny knew evil had little regard for things like locks and optimism. It always found a way in, existed in places you might never think possible.

He went inside and found a corner table by the window overlooking the street. Just past the façade of the buildings opposite, he could see the metallic sheen of the ocean, each wave driven by the wind and capped with white, and the blue bulk of the Land and Sea Welding company. He checked his messages and flicked through a copy of the *Evening Telegram* that someone had left behind. A public-housing building in St. John's had burned to the ground, the fire quite possibly arson, and a local member of the provincial legislature was in hot water for some unsavoury remarks he'd made about the indigenous community. He could kiss his political career goodbye, Danny thought. He glanced out the window, but there was still no sign of Ford. Then a large heavy-duty pickup truck with all the bells and whistles pulled up to a meter across the street, and Ford got out. He glanced up and down the street, although there was no traffic whatsoever, then crossed to the restaurant and came inside.

"Sorry," he said, sitting at Danny's table. "Think I'd know the layout of this damn place by now, but I still keep getting lost." A strong smell of booze wafted from him. Danny wondered if he'd stopped into a pub on the way. Surely Ford wasn't stupid enough to drive under the influence. He was about to say something when the waitress, a smiling middle-aged woman, appeared at their table.

"Now then, gentlemen," she began, taking out her notepad, "do the two of ye want coffee or tea this morning?"

Danny glanced at Ford. "Coffee?" he asked. Ford nodded. "Two coffees," he told the woman.

"Right away," she said and headed back behind the counter where a fresh pot was just completing its drip cycle.

"Nice truck you got," Danny observed, nodding at the vehicle across the street.

"Yeah. It's a Ford." He grinned, but it didn't reach his eyes. "What else would it be, huh?"

They both fell silent for a moment. Danny searched his mind for something suitable to say while Ford fiddled with various items on the table, seemingly unable to meet his gaze. He rearranged the salt and pepper shakers, the ketchup and vinegar bottles, stroked the smooth surface of the shiny metal napkin holder.

Danny asked, "Everything all right?"

Ford looked up. "Yeah, sure." He pulled a napkin from the holder and began folding it into tiny, precise pleats, aligning each pleat with the edge of the table and squaring it off before beginning another. It reminded Danny of a methamphetamine addict he once knew, a shy, cadaverously thin young man who seemed to always be in motion— touching his face, his hair, the buttons on his sweater, drumming his fingers on the table when he sat opposite Danny in a police interview room. He practically shimmered with nervous energy, like Ford was doing now.

"You seem uncomfortable," Danny started, but Ford made no reply. His hands were trembling very slightly.

The coffee machine finished brewing with a hiss and a gurgle. The waitress lifted the pot, plucked two clean mugs off a pyramid of them on the counter, and approached their table. She put the mugs down, deftly filled them, and placed a pitcher of cream on the table. "Something to go with it?" she asked. "We've got some lovely banana bread. And carrot cake, if that's what you'd like."

Danny remembered Ford's love of his grandmother's banana bread and ordered them a slice each, hot, with butter. Ford added cream and a liberal helping of sugar to his coffee, then stirred vigorously, the spoon clanking against the cup. He stirred and stirred, the endless clamour wearing on Danny's nerves.

"Sure, you'll have the bottom beat out of that if you keeps on," Danny said, trying for humour.

Ford gazed at him, lips parting. He drew a breath, seemed to think better of speaking, then let it go. He pulled another paper napkin from the dispenser and put it on the table, laying the spoon down on it. After a moment, he adjusted the handle so that it was square with the edge of the napkin, then adjusted both the napkin and the spoon to align with the side of the table. He reached for his coffee, then drew back.

"Danny, it's like this."

Danny tasted his own coffee. It was hot, delicious, perfectly strong and bracing. "I'm listening." He sensed imminent disclosure and wondered what Ford wanted to tell him that required such an elaborate preparatory ritual.

"I've had a hell of a hard time, and I don't mind telling you." Ford reached for the spoon and turned it over so the convex bulge of its bowl was facing him. He traced the handle with his index finger, as if smoothing some invisible imperfection. "Kinda strange me saying that and we ain't seen each other for, what? Must be thirty years now."

Danny nodded. "Thirty years, give or take."

"I been away for a while. Working in South America. Texas." Ford laughed. "Even found myself in by-God Australia, if you can believe that."

"I always knew you'd do well," Danny said. He was being generous. In truth, and knowing Ford's history, a long stint in jail wouldn't have surprised him.

"I have been—" Ford broke off as the waitress appeared with their banana bread. "Oh, that sure smells good, ma'am." He offered her a dazzling smile. It faded abruptly the moment she turned to go. "Ain't had banana bread in forever." He picked up his fork and neatly sectioned off a corner.

"You've been what?" Danny probed. "What were you about to say?" He laid his palms flat on the table. "Tell me."

Ford put his fork down and dropped his head into his hands. There was a pause, a moment of awful, infinite stillness; then he began to weep. Stunned, Danny reached out a hand and took hold of Ford's wrist. He remembered the first time he had ever seen Ford, a sad little boy who came to the elementary school in Kildevil Cove and sat in his seat with his snowsuit pulled down to his waist, crying silently. Danny was only nine, but the sight pierced his heart. Over the years, many foster children had come and gone, but the image of Ford, weeping in his snowsuit, stayed with him. Seeing him cry now, his head in his hands, made him feel as useless as he had felt back then.

"I'm in trouble, Danny," Ford whispered. He plucked a handful of napkins from the dispenser and wiped his eyes. "Goddammit, I'm coming apart."

"Tell me." Danny squeezed his wrist and let go. "I'm listening."

"It's… I don't know where to start." Ford sipped his coffee, ignored the banana bread. "Look, Danny, this isn't your problem, okay? I don't expect you to—" He stopped, and his face crumpled.

Danny pretended interest in his banana bread while Ford composed himself.

"I've been…." He seemed unable to go on.

"Maybe this isn't the best place for it," Danny said. He caught the waitress's attention, and when she came over, asked if they could have their food and coffee packaged to go. She came back with a brown paper bag, and he paid her, then reached to help Ford out of his chair. "Let's get some fresh air."

They went outside, and Danny bundled Ford into his car—Ford was in no fit state to drive—and headed towards Beach Road. He parked at the old railway station across the way, and they both got out. A cool breeze had sprung up, smelling of salt-sea air. Danny hoped it might revive Ford's spirits, refresh them both. Ford was shivering, his hands jammed into his pockets. Danny stepped over to him and zipped up his puffer vest.

"Catch your death out here today," he said, attempting a smile. They walked side by side in silence for a while, watching the seagulls dip and wheel.

"I've been seeing a doctor," Ford said. "A psychiatrist." He waited, as if expecting Danny to say something, then continued. "When we were living in the States, my mother divorced my old man and got herself remarried. The new guy didn't like me. No, that's not completely right." He glanced at Danny and gave a bleak grin, like the smile of a skull. "He liked me too much. Started coming into my bedroom at night, putting his hands under the covers—that sort of thing."

Danny wanted to ask what sort of thing? But he was reluctant to interrupt. The entire conversation had the air of a confession. And it was pretty clear what Ford meant by "that sort of thing" anyway.

Ford stopped walking and stood for a moment, gazing out to sea. A lone fishing boat was putting out lobster pots, moving in a slow circle around the harbour. He hunched his shoulders. "It really fucked me up, but once we came back to Newfoundland, I figured I could put it all behind me." He shook his head. "Didn't work out that way."

"I had no idea," Danny said. "When we were in school—"

"He was dead by then," Ford said abruptly. He turned around, began walking back the way they'd come. "You know, I did real good in university. Got good marks, despite all the rest of it." "The rest of it" probably meaning his dealing of drugs, Danny thought. Ford was well known on the campus of Memorial as the go-to guy for whatever chemical high you wanted to pursue. "Figured I was free and clear, and I was, for a good long while. I got married, had a son. He's nineteen now. Wants nothing to do with me, but that's another story."

Danny wondered what—if anything—he could say.

"This doctor, he's got me on some heavy-duty medication. Real military-grade stuff. Experimental. Does weird shit to my head. Fucks up my sleep too. You know what I mean?"

Danny knew all too well about psychiatrists and their drugs. "Of course," he replied noncommittally. As they reached Danny's car, his phone rang. "Sorry," he said, pulling the phone out of his inside pocket. "I have to take this."

It was Kevin Carbage, and he was upset. "Sir, there's some RNC sergeant here, trying to take over the whole bloody show. He says Moira Fraser sent him."

Danny sighed inwardly. "I'll be there as quick as I can. Just keep processing the witnesses. I'm on my way." He rang off and offered Ford an apologetic smile. "I can take you back to your truck," he said.

"No, it's only spittin' distance from here," Ford replied. He held out a hand, and Danny took it. "Thanks for listening to me," he said. "Maybe I'll call you sometime."

"I wish you would." Danny gave Ford one of his business cards. "My cell number is on there. Call me anytime." He shook Ford's hand. "I mean it. Day or night."

"Thanks." Ford offered him a watery smile. "Think I'm going to walk on the beach some more."

Danny turned to go, leaving him there. "He was dead by then." Something about the way Ford had said that made Danny's scalp tingle unpleasantly.

KEVIN CARBAGE was waiting at the New Melbourne United Church when Danny arrived half an hour later. "Good to see you, sir. We've got everybody inside." Danny followed him into the church, which smelled of damp and old hymnals. He didn't particularly care for churches, with their thinly veiled hypocrisies and lingering air of silent disapproval. Christ had apparently preached love, a fact many of his followers had forgotten. All the really religious people Danny had ever met had a long list of biases and strictures by which they measured the virtue of others. He wondered how they'd react to him, an agnostic police officer and an openly bisexual man in a committed relationship with another man. Not well, probably.

Most of the Harvesters were seated in the pews, although a small group of younger people lingered near the altar, the girls sitting on the edge while several teenage boys hovered nearby. A uniformed police officer stood near them, his back to Danny, while a second took individual close-up shots of the young people. The digital photos would be downloaded later and matched to each witness's statement.

"I thought you were taking statements," Danny said. He glanced around. "Where's June?"

"She went with the Salvation Army ladies. The corps in Winterton is sending down some blankets and hot food for these people."

"Any sign of Tommy Power?" Danny asked. He couldn't see the old man anywhere. "I figured he'd be here supervising."

"Not Tommy," Carbage replied. "He's a queer hand, that one. Don't mix with no one."

Danny smiled involuntarily at Carbage's lapse into local dialect. In any other place "queer hand" would be readily misinterpreted as a homophobic slur. Here, it simply meant a strange person, someone other cultures might term "an odd duck."

"He's a recluse?" Danny asked.

Carbage shrugged. "More or less. He used to fish a bit, back before the moratorium, but not now. He goes into the woods to cut firewood in the winter; that's about it."

This didn't describe the Tommy Power Danny had known. That man was gregarious, frequently loud, and often rude, but well-known around Kildevil Cove and welcome in people's homes. What had happened to make him shut himself away?

"How long have these people been camping on his land? Sure, it's hardly warm enough to be sleeping in tents this time of year." This was no green and pleasant land; April in Newfoundland was still winter, and nighttime temperatures usually dipped well below zero.

"One of the women I talked to said they've been here since the middle of March." Carbage seemed to shiver at the thought of it. "Wouldn't be me."

"Nor me," Danny replied. "I'll take my warm bed any night." *With Tadhg in it*, he added mentally. "How many are left to interview?"

"Himself there came in and took over." Carbage nodded at the officer taking the pictures. "Said Chief Inspector Fraser sent him. Him and that other one pushed me out. Said they have 'a system' and I wasn't to interfere. Who died and made him God, I'd like to know."

Danny laid a hand on Carbage's shoulder briefly. "I'll go and have a word." He went towards the altar, resisting the urge to genuflect. As he neared the dividing rail he called out, "Sergeant—" and fell abruptly silent, shock reverberating through him like a blow.

Cillian Riley. Of all the churches in all the fishing villages on any island in the world, Riley had to walk into this one.

"Sir." He blinked, obviously ill at ease. "Chief Inspector Fraser sent me."

"So I see," Danny replied. Did his voice sound that strangled, or was he imagining it? "Are they cooperating?"

"All except that one." Riley pointed towards the first row of pews. A man in his late fifties or early sixties sat propped against the wall, with what looked like two logs beside him, tied together with a length of twine. Danny's gaze travelled downwards, and he realised that what he'd assumed were logs were actually the man's useless legs. "He's been nothing but trouble," Riley said. The man returned their attention with an openly hostile stare. "Won't give a last name. Says his name's Malachy, and that's all anybody can get out of him." He moved closer to Danny and, lowering his voice, asked, "How have you been? I don't like the way we left things. I think—"

Danny cut him off. "I'm with Tadhg now."

A shutter came down behind Riley's eyes. "Tadhg Heaney?"

"Yes."

"I see." Riley gazed at him for a moment, then turned and nodded at the group of people. "Your new constable is pissed off with me," he said. He ducked his head and smiled. "And now you're pissed off with me and all." Riley's Newcastle accent burred the edges of his words a little.

"I'm... not pissed off with ye," Danny told him. His unplanned meeting with Ford Maddox had unsettled him. He felt as if something deep inside had been flayed open, laid raw. Maybe he should have tried harder to keep in touch with Ford after university, check in on him now and then, see if he was okay. "It's shaping up to be that sort of day. Old home week, you know how it is."

"Sir." Kevin Carbage appeared behind Danny. "I think we should work on finding these people alternate accommodations. The weather report says there's a blizzard coming." He and Riley stared coldly at each other. *No love lost there*, Danny thought.

"A blizzard," he said.

"Yes, sir."

Great. A blizzard in April. Not unheard of on the island, Danny knew. "Let's see what the Salvation Army can come up with," he said. "Maybe we can set them up in the school gym." He glanced at his watch. It felt like days since he'd climbed out of bed, but it was just past two in the afternoon. "I'm going back to the station to write up some reports. Let me know if you hear from Tommy Power. If not, I'll go have a word with him this evening."

TOMMY POWER'S house had once been the rural Newfoundland equivalent of a grand manor, a stately saltbox set on a rise overlooking the sea, but time and weather had reduced it to little more than a shack. Its narrow clapboard exterior had once been painted white, but was now faded to a feathery grey, the entire structure leaning perilously to the side as the foundation crumbled and gave way. It reminded Danny of a drawing he'd once seen in a museum: a ramshackle house perched on the edge of a cliff, perhaps a metre from the sea, its door and windows left open to the weather. He parked at the end of Tommy's gravel drive, careful to keep his car's tires off the grass, and went around to the side.

Few people in this area ever used the front doors of their houses, and most were blocked off by furniture on the inside. Since most of daily life was lived in the kitchen, it made more sense to go in that way. He mounted a set of sagging wooden steps and rapped on the door, waited. "Tommy? Are you in there? It's Danny Quirke. I want a word."

He waited, listening carefully, but there was no sound, nothing stirring besides the wind. He tried again. "Tommy? Is it all right if I comes in to see ye?" Still nothing. He went around to the front of the house and tried looking in the living room window, but the interior of the house was so dark he could make out nothing. The ground was soft, owing to the recent wet weather, and there were several fresh footprints—a mature male, to judge by the size and depth, which meant Tommy had probably made them himself. Danny moved to the rear of the house and checked the garden shed, but it was empty, the door hanging open on its hinges. If Tommy had become a recluse in recent years, as Carbage asserted, wouldn't he be at home most of the time?

The door opened easily when Danny tried it. He stepped inside the house and called again. The late-afternoon light was weak, the interior windows covered with ornate lace curtains whose folds were heavy with dust. The kitchen table had been piled high with magazines and old newspapers, advertising flyers, and stacks of unopened mail. Some of the envelopes read Final Notice or Past Due. The old-age pension didn't go very far these days. An electric kettle, its base scorched and blackened, sat on the countertop next to an old-fashioned chrome toaster, the sort his grandparents had used. An empty cup had been placed on the edge of the sink next to the taps. It, too, was crusted inside with dirt.

"Tommy?" Danny called. No answer.

A plastic container about the size of a shoebox sat in the middle of the table; it was filled with prescription medication bottles—blood pressure pills, heart medication, low-dose aspirin, something called donepezil, and levetiracetam, an antiseizure treatment. He recognised the latter because Alison's doctor had prescribed it when her fatal insomnia had progressed to violent convulsions. Even with this powerful pharmaceutical intervention, she still suffered occasional breakthrough seizures that ravaged her with their violence. If Tommy was taking it, his epilepsy was probably serious. It was important that he not miss a dose. The donepezil, that was one he didn't know. He made a mental note to look it up later.

He went down a narrow passageway to the living room, a similarly squalid space with dull green carpet worn thin, its pile trodden down and blackened by the passage of unwiped feet. A small black-and-white television set sat on top of a wooden crate, and next to it an outdated copy of the *Newfoundland Herald* TV guide. An ashtray, overflowing with butts, sat on a side table near an ancient recliner chair, the only piece of furniture in the room. Danny bent and laid his palm over it, but there was no sensation of heat. These cigarettes had been smoked ages ago. Like the kitchen, this room was full of old newspapers and magazines, plastic shopping bags rolled into balls or tied into complicated knots.

"Tommy, are you here?" He listened, straining his ears for even the slightest noise, wondering if perhaps the old man had taken ill or was incapacitated and unable to call for help. "It's Danny Quirke. I'm coming upstairs."

He put one foot on the lowest tread of Tommy's rickety stairs and leaned forward, applying a portion of his weight before trusting the whole of it. The stair held, and he started forward, easing himself cautiously upwards, one hand holding tight to the bannister. At the top he saw four separate doors arranged around the elongated rectangle that was the upper hallway. The first door to the left opened onto a small bathroom, containing a toilet and sink but no bathtub. The single window was tiny and set high on the wall. Like the rest of the house, it was filthy with grime and many years' accumulation of dust. Two of the other doors opened onto bedrooms, one of which contained only an empty bed frame and an old-fashioned slop pail with a lid. Danny remembered its like from childhood, in the home of a friend with no indoor plumbing. He could still feel the bite of its cold metal lip against his bare arse.

The second bedroom was obviously Tommy's. It contained a sagging double bed covered by a dusty hand-sewn quilt and two pillows, sans cases. Both were stained yellow by the oil from the old man's hair, and both smelled fusty and altogether unpleasant. He pulled back the quilt and saw there were no sheets, merely the bare mattress and the remnant of a satin-bound blue blanket, much used and full of holes. A small table to the side of the bed held a box of matches, a stub of candle, and a slim yellow-backed erotic novel, *School for Courtesans*.

Danny tutted. "Dirty old bugger," he said aloud. His grandfather had had the very same one; as young boys, he and Tadhg had regaled each other for hours reading the lurid descriptions of improbable sex acts depicted in it.

The final door, at the far end of the hall, opened onto a walk-in closet or box room like the one his grandparents had. His grandmother used it to store her winter clothing during the summer months, along with the one moth-eaten raccoon fur coat his grandfather had purchased for her as a wedding present. The room had always smelled of mothballs and cardboard boxes, and there was an old steamer trunk in which his nan stored her hoard of strong British tea and old copies of the Scottish newspapers she'd had sent from overseas.

Tommy didn't have a steamer trunk, but there was a large plywood box set against the wall in one corner of the little room, half-hidden behind a closet rail crammed with hanging clothes. Danny dropped to his knees and crawled under the coats to retrieve it. He pulled it out into the middle of the floor. The lid had one of those latches designed to take a padlock, which was missing, but the metal straps were so rusted he had to exert significant pressure before it would yield. The interior was subdivided into separate compartments and lined with old newspapers; there was a top tray that lifted out. Underneath he found a stack of ancient letters bound together with butcher's twine, the paper so old it had begun to crumble. The ink had faded almost to invisibility, but the first envelope in the pile bore a return address in Boston. The style of the handwriting was elaborate and ornate, like something from the mid-twentieth century, and quite possibly written with a fountain pen. He untied the knot with some difficulty and carefully separated the first envelope so he could look through the others. They were all from the same Boston address. This wasn't particularly unusual. Many Newfoundlanders left the island for "the Boston States" to work aboard large American schooners or whaling vessels, and some never returned, preferring to put down roots in New England instead. These were probably from some ancestor who'd done exactly that.

He laid the letters aside and took up a cloth-wrapped bundle, opened it to reveal an old-fashioned doll, the sort that little girls might have played with in the 1950s. It had a hard-plastic head, plastic legs and arms, and a cloth body, and was wearing a frilly yellow party dress. Someone had knitted yellow booties for it and tied a scrap of ribbon in its hair. The face was expressionless, the lips fixed open in eternal expectation, the cheeks appealingly pink. The bright blue eyes clicked shut when he laid the doll down. It was the standard sort of doll that any little girl of that era might have played with and had probably belonged to one of Tommy's relatives. Danny had heard talk in the village that a young cousin of Tommy's, a little girl named Marion, had gone missing many years ago. According to the gossip, she'd wandered into the woods and was never seen again. It was a sad story, but there wasn't necessarily anything sinister in it. Children sometimes wandered away from their homes and met with tragedy, falling into the sea or getting lost on the barrens in winter.

There was a small wooden box at the bottom, perhaps ten centimetres wide by fifteen centimetres across and about five centimetres deep. In it he found a glass bottle half-full of mouldy earth and stoppered with a cork that had been sealed in wax, a broken pocketknife with an inlaid ivory handle, a small round mirror of the type a woman might carry in her purse, and a single iron nail, hand cut and archaic. Finally, there was a continuous strip of something resembling cured leather, about two metres long unrolled, curiously yellowish, its edges curling under. He bundled it up and returned it to the box, then took the box and the letters with him.

At the foot of the stairs, he stopped and called out, but there was no sign of Tommy anywhere in the house. In the back porch, two empty water barrels stood against a wall, with a metal dipper hung on a hook just above. Tommy's well had never been the best, the water brackish, unfit to drink. For years he'd been hauling water from a natural spring in the woods, so maybe that was where he'd gone. Danny had no way to get hold of him. Tommy didn't have a mobile, had never even installed a landline in his house. "If anyone wants me," he once said, "they can come and knock on me door."

Tommy clearly wasn't home, and Danny could think of no good reason to hang around. He'd turned to go when something caught the tail end of his attention. A scrap of something yellow was wedged between the doorframe and the door. He bent and looked at it, saw it was a piece of fabric, and pulled it out. It had been folded, almost as if whoever had placed it there meant to conceal it, but he couldn't imagine why. He put it in his pocket and took it with him. Perhaps it was nothing.

Danny's mobile phone shrilled into the silence, startling him. He didn't recognise the number, but he took the call anyway. Sometimes people called the police from public telephones or the cheap, disposable mobiles known as burners. It could be important information.

"Deiniol Quirke." Nothing. "Hello?" He pressed the instrument closer to his ear, wondering if there was something wrong with it. "Is someone there? Hello?"

At first he thought he was listening to the ocean, the faint huffing of sea on shingle. Then he realised it was the sound of someone breathing. "I know you're there," he said. "I can hear you. What do you want?"

The breathing trailed away and stopped, then burst abruptly into what sounded like a child's raucous laughter. The connection dropped, and he was left listening to a dial tone.

Weird.

The sun had disappeared by the time he stepped outdoors, and a rank of angry-looking dark grey clouds had piled up against the horizon. He shivered and buttoned his coat around his neck. He hated the spring here. There was no warmth, just months of damp misery and a biting wind. Oh, summer was glorious—when it finally deigned to appear—but so short it was barely worth the name. He sighed and opened the car door.

A snatch of song, carried on the wind, as faint as a whisper but so distinctive:

See see my playmate
Come out and play with me

It had to be his imagination.

CHAPTER THREE

THE PATH wasn't clearly marked, but when had it ever been? Tommy Power knew these hills like the backs of both his hands. It was getting on for dark, though, and he'd never mistaken the location of the spring before now. It had to be here. Maybe if he went to the end of the old woods road, where the big boulder was, he could retrace his steps and find his way to the spring. He'd decided on it earlier that day, after he'd come back from the doctor, knew this was the perfect time to put his plan in motion. Some things you didn't wait for.

He had no watch, had never bothered with one, so he wasn't sure what time it was, but this was April, and the clocks had gone forward for daylight savings time, which meant the sun didn't set until nearly eight o'clock in the evening. Lord Jesus, he'd been out here all day, probably going in circles trying to find the spring. The spring was where he needed to be—it was always best to cross water when you needed to accomplish something important—but he'd slipped down a narrow incline between two immense fir trees, skidding on his knees and falling face first onto the loamy ground. The size of the trees didn't make any sense, either: fir and spruce around here didn't even grow that big. The soil was too poor for anything to make good roots, and so the few straggly fir and spruce and tuckamore clung to earth mere centimetres deep. How could the trees ever get so big? Surely to God there was devilment in it.

The setting sun plunged the forest into blackness, and he was forced to feel his way forward, his hands outstretched in front of him like a blind man, like poor old blind Uncle Paddy from Southwest Path in Kildevil Cove. Uncle Paddy had been old for as long as Tommy could remember. Even when Tommy was a very small boy, he remembered seeing Uncle Paddy feeling his way along the path in front of him with a long stick, probing the ground for obstacles. Occasionally the boys would place objects in front of him—cardboard boxes and empty barrels, a dirty old puncheon tub half-full of brine—to see if he would trip up so they could laugh at him. They didn't mean nothing by it; it was just for devilment, and it was funny to watch the old man flounder in the road, feeling around for his stick and cursing the boys up in heaps.

It wasn't funny now, staggering around the way he was, feeling his way along in the dark. No, it wasn't funny at all. He would go back to the boulder and try to find his way from there. Surely he wasn't that lost. He'd never been lost in these woods in his life. But the spaces between the trees grew progressively narrower, until there was barely room for him to put one foot in front of the other. *I don't want it to be this way*, he thought wildly, as coloured lights began to flicker at the edges of his vision. This was the sickness coming on. That's what it was. His sickness always came on this way. It started every time. Every time.

He sat down on a fir stump to catch his breath, the air rasping hard in his lungs. The forest was wavering in and out of focus. Next thing he'd pass out. Sometimes he'd faint and come to in a different place from where he started. That always frightened him, especially if he wandered outdoors at night. Some years ago the doctor had told him it was the drink that was doing it. "You got to leave off the drink, Tommy. It's rotting your brains away."

"Don't cry," a voice near him said. "I'm lost too." He looked up to see a little girl, standing about a meter away and gazing at him with a sombre expression that looked out of place on someone of her scant years. "Is ye sick or something?"

"Who's you?" he asked. It was dark, and her face was hard to see. He couldn't be sure what he was looking at. "Is ye Marion? Ye looks like Marion." But she couldn't be Marion, could she? Sure, Marion was gone. He remembered, even though it was so long ago. He'd waited for her outside the school that day. In October it was, a lovely sunny day but cool enough to keep the flies away. He showed her the tin jug he brought to pick their berries in—partridgeberries, red as blood and delicious now the frost had touched them, turning their pale insides to a tart and juicy wine.

"I knows where to get the good ones. We'll pick a jug full, and there's bound to be a pudding then on Sunday." He knew the way, and so did Marion. There was nothing to be afraid of. He led her past familiar fishing huts and pasturelands, deep into the forest, always keeping to the path.

"I bet I knows the way," Marion had said, skipping ahead of him so he was forced to run to keep up with her.

"You stay with me if you knows what's good for ye." He'd grabbed her by the arms and shook her then. Not to frighten her or hurt her but to make her understand. "There's things in these woods, my dear. You minds I'm telling ye."

Sometimes youngsters went away. Sometimes they fell over the cliffs and drowned or wandered so deep into the woods they were never found again. Sometimes grown people did as well. Lucy Squires went in over Sibley's Marsh looking for cloudberries one afternoon in August and was gone for ten days. When she came to herself, she was wandering on the Heart's Content barrens forty kilometres away, her dress and stockings torn, with no notion of how she'd come to be there. Llewellyn Single was fishing for capelin one hot day in July when he fell into the water. His body was never found, or so people said.

"I bet I knows the way," Marion said, and try as he might to keep her alongside of him, she wouldn't listen but ran ahead, away. He caught up with her beside the brook, then swollen with autumn rains and impassable for a girl her age and size.

"You go on home," he told her. He turned her around and pointed her in the right direction. "Follow the path and don't go off it. You mind I'm telling ye."

Where was Marion? *I bet I knows the way.*

"I bet I knows the way," the girl said now, holding out her hand to him. "Sure, come home with me. Mam'll put the kettle on."

He shouldn't go with her. He knew better than that. His mother told him not to go anywhere with them, not the Good People, not the ones living in the woods, and him without any bread in his pockets. But she couldn't be one of them, could she? Sure, they were all gone long ago. Some people said they'd never been here in the first place. Not here. Gone, the whole works of them. But he couldn't go with her. He had something important to do.

"I'll help ye up." She put her hands in his and hauled him to his feet, her grip surprisingly strong for a small child. "Come on, then," she said. "I'll show ye."

He rose and went with her. The way they took was circuitous, a wandering route that turned in upon itself until he was sure they were walking an unmarked labyrinth, proceeding by sense and intuition, the little girl always in front and him behind. What did it say in the Bible? "A little child shall lead them." But Tommy hadn't been to mass in ages. Maybe that wasn't from the Bible at all. Now and then the girl stopped and looked behind her, as if making sure he was still following.

"Come on, then," she said, "Mam'll put the kettle on for ye."

The clouds blew away, and the stars came out, and a fingernail scrap of moon. "That moon's waxing," Tommy said aloud. He'd fished for years. He knew to keep an eye out for the weather. "Old Elihu Single won't be going out, no sir. That he won't." Why had he said that? Elihu Single was twenty years dead, had seemed old even when Tommy was a boy. There were so many more old people back then. You never saw them anymore, not now. They took old people and shut them up in special hospitals. The girl was taking him somewhere he didn't know, and his fear of her made him say things he never meant to say.

They rounded a small hillock with the sound of the sea behind it, and suddenly a young man loomed out of the darkness at them. "I knows you," he said to Tommy. He was tremendously tall and very thin. His long arms had enormous pale hands hanging at the ends of them, dangling down by his knees. "I knows who you are." He came closer, bent down and peered into Tommy's face. "Sure what'd you bring him for?" he asked the little girl. "He's no good."

"Don't be an idiot," she replied, her voice suddenly sounding more like a grown woman's than a little girl's. "He's as good as any of them around here. Besides, he got money."

"No, he don't," the man retorted. Tommy wondered if they were talking about him. By now the coloured lights in his head were flashing and spinning, and nothing seemed real. The trees had grown enormous and the ground was a long ways away, so far below that he could barely see it. He was getting sick. He needed to go home and take his pill. "We checked all through that fucking shack he lives in, and there's nothing there." The man was not much more than a teenager, and his face was a constellation of pimples under a thin growth of new beard. "You should have finished him off yourself."

"Don't be like that." She went to where the man stood and held his hand. "It's going to be just us, remember? You and me."

The young man fixed Tommy with a penetrating stare. "And what's we supposed to do with him?"

"We'll bring him home with us." Her lips parted in a smile of absolute malice. "We'll have a bit of fun with him."

"You're not taking me nowhere!" Tommy shouted. "I got things to do here, and it's nothing to do with either one of ye." The skin of Tommy's face and head prickled, and the lights were much too bright, the oncoming seizure heralded with a clanging noise that always sounded to him like someone beating on tin cans with a spoon. He turned to go, knowing that his coming here had been a mistake, that this little girl was not a child at all but some demon of the pit who meant to do him harm. But it was much too late to turn around and flee, even if he could. Another youth appeared out of the darkness and seized his arms, pinning them behind him, and he was stumbling forward over the frozen ground, moving faster and faster, scarcely able to keep up. Someone was singing in a childish voice, a song he knew from his own younger days, the clapping game Marion and her friends would play, sitting on the front steps of Nan's house.

See see my playmate
Come out and play with me....

"Let him up," the little girl—the demon—said. "He's got business here." Tommy's legs were suddenly too weak to hold him, and he sat down heavily. His back came to rest against the trunk of a tree with a sickening thump that drove all the air from his lungs. The girl's face was there before him, filling the whole of his vision. "You can do it," she said, pressing something into his hand. He'd seen the thing before; he knew the shape of it. "You have to do it," she told him. "You know you have to do it." She smiled. "It's what you came here to do."

THE PHONES were ringing off their collective hooks when Danny arrived at the station early the next morning. The promised blizzard hadn't arrived yet, but the weather forecasters expected it within the next few hours. He'd hoped to get over to Eigus to see Tadhg, but it was unlikely he'd find the time now, never mind the impending weather. They'd spent some time on the phone together the night before, but Tadhg was sick with a heavy chest cold, and Danny was so tired he fell asleep with the phone next to his ear. Maybe romance was better left to the young.

He had taken a detour to stop by Tommy Power's house, but there was still no sign of the old man. A look inside revealed that nothing had changed since Danny's previous visit. The dwelling was deserted, and Tommy was nowhere in sight. This was concerning. Tommy was an old man, not in the best of health, and if he had spent the night on the barrens in the cold of early April, he was probably in bad shape. People had gotten lost in the woods and died of hypothermia or wandered away in the fog or fell into sinkholes and drowned. The area's vast, featureless peatbogs weren't safe unless you knew them well, and even then many an unwary berry picker or poacher had met with misadventure. There were even stories....

Here Danny stopped his train of thought. He didn't believe in fairies. His Scottish grandmother had always made him and Sandra carry bread in their pockets whenever they went into the woods, supposedly to avoid being led away by the Good People. In truth, he suspected her carefully wrapped jam sandwiches were intended as snacks, in case they got hungry while playing. Surely to God no full-grown adult actually believed in fairies.

He hung his coat on a hook by the door and found Marilyn, the desk sergeant, fielding calls like a veteran telephone operator. "What the hell's going on?" he asked. "It's like the Second Coming around here."

She grimaced. "Don't I wish. Someone got the word out about the girl in the bog, and the phones are going cracked. Everybody and his mother knows who she is and how she got there. Too bad their so-called evidence is a load of old shite."

Danny didn't know Marilyn Dobbin well—like the rest of his staff, she'd been seconded to the new station from another police force—but what he did know of her, he liked. She was in her midfifties, immaculately turned out, with perfect nails, hair, and makeup. When it came to dealing with members of the public, she had the patience of a saint, but she didn't suffer fools at all and had no time for anyone who considered themselves above the law. She was ridiculously efficient, able to multitask with ease, and made the only drinkable coffee in the station.

"There's people waiting to see you," she said. "Outside your office. Grim-looking bunch too. Bet they wish it was the Second Coming."

Danny handed her the scrap of ribbon he'd found stuck in the doorjamb at Tommy Power's house, holding it carefully by one corner. "Can you ask Bobbi Lambert to have a look at that? It might be nothing, but then again it might be something."

She held it up between her fingers. "A girl's hair ribbon. Mam wouldn't let us out the door on a Sunday without we had our hair done up nice. Where'd you get it?"

Danny told her.

"What?" she asked, incredulous. "Sure, the youngsters are frightened to death of him. They'd run a mile just to get clear of him."

"Why?" Perhaps, given the state of the modern world, this was an idiotic question. "Does he… does he hurt them?"

Marilyn stared at him for a moment. "Lord Jesus, nothing like that. No, he's just…." She paused, searching for the appropriate word but, finding nothing better, said, "Different."

Danny was intrigued. "Different how?"

"Tommy is the seventh son of a seventh son," she replied.

"Oh," Danny said. "So he has the power to heal."

Marilyn glanced away, pretended busyness with something on her desk. "Or kill."

The hair prickled on the back of Danny's neck, but he ignored it. This was nothing but talk, and idle talk at that. He gestured at the ribbon. "Can you get Bobbi to come and pick that up?"

Marilyn plucked a plastic evidence bag out of her desk drawer and dropped the scrap of ribbon into it. "Right away," Marilyn said.

Danny swiped his key card at the security door and went inside. His office was towards the back of the building and would have been quieter if he had any actual walls. He didn't. The wall of the makeshift temporary barrier erected around his desk was thin, and every single sigh and whisper could be heard clear to the other end of the station. Three people were sitting in the hard plastic chairs he'd placed in the corridor. They rose as they saw him coming.

"We needs to talk to you." The first to speak was a young man, perhaps thirty years of age, dressed in a three-piece suit and tie, as if he were going to church. An older man stood next to him, similarly dressed and wearing a flat cloth cap. The third member of the party was a hard-faced woman about sixty years old, her sparse grey hair pinned into a coil at the back of her neck. She wore a long cotton dress to her ankles, dark blue with a pattern of small flowers, and the kind of lace-up shoes his grandmother had worn. Nun's shoes, he and Sandra had always called them. He'd never seen them worn by anyone under the age of fifty.

"I'm Inspector Deiniol Quirke," Danny said by way of introduction. He held out his hand, but none of them approached. The old woman glared at him while the two men lowered their gazes. No trouble to tell who wore the pants in this family, Danny thought. He wondered if they were part of the Harvesters sect who'd been camping on Tommy Power's land.

"Please, step into my office." He indicated the open door. They filed inside, the old woman in the lead, and stood in a line along the wall. "Won't you have a seat?" He himself sat behind the desk and took out a notebook and pen.

"We'll stand, thank you," the old woman said, "and be thankful to the Lord we got our health."

"Can I get you anything?" Danny asked, determined to be polite. "Coffee, tea?"

"We don't agree with taking stimulants," the woman replied in a chiding tone. "The joy of the Lord is our strength." She looked him over as if seeing him for the first time. "Do you know the Lord Jesus Christ?" she asked.

Danny ignored the question. "Now then, how can I help you today?"

"We heard about that girl," the younger man said. "And we don't think our women are safe anymore. We wants to know what you're planning to do about it."

"I have my best officers on it," Danny replied. "We're working to solve this case as soon as possible." He gazed at the three of them, allowing the silence to grow. It was an old trick, but one that had worked well for him in the past. Nervous people, suspicious people—people with something to hide—would rush to fill the gap in conversation. What they blurted out was often very telling.

"It got nothing to do with us," the older man said. He reached to take off his cap, squeezing it between his hands and wringing it like a wet dishcloth. "We keeps to ourself. We got nothing to do with that other crowd."

"What other crowd?" Danny asked.

The old man glanced at the woman, then back to Danny. Interesting. What was he looking to her for? Permission? "Them Harvesters. They're a queer bunch. Not right in the head, the whole works of 'em. Do you know what they does? In church? It's enough to turn your guts!" This last was spoken with surprising vehemence.

"We don't want nothing to do with it," the woman said. "But there's some that thinks we're mixing in with them, and it's not right."

"I don't see how this is a police matter." Danny was beginning to lose patience. They hadn't come to see him for any legitimate reason. Instead, they were wasting his time with some ridiculous sectarian squabble. "You'll have to sort this out for yourselves," he said, rising from his chair. He went to the door and called for Carbage, remembered he'd been told Kevin had stayed in New Melbourne until nearly four in the morning, getting the situation with the Harvesters sorted. He wouldn't be coming in until later.

"We're not safe!" the younger man said, rounding on him with clenched fists, his anger so violent that Danny stepped back a pace. "They're going to think—"

"Azariah!" The old woman's voice snapped like a whip. "You be quiet, now. Mind I'm telling you."

"Our women aren't safe," Azariah continued, ignoring the warning. "Some demon from hell is out there stalking the land like a hungry lion, seeking whom he may devour, and ye crowd aren't doing nothing about it."

June Carbage put her head around the door. "Anything I can help you with, sir?"

"Constable, these people are just leaving," Danny said. "Could you show them out?"

Her glance took them in, the corner of her mouth curling in scorn. "Happy to, sir." She reached towards Azariah, who jerked away like he'd been scalded.

"Don't you go putting your hands on me," he snarled. "I knows what you are. You're not touching me. Don't be at it!" His face had gone a startling shade of puce from his neck to his eyebrows, and flecks of spittle had gathered at the corners of his mouth. "I rebuke thee in the name of the Lord Jesus Christ!"

Danny's fists clenched involuntarily. "Carbage, get these people out of here, would you?"

"Come on," the old woman said. She gestured that the two men should leave and then followed behind, probably so she could keep an eye on them. Danny went as well, just in case they decided to start a revival meeting in the middle of the station. But they allowed June Carbage to escort them to the door without incident and went quietly on their way. Danny had turned to go back to his office when Marilyn spoke up.

"Do you know who that was?" she asked. Her face was grim, her mouth a hard line.

"No, I don't believe I've had the pleasure," Danny replied.

"Oh, that's the Harrises," Marilyn said. "No trouble to tell you've been living away for a while."

"The Harrises?" Danny asked. "I don't remember them."

"Just as well," Marilyn said. "You're not missing much. Religious nutcases, the whole crowd of them. 'Come out from amongst them,'" she said, quoting the Bible, "'and be ye separate.' They don't mix with no one outside their church. Thinks the rest of us are filthy sinners. That young fella, he married a girl from town. Deborah something, I believe her name was."

"He married a St. John's girl?"

"Met her down on George Street, if you can believe that. Witnessing for the Lord."

"What was she doing down there?" Danny asked.

"Deborah?" Marilyn smirked. "Pole dancer. Try getting your head around that, my son." The phone at Marilyn's elbow shrilled, and she reached to pick it up.

Danny stopped by June Carbage's desk, where she was studying the New Melbourne area on Google Maps. "Have we heard anything from Tommy Power?" he asked.

"No, sir." She gestured at the satellite view of the surrounding barrens. "There's nothing there but trees and bog. If he's gone into the woods, he could have gone in any direction. I mean, it's not like there are roads. It's just empty land." She turned away from the computer to look up at Danny. "Do you think he might have gone into the water?" she asked.

"Why would he?" Danny couldn't see it. "He's not one of these surfing types that come out from the city with their longboards and their wetsuits. Tommy was a fisherman all his life. He knows what the sea can do. He'd be unlikely to venture into it for pleasure." He shook his head. "No, I don't think he's gone that way. I think he went into the woods."

"Do you want me to contact the Rovers Search and Rescue?" She was already reaching for the phone.

"Let's get some of the local people together first," he said. "They know the land better than anyone." He made to turn away, then thought of something. "Heard from your brother yet?"

"He's on his way in," she said.

"He doesn't have to come in yet," Danny protested.

She shrugged. "You don't know Kevin. He's a queer hand."

"By the way… why did Azariah Harris go aboard of you like that?" Danny asked. "I thought he was going to get the holy water out and start flinging it around."

She smiled. It was a lovely smile that showed the dimples at either side of her mouth. "My guess is he doesn't see too many lesbians around here," she said. "He might have caught sight of Amy and me at the supermarket."

"Amy's your partner?"

"Yes, sir. Twelve years now. We're like an old married couple."

"Good for you," Danny said. "Do you want to round up some people for a search party? The sooner we start looking for Tommy, the better. He's not a well man."

"I'm on it," she said.

His mobile phone buzzed in his back pocket, and he pulled it out to look at the display: Regan Lampe, MD.

"Oh, great," he said aloud to no one in particular. He swiped right on the screen to take the call. "Regan, what can I do for you?"

"I've done a preliminary on the baby's body," she said. "There's no way that baby belonged to the bog girl, if that's what you were thinking."

"Oh?"

"The body is very well preserved, but she's been dead a long time. I mean, decades." She paused. "Well?"

"That's… uh, well, that's surprising," Danny replied. This was not good news. He'd hoped the baby was connected to the girl so he could at least close off that particular loop in the investigation. This discovery had thrown a wrench into the whole bloody works.

"There's no way our bog girl could have birthed that baby unless she's a time traveller," Regan told him.

"When can I expect the full autopsy?"

"Are you being serious right now?" she asked testily, then swore at him in Inuktitut. Danny didn't know any Inuktitut, let alone swear words, but it sounded pretty bad. "In case you've had your head up your arse, there's a bacterial infection running through three of the old-age homes. One in Old Perlican, one here in Carbonear, and another in Shearstown. I've got bodies coming in here every damn day."

"I'm sorry. I didn't know."

"Well, now you do. You'll get your complete autopsy when I get around to it and not before."

Then his ear was full of dial tone. "Thanks, Regan," he said belatedly.

DANNY MADE his way to the break room, where the new Keurig machine sat waiting. Someone—probably Marilyn; such things seemed to be her purview—had installed a rotating carousel on the countertop, full of various coffee and tea blends. He selected a Columbian dark roast and put the pod into the receptacle, then waited patiently while the device whirred and gurgled fresh hot coffee into his cup. When the cycle completed, he took his cup and, holding it close to his face, inhaled gratefully. The Keurig was a godsend.

He had just taken his first sip when his phone rang again. He fished it out of his pocket and smiled at the caller ID display: Tadhg. "Good morning, my love."

"Ye're chipper this morning." Tadhg sounded cranky and resentful, but Danny could hardly blame him. He'd been battling a nasty chest cold for nearly a week now, was reduced to accepting help from his teenaged daughter, Lily, a fifteen-year-old with an acerbic tongue and wisdom beyond her years. "All right for some."

"D'ye want me to come over with hot soup?" Danny asked. "Mustard plasters for your tender parts?"

"Keep it up," Tadhg growled, "and it'll be a cold day in hell the next time you get near my tender parts."

"So how are ye faring?" Danny asked. "Are ye resting like the doctor told ye to? Let me guess: you figured now would be a good time to catch up on some work, so ye've got Lily acting as your secretary while you wheel and deal from the confines of your sickbed."

"It's got to get done," Tadhg said. "I've got the final plans from the architect for the house I'm going to build on your grandfather's land. D'ye want to see?" He paused for a moment, and Danny could hear him talking to someone in the background before continuing with "Lily thinks you should come for the weekend."

Danny groaned. "It's only Wednesday," he said. "I can't even plan that far ahead, not now. I'm face and eyes into a missing persons case."

"I heard about the girl," Tadhg said. "Any idea who she is?"

"You know I can't talk about it," Danny said, irritated that Tadhg saw fit to press the matter. "Why d'ye keep asking me such things?"

"Maybe I'm interested in your work," Tadhg bit back, "and proud of what you do for a living. Pardon me if I'm treading on your toes."

Danny sighed. "I'm… I'm sorry. Everything's a bloody mess here. I'd love to see you, but I can't leave." He took another sip of his coffee. It was hot and delicious. "How's Lily? Everything okay?" This was a cautious reference to her current remission. Lily had been diagnosed with neuroblastoma when she was a little girl. Her prognosis seemed dire until a bone marrow transplant from Tadhg had finally set her on the path to recovery.

"She's a pain in the arse," Tadhg said flatly. "Thinks she's old enough to have a steady boyfriend. I was hoping you'd be able to talk some sense into her."

"You're her dad," Danny said.

"And you're the only one she listens to," Tadhg replied. "D'ye want her? You can have her. I'll send her over on the boat."

Danny laughed. "I'll try and come over this weekend, but I can't make any promises." He paused. "I love you."

He heard Tadhg huff out a sigh. "I love you too," he said.

"You'll never guess who I ran into the other day. Ford Maddox." He wasn't sure Tadhg would even remember him.

"Our weed dealer from university?"

"The same. He's an engineer. Done really well for himself."

"Huh." Tadhg didn't sound impressed. "I always figured he'd end up dead in a ditch somewhere."

Danny was stung by the acid in his tone. "What makes you say that?"

"He was a drug dealer, Danny. Jesus Christ, that's hardly a guarantee of success."

Last time I checked, you weren't exactly on the straight and narrow, Danny thought, but he didn't say this. They had a tacit understanding that Tadhg's misdemeanours were a thing of the past. "People can change" was what he said instead. *You did.*

"Don't count on it with him," Tadhg replied. "He'd cut your throat and walk away whistling."

"Tadhg, I don't understand why you're so—"

June Carbage appeared and interrupted him. "Sorry, sir, but I thought you'd want to know some local people are forming a search party to look for Mr. Power."

Danny nodded at her to indicate he'd heard and understood. To Tadhg he said, "Listen, I have to go. I'll try and get over to see you this weekend, all right?"

"Mmm."

"Tadhg?" His question fell into silence. "Are we okay?"

"I've got a call on the other line," Tadhg said. "It's Sandra's man, Malcolm. We've been working out the terms of his investment in the project on your grandfather's land. I'd best take this."

"All right, then. I'll—" But Tadhg had hung up. Danny stared at the phone in his hand, as if it were some foreign object that had materialised from nowhere. What the hell had just happened? Had he missed something Tadhg was trying to tell him, failed to read between the frequently indelible lines of their unconventional relationship?

June was still waiting for him. "They wanted to know if you'll be joining them, sir." She looked apologetic. "Sorry to break into a private conversation." Her expression said she'd rather be anywhere else but where she was.

Danny slipped the phone into his back pocket. "It's fine, Constable. I'd best be on my way."

A CROWD of about fifty local people, mostly fishermen and their wives, had assembled in front of Tommy Power's house when Danny arrived. Several of the Harvesters had shown up too, wearing thick winter jackets and woolly hats, likely donated by the Salvation Army. He was surprised to see Ford Maddox standing at the rear of the crowd, talking to someone on his mobile phone. He raised his hand and waved Danny over.

"I heard you were getting together a search party," he said, "and figured I'd come and help out. I know these woods pretty good. Can't say my tracking skills are what they were when I was in the Corps."

"You were a Marine?" Danny was surprised. "Since when?" And how had Ford heard about the search party?

"Joined up after college," Ford said. "I was at loose ends, and they agreed to pay off my student loans in exchange for my service. Guess they needed engineers. Figured I'd get some good experience working around the world, and I did, but not exactly the kind of experience I was expecting."

Danny wondered what he meant by that, but Ford had moved on. He seemed more cheerful than he had when Danny saw him in Carbonear. What had changed? But now wasn't the time to ask.

"Okay if I take part?" Ford prompted.

"God, yes," Danny said. He reached out and squeezed Ford's shoulder. "I'll pair you up with one of my constables." As if on cue, Kevin Carbage pulled up in a patrol car. He got out, and Danny waved him over. He looked tired, but that wasn't surprising, all things considered. Carbage had pulled a double shift and then some. Danny introduced him to Ford Maddox, told him Maddox had tracking experience and asked could they work together.

"Of course, sir." The young constable held out his hand, and Maddox took it, holding on a moment longer than was strictly necessary. Something kindled between them, a spark of an elusive quality Danny couldn't put his finger on.

Huh, as Tadhg would say.

Huh, indeed.

Danny got the attention of the gathered volunteers. "Fan out, two to four metres from each other, and move forward in a straight line," he instructed. "The man we are looking for is elderly and in poor health, so go slowly. He may be injured or… otherwise. If you find something, stop immediately and blow the whistle you've been given. Someone will come to you. Is there anybody who doesn't understand any of what I just said?"

The assembled group shuffled their feet, and someone mumbled something Danny couldn't make out, but that was it. "All right, Carbage. You and Maddox go ahead and lead the others. Let me know if you find anything at all."

Carbage nodded. "Will do, sir." He turned to gaze at Maddox, and there it was again, Danny thought, that weird something kindling between them. What the hell was going on?

"You're an idiot," Alison's voice said inside his mind, "if you don't recognise attraction when you see it. Wise up, Danny."

He glanced over as a dark SUV pulled up and stopped. The dog unit had arrived from St. John's. The handler, an old friend from Danny's training days, got out and opened the back of the vehicle, releasing a trim Belgian Malinois from her cage. He saw Danny and raised a hand in greeting. "How's ye getting' on, Quirke?"

"Chris Tremblett! Good to see ye." Danny shook his hand, then ruffled the dog's fur. "Sheena looks great. How's she been?"

"Oh, she's finest kind," Tremblett replied. "We bred her for pups last winter." Sheena looked up at him with warm, intelligent eyes, as if she understood every word being said. "She had some beautiful babies."

"I bet she did." Danny smoothed the soft fur on her head. "Think she can help us find Mr. Power before the weather turns?"

"We'll certainly try, won't we, Sheena?" Tremblett said. He bent to fit a halter and leash to her. "You got something with his scent on it?" he asked Danny.

Danny produced one of Tommy's worn flannel shirts and handed it to him. Tremblett offered it to Sheena, who sniffed at it, then raised her head to look at him. "She's ready to go," Tremblett said.

"See you on the other side," Danny remarked as Tremblett and Sheena set off towards the forest.

The searchers spread out, everyone with their eyes on the ground, moving steadily forward, and Danny followed, bringing up the rear. He knew the tendency of non-professionals to see only what they expected to see and to overlook things a trained police officer would notice. The strong coffee was singing in his veins, energising him and propelling him forward; he forced himself to concentrate and to move slowly but steadily, overlooking nothing. He knew even if the others did not that their chances of finding Tommy alive diminished by the hour. Tommy was old and in poor health, and the darkening sky indicated the blizzard would be upon them much sooner than predicted. Danny had participated in many similar searches in the past, and only once had the missing person—a small boy who'd wandered into the woods while his grandmother was distracted—been found alive. He claimed to have followed a bright yellow bird deep into the forest, where he danced with a cheerful group of little men who fed him bread and molasses and sang songs to keep him company until searchers could locate him. Danny seriously doubted any little men would be feeding Tommy anything.

He moved steadily, slowly, paying careful attention to where he placed his feet, wary of treading on anything that might lead them to Tommy. He saw a discarded cigarette butt, two or three bottle caps, the pull tab from a tin can, and nothing more. How far could Tommy have gone, an old man in poor health and without the energy or stamina to travel very far? At most he'd wander a mile or two before he got too tired to go on, and much of that would probably be in circles as he tried to find his way out. The thick stands of fir and spruce were hardly the vast primordial forests of Europe, but even the most familiar woods path could be overtaken with fast-growing alders, and known shortcuts obscured by tenacious raspberry canes and invasive knotweed. In the dark, exhausted, probably dehydrated, even a young man might stumble and fall, injure himself. Almost everyone Danny knew in Kildevil Cove had gotten lost in the woods at one time or another, and there were myriad stories of local people who'd gone berry picking in the country, and were missing for hours and sometimes days.

A smattering of yellow near the base of a black spruce caught his eye: a spray of coltsfoot, bright against the dark dun colour of the trodden earth. The ribbon he'd found at Tommy's house was yellow. A girl's hair ribbon, Marilyn had said. Forced into the doorjamb a foot or so above the threshold. Why? He knew some people claimed you could cast a curse on someone by placing particular knots in a length of cord and laying it across the doorstep. Was that what it was? Why would someone curse Tommy?

By NOON, there was still no sign of Tommy Power, and Kevin Carbage was beginning to wonder if the old man hadn't vanished into thin air. He and Ford Maddox had split off from the main group, agreeing that they could make faster time and cover more ground that way. They were both experienced searchers, trained to spot the subtle signs and signals of human presence in an area, but so far neither of them had seen even the slightest indication that Power had passed this way. Kevin sat down on a convenient boulder and took out a canteen of water, offered it to Ford. "Thirsty?"

"As fuck," Ford said and chuckled. "You do know that's got an alternate meaning," he said, reaching to take the canteen.

"It does?" Kevin watched as Ford drank, the muscles of his throat rippling. Uh, yeah, this was going to be trouble. *You love Karen*, he told himself. *Karen is your girl. You're going to get married to her.*

"Thanks," Ford said, passing back the canteen. His lower lip glistened with moisture, and Kevin had to look away. "Yeah, it does," Ford said, and added, "Why won't you look at me?"

"We should keep going," Kevin said, glancing at the sky. "There's weather coming in, and I don't want to be caught out here in the open." They had stopped at the base of a hill Kevin remembered from childhood hiking trips with his class in school. There was a pond behind it, full of trout, and he'd often come fishing here as a teenager, sometimes catching as many as a dozen fat fish in one go. Mr. and Mrs. Hapgood, friends of his parents, had a cabin out this way, but they didn't use it much now that Mrs. Hapgood was confined to a wheelchair with a badly broken hip.

"You didn't answer my question," Ford said. He caught hold of Kevin's sleeve. "You got something against me?"

"No, of course not." The top two buttons of Ford's plaid shirt were undone, revealing a patch of dark chest hair and the tanned hollow of his throat. So he was an outdoorsy type, liked being in the wilderness, far from civilisation. Was probably good with his hands, knew how to tie all kinds of knots and things, chop wood and carry water. Kevin's gaze wandered to his hands. They were tanned, too, strong-looking, with long fingers, neatly trimmed nails. Hadn't Danny said that Maddox was an engineer? So he worked with those hands, was probably a very physical person.

"Ah, I get it." Ford's amused voice broke into Kevin's thoughts. "If your feet are wet and you can see the pyramids, huh? Is that it?"

"What?" Kevin tucked the canteen back into his knapsack. "If my feet are wet?"

Ford assumed a patient expression. "If your feet are wet and you can see the pyramids—" He broke into a broad grin. "—well, son, you're in de Nile." He chuckled. "Get it? Denial." He reached out and poked Kevin in the shoulder. It hurt. "Come on," he said, turning to go. "There's weather coming in."

They walked for a long time in silence, following a ridge of fir trees to the north and keeping the ocean on their left. About one in the afternoon it started to rain, and the temperature dropped so that the rain began to freeze and stick to the trees. The ground below their feet grew dangerously slick, and several times they had to grab on to each other in order not to fall. The daylight this time of year was long, but the clouds overhead were so thick there was scant illumination to penetrate the heavy growth of forest. Ford stopped near a stream and bent to look at something.

"Check this out," he said. Kevin leaned over and peered at it—a scrap of yellow fabric. "Think that might be something?"

"I don't know," Kevin replied. He fumbled in his pocket for a pair of tweezers and a plastic evidence bag. "I'll collect it just in case."

"You lean too far over that stream, you'll fall in," Ford said. "Here." He indicated the space in front of him. "I'll keep hold to ya. Damn rocks are slippery." He waited until Kevin had moved into position, then wrapped his arms around the constable's waist. "Go on, now. You can get it."

Kevin plucked the scrap of material from the water and dropped it into the bag, careful not to touch the sides. He leaned back, his heels slipped on the slick rocks underfoot, and he was falling—

"I got ya." Ford's voice, with its soft American accent, was at his ear, and Ford's warm breath was ghosting over the back of Kevin's neck. Ford's hands tightened on Kevin's waist. "Okay?"

His touch burned like fire, even through Kevin's jacket and sweater. He swore he could feel Ford's hands on his skin, and it disturbed him. Even more disturbing was the knowledge that he liked it.

"Fine." Kevin stepped backwards onto the grass, breaking Ford's hold, and stowed the evidence bag in his pocket. "We should keep going."

They had been walking for a while when the freezing rain thickened into snow, the huge, wet flakes coming dense and fast, obscuring the view in front of them.

"Oh, fuck," Ford muttered. "I hate snow. Where the hell are we?"

Damned if I know, Kevin wanted to say. He could just imagine Danny's reaction when he told him they got lost. "Let me check the map." He pulled out his phone and thumbed through to Google Maps, waited with a pounding heart while the screen filled with the familiar graphic, but when he tried to enter something in the search box, it returned an Offline warning. "I can't get a signal," he said. He nodded at Ford's pocket. "Try yours."

Ford did. There was nothing. "Fucking Jesus," he swore. "Ain't this wonderful." He peered through the falling snow, squinting. "If that old guy's still out here, I sure hope he found somewhere warm to hunker down. It is colder than a witch's tit."

He wasn't really dressed for inclement weather, Kevin thought. Neither of them was. He'd taken the precaution of wearing a midweight parka with a thick sweater underneath, and fleece-lined jeans, knowing how capricious the spring weather on the island could be, but Ford was wearing a padded plaid shirt under a down vest and ordinary chinos.

"We're going to need shelter," Kevin said. "And soon." It irritated him, what Ford was wearing. He should have known better. "Didn't someone tell you to dress properly?"

"Didn't think we'd be out here all goddamn day and night," Ford snapped. "Or that you were such a fucking amateur."

Kevin bristled but said nothing. They didn't have time for this. The snow was getting heavier, the wind was rising, and the full-blown blizzard the weather office had promised had most definitely arrived. "There's a cabin just through there," he said, pointing ahead of him into the swirling snow. "It'll do until the weather clears. Stay close to me."

Ford said nothing, merely nodded. Kevin set off, head down and shoulders squared. The snow blew into his face, blinding him, each individual flake feeling like a tiny knife against his skin. It would be easy to get lost here. Even people who knew the lay of the land got lost all the time, and some of them never came home. Hunters set out across the barrens in search of moose and stumbled into sinkholes in the bog and drowned, their bodies never recovered. The old people would say they'd been fairy-led, but Kevin didn't believe in such nonsense. His religious father always said there was nothing in heaven or earth that the Lord God hadn't made with his own hands, so therefore nothing natural was to be feared. Fairies were demons from hell who had assumed the shape of men to lead people astray and damn their souls to darkness. If a man was right with God, no manner of evil could harm him.

But Kevin knew better. Evil came in different guises, each one as capable of harm as any other. He stole a glance behind him at Ford Maddox, walking with his head bent, his arms wrapped around himself. He was shivering. Maddox sensed Kevin's gaze and nodded. "How much farther?" he shouted over the tumult of the storm.

"Almost there," Kevin lied. In truth he had no idea where the cabin was. He'd long since forgotten how to get there, if ever he knew it in the first place. He was wandering alone and unprotected in a storm with a man he didn't know. Someone whom Danny Quirke had vouched for, but then, Kevin didn't really know Danny either.

"What's up there?" Maddox called. He nodded at a dim shape ahead of them. "Looks like that might be it."

Kevin peered into the falling snow. "Hard to say," he shouted. "I need to get a closer look." But it wasn't the Hapgood cabin. It was a tumbledown shack, an abandoned hunting cabin in the middle of nowhere, and would probably provide little if any shelter.

"Better than nothing," Maddox said. "Come on!"

They approached the building and searched around it for the entrance, but there was nothing. The swiftly falling snow was piling up, obscuring the shack's external features. Kevin got down on his hands and knees and scraped at a slab of stone with his bare hands.

"I think it's a doorstep," he said to Maddox, who bent over him to see. "The door should be here."

They put their shoulders to it and pushed, but it resisted. The wind had risen to an eldritch howling, flinging icy handfuls of snow into their faces.

"Try again," Maddox urged, his face very close to Kevin's. His eyelashes and eyebrows were coated in ice, and he was shivering violently. "I'll be damned if I'm freezing to death out here."

"Look. Up at the top." Something had caught Kevin's attention. "It's a hook." He reached up and eased the rusted metal out of its corresponding eye, feeling along the doorframe for any other impediments. When he and Maddox pushed this time, the door swung suddenly inwards, nearly spilling them to the ground. Kevin caught hold of it and shoved it closed. He grabbed a long bar off the floor and slotted it into a pair of wooden brackets on the back of the door, pinning it closed. The sound of the wind died away to the level of a whisper.

"Shit," Maddox breathed. He tucked his hands into his armpits. "It is cold in here." There was an old-fashioned pot-bellied wood stove against the opposite wall. "Think I might be able to get that going," he said, "if we've got something to start it with."

"I have a lighter." Kevin brought it out and handed it to him with shaking hands. "Keep it on me just in case. It looks like somebody left us some wood." He indicated the neatly stacked pile of logs next to the stove. It was a ridiculous situation, stumbling upon an abandoned hut in the middle of a storm and finding it already supplied with firewood, as if someone had been expecting them to come this way. His father would have called it "an answer to prayer." His old man believed in things like that, God intervening when you least expected him, coming to the rescue of his chosen people. If you called on God in your hour of need, he would help you. Except that one night all those years ago. That night….

Kevin shook his head, willing the memory away. It was bad enough he relived it in his dreams; he refused to let it colour his waking hours as well.

"Well, thank you, somebody," Maddox said. He was shivering so hard his entire body was vibrating. He opened the door of the stove and laid in some kindling, lit a piece of old newspaper, and coaxed the whole lot into flame. Once it was going, he added two logs crosswise so the air could circulate and closed the door. They crouched near the stove, warming themselves in silence as the fire got going. Maddox didn't look good, his lips and fingertips nearly blue.

"Stay here," Kevin said, getting up. "I'm going to get the blankets off that bed so you can wrap up." The sagging double bed was of a similar vintage to the stove, with an iron bedstead and a mattress so thin it could have been slipped under the door. Kevin dragged it and the blankets over to the stove and made up a pallet. "Come on, get in," he said. "We can keep each other warm."

Ford looked at him. "Oh, I see," he said, and his grin was back. "That old chestnut."

Kevin stared. "I don't…. Listen now, I'm not…. I'm engaged to be married, you know."

Ford stood up and started taking off his wet clothes. "Is that so?" He laughed, not unkindly. "I was married once myself, son." He toed off his hiking boots and pushed them closer to the fire, unzipped his pants and slid them down his legs so he was standing in front of Kevin in his boxer shorts and socks. "Never believed in labels, myself."

Kevin stood up. He and Ford were of a height, and he was now looking the other man in the eye. "I'm engaged," he said, "to a woman."

Ford swayed close to him, taking Kevin's face in his hands. "Son," he whispered huskily, "right now, I don't give a shit."

DANNY ABANDONED the search once the snow became too thick for him to see more than a foot or so in front of him. He called the searchers in and met Chris Tremblett and Sheena back at Tremblett's truck.

"Just as well to give it up for a bad job," Danny said. "At least until the weather clears." He nodded at the dog. "Did she get anything?"

Tremblett shook his head. "Thought she might be on to something just the back of Buckler's Hill there, but I think it was too faint for her. If he passed that way, it was a while ago. Do you want us to hang around?"

"No." Danny shook his head. "Weather says this is going to last through the night and possibly into tomorrow afternoon." He didn't say it out loud, but they both knew it would be too late for Tommy Power. "You okay to get back to St. John's?"

"We'll be fine," Tremblett said. He clapped Danny on the shoulder. "Sorry it didn't work out."

"Thanks for coming." Danny reached out and rubbed Sheena's side. "You did a good job, my darling, you did so." He stepped back to let Tremblett put her in the back seat. "If I hear anything, I'll let you know."

The remaining searchers were filtering out of the woods now, many of them with their heads bent against the storm. Danny instructed them to check in with the duty constable and give their names so he'd know everyone had made it back safely. The constable, a young woman in her midtwenties, handed him the muster list. "Everybody present and accounted for, sir, except for Constable Carbage and Mr. Maddox."

Danny looked up from the list. Kevin and Ford hadn't returned? That was worrisome. But of all the searchers, surely they were the least likely to run into problems. No way he could send people back out to look for them now. He'd have to hope they'd get back soon, and if they didn't, well, that'd be three people to search for tomorrow.

"Okay." Danny gave her the list. "You go on back to the station. We've done all we can do for now."

He waited till the others had gone, then climbed into his car and called Tadhg. "We didn't find him," he said. "The weather's after turning off bad. I sent everybody home out of it."

"Poor old bugger," Tadhg replied. "I expect he never figured he'd go this way."

"No."

"And ye're gutted about it, aren't ye?"

Danny smiled. Tadhg knew him too well. "Yes."

"D'ye want me to try and get over to see ye?"

Danny peered through the windshield. "It's not fit, bhoy. Stay where you're to, sure." He wanted—needed—to see Tadhg, but it wasn't in the cards, not today. "I'm off home. Call me later on?"

"Sure, you knows I will." It was so good to hear Tadhg's voice, to feel his familiar warmth, even though he was many kilometres away and there was an expanse of dark water between them. "I love you," Tadhg added.

"Me too."

Danny closed out the call and headed for home. The roads were already well covered, and visibility was almost down to nothing. He drove slowly and cautiously, but the car still slipped and slithered, fishtailing dangerously on the turns. The journey to his rented house took three times as long as normal, and pulling into his driveway nearly sent him sliding over the cliff into the sea. His hands were shaking as he retrieved Tommy's wooden box from the back seat and went into the house. Inside, he set a match to the fire he'd laid that morning and coaxed it to a fierce blaze, then went into the kitchen to put the kettle on. He placed a quick call to the station and got hold of Cillian Riley, told him he'd be working from home for the rest of the day, but Riley could call him if something important cropped up. Then he changed out of his sodden clothes and into a warm sweatshirt and jeans, pulling a pair of wool socks on over his ice-cold feet. He poured boiling water over a willing bag of TyPhoo Extra Strong and sat down at the kitchen table with Tommy Power's wooden box.

He untied the knot in the twine that held the bundle of letters together and carefully spread the envelopes out on the table. There were ten—no, twelve—in all, the postmarks spanning approximately a year, from 1954 to 1955. The return address read simply Boston, MA; all the letters were addressed to Tommy Power. Danny did the mental arithmetic. Tommy would have been about twenty years old when these were sent. Danny arranged the correspondence in order of date and slid the first letter out of its envelope.

> *My dear Thomas,*
> *I received your letter of the fourteenth but owing*
> *to circumstances beyond my control I was unable to*
> *respond until now. I have been very ill with what the*
> *doctors say is nervous exhaustion but which I know*
> (the word 'know' was underlined several times) *is the*
> *result of supernatural influence. I have exerted all my*
> *powers to turn this malignity back on the one who gave*
> *it, but have so far been unsuccessful. As a result of this*
> *unfortunate event, I have lately been hospitalised in the*
> *MacLean, to my great distress.*
> *I shall attempt to aid you in whatever way I can,*
> *but be warned: my help may be some time in coming and*
> *may not be in the form or manner you might expect.*
> *Fondly,*
> *Aunt Ditti*

A quick Google search indicated what Danny suspected: the MacLean Hospital was a psychiatric institution. He wondered what the "nervous collapse" entailed, but resisted the urge to speculate based on the contents of a single piece of correspondence. The second letter, dated six weeks later, contained more of the same.

> *Now you must do* exactly *as I tell you and not*
> *deviate from my instructions in the slightest. On the first*
> *day of the full moon, take a length of common cord—*

Danny laid aside his tea. Something about the phrase "a length of common cord" resonated with a particle of memory. Him and Sandra, both very young, sitting in his grandfather's open boat. They were wrapped in a tartan blanket belonging to his grandmother, who herself entered the boat with a loaded picnic basket and a Thermos bottle of hot tea. Before any of them were allowed to get aboard the boat, his grandfather handed in a piece of twine, into which three distinctive knots were tied. This was laid on the floor of the boat, underneath the plank where he and Sandra sat.

"What's that, Grandar?"

"That's a charm and never you mind."

But there was another name on it, something more esoteric and probably sinister. He squeezed his eyes shut, willing the memory to surface. What was it called? He remembered reading about it in a folklore course while he was at university. You took a length of cord and you tied knots in it and attached things….

The image swam into his consciousness, something at once familiar but dimly seen, and all at once he knew the thing and understood its meaning. That obscure part of him that made unusual connections between seemingly unrelated things lit up and clanged like a church bell. The length of cord, the knots, the feathers from a bird, tiny stones gathered off the beach, bits of shells….

A witches' ladder.

WHEN KEVIN woke it was hours later, and the sound of the wind had died away. He was lying on the mattress in front of the wood stove, which seemed to have gone out. What time was it? How long had he been here? He sat up and glanced around, saw Ford across the room, pulling his shirt over his head.

"Good morning," Ford said. He reached for his puffer vest and slipped it on. "Looks like the storm's stopped." He sat down on a rickety wooden chair and reached for his boots. "You want me to build the fire up again?"

"No." Kevin pushed the blankets away and got up. He was fully dressed, and this surprised him. When had that happened? His memory of the previous night was a jumble of sensations and emotions he wasn't ready to think about. "Thanks anyway."

"You sure slept well." Ford bent to lace up his boots, then stood and came towards Kevin. "What's that they call it? Sleepin' the sleep of the just?" His gaze flickered over Kevin's face and darted away. "Um, look…." He scratched his head. "I don't want you to think—"

Kevin cut him off. "I don't think anything," he snapped. He searched around for his boots, found them next to the woodstove. Someone—Ford—must have put them there to dry. He shoved his feet inside and laced the boots up savagely. "We should get back. Inspector Quirke probably thinks we fell off the face of the earth." Not to mention his sister, June, who would likely be freaking out about now. Older than him by five minutes, she regarded Kevin as a lifelong simpleton whose safety she was personally responsible for.

"I was going to say we can resume our search," Ford replied. His face had closed down, and his eyes were cold. "That poor old man is lost out here somewhere, and we said we'd find him."

Before he could speak further there was a knock on the door. Kevin quickly removed the bar, and then someone pushed their way inside.

"Kevin!" A tall figure swaddled in heavy clothes and a fur cap peered at them over the edge of a scarf. Gord Janes, a local man whom Kevin remembered having seen in the search party the previous day. "Lord Jesus, bhoy, we thought you was after falling down a hole." He glanced at Ford, nodded. "Got a bit of bad news. They found poor old Tommy." He took a breath. "Dead, he is. God love him, the poor old soul."

"Did he die of exposure?" Ford asked.

Gord shook his head. "Had his throat cut. Danny says it's murder."

CHAPTER FOUR

THE DAY of Tommy Power's funeral, the Wednesday not quite a week after he was found, it rained—violently, copiously, driven by a cold wind from the east. Danny stood at the graveside with Tadhg and Lily. He'd asked Tadhg to come. Tommy had no living relatives or friends, and the thought of him being buried with no one in attendance was more than Danny could bear. It was bad enough the way he'd died; to have no one at his funeral seemed like a final insult.

Danny was surprised when Tadhg arrived from Eigus with Lily, given it was a weekday, but Tadhg explained it was a school holiday. Danny was pleased to see her, although she looked less than thrilled to be there.

Until the very last moment, Danny had hoped the old man would be found alive. Cold, perhaps, and disoriented, probably having wandered some distance from his home, but not this. Never this. His body had been found in a grove of fir trees, propped up cross-legged with his head leaning forward in a grotesque parody of someone sleeping in the open. His throat had been slit from ear to ear.

The two searchers—local couple Dan Tucker and Harry Jamieson—had called the police station. June had taken the message and alerted Danny. Since the body was so far in the woods, it was impossible to take it out on foot, but luckily the recent blizzard had dumped a good twenty centimetres of fresh, powdery snow on the ground, and they were able to bring Tommy out with the help of a horse and sleigh. Regan Lampe had sent the ambulance from Carbonear, and the body was duly dispatched to the morgue for an official autopsy, although there was no doubt in Danny's or anybody else's mind about the cause of death.

He and June Carbage had searched Tommy's house immediately afterwards for clues to his murder but found nothing of any use. The forensics people had been through it with their fingerprint powder and their tweezers and bags, but no one besides Tommy—and Danny himself—had been in or out of his house in recent memory. Danny vowed not to give up on finding Tommy's killer, but in the meantime, the old man deserved the respect of a funeral.

Kevin took up a collection in the town, and Danny used the money to purchase a coffin from a company in Port de Grave that made beautiful caskets out of local wood. He paid for the minister and the gravedigger out of his own pocket. Normally the hearse with Tommy's body in it would have travelled from the church to the cemetery, but Tommy had no religion, so Danny opted for a simple graveside ceremony and the dignified interment of Tommy's body. If the United Church minister—a fiftyish woman from Nova Scotia—thought the lack of a religious service strange, she didn't say so.

The hearse had arrived at Carbonear hospital the previous morning and retrieved Tommy's body from Regan Lampe's cold storage locker to convey it to the funeral home in Winterton, where Hap Green prepared it for burial and placed it in the casket Danny had picked out. The money Kevin had collected wasn't much, but Tadhg wired Danny a sizeable donation, out of which he purchased a simple, beautiful coffin made of local birch with inlaid panels of white pine and a dark green lining that reminded him of the deep spruce woods Tommy had loved. For the top of the casket, he purchased a spray of mountain-ash berries and cinnamon ferns, bound together with simple twine.

Danny was emotionally unaffected during this entire process, something that surprised him, especially considering Alison had died only two years previous and that hers had been the most recent casket he'd had to purchase. Perhaps it was because he had no emotional connection to Tommy, barely remembered him from childhood. Tommy's death saddened him the way any death saddened him, but he didn't feel as if he'd been punched in the chest.

Tadhg and Lily stood together, miserable in matching yellow waterproofs, huddled against the rain. There was no point to an umbrella, not in Newfoundland; the violent wind tore umbrellas to shreds and sent them flying over the sea to Ireland. Today felt more like December than April, but that was typical. You didn't come to the island for the weather, you stayed in spite of it.

"Thanks for coming," Danny told Tadhg. "I really appreciate it."

"God love him, the poor old bugger," Tadhg replied. "Somebody got to stand up for him. It's a hard thing when a man's got to go out of the world alone." He shivered. "Could have picked a better time of the year to die." He realised at once how inappropriate this was and blushed. "Sorry."

Danny wasn't offended. Tadhg had a remarkable ability to put his foot in his mouth. "No," he said, "you're right. It is a hard time of the year to die." Anytime was a hard time of the year to die. "And how are you doing?" he asked Lily. She was obviously going through a Goth phase, judging by her cosmetics-induced pallor and the thick black eyeliner that ringed her eyes.

She shrugged and rolled her eyes. "Whatever."

Tadhg rounded on her. "Lily!"

"What am I supposed to say?" she asked. Danny suspected she didn't really care about the answer. As he watched, she took out a mobile phone and swiped a finger across the screen, then turned and wandered away.

"She's…." Tadhg watched her go, clearly annoyed. "She's been a little pain in the arse lately."

"She's a teenager," Danny said. "Remember what you were like at her age?"

Tadhg smirked. "Too big for my boots," he replied, "and thinking I was God's gift to the world."

"I remember," Danny said. "Here's Elizabeth."

The United Church minister had a shock of white hair dyed purple in the front and a ring in her bottom lip. She reached to shake Danny and Tadhg's hands. "We can get started whenever you're ready," she said.

"I guess we're ready now," Danny replied.

Tadhg called Lily back, and the three of them followed Elizabeth to stand in front of the yawning hole in the ground. Danny hated funerals—did anyone really like them?—but understood they were for the benefit of the mourners and not the dead. The church at Alison's funeral had been packed with everyone who had known and loved her, and afterwards they had all come to shake Danny's hand or hug him and offer their condolences, but he was numb to it. There had been nothing beautiful or transcendent about Alison's death. It was merely the long-overdue end of her horrific suffering. Until Alison's illness, Danny had never heard of fatal familial insomnia, a vicious disease that slowly drove its victims into dementia and insanity from lack of sleep. At least Tommy Power had died relatively quickly.

Danny only half listened while Elizabeth read the Order for the Burial of the Dead: "I am the resurrection and the life, saith the Lord…." His thoughts drifted not to Tommy or Alison but to Tadhg, standing across from him, the hood of his yellow waterproof partly obscuring his face. He loved Tadhg. He was as sure of this as he was sure of anything. Tadhg was his past, his present, and, he hoped, his future. Did Tadhg feel the same about him? Always there was this nagging doubt in the back of his mind that Tadhg was only with him because he was familiar and convenient. Maybe Tadhg would leave him someday, meet someone else who suited him better, someone who excited him. Did Danny excite him? They were two middle-aged men, for Christ's sake, hardly in the first flush of youth. Maybe Tadhg would meet someone younger, more vital, with more to offer than Danny. As if sensing Danny's gaze on him, Tadhg lifted his head. The corners of his mouth quirked upwards in a smile. "I love you," he mouthed.

Danny let out the breath he'd been holding. "I love you too," he said silently. Lily, head bent over the screen of her mobile phone, was oblivious to this exchange, and Danny found himself wishing she might take herself off somewhere for an hour or two after the funeral so he and Tadhg could be alone. He suddenly wanted Tadhg with a fierceness that surprised him, and he was glad the hem of his raincoat effectively hid the evidence. He forced his attention back on Elizabeth, who was reading a prayer about the resurrection and the repose of the soul, and then the ceremonial part of the funeral was done. He and Tadhg moved to help the gravedigger lower the coffin, letting the straps slip slowly through his hands.

"Oh for fuck sake!" Lily exploded. "Just drop the old fucker in the hole already!" She burst into a flurry of giggles.

Tadhg's head jerked up, and Danny was momentarily shocked into open-mouthed silence. They managed to lower the coffin the rest of the way, and the gravedigger, with a quiet word to Elizabeth, began filling in the grave.

As soon as he was able, Tadhg stormed over to where Lily was and grabbed her by the arm. "What the hell is the matter with you?" he asked. "You show some respect, or I swear to God I'll smack your arse!"

She wrenched away from him, rolling her eyes, and stomped off in the direction of Tadhg's car.

"Do you want me to talk to her?" Danny asked. He wanted—needed—to see Tadhg alone, but perhaps that wasn't possible.

"No, just...." Tadhg gestured wearily in Lily's direction. "Let her go. I'm black in the face talking to her."

"Come over to the house for a drink," Danny said, "you and Lily."

Tadhg laughed. "Are you sure you want her in your house?"

Danny moved close to him, caught hold of his bicep and squeezed gently. "I'm sure," he murmured.

He got into his car and pulled out of the church parking lot. When he arrived at his rented saltbox on the point before Tadhg, he went inside and fetched a bottle of Glenfiddich and two glasses. Lily could have Pepsi or fizzy water if she wanted it. Maybe he'd even put the kettle on, make a pot of strong tea, something to take the chill out of all their bones. But a few minutes later, when Tadhg's car pulled up, only he got out.

"She's gone to visit a school friend," Tadhg explained, stepping into the front hall. "She sends her regrets."

He followed Danny into the kitchen and gratefully accepted the glass of whisky. Danny found a bag of pretzels in the cupboard and dumped them into a bowl.

"Unless you want me to cook something?" Danny asked.

"Your cooking is shite," Tadhg replied, leaning in to give him a whisky-flavoured kiss. "And I'm not interested in food." He caught hold of Danny's arm and tugged him close. "You, on the other hand...."

Danny wasn't of a mind to dispute it.

"SORRY," DANNY murmured. "Didn't mean to crush you." He was unaware of how much time had passed, how long they'd spent reveling in each other, and he didn't really care. After a moment he asked, "What's up with Lily?" He snuggled close to Tadhg and laid his cheek against the other man's shoulder. "She's not herself at all, is she?"

Tadhg seemed discomfited by this, judging by the slight quickening of his heartbeat. "It's nothing," he said. "You know what the young people are like."

Danny leaned up on his elbow so he was looking at Tadhg. "I've never known Lily to act like she did today."

"It's puberty," Tadhg said uncomfortably. "The chemo delayed it for ages. I guess now she's just a walking cascade of hormones."

"She's seeing someone?" Danny asked. "A doctor, I mean. It can't be easy on her."

"She's seeing a psychiatrist in St. John's," Tadhg replied. "A Dr. James Fahey. He's the best money can buy."

"But we've got universal health care in this country," Danny reminded him. "So cost isn't even an issue, is it?"

Tadhg shifted in the bed. "Dr. Fahey's a specialist in private practice," he said, his tone resentful, shading into angry. "He's not part of the government medical care program."

"So he's a quack," Danny stated flatly. He had an innate distrust of private practitioners, the kinds of doctors rich people went to when they didn't want to wait to see a public physician. The Quality always felt they had the right to jump the queue.

"He's not a quack," Tadhg protested. "He's developed a unique homeopathic protocol that uses… native herbs and… plants and things. It's called complementary medicine. He uses things that come from the same geographical area as the patient to encourage the patient's body to heal itself."

"The same geographical area," Danny said. He could feel his eyebrows crawling up towards his hairline. "So if you have a headache, I give you a beach rock to suck on and that'll be all right?"

"Jesus, Dan! Not every kind of treatment has to take place within the walls of a hospital. Since when are you so fucking parochial?" Tadhg rolled away from him and got up. "Mind if I take a shower?" he asked, changing the subject. It was typical Tadhg in all his evasive glory.

"Sure," Danny replied. He threw the covers back and got up himself. "Room in there for two?"

"It's your house," Tadhg said. It was hardly the enthusiastic response Danny had hoped for.

"Never mind," Danny said tartly. "I'll wash up in the downstairs bathroom." He descended to the lower level, the shock of sudden cold pricking gooseflesh on his naked skin, and went into the small room at the rear of the dwelling. It seemed to have been added to the house as an afterthought, almost like a lean-to, with a low ceiling that sloped towards the ground and barely enough room for a toilet and a sink. It was conveniently situated near the kitchen, so perhaps whoever was doing the cooking could nip in for a quick pee as the situation demanded. But it was a charming little room, painted dark gold, with shiny brass fittings on the sink and toilet and a tissue holder in the shape of a Scottie dog. His grandmother, a war bride from Fife, would have been absolutely wild about it.

He couldn't figure out Tadhg's weird mood. He seemed to blow hot and cold without provocation these days. Was there more on his mind than Lily? Perhaps the new project wasn't going well and he was ashamed to say anything about it. It was like Tadhg to keep things to himself. He'd kept the secret of Sandra's pregnancy for thirty years, willingly taking the blame instead of revealing the dark rot of incest that lay at the heart of their family. It had been her grandfather who'd impregnated her, not Tadhg, but he'd kept quiet rather than shame Danny and Sandra.

Danny sighed, turning on the tap and letting the warm water flow over his hands and into the small basin. For Christ's sake, why was Tadhg so prickly? Danny was concerned about Lily. He cared about her, would even venture to say he loved the girl like she was his own daughter. Was he so wrong to ask the questions he'd asked?

He washed himself quickly and wrapped a towel around his waist, went back upstairs. Tadhg was already dressed, his hair still damp from the shower. He was sitting on the edge of the bed, pulling his socks on.

"Hi," he said, when Danny appeared.

"Hi," Danny replied. What a bloody ridiculous conversation for two grown men to be having. He passed by Tadhg and went to take clean underwear from his bureau drawer. From where he was standing, he had an unobstructed view out the bedroom window, could see his and Tadhg's two cars parked side by side. Was this how it would be forever? The two of them running back and forth between their houses, meeting up for a quick-and-dirty rendezvous before dashing off to wherever it was life took them?

"Hey." Tadhg touched his shoulder from behind, and Danny turned. "I'm sorry," Tadhg murmured.

"I know," Danny said.

"Ye should put your underpants on," Tadhg said. "Ye're freezing your arse off like that." He grinned, and Danny's anger vanished. He bent to slip the shorts on, then donned the rest of his clothes.

"Come here," he said when he was dressed. He pulled Tadhg into a tight, lingering hug. "Ye knows I loves the bones of ye," he said.

"Just my bones?" Tadhg asked playfully. He released Danny with a sigh. "She's… she's been having a hard time, Danny. Lily is so far behind all the other girls her age. There's girls in her school who've got full-time steady boyfriends. Who are already on the pill, for Christ's sake! She's got all this catching up to do. It's tough for her." He shrugged. "Dr. Fahey is helping her. He's prescribed these new medicines that help her manage the mood swings and all the rest of it." His eyes begged Danny to understand. "He's helping."

"All right," Danny said, nodding. "All right." He wondered aloud if something as normal and natural as puberty required medication.

"You're not a parent," Tadhg said. "I mean, no offence, but you don't understand a thing about it."

Danny drew back, stung. "I realise that."

Tadhg looked at his watch. "I have to go." He leaned in and kissed Danny—a slow, hot, dangerous caress that thrilled him to his core. "Will ye come over to Eigus for supper some night?" he asked.

"Kiss me like that again," Danny said, "and I'll go anywhere you like."

He saw Tadhg to the door, where they shared another dozen or so kisses, until finally Tadhg broke away with a grin. "I'd better go get her," he said. "I'll call ye when we get home."

"Okay." Danny hugged him hard. "Give my love to Lily."

"Only if she behaves herself," Tadhg said wryly. "Otherwise she's getting a good boot up the arse."

Danny stood and watched him drive away, raised a hand he hoped Tadhg could see in the rearview mirror. Why hadn't he asked them both to stay the night? Lily could bunk in the spare room if she wanted. They could all sleep in the next morning. Except—no, that wouldn't work. There was too much to do at the station, and God help him if he wandered in late. That would set tongues wagging. People in Kildevil Cove, like people on the rest of the island, loved gossip. It was like meat and drink to them.

He'd closed the door and gone upstairs to strip the sheets off the bed and throw them in the washer when his phone shrilled. It was June Carbage. If she wondered why he was so late back from Tommy's simple funeral, she didn't ask.

"A Dr. Fahey's been mad savage to get hold of you," she told him. "He's been calling all morning. Wanted me to give him your mobile number, but I didn't."

"What does he want?" Danny asked. He wondered if this was the same Dr. Fahey Lily was seeing.

"He wouldn't say, sir. Refused to disclose it to any member of staff. Said it was a 'private matter.'" June's voice was laced with sarcasm. "Some people loves putting on airs."

"It might be nothing," Danny allowed, "but give me his number, and I'll call him anyway."

He keyed in Fahey's number; the doctor picked up on the first ring. "Dr. Fahey, my constable says you were looking for me. What can I do to help?" He fought to keep a note of civility in his voice. It irked him that Fahey had refused to deal with June Carbage, who he knew was more than capable of handling the matter, whatever it was.

"Inspector Quirke, I apologise if I'm disturbing you." Fahey had a pleasant, well-modulated voice and a St. John's Irish accent, that Waterford/Wexford lilt that sounded as if he'd come straight from the Ould Sod. "A patient of mine has gone missing, a young mother with… serious psychological problems. She's been under my care for a while, and her condition worsened after the recent birth of her baby boy."

Danny reached for a notepad and pen. "When is the last time you saw her?"

"She missed her last two appointments, and no one has seen her for over a week," Fahey said. "My office tried contacting her, but she lives with her in-laws, and they don't have a phone. Something about their religion. They don't believe in modern technology of any kind."

"What's her name, this young woman?"

"Deborah Coyle—no, that's her maiden name. I believe she took the husband's name when they married. Deborah Harris."

Harris. The hair on Danny's forearms prickled.

"She's from St. John's originally," Fahey continued. "I don't know if she has any family there or not. We never spoke of it."

"Do you happen to have a photo of her that I can circulate?" Danny asked. Fahey didn't. "Well, can you give me a general description?"

"She's medium height, slender build, dark wavy hair, and green eyes. She has a very confident way of speaking… brash, you might say."

"You might say," Danny repeated. "I'll look into it, Dr. Fahey."

"It's vital that she's found," he said. "She's very vulnerable. Please do your best, Inspector. For all you know, there could be a killer in your town."

"A killer?" This was a strange thing to say. "D'ye have someone in particular in mind?" Danny wrote Fahey in block letters, drew a circle around it.

"Well… no. I don't like to point fingers," Fahey said, retreating from the accusation. "Perhaps I spoke out of turn."

"No, wait a moment, Dr. Fahey." Danny wasn't quite so ready to let it go. "You said there could be a killer in town. Has someone been talking to you?" As a psychiatrist, Fahey probably heard all sorts during his sessions with patients. It was very possible someone had confided in him, confessed to a crime.

"No one has said anything!" Fahey huffed out an exasperated breath that Danny could almost feel against his ear. "Inspector, my patients are very troubled people. They have great difficulty coming to terms with their pasts. One simply can't move forward in life until the past has been dealt with. That is what I do."

"I understand doctor-patient confidentiality," Danny said, "but if you have knowledge of a crime, you are morally obligated to inform the police."

"For the love of God." Now he was becoming distraught. "Inspector, I really must go. This has already taken far more time than I have. Please tell me you will do your best to find Deborah Harris. It's vital that she be found before it's too late."

Danny wanted to tell him that he always did, but that would sound trite, and it wasn't true. If he'd done his best, Eamonn Nolan wouldn't have died in Dublin the year before, and Danny wouldn't have the stain of that death on his conscience.

"I'll get right on it," Danny said and closed out the connection. He sat for a moment, staring at the phone in his hand. His mind was swarming with a dozen different things he needed to do, items on various mental lists that wanted ticking. He supposed he could have gone into the office directly after Tommy's funeral instead of inviting Tadhg back to the house, but didn't he deserve to have a life of his own? He was the sole senior police officer in a tiny fishing village with a supposedly nonexistent crime rate, yet things kept cropping up, and there was always some new thing tugging at him, demanding his attention.

The phone buzzed in his hand, signaling a text message. He sighed, tapped the appropriate icon to open it. It was a web URL that opened a page on the anatomy of the eyeball. This made no sense. Why would someone send him a web link to a page about an eyeball? The number from which the message had originated was listed as Unknown. Before he had a chance to investigate this further, the phone buzzed again with a second text message, another web URL, this time to a page detailing the various ways of—*oh Christ*—gouging out someone's eye. He stabbed at the screen, deleting both messages. He knew better than to think it was a coincidence or a simple mistake. Someone had heard about the woman in the bog.

THE MOOD at the station was subdued, everyone going quietly about their business without any of the usual piss-taking and banter typical of a weekday.

Kevin Carbage had slept badly, dreaming of Deborah Harris. He was standing in the aisle of the old United Pentecostal Church in Kildevil Cove, holding a stack of hymnals, breathing in the musty scent of the building and the smell of old paper. Deborah approached with her baby in her arms, wrapped in a white christening shawl. "Look what they're after doing to me," she said. She thrust the baby at him. "Here, you take it." But when he pulled the shawl aside, it wasn't Deborah's infant boy at all but the baby from Tommy Power's land, grey-skinned and dead, the eyes sunk into the ruined skull, destroyed... and Deborah herself was dead, her left eye missing, the creamy flesh of her pretty face fallen in on itself. "You don't belong here either," she said. "Get out while you can." The baby in her arms began to wail, the screaming rising to a crescendo and merging with his own terrible memories.

He had woken with a headache that seemed to intensify as the day went on. By early afternoon it had settled behind his eyes and throbbed like a secondary heartbeat. He went to the break room to get a coffee and found his sister in there.

"Who pissed in your cornflakes?" she asked as soon as she saw him.

"Don't start," Kevin moaned. "My head's fit to bust."

The Keurig machine gurgled to a finish, and June reached to hand him the cup she'd been making for herself. "Here," she said. "You look like you need this more than I do." She peered into his face. "Have the nightmares started again?"

He nodded, stirring sugar and cream into his coffee. "Yeah." There was no sense lying to June. She'd lived through it all, the same as him.

"Oh, Kev." She reached out and draped her arms around his neck, hugging him gently. "You've got to see somebody. Ye can't keep going like this. Mind I'm telling ye."

He sipped the coffee. It was hot and strong, just what he needed. "You're my favourite big sister," he said.

"Pfft." She put another coffee capsule into the machine. "Your favourite big sister is going to kick your arse if you don't see the doctor. Suffering isn't going to help ye. Come down off the cross, bhoy. Somebody needs the firewood."

Kevin shook his head. "The pills make me sick to my stomach. I feel like I'm sleepwalking through the day." He didn't add, even though he wanted to, that medicating away the dreams didn't work. The bad memories, the intrusive thoughts and images, they all persisted, blooming in his waking hours like poisonous poppies. He would never forget that night for as long as he lived; the sound of her screaming had seemed to split the world apart. It reverberated through his nightmares, and sometimes through his waking thoughts as well. He was forever walking down an endless dark corridor, hands clutched in front of him, body vibrating in abject terror. "No… stop…. Please stop…." He woke with these words on his lips, night after night.

When Kevin got back to his desk with his coffee, the phone was ringing. It was Danny.

"Kevin, we've got a missing woman in the Kildevil Cove area, a Deborah Harris, née Coyle. She missed her last appointment with her psychiatrist, Dr. Fahey, and he's concerned. I think she might be related to the Harrises in New Melbourne. The description loosely fits the girl we found in the bog. Can you check it out?"

"You want me to go now?" Kevin could have kicked himself as soon as he said it.

"Yes," Danny said sharply, "I do. Why? You got something else on today that's more important?"

"I'm… I'm o-on my way," Kevin stammered, feeling foolish.

"Go door to door," Danny said, "Call up the Carbonear and Old Perlican hospitals and the RCMP detachment in Harbour Grace. Ask June to do an internet search and the usual databases. I'll go to the Harris house first thing tomorrow to ask about Deborah and why they haven't reported her missing."

"Yes, sir," Kevin replied, annoyed that Danny saw fit to tell him how to do his job. "I'll get right on it."

"See that you do," Danny replied and hung up. Kevin, angry and rattled, swallowed half of his coffee in a monstrous gulp, burning a hot streak all the way to his stomach. He cursed aloud and pulled his jacket on, found half a damp tea bun in the right-hand pocket. "For Christ's sake…."

He passed June in the hallway as he was tugging on his uniform cap.

"Bad news?" she asked. Like most twins, they were highly attuned to each other's moods. "Ye got a face on ye like a slapped arse. What's on the go?"

"That was Danny," he told her. "That Dr. Fahey you were talking to is after losing one of his patients, a Deborah Harris. Deborah Coyle she was, before she married. Said she didn't show up to her last appointment, and no one's heard from her in donkey's ages. Can you do the computer work on it, and I'll go door to door?"

"Of course I will," she said. She offered him a fond smile, the sort of smile his mother used to give him when he was feeling like absolute shite and there was nothing to be done about it. Kevin missed his mother. Some days, like today, he missed her so much it was like a hard punch in the guts. "You going to be all right?"

"Eventually," he replied, and stepped out into the pouring rain. The temperature had warmed slightly, and most of the snow left over from the blizzard had disappeared. The grass was just beginning to turn a tentative pale green after the ravages of winter, and the sight cheered him. He loved summer, never felt more at home than when he was outside in the sunshine, when the weather was finally not cold enough to kill you for a change. Good things happened in summertime, when it was warm and the light was long in the evenings, fading through a late sunset to a pale blue glow along the horizon for most of the night.

He used the hands-free attachment in his car to call the RCMP detachment as he drove. Danny had already forwarded the missing woman's details, so what Kevin was doing was merely follow-up, a small job to do as punishment so he remembered his place. The call was answered by Angus Swyers, a former classmate from Kevin's university days.

"Kevin Carbage. Whatta ya at?" Angus asked with cheerfulness Kevin knew was feigned. He and Kevin couldn't stand each other.

"I'm checking on a young woman who's missing over this way," Kevin said. "Wondering if there's anything on your end."

"You get in Karen's pants yet?" Swyers asked. Kevin swore under his breath. This was hardly a conversation to be having over official channels. "Figured as much," Swyers said when Kevin didn't reply. "Sure, you're probably gay, bhoy."

"Have you seen her?" Kevin asked, forcing himself calm. He stopped at the intersection leading onto Kildevil Cove's main road.

"Not a whiff, my son."

So that was that. Next Kevin called the hospital at Carbonear, and then the one in Old Perlican. No one matching the woman's description had been in, nor had anyone like that been admitted. He started canvassing houses on Southwest Path in Kildevil Cove, then moved to the houses along the main road, knocking on doors and asking if anyone had seen the missing woman. No one had. He extended his search southward as far as Winterton and Heart's Content, then headed north into New Melbourne, Brownsdale, and Sibley's Cove, but again his search came up empty. Maybe Danny's suspicion was right and this Deborah Harris was the woman in the bog—in which case looking for her was a futile endeavour. He finally returned to the station at five that afternoon, wet and dispirited, stopping long enough to write up a quick report that he emailed to Danny before leaving for the day.

He stripped off his sodden uniform inside the front door of his rented house and left it in a heap on the floor. The house was a traditional biscuit-box design, smaller than was usual, and until recently had been the home of Aunt Suze Pilgrim. When Aunt Suze had gone to her reward the previous summer, her sons had refurbished the house inside and out and offered it as a holiday rental for tourists from the mainland and the States, but they were happy enough to rent it to Kevin on a year's lease. He could have stayed in his parents' old house, which had lain empty since his mother's death several years before, but there were bad thoughts trapped inside those walls, where terrible things had happened. As June so often said, "You're better off out of it."

He was seeing Karen tonight, although considering the day he'd had, he'd rather have a swift kick up the arse. He reached in to turn on the shower taps and caught sight of himself in the mirror. He looked tired and haggard, older than his years. His habitually sombre mood had deepened into genuine sadness. Maybe seeing Karen would lift his attitude a little.

KEVIN ARRIVED at Karen's house in Winterton shortly after seven, bearing a half-dozen bottles of beer and just in time for the second half of the supper-hour news.

"Will wonders never cease?" She greeted him at the door, still in her workday nursing scrubs and wearing woolly slippers on her feet despite the mild weather. Karen was a nurse at Carbonear General Hospital, and she was forever complaining about the state of her feet. Lately she seemed to be complaining about anything and everything, including him. "I was after giving up on you. Figured you weren't going to bother."

"Bad day at work," he said shortly. He didn't feel like explaining it to her beyond that. "You're looking good." This wasn't strictly true. In the past several years, Karen had put on a significant amount of weight, most of it settling around her middle. Her once-dewy complexion was now dull and sun damaged, due to her love of tanning beds, and her hands were raw and red from frequent washing. She was still pretty, and he still loved her... didn't he? He was almost forty years old. Maybe it was time to press the marriage issue, get her to decide on a date, get it over and done with, move on with their life together. She still wore the small sapphire ring she'd accepted from him several years before, but any idea of romance between them had died a hard death.

He took off his shoes in the front hall and moved to kiss her, but she turned her head at the last minute and he got her cheek instead.

"Dad's home," she said. "We're watching TV in the front room."

He followed her through the kitchen, pausing to put the beer in the fridge. The entire house smelled powerfully of Lysol and bleach; Karen liked to clean when she was pissed off. He wondered what he'd done—or failed to do—this time. Roger, Karen's father, was a long-haul truck driver, a French Canadian originally from Sept-Iles, Quebec. He was short and rotund, with an enormous beer gut.

"Eh, Kevin, come in and watch the news," he called. He extended a hand from the comfort of his recliner chair, and Kevin shook it. "You and Karen still got no babies, eh? You got to get busy."

Kevin had heard this speech so many times he didn't even bother to blush anymore. "Where'd you go to this week?" he asked, to change the subject. He didn't really care, but Karen was sitting in stony silence on the other side of the room, and at least this was conversation.

Roger launched into an enthusiastic tale of his latest run down to the French island of St. Pierre, off the southern coast of Newfoundland, while Kevin only half listened. The news reader on the television was talking about the missing woman, Deborah Harris, and someone had created an artist's impression of her based on the available description. She looked like the woman they'd found in the bog. Danny was right, but this was only half the story. How had she ended up in the middle of nowhere with one eye gouged out?

"That young woman, she run off with her boyfriend," Roger said, gesturing at the TV. "That's how they do it nowadays. No respect for family or home."

"She was married, Dad," Karen said. She shot Kevin a glance. "Married with a baby. I don't think she was after running away with anyone, although God knows these days."

Kevin raised his eyebrows at her. What the hell was that supposed to mean?

"Maybe one of these bad boys come along on a motorcycle and took her off with him," Roger opined. He yawned hugely, not bothering to cover his mouth.

He looked like a potbellied pig someone had dressed in human clothes, Kevin thought, his gaze fastening on Roger's short, fat legs ending in plump little feet that reminded him of hog's trotters. He had a sudden mental image of the feet floating in a jar full of pickle brine and had to bite down hard on his bottom lip to avoid bursting into inappropriate laughter.

"These girls, they want a big bad boy can give them a good ride, vroom-vroom!" Roger twisted his hands like someone revving a motorcycle. "Eh, Kevin, you got to give Karen a good ride sometime. She got no babies."

The headache Kevin had been nursing all day began throbbing again at the base of his skull, and he felt momentarily sick. He saw himself many years from now, married to Karen and living with Roger in their tiny house, arriving home from work every night to Karen's mediocre cooking, spending his evenings sitting in front of the TV listening to Roger complain about the news. *I'd rather be dead.* The thought, coming as suddenly as it had, startled him. Moreover, it wasn't true. He was happy with Karen. They were going to get married and have a nice life together—

But you'd rather be dead, his mind whispered.

Later, after finishing three bottles of Kevin's beer, Roger fell asleep in his chair. Karen got up and went into the kitchen. Kevin followed.

"Do we need to talk?" he asked. He approached and put a tentative arm around her. "If I did something to make you mad, I'd like to know what it is."

"You knows what you did, sure." Karen pushed him away, went to the sink and started filling it with water.

"I really don't," Kevin said. He was suddenly very tired. "I wish you'd tell me, Karen. God knows I can't read your mind." He studied the set of her shoulders, her stiff posture. "Do you think we should…." He couldn't even say it. "If you want to, I mean. We could…." He drew a slow breath, trying for calm even as his heart thudded and leapt in his chest like a netted bird. "We could go away for the weekend, somewhere nice, check into a hotel. I don't know if you're on the pill or not, but I can certainly pick up some condoms." Was this what he wanted? *I'd rather be dead.* He tried to imagine being alone in bed with her, uncovering what his mother had always called her "maiden modesty," but his mind refused to go there. Kevin had never seen her unclothed, had never even touched her breasts inside her clothes. And even if she had kept to their agreement of mutual chastity before marriage, he hadn't.

"Son, right now, I really don't give a shit." Ford's voice in his head and Ford's hands on his body, as vivid now in memory as the night of the blizzard. Ford's mouth on his, kissing him like he'd never been kissed before. Kissing him until Kevin fully understood that this act was more than merely the meeting of two bodies, that it had a particular importance entirely apart from the quotidian necessity of human reproduction. Until he'd spent the night with Ford, he never knew what real pleasure was, or how one person could give and take in gorgeous tandem from another.

"I'm after hearing stories," Karen said. She shot a look at him over her shoulder, eyes narrowed. "You were in the woods with some fella all night."

It struck him full in the face like a splash of ice water. "We were searching for Tommy Power." He felt himself reddening under her scrutiny, hot colour mounting into his cheeks. "We got caught in the storm."

She reached to shut off the tap, plunged her hands wrist deep into the sudsy water. "Oh? Queer thing nobody else did."

Queer thing. He was pretty sure that was deliberate. "Are you accusing me of something?" His pulse speeded up, fluttering in his wrists and at his temples. The room felt smaller, as if the walls had shrunk, and he himself was smaller too, diminishing in size, becoming invisible. If Karen knew what he'd done with Ford that night, then everybody else in Kildevil Cove would know as well. The rumours would spread, and there would be no stopping the tsunami of idle talk. "Because whatever you're thinking—"

"Kevin." She cut him off. "This conversation is over." She half turned from the sink, her hands full of suds. "Go on home out of it. We'll talk some other time." She dumped a stack of plates into the sink with a thunderous crash, and Kevin took this as his cue to exit.

OUTSIDE KAREN'S house, Kevin sat in his car for a while, not sure what had just happened. Had he and Karen broken up? They'd been together for so long. It seemed impossible that they should break up over something so meaningless, so undefined. Lots of people lost interest in the physical part of their relationship as time went on. Why was she so pissed with him? Just because he and Ford had gotten cut off from the rest of the search party and spent the night together in the woods didn't mean....

But Karen wasn't stupid. She was popular in Kildevil Cove and knew a lot of people. Whoever had reported this to her knew they would be believed, and why shouldn't she believe it?

It was true.

He started his car and pulled out onto the main road between Winterton and Kildevil Cove. Everything was quiet at this hour, most people having gone home ages ago, now sitting in front of their TV sets, watching reality shows or cop dramas from the States. Something at the edge of his vision made him slow down; he stopped to let two moose, a bull and a cow, cross the road. The big animals plodded silently past him, the female turning at the last moment to fix him with her soft brown eyes before fading into the forest. He moved forward cautiously, aware there could be other moose waiting by the sides of the road, but saw nothing further. As he passed the softball field on the outskirts of Kildevil Cove, the lighted sign of the Circle Club, a local watering hole, came into view. On impulse, he pulled into a parking spot, shut off his car, and went inside.

Kevin wasn't a drinker by nature, but tonight the shabby pub, with its decrepit booths and too-loud country music, called to him. He went to the bar and ordered a beer, something he could sip slowly and still be sober enough to drive. He scanned the room while he waited for the barmaid to pry the top off his Miller Genuine Draft and saw Ford Maddox seated by himself in a booth at the back, typing something on his phone. Kevin took the beer, paid for it, and tipped the girl, then went over to where Ford was.

"Hi," he said. "Can I sit with you?"

Ford looked up. The dim bar lighting caught the strands of silver in his hair. "Hey," he said, and broke into a grin. "Yeah, sit down." Kevin slid into the seat opposite and set his beer down on the table.

"Been trying to get hold of you," Ford said. "I musta left a dozen messages on your voicemail. You avoiding me or something?" He didn't seem angry, but there was an undertone of subtle hurt in his voice.

"Yeah…." Kevin felt himself blush. "Sorry about that." After the night of the blizzard, he'd found himself at a loss for what to say to Ford, deliberately blocking out the memories of their time together in the abandoned cabin and what Ford had made him feel. He wasn't like… that. He wasn't into sleeping with men, being close to them. No, not men. Man.

A man. Ford.

"You took off the next morning," Ford said. "After that guy showed up. Didn't hardly give me a chance to say goodbye."

Kevin began peeling the label off his beer bottle. "That was bad manners," he said. "I shouldn't have done that. Not to you."

"So I warrant special consideration?" Ford asked. He reached his hand across the table, not quite touching Kevin. "I'm flattered. I really like you, Kevin. You're just about one of the nicest people I've ever met, but I gotta tell ya—" He glanced around the bar. "—I can't live my life ashamed of who I am. I did that for years, and I won't do it no more. I'm done hiding."

Kevin considered this, drank some of his beer. He understood what Ford was telling him: he was gay. Did Ford think Kevin was gay as well? Was that what this was all about? The jukebox in the corner was playing Hank Williams Jr. singing "Walk On By." The beer was icy cold, refreshing. Kevin looked up to see Ford watching him, waiting for a reply. Maybe you could be yourself with someone you trusted, someone who wasn't going to tell on you or spread dangerous rumours, someone who genuinely liked you, who wanted you.

"Let's get out of here," Kevin said. He drained the rest of his beer in one go and got up.

"You got any place in mind?" Ford asked, looking bemused. "Maybe we can drive somewhere, away from prying eyes."

Kevin nodded, his whole body thrumming with barely suppressed excitement. "Sure."

Ford got up, threw some coins down on the table for a tip, and they left the bar together. The cold night air was a shock after the warm, fuggy atmosphere inside the pub, and Kevin shivered.

"You cold?" Ford asked.

"No," Kevin said. No, he wasn't cold. They crossed the parking lot together to where Ford's pickup truck was parked. He waited, impatient, as Ford unlocked the vehicle, then climbed up into the cab, trembling.

Wasn't the road to hell supposed to lead downhill? And be paved with good intentions?

"Where to?" Ford asked. He started the truck and put it in gear, then turned to gaze at Kevin with eyes that burned like long-banked embers.

"Take the road down to the Point," Kevin told him. That was all he needed to say.

"I SHOULD be getting home," Kevin said, turning to smile lazily at Ford. His body felt absolutely boneless, and he was warm all over. "Give me a lift to the pub?"

They were silent on the ride back, but Ford drove with one hand on the wheel and the other lying on Kevin's thigh. He pulled into the parking spot next to where Kevin had left his car. "I'd love to kiss you right now," he said quietly, "but we both know that ain't a good idea."

"Yeah," Kevin said, sighing. "Maybe someday this place will catch up to the rest of the world." He unbuckled his seat belt and moved towards the door. "Call me?"

Ford turned and smiled at him, but there was something sad and distant in his eyes. "Sure," he said. "Sure I will, baby. You take care now."

Kevin stepped down from the cab of the truck and shut the door behind him. His own car felt chilly and foreign when he unlocked it and got inside, the driver's seat cold against his buttocks. He sat there for a moment, hands lying loosely on his thighs, his mind and body full of Ford—the feel of him, the smell of him, his touch.

Kevin shuddered deliciously and started the car. He had an early rise the next morning too. He should follow Ford's lead and get home. At the parking lot exit, he stopped, looked left and right, wary of any wildlife traffic that might be passing, but nothing moved in the still landscape of the night. He pulled onto the main road.

He was passing in front of the elementary school in Kildevil Cove when he felt something hit the underside of his car—violently and with a sudden thump. *Jesus Christ*, he thought, *I hit someone. I killed someone.* He stamped on the brakes, bringing the car to a shuddering halt, slammed it into park, and got out, terrified of what he would find. He'd had one beer, just one, but maybe one was enough to register as impaired if they made him take a breathalyser. He knew what the legal limit was, but he'd never stopped to consider his own metabolic rate, whether a single beer would be processed quickly enough to be out of his system by now.

He'd have to call an ambulance; he was a police officer, and he was required to do so. They'd notice something was amiss and question him about it, maybe even make him perform those humiliating field sobriety tests you saw on American cop shows.

Kevin had never been arrested before, had never been touched by even the slightest whiff of suspicion. His personal record was spotless. His Pentecostal upbringing made sure of that. As a teenager, he'd been in church or Sunday school while the other kids his age were out drinking and causing all kinds of devilment. He attended Tuesday night prayer meeting, young men's fellowship on Wednesday night, and youth group on Friday evenings. He sang in the choir, taught Sunday school, read his Bible diligently every single night of his life, until….

When he crouched down and looked underneath the car, he saw nothing. He checked all four tires, wondering if perhaps he'd hit some poor stray animal, but there was no blood. He did a slow walk around the vehicle, checking it the way he'd been taught, crouching to examine the wheel wells and both bumpers. Nothing. When he ran a hand under the front bumper, his questing fingers snagged on something. He caught hold of it and pulled it free, held it up to the light. It was a scrap of yellow ribbon or fabric, a trimming from a young girl's party dress. So where was the girl? If he'd hit someone, shouldn't they be lying in the road? Unless she'd taken fright and run off into the woods. Traumatised children often behaved in unexpected ways. A child who'd been hurt or frightened might have run away.

He got back into his car, pulled it safely onto the shoulder, and set the hazard lights. He took a flashlight from the glovebox and switched it on, searched the ground around the car for any trace, but there wasn't even a footprint in the dust. Where might a frightened child have gone? On one side of the road was a pond; on the other was a thick, nearly impenetrable forest of spruce and fir. He'd go that way.

Without the benefit of a path, he was forced to pick his way through the woods by instinct, stopping frequently, bending to examine twisted branches and overturned rocks by flashlight. A foraging rabbit startled at his approach and bounded away into the darkness, white feet flashing. There were coyotes in these woods, he remembered, but they were probably more afraid of him than he was of them, urban legends notwithstanding. At the edge of a stream, he bent low to examine what he thought might be the impress of a foot, but he couldn't be sure. Whoever had made it had been barefoot. He could clearly see the imprint of the heel and five individual toes, the print no larger than what a child might make.

Then something hard came down on the back of his head and a darkness as profound as death closed over him.

CHAPTER FIVE

DANNY HAD just pulled into the driveway of the Harris house in New Melbourne the next morning when his mobile phone rang. It was June. "Is Kevin with you?" she asked.

"No." Danny had only gone into the station long enough to check his messages before heading down to New Melbourne. If Kevin had been around, Danny hadn't seen him. He told June this.

"That's the trouble," she said. "Nobody's seen him. Ye know what Kevin's like, sure. He's up every morning putting the birds on the wires. He should be here by now."

"Maybe he overslept," Danny said, getting out of the car. "Have you tried calling him?" Something moved behind the curtains in the front room window of the Harris house. "Listen, June, I've got to go." He rang off before she could answer and went around to the side to knock on the kitchen door.

Like most houses on the island, the front door lacked steps or a landing, opening onto empty air. In local parlance it was known as a "mother-in-law door"—the door you asked your annoying in-laws to use as you put them out of the house. In most Newfoundland homes, the bulk of family life and interaction took place in the kitchen, so it made sense to enter by that door instead—and until very recently, it was traditional not to knock at all, but to simply walk right in.

"Hello?" Danny called, rapping on the door and opening it. "Mr. Harris? Mrs. Harris?" There was no answer, so he proceeded into the kitchen. "Hello? Is anyone here?"

The kitchen looked as if it had been invaded by wild animals, many of whom had decided to nest there. The sink overflowed with dirty dishes, cups, and drinking glasses, all of them foul and absolutely filthy. The refrigerator door had been partially wrenched off its hinges and hung open; it was empty inside except for a smashed carton of eggs and a large ginger tomcat, who meowed in an aggrieved fashion when Danny reached to pet it.

"Ye poor old bugger," he said, rubbing the cat under his chin, "did they go and leave ye all alone?"

"That's my cat," a voice said.

Danny turned to see a small boy of about three or four, dressed in a filthy undershirt and a pair of socks and nothing else. "Where are your parents?" he asked. "Are your mam and dad here?"

"Ambrose!" a voice roared from another room, and the boy startled violently, turned, and ran, nearly colliding with Malachy, who was making his way into the kitchen on his hands. He glared up at Danny. "What the hell do you want?"

"Are you living here?" Danny asked. "Without permission?"

"I got permission," Malachy said, puffing out his chest. "From our Lord and Saviour, Jesus Christ."

"Last time I checked, his name wasn't on the lease," Danny commented dryly. "Where are the Harrises?"

"I got no fucking idea who ye're talking about," Malachy replied. "We come along here, and this house was empty with no one in it, so we come in. We come in, sir, and we made our home here, and this is where we're going to stay, and you got nothing to say about it."

Danny ignored him, pushing past the man and going into the front room. A group of children, ranging in age from very young toddlers to teenagers, were sitting in front of the television set watching a religious broadcast from the States. A red-faced evangelist with hair dyed an improbable black was striding up and down the stage, waving a green handkerchief and ranting about sin. Danny resisted the urge to roll his eyes.

"I'm Inspector Deiniol Quirke," he said and showed them his badge.

"We knows who you are, sure." A young woman wearing a long flower-printed dress stood up and came towards him. She smelled of body odour and dirty hair, and her bare feet were none too clean. "Malachy told us about you." She drew back and, without a word of warning, spat full in his face.

"For fuck's sake!" Danny shouted. He fumbled in his pocket for a handkerchief and wiped the spittle from his cheek, barely repressing a shudder. *Christ.* Tadhg mocked him for still carrying handkerchiefs "like a 19th-century fop," but Danny was grateful he'd one to hand. The warm saliva recalled unpleasant memories of Eamonn Nolan's suicide in

Dublin the year before, the young man standing so close that Danny had been spattered by his blood when he'd shot himself. It had taken months for him to lose the phantom sensation of it sliding down his face.

Malachy propelled himself into the room, saw what was going on. "Flora!" he yelled. "That's no way to act! What have I told ye? Go on, get." He jerked his head towards the stairs. "Get out of me sight. Go on, ye turns me guts, ye do."

The girl—Flora—turned and ran out of the room.

"There's such a thing as hospitality," Malachy said to no one in particular. "Acting like a friggin' savage, now, that's uncalled for."

"Where is the Harris family?" Danny asked. He clenched his jaw and ground his teeth together. "This is their house. Where are they?"

"We don't know nothing about no Harrises," Malachy said. He humped himself across the room and swung his body up into a chair, settling his useless legs beside him. "We come here and seen nobody in this house, so we figured to move in." He nodded at the TV set. "Sure, the electric is still on and there was food left and everything. We took it for the blessing it was and asked no questions."

"Who owns the cat?" Danny asked.

"He's a stray," Malachy replied. "The youngsters been feedin' him."

"When was he last fed?"

"He gets fed plenty," Malachy said. "Listen, we're not hurting anybody—"

"You're trespassing," Danny told him. "You're here without permission of the homeowner." But this was a weak argument at best, and he knew it. What the Harvesters were doing was squatting, if Malachy was telling the truth and the house really was abandoned. "You haven't seen the Harrises at all? They weren't here when you came?"

"Nobody was here." Malachy was getting fed up. Then again, Danny reasoned, that was more or less Malachy's permanent state. "We got the right to be here. Squatter's rights, bhoy."

"Not unless you've been here for twenty years or more prior to 1977," Danny told him, paraphrasing the statute in question. "And even then you'd have to apply to the Crown. I want you and your gang of—" He sought for an appropriate phrase and found one his Scottish grandmother often used. "—god-botherers out of here. You have no legal right to squat in this property."

"Come back with a sheriff's officer and make it happen." Malachy sneered. Danny ignored him, turned on his heel and left. He made a mental note to drop off some food for the cat.

Back in his car, Danny called Moira Fraser. He'd reported the missing Deborah and his suspicions about her possibly being their bog girl, and as usual Moira had insisted upon being kept in the loop.

"The Harrises are not in their house," he told her, "and I have no idea where they went." He told her about Malachy's Harvesters and how they had taken illegal possession of the property.

"Well, get them out of there!" she said.

Danny bit down hard on an impulsive reply. "I'll see what I can do," he said. Maybe he could send June or Riley to speak to the group, advise them to move on and threaten to report them to the Department of Children, Seniors and Social Development on account of their unfit living conditions. Surely to God youngsters couldn't be expected to thrive in the midst of such absolute squalor. "Should we broadcast a missing persons alert about the Harrises?" he went on.

"How long have they been gone?"

Danny shrugged, even though she couldn't see him. "I'm not sure. They're very reclusive. The last time I saw them was when they came into the station, but any number of people could have seen them since then. I'm going to check with their religious congregation, see if anyone knows anything."

Next he called the station, got June on the phone, and told her to contact the United Pentecostal church office and see if anyone had heard from the Harrises.

"I can't find Kevin," she said. She sounded on the verge of tears, and Danny was alarmed. June wasn't a weeper. Apart from her general air of amused tolerance, she rarely showed any emotion at all. "I've looked everywhere. Nobody has seen him."

"Did you call his mobile?" Danny asked. "What about his house?" He wanted to ask her what she'd learned about Deborah Harris, but now wasn't the time.

"Of course I did!" she retorted. "For Christ's sake, something's happened to my brother. I know it…." He heard her draw a shaking breath. "Something's wrong. This isn't like Kevin at all."

"I'm coming in," Danny told her. "Look, June… I'm sure he's fine." He cast about for something reassuring to say, wished Tadhg were there. Tadhg did reassuring so much better than he did. "I'll be there in a few minutes."

Wasn't Kevin friendly with Ford Maddox? Maybe he might know where Kevin was. Danny used his hands-free device to call, but it went to voicemail immediately. He left a message anyway, asking Ford to call him if he heard from Kevin. It was just possible Ford was on the job site in Bay Roberts, supervising the new bridge span he was building over the Veterans' Memorial Highway and not answering his phone.

The station was unusually sombre when Danny arrived. He found June seated at her desk, a pile of soggy tissues crumpled in her hand. He touched her shoulder, and she stood up, flung herself into his arms. The gesture tore at his heart. "That's your trouble," Tadhg often told him, "you feel other people's pain too much." It was the truth. "We'll find him," Danny said. He patted her back, then released her. "He probably just overslept."

"He takes medication." She sniffled and blew her nose. "To help him sleep. He's had trouble sleeping ever since Dad—I mean, he's had trouble sleeping for years. Maybe he took too much?"

Danny didn't know Kevin very well, but he thought it supremely unlikely. He seemed methodical and steady, not someone who'd take a dose of medication and then forget about it.

"I don't see that happening," he said. "I'm sure he's fine. He'll show up soon with a perfectly good explanation."

He went to the kitchen to make her a cup of tea—didn't his nan always say that tea solved everything?—hoping that this would make June feel at least a little better. He waited while the kettle boiled, mulling over the situation with the Harrises. Where had they gone? And why? Were they away on some religious retreat? Danny himself had been raised Roman Catholic. Sunday Mass was something you attended as a matter of course, and he'd dutifully gone to Confession as well, even if it meant he had to invent sins to confess. There wasn't much to get into in Kildevil Cove, so his sins were few in number, unless you counted impure thoughts and furtive wanking underneath the covers. He'd never done anything that would cause him to flee his home in shame. Except Llewellyn Single's death… that event had him out of Kildevil Cove in jig time.

When the tea was ready Danny carried it back to June's desk and laid it at her elbow. She was on the phone. "Here," he murmured, "get that down ye."

She nodded, smiling her thanks at him. "Sir," she said, putting the phone down as Danny turned away, "I did have a look for Deborah Harris. I've printed out some things for ye. I put them on your desk." She'd soldier on, June would, no matter what. He turned back to squeeze her shoulder.

"We'll find him," Danny said. "I give you my word." Privately he thought she'd be better finding something to take her mind off matters, but he wasn't about to suggest it, fearing it would sound callous.

"Maybe after I'll go have a look at the spot where the baby was found," June said, as if she'd read his mind. "On Tommy Power's land." She hoisted the cup he'd brought her. "Soon as I finish this."

"Only if you feel up to it," Danny said.

"It'll help keep me busy," June replied. "And Kevin's bound to be somewhere, right? Sure as shooting the silly bugger's lost in the woods or something." She offered him another watery smile. "Thank you, sir."

He went back to his own office and closed the door. The clock on the wall said it was twenty minutes past ten. Kevin Carbage's shift started at eight. Where the hell was he?

The printouts June had left for him were nearly three centimetres thick, printed on both sides. She certainly wasn't someone who did things half-arsed, that was for sure. Danny thumbed through the sheaf, noting where June had marked pertinent information with a yellow highlighter pen. Deborah Harris, née Coyle, born in St. John's, lived in the Shea Heights region of the city until she left to marry Azariah Harris of Kildevil Cove. Danny wondered where they could have possibly met. Maybe young Azariah had temporarily cast off the shackles of his fundamentalist faith, venturing into the fleshpots of George Street to see what he'd been missing. They were certainly an odd couple, that was for bloody well sure. Or maybe Azariah had gone there with his church, a kind of soul-saving mission, lift up the fallen and all that.

Deborah Coyle had been educated at Holy Heart of Mary High School in St. John's, had been accepted to the School of Nursing at Memorial and had completed three semesters, but left before finishing her degree. That was interesting. He paged through the printed sheaf, idly noting where June's highlighter pen had done its work, and stopped at a section she'd not only highlighted but circled in red. It was a copy of Deborah's medical history: *late stage miscarriage of 8-month fetus.* Had she found herself pregnant while she was at university and had to drop out?

Danny went to look for June and found her still at her desk, sniffling into a handful of tissues. "I'm just going, sir. Don't worry."

"Got a minute to talk about Deborah Harris?" he asked.

"Of course." She blew her nose loudly, then blushed. "Sorry, sir."

"Come back to my office." He stood back to let her go ahead of him down the corridor, then ushered her into his space and sat down behind his desk. "Constable, you've lived in Kildevil Cove for a while, am I right'?"

"Yes, sir." She sniffled and dabbed at her eyes.

"Do you remember when Deborah Harris first came to the area?"

"I do, sir." She took a breath and cleared her throat. "He brought her here, Azariah did. They were married in St. John's, he said. Nobody here even knew he had a woman. Az was always a queer hand, growing up."

Danny smiled reflexively at the colloquialism. "So he just... appeared one day with a new wife," Danny said.

"Yes, sir. Proud as a peacock he was too. We didn't figure he was ever likely to marry, not Az. Sure, none of the girls around here would have him."

"Did she make an effort to fit in?" he asked. "You know, make friends with the other women her age."

"Not that I could see. Always acted like she was above all of us because she was from town."

Danny shuffled through the pile of computer printouts and slid a photograph of Deborah Harris across the desk to her. "She looks like the girl we found in the bog," he said.

"She does, sir. I've also had a look at the autopsy photos Dr. Lampe uploaded to the system. I think Deborah Harris is our girl."

"Yeah, I do too." He drew a slow breath. "The poor thing. I'll tell Dr. Fahey we've found his missing patient." He stood and went to open the door. "Thank you, Constable."

When June had gone, he pulled the autopsy files Regan Lampe had sent him. As usual, she'd done a very thorough job. He'd have expected nothing less from her. In their university days, Regan had been a stellar pupil, winning all the most lucrative scholarships and carrying off all the prizes. She was beyond brilliant, and not shy about letting others know. Her detailed report of Deborah Harris's stomach contents was interesting, building on what she'd initially told him: *Datura stramonium*— commonly known as jimson weed—*Amanita* mushrooms, and something called ayahuasca, a word he wouldn't even try to pronounce aloud. There was also a small amount of Labrador tea and some form of ethyl alcohol, likely as part of a homeopathic tincture. More quackery, he supposed. More of Dr. Fahey's kitchen-sink remedies. How in the hell the man had escaped prosecution all these years, God only knew. It still didn't answer the question of who killed Deborah Harris, and the more he thought about it, the more it irritated him. She might have run away from her husband after a row—was that why the family hadn't reported her missing themselves?—but how had she ended up in a bog with one of her eyes gouged out?

There was a knock on his door, and June poked her head in. "Sir, someone found Kevin's car up near the Circle Club." Her face twisted as she fought with her emotions. "It's been abandoned."

THE AIR smelled like spruce needles, sap, and damp earth. He was lying on something soft that prickled, like a bed of boughs and moss. When he opened his eyes, he saw nothing but a grey dimness, and for a moment he fancied he'd gone blind. Then something moved into his field of vision: a little girl with her hair in long curls, like an illustration from a child's book of fairy tales. She was weaving back and forth, her hands dancing in the air, and she was singing as she did this.

"See see my playmate, come out and play with me…." She leaned close to his face. "Didn't ye just go the wrong way, young Kevin? Too bad for you."

"Come out of that." An old woman caught hold of the girl's shoulder and pulled her away. "Go play with your toys."

"Go fuck yourself," the girl snarled, but she did as the woman said. Kevin made to sit up, but the old woman pushed him gently back down.

"Not too quick," she said. "You've done yourself an injury."

It came back to him then—drinking beer at the Circle Club with Ford, then going to the Point in Ford's pickup truck and….

"How did I get here?" He was in what looked like the back room of a house, a bedroom or a porch, lying on a sagging cot that smelled like spruce boughs, like the bough houses he and June used to build up in the hills when they were children. That was their escape, going into the forest where it was peaceful.

Right. "Someone hit me in the head," Kevin said angrily. "I bloody well didn't do it to myself." He'd been walking through the woods with a flashlight in his hand. That was all he remembered. "Where's my phone?" He felt about in his pockets for it. "And my car keys?"

"She didn't mean no harm," the old woman said. "She didn't realise you were the wrong kind. No good to us, not now. Got to be pure in heart and mind, in soul and body, and you're not, are ye? You've lain with another man."

Kevin pushed her away and sat up. The back of his head throbbed like he'd been kicked by a bull moose. He located his phone in the inside pocket of his jacket and tried to switch it on, but the battery was dead. "Fuck," he murmured. He stood up. The room spun around him, and for a moment he thought he might be sick. He forced himself calm, drawing in deep lungfuls of air until his head stopped swimming.

"We gave you a little drink," the old woman said, "to help with the healing."

"I'll take an aspirin when I get home," Kevin told her. "I don't need nothing else."

"We already gave it to you when we put you to sleep," she said. She smiled, showing a mouth full of beautiful white teeth, probably not her own.

Panic hammered at him. "What?" he asked. "What did you give me?"

"Just a little drink," she said. "A little drink, and then we put you to sleep."

He pushed past her, out of the room and down a narrow hallway. He could see light at the end of it, and an open door admitting a waft of cool, wet air. To one side was a sitting room, several people of various ages grouped around an old man who was listening to the radio, some phone-in show. Kevin scarcely glanced at them.

"What time is it?" he asked no one in particular. When he got outside, he saw that it was daylight. He was standing in a small clearing, surrounded by larch, spruce, and fir trees. To one side was a large boulder, abutting a cliff that rose several hundred metres into the air. A wooden ladder had been affixed to its face.

He fought back the incipient panic. He couldn't be all that far from Kildevil Cove, especially if he'd walked. He must have walked. He'd seen no other means of conveyance in the house. No way could the old woman or the girl have brought him to this place. Judging by the angle of the sun, it was anywhere between eleven in the morning and noon, which meant he'd been here about twelve hours—the entire night. The average man could cover about five kilometres of wooded ground in an hour, and he doubted he'd gone even that far. Perhaps a kilometre or two off the main road, no more, so where he was now ought to seem familiar. Jesus God, he'd spent his childhood in these woods, playing with June or picking berries with Mam before....

It ought to be familiar, and it wasn't. Even the air felt different: thick, overladen with moisture, the scent of the trees heavy and cloying. The winter's snow had retreated, leaving bare patches of ground, some a bright emerald green, with tender new coltsfoot flowers already blooming. In the distance he could hear the suck and pull of the ocean, the gurgle of the retreating waves streaming through the shingle, the call-and-response of herring gulls.

I know this place, he thought, but he was lying. He'd gone to a place quite like this many times in his imagination, in daydreams and at night, when he needed to shut out the harsh realities of life. He'd invented all of it: the cliff, the bright green grass, the wooden ladder, the sound of the sea. He wasn't popular at school, not like June. As a child he'd been slow to catch on to lessons, and it wasn't until much later, when he was in high school, that his dyslexia had been correctly diagnosed. For years he'd been told that he was lazy, stupid, wasn't applying himself, could do so much better if only he paid attention. With the appropriate help, his intellectual abilities blossomed, and he was surprised and delighted when further testing showed he had a remarkably high IQ. None of it erased the pain of a childhood spent in the "special" class, being taunted by his schoolmates, called "retard," and shunned on the playground. So he created his own world where he could retreat and be comforted, a place where he was left alone in peace. A beautiful place.

This place.

The wound on the back of his head pounded, and he sat down on a rock, rested his head in his hands. He had to find his way back to the car, and from there he could go home. Somebody had to be missing him by now. June would be frantic. But the pain intensified, blotting out everything, and he was on his knees, retching, heaving up everything he'd eaten and drunk. Someone was watching him; he was certain of it. Watching him and judging him. They could see everything he'd ever done, and none of it was good. He was sinful, the way his father and the church had always said, and Jesus was coming back, and he'd be left behind to face the Great Tribulation alone.

His vision narrowed to a tunnel with blackness all around. The air was thicker now, too thick to breathe, and his throat was closing. He fell over on his back, gazing up at a sky full of blackbirds, crows, and ravens, all circling, making complex patterns in the air like a murmuration of starlings. He was going to die; he had no doubt about it…

And then the world was a white room, with muted noises far off in the distance and a hazy light hanging in the air. His head hurt even worse than before, and he blinked a few times, wondered vaguely if this was hell or heaven. The back of his left hand itched, and he reached to scratch it, but someone moved to stop him.

"Don't touch that, baby. You leave that be, now." Ford's voice. Ford's hand, holding his wrist. "You scared the hell outta me. Hell, outta all of us."

He had the sense that time had passed, possibly a great deal of time, but he didn't know how much. "Where'd they all go?" Kevin asked. His throat was sore.

"Where'd who go, sweetheart?"

"Old woman… little girl in a yellow dress." He'd been in their house in the woods. What was that fairy tale? He'd had it in a book when he was little, a story about a house in the woods that walked around on chicken legs, and an old woman in a flying mortar and pestle. The old woman had given him something to drink… the old woman in the chicken house. Was there a chicken house?

"There was only you." Ford sat down next to Kevin's bed. "You're in Carbonear hospital. Couple of young boys found you walking down the main road in Kildevil Cove, raving about being lost in the woods. You were out of your mind, they said."

"I don't remember." The shapes in his mind were hazy and indistinct. He might have dreamt the things he'd seen. It was good that Ford was here. Ford made him feel safe.

"They called the police. Inspector Quirke himself brought you to the hospital." Ford examined him critically, his gentle gaze on Kevin's face. "Dunno what it was, but you were fucked up on something."

After a while Ford left, and Danny came in with June, who looked like she'd been crying. She flew at Kevin and hugged him, bursting into floods of tears, telling him repeatedly how scared she'd been. "You missing for all this time, sure, and nobody knowing if ye were in the world or out of it." She squeezed him so hard his bones creaked. "We had everyone out looking for you. All up and down the shore."

He struggled to sit up in the bed. June reached across and pressed the button that raised him into a sitting position. "But I was only gone for a few hours," Kevin said, confused. The old woman and the little girl in the yellow dress. Had they done something to him?

"A few hours?" June gaped at him in disbelief. "A few hours? Lord Jesus, Kevin. You were gone for three days."

DANNY HAD just let himself in the front door of his rented house in Kildevil Cove when his mobile phone rang. It was well after nine o'clock in the evening, and he was tired, so he debated for perhaps half a second whether to answer it or not. It was Tadhg.

"I need you," he said, sounding panicked. "I've tried everything I can think of, and she won't come out." He paused long enough to draw a ragged breath. "She won't listen to me. She's been in there all day long, ever since this morning."

Danny didn't have to ask who he meant. "Did the two of you have a fight?"

"No."

Tadhg was lying. Danny could always tell. Over the years, he'd despaired of Tadhg's lifelong habit of prevarication. Why bother lying when it was so much easier to just tell the truth?

"Do you want me to come over?" He squeezed his tired eyes shut.

"Ahhhh…." Tadhg let out a strangled laugh. "Ye know, Danny, it's these new meds the doctor's got her on. It's completely changed her personality." He was silent for a moment, and Danny imagined the long stretch of dark water between them, him here in Kildevil Cove and Tadhg over on Eigus. "I know you're probably beat to a snot after all day at work, but—"

"If I go down to the wharf in Kildevil Cove, can Jesper come in the boat and pick me up?" He couldn't face driving all the way to Portugal Cove to wait for Tadhg's motor launch. Not at this hour of the night, and not when Tadhg's fast boat could do it in a couple of hours. The whole past week had been surreal, from Kevin Carbage's disappearance and mysterious reappearance, to Tommy Power's death, to Dr. Fahey's anguished insistence that Danny find his missing patient. All he wanted was to pour himself a couple fingers of Glenfiddich and sink into his armchair with a book.

"Of course," Tadhg replied, sounding relieved. "He'll be there in an hour. Pack your things for overnight, okay?"

Danny smiled, despite knowing Tadhg couldn't see him. "Of course. See you in a bit."

"I love you," Tadhg said.

"I love you too."

Danny went upstairs and packed a holdall with a change of clothes, clean underwear and socks, his toothbrush, and the Ken Bruen novel he was currently reading. He'd just gotten to a good part, where Jack Taylor had been attacked by a trio of murderous goths intent on cutting off his fingers. Hopefully there would be time to read a little more before he slept tonight. If he slept tonight. He layered thick corduroys over his merino-wool long johns, put on a wool undershirt, a warm Fair Isle sweater, and his thickest pair of socks. Tadhg's boat, the *Day Lily*, was fast, but even in the protection of the cuddy, it was cold out on the water. The wind tonight was straight out of the northeast, full of tiny snowflakes that struck the skin like needles. He didn't relish the idea of being out in it, but needs must. He would do this for Tadhg. He would do almost anything for Tadhg.

Alison's painful and protracted death had left him broken in ways he'd never considered possible. He'd expected to grieve, to mourn her, to miss her daily presence in his life, to succumb to loneliness. Her loss had paralysed him, and when he was finally able to regain some tiny sense of equilibrium, he'd vowed never to open his heart again. Then along came Tadhg. Falling in love with him was the most unexpected thing that had ever happened. At his age—hell, at both their ages—the idea of romance was ridiculous.

He and Tadhg hadn't even seen each other for years, and their first meeting after more than thirty years was acrimonious, full of resentment and long-buried regret. It was amazing they'd found their way to friendship and from there to love. Tadhg reassured and steadied him, even if he at times tested Danny's patience to the limit, and though he'd never really considered having children of his own, he'd come to look on Lily as a stepdaughter, part of his family. Their family. A family of three.

He went downstairs and set a pot of coffee to brew. He'd take a Thermos with him on the boat. Tadhg had been sparing with details, and like as not the situation with Lily was nothing to worry about. Young teenagers tended towards the dramatic. He remembered Sandra at that age, flouncing about the house, rolling her eyes and sighing, continually lamenting that none of them truly understood her. More than likely Lily had wanted something Tadhg denied her, and she'd locked herself in the upstairs bathroom as a protest. She'd come out when she got hungry. They almost always did.

At the appointed hour, he took his insulated Thermos and his holdall and went out, locking the door behind him. He paused to pull his knitted cap down over his ears, shivering as the howling wind snaked a chilly arm around his shoulders, and walked the thirty metres or so to the wharf. In the distance, he could see the lights of Tadhg's motor launch as it navigated the coastline of New Melbourne. Not long now. There was a little flutter of excitement in his belly at the thought of seeing Tadhg.

He climbed aboard as soon as the boat drew alongside, and greeted Jesper, Tadhg's boat captain and habitual marine pilot. Jesper was somewhere between twenty and forty, a Mexican who had fled the treacherous hinterlands of Sinaloa for the island's rocky, windswept shore. He had originally studied naval architecture at the Marine Institute in St. John's, but dropped out in favour of a life spent on the water. Before he'd joined Tadhg's staff, he'd been a ferry boat captain on the Portugal Cove to Bell Island run. That was where Tadhg met him, on his way to Eigus via Bell Island.

"Cold night, Jesper," Danny said. Jesper took his holdall and stowed it away in the boat's cabin.

"Freezing," Jesper agreed. "No sane person would be out in this."

Danny poured them both hot cups of coffee from his Thermos, and they chatted while Tadhg's powerful boat ate up the distance between Kildevil Cove and Eigus. It would take a little while for them to reach their destination, so Danny settled himself in a comfortable seat and watched Jesper ably handle the big boat's controls. His thoughts drifted to Tadhg on Eigus, then to Kevin Carbage in hospital at Carbonear after his apparent poisoning. How on earth did someone vanish into the woods for days without anyone knowing where he was? Had he genuinely been missing, or was his ostensible disappearance an attempt to escape something he'd prefer not to face?

June probably knew, or at least suspected. They had that twin thing between them, just like he and Sandra. He remembered something June had alluded to when she'd first told him Kevin was missing, that Kevin took medication for insomnia. Far be it from Danny to delve into someone else's personal life, but Kevin didn't give the impression of someone carrying a heavy psychic burden. So what was keeping him awake at night? When he'd asked June, she'd pretended not to hear him, turned back to her computer.

TADHG WAS waiting at the wharf with his Range Rover when the *Day Lily* pulled in. He helped Danny ashore, enfolding him in a hug as soon as his feet hit solid ground. "I'm so glad you're here," he murmured. He let go, reaching to open the car door for him. "Come into the warm," he said. He watched in amusement as Danny did up his seat belt. "It's only up the road, sure. I'm quite literally the only traffic on this island."

"It's the law," Danny reminded him and stared pointedly at Tadhg until he fastened his as well.

"She's not been herself for ages now," Tadhg said when they were underway.

"I remember how she was at Tommy's funeral," Danny replied. Lily's uncharacteristic rudeness had shocked him, her blatant disregard. She wasn't the Lily he knew.

"That's nothing," Tadhg said. "She's gone full-on teenager now. I might see her half an hour a day, if she deigns to open her bedroom door." He glanced across at Danny. "She's sooky, crooked as sin, and the mouth on her! Saucy as a dog." He pulled up in front of a looming Nordic-style house and shut off the motor.

"Lily?" Tadhg called when they were inside the house. "Danny's here. You going to come down and see him?"

There was no answer. The big house was uncharacteristically silent. The absence of noise made Danny uneasy. Usually the walls would be pulsing to the beat of Lily's favourite techno-pop. "Is she asleep?" Danny asked.

"Locked herself in the bathroom," Tadhg said wearily. He nodded at the stairs. "Come on."

Danny shrugged out of his heavy coat, peeled off his hat and gloves, and dropped them on a chair. Tadhg lifted Danny's case, and they went upstairs and along the hall to the alcove at the back end of the house where Lily's room was. Tadhg tapped on the door and called her name, but there was no reply, and when they went inside, the room was dark. The only illumination came from her bathroom, where a thin seam of light was showing underneath the door.

"In there." Tadhg gazed at Danny for a long moment. "I should tell you, she's been talking old foolishness lately…." He swallowed, and the next words, when they came, were barely above a whisper. "Saying she wants… she doesn't want to live anymore."

The skin of Danny's face felt suddenly too tight. "She's suicidal?"

Tadhg shook his head. "I don't know. I… maybe she's just being dramatic. You know how teenage girls are. She's probably got something in her head from one of the girls at school." Lily attended a progressive private school in St. John's called Havencrest. The per-semester fees were the equivalent of a year's mortgage payments for most people. Danny had often wondered—privately, of course—how the hell Tadhg was paying for it. She lived in the dormitory during the week, coming home at the weekends. "Place costs the friggin' earth," Tadhg had once said, "but she's happy there." She could have been just as happy at an ordinary public school, Danny thought, but didn't dare say this to Tadhg, who could be touchy about money.

"Lily?" Danny called through the door. "It's me, Danny. Do you want to come out and say hello?"

"She's been in there all day," Tadhg said. "She was crying and shouting for a while, but the past hour or so there's been nothing. I threatened to get a locksmith in, but she said she'd kill herself." He looked sad and lost, and more confused than Danny had ever seen him. "I've no idea what to do."

Danny rapped on the door. "Lily, why don't you come out and talk to me? I haven't seen you in donkey's ages."

There was nothing but silence, an ominous silence that boded ill. Danny stepped back. "We have to get in there," he said quietly. "If she's been in there for hours as you said…." He didn't bother to finish the rest of the sentence.

"Should we just… I don't know, bash it in, like they do in the movies?" Tadhg asked.

"We might be able to kick it in," Danny said. He'd done it plenty of times in his younger days and during his secondment to the Garda Síochána in Dublin. Some people were reluctant to open the door when the Gardaí came calling. "Lily?" He put his mouth close against the door. "Your dad and I have to come in, my darling. Ye can't be in there all by yourself." He glanced at Tadhg, who seemed to be thinking. "What?" Danny asked.

"That door's imported Brazilian mahogany," Tadhg replied. "Maybe I should call a locksmith."

"Stand back out of my way," Danny said. He swung his leg and kicked the door, just above the lock. The shock of the blow ran up into his pelvis and lower spine. He swung and kicked again, saw the panel above the lock buckle with the force, and by the third kick he was in. Lily was sitting on the floor next to a pretty pedestal sink. At the base of the pretty pedestal sink was a pool of blood. She held what looked like a nail file in her right hand and had used it to mangle her left arm.

"Oh sweet Christ—" Tadhg rushed to her, knelt at her side, and gathered her into his arms. Her eyes were wide open but unseeing. She was conscious but completely unresponsive, in an almost catatonic state.

"She has to go to the Janeway," Danny said, reaching for his phone. "I'll get an ambulance to meet us in Portugal Cove. We can—"

"No." Tadhg reached out a hand to stop him. "They'll… she'll end up on the psych ward. I can't bring her there."

"Good Christ, Tadhg!" Danny was exasperated. "She's torn the bejesus out of her arm. It's got to be looked at." He gazed at Tadhg in astonishment. "She'll need stitches in that." Something occurred to him. "What about Dr. Fahey? Can he come here and see to her? She's his patient, after all."

"He doesn't make emergency medical calls," Tadhg admitted. "His practice is highly specialised, and—"

Lily stirred in her father's arms. "Dad? I couldn't get it out. I tried to cut it, but I couldn't get at it. It was too deep. She said it was already inside me, and I had to get it out." Her torn and bleeding arm had stained the front of Tadhg's light grey pullover. That would never come out, Danny thought abstractedly. You could soak blood out, but even then there were no guarantees.

"I'm here, my darling," Tadhg said. He appealed to Danny: "Isn't there someone you know who can come here and help her privately? I'll pay whatever it costs."

"I'm sure you will," Danny replied grimly. "That's your answer for everything."

"Call them," Tadhg begged. "I'll charter a helicopter if that's what it takes." Tears shimmered in the rims of his dark green eyes. "She spent so much time in hospital, Danny. I can't bear to send her back there again."

"Okay," Danny said, resignedly. "I'll see what I can do."

IT WAS well past midnight by the time Regan Lampe finished stitching up Lily's savaged arm. She'd painted the wound well with betadine and dressed it securely. Afterwards, she drew a blood sample for analysis before giving Lily a sedative injection, and Tadhg carried his daughter up to bed. Danny took the time to slip into the bathroom and clean up the blood, wiping down the floor with disinfectant and disposing of the soiled rags. He also took the opportunity to rummage around in Lily's medicine cabinet. Tadhg had mentioned she was on some new drug protocol, courtesy of this Dr. Fahey, but the only pharmacy-labelled bottles he found were left over from her cancer treatment the year before. Apart from an expired bottle of common aspirin, the only thing he found was a plain brown vial of some earthy-smelling liquid. If it was a drug, it wasn't one he recognised. He met Regan in the kitchen, where she'd put the kettle on and was waiting for it to boil.

"Anytime is teatime," he said. He reached past her into the cupboard and fetched down a cup for himself. He waited for Regan to jump in with some acerbic comment, but she was quiet. "Penny for 'em?" he asked.

"That girl," she said. The kettle automatically shut off, and she reached to pour water into their cups. "She's fucked up on something. I don't know what it is, but it's something." She paused for a moment, thinking. "She kept talking about a new girl in her school saying things to her."

"Like what?" Danny asked. The ways of young girls were a mystery to him. As a child, Sandra had been popular, with a large group of friends who seemed to spend more time at his house than their own. He assumed most girls Lily's age had a loyal cohort of pals to insulate them against the world.

"She told me this girl said she was dirty." Regan scoffed. "The usual bullshit they say to each other, you know how it is."

Danny didn't know how it was. "So is she messed up on drugs?" he asked, although he didn't think it likely. Tadhg would come down on her like a ton of bricks. "Weed?"

"Nobody gets that fucked up on weed, stun-arse." She scoffed. "This was hallucinogenic." She paused, thinking. "She said there was something in her arm? Something she was trying to dig out?"

"Yes." Danny shuddered, remembering. "She said it was too deep, and she couldn't get at it. I don't know what she meant by that."

Regan shook her head, her dark hair swirling around her face. "I got some blood samples that I'm going to have tested. I'd like to know what the hell she took."

He showed her the vial he'd taken from the medicine cabinet. "I found this. No idea what it is."

She took the lid off and sniffed it, shrugged. "I can't tell. Smells more herbal than medicinal. Could be some kind of homeopathic shite. The organic compounds might not show up in the blood sample, depending on how good her liver is at clearing toxins."

"So there might not be anything to find, is that what you're saying?" If Fahey had indeed been dosing Lily with vegetable alkaloids, Danny wanted evidentiary proof. "You'd need to test the liquid itself."

"Lily is very young," Regan replied. "Her body is probably pretty efficient. If you want to know for sure, yes, I'd recommend testing a sample." She held the bottle up to the light. "Where did it come from, anyway?"

"I'm not sure, but she's been seeing this new doctor, a Dr. Fahey. Tadhg thinks he's the best thing going." Danny opened the fridge and took out a carton of milk.

Regan frowned. "Never heard of him. Is he from around here?"

"He's in St. John's," Danny replied. "A psychiatrist who fancies himself a naturopath or some shite."

"Hm. I'll have to look him up," she said. She held up the little bottle. "Is it okay if I take this with me?"

"Yes," Danny replied cautiously, "but don't tell Tadhg. I'd rather not have yet another row with him if I can avoid it." He rummaged through the cupboards and found a biscuit tin full of Peek Freans favourites, but all the bourbon creams were gone. Tadhg couldn't resist a bourbon cream if his life depended on it. Danny offered the tin to Regan, but she shook her head. There was a noise on the stairs, and they both turned as Tadhg came into the kitchen. He looked exhausted, worn through with the stress of worrying about Lily.

"She's asleep," he reported. He nodded at the kettle. "Any hot water left in that?"

Danny got another cup and a teabag, poured hot water in. "Someone's eaten all the bourbon creams," he said, indicating the tin. "Can I interest you in a chocolate digestive?"

"Just tea's fine," Tadhg replied. "You did an excellent job with her," he said to Regan. "Thank you. Please let me know what I owe you."

"There's no charge," Regan said tightly. "It was a favour to Danny."

"Oh," Tadhg said, raising his eyebrows. "A favour to Danny, is it? That's different, then." There was a subtle amount of vitriol in it, and Danny was surprised. Was Tadhg actually jealous?

"Danny and I go way back," Regan said.

"Good to know," Tadhg replied archly. Danny shot him a warning look, but Tadhg ignored it.

Regan laid her unfinished cup of tea down on the worktop. "Now," she said briskly, "if your man can take me back to Portugal Cove, I'd like to be on my way."

"Of course." Tadhg pulled out his mobile and called Jesper. In moments, Regan was at the door, slipping into her sealskin coat. "Are you sure I can't at least pay you for your time?" he asked. "I realise I owe you quite a lot."

She glanced sharply at him, eyes narrowed. "No need. We don't owe each other anything at all." She reached past him to shake Danny's hand. It was a deliberate snub. A horn tooted imperiously outside the front door. Danny didn't envy Jesper having to be at Tadhg's beck and call… but he supposed Jesper was being paid well. If the rest of Tadhg's employees were anything to go by, Jesper was getting a good salary and then some.

"Jesper'll take ye down to the pier," Tadhg said, "and drown ye," he added, sotto voce and behind her back. Danny glared at him, astonished. Tadhg was behaving like a spurned lover. "That's some sealskin coat," he continued, watching through the door as Regan got into the car. "I bet if she loses that she can never go back to the sea."

"She's not a selkie," Danny said, referring to the old Scottish legend about seal people.

"She's not?" Tadhg turned away and shut the door. "Are ye sure?"

"What the hell is wrong with you?" Danny asked. "She came a long way to help you, in the middle of the night. She didn't have to."

"Oh, but she did," Tadhg snipped, "as a favour to you."

"Don't be such a spoilt brat," Danny said. He turned and went back into the living room, stood in front of the floor-to-ceiling wall of glass that made up the eastern side of Tadhg's house. *We are fucking up this relationship*, he thought. He gazed towards Portugal Cove, at the twinkling array of lights visible along the shore. The view from here was magnificent, no matter what the weather.

"I'm sorry." Tadhg spoke from behind him. "I've… got a short fuse lately." He came to stand behind Danny, close but not touching him. "She really went above and beyond. I should give her something. What do ye think she'd like?" This last was phrased as a plaintive question.

Danny sighed, all the anger suddenly gone out of him, and turned around. "You really haven't got a clue," he said. "How's Lily?"

"Sleeping still," Tadhg replied. He tilted his head towards the sofa. "Come sit with me and have a little drink before bed."

"Sure." Danny went to the big leather sofa and sank down onto it. He took the glass of Glenfiddich that Tadhg poured for him and sipped it gratefully. Tadhg poured one for himself and sat down beside Danny.

"Tadhg, what sort of drugs is this Dr. Fahey giving Lily?" Danny asked. "I found a bottle in the medicine cabinet. There was no label on it."

Tadhg gazed at him over the rim of his glass. "You looked through Lily's medicine cabinet?"

"I was curious."

"You're a fucking nosy bastard is what you are," Tadhg said mildly. He drained the last of his Scotch and set the empty glass on the end table. "It's a natural tincture. Dandelions, catnip, some other things. It's to help with the hormonal fluctuations."

Danny couldn't believe what he was hearing. "Dandelions."

"Sure, dandelions are highly nutritious," Tadhg said.

"You said catnip and some other things." Danny caught and held his gaze. "What other things?"

Tadhg huffed out a sigh. "I don't know, Danny. Herbs and stuff like that." He closed his eyes and rubbed them with the heels of his hands. "Christ, I'm tired."

There was no point in pursuing the matter. Danny knew he would get nothing more from Tadhg on the subject. Not at the moment. "Good night's sleep is what you need."

He waited while Tadhg put out the lights, and then they made their way upstairs together, footfalls silent on the lush carpets. Tadhg paused at Lily's room and pushed open the door. She was lying on her side, her damaged arm cradled against her body, the white of the bandage gleaming faintly in the dimness. The hair she'd once lost to chemotherapy had grown back lush and full, the same dark brown Tadhg's had once been.

"The sleep of the just," Tadhg murmured.

In the bedroom, he and Danny undressed in silence and got into bed together. Danny lay on his back and opened his arms. "Come here," he said, and Tadhg went into his embrace, nestling with his head against Danny's shoulder.

"I'm sorry for being such a prick," Tadhg said. His arm tightened around Danny's waist. "I don't know what comes over me."

"You're worried about Lily," Danny replied. A sense of disquiet settled over him. If Dr. Fahey's drug protocol was making Lily harm herself, what might she do next? "Find her a different doctor, Tadhg. This Fahey character.... God only knows what he's been giving her. It could be anything. Please don't give her any more of that stuff."

"He's been helping her, though," Tadhg said, "that's the thing." He turned his head. Danny could barely make out his features in the moonlight filtering through the windows.

Danny was gobsmacked that Tadhg could still think this after everything that had happened. "You know, ye make me absolutely mental sometimes." He moved to sit up, dislodging Tadhg. "The girl's just cut her friggin' arm to pieces and you think he's helping her?"

Tadhg sat up as well, eyes narrowed as he looked at Danny. "It was helping, Danny. This is a hard time for her—"

"Puberty is a fuck of a hard time for everybody," Danny replied. "Christ, I remember it myself. I didn't know if I was punched, bored, or shot out of a gun most of the time. You've got all these hormones surging through you, dragging and pulling you into adulthood."

"It's different for her," Tadhg countered. "She's years behind others her age." His brow wrinkled. "I just... I want her to be like all the other girls." The corners of his mouth pulled downwards violently. He was on the verge of tears. "It's not fair what happened to her. Her classmates are young women, and she's still a child." He turned away, scrubbed a forearm across his eyes. "I want to make it up to her."

"Her cancer," Danny said, softening, "was not your fault, Tadhg." He leaned over and kissed him gently. "She couldn't have asked for a better father than you." He lay down again and drew Tadhg into his arms. "Try to sleep."

"I will."

"And maybe find her a different doctor," Danny said.

"I will," Tadhg promised. "I'll do that."

CHAPTER SIX

JUNE CARBAGE pulled her car up on the gravel shoulder of the road and shut off the engine. It was an unusually warm morning for April, with light winds, and the air was filled with the scents of damp earth and salt water. She checked that her mobile phone was switched on, then got out.

From the road, Tommy Power's land stretched away into the distance. Standing where she was, she had a full three-quarter view of it, bounded on one side by a copse of stunted fir trees and at the far boundary by the sea. The area where the baby's body had been found was inland, where the land rose towards the trees. It was boggy and very wet, the ground saturated with the spring rains, and she'd taken the precaution of wearing knee-high rubber boots. "Goat boots" her grandfather had called them. She'd inherited them from him, along with her love of Irish whiskey.

Bobbi Lambert's forensics team had marked off the area with yellow tape, so it was easy to find, but June didn't go there immediately. Instead, she walked the area slowly, her eyes scanning the ground, looking for something that Bobbi's team might have missed. It was unlikely—they were very thorough—but June believed there was no such thing as too much investigation. But she found nothing, not even a dropped cigarette butt, and the shallow grave where the body had been yielded little. Until Regan Lampe came back with an autopsy report, they didn't even know how the baby had died. She took some photos of the site and headed back to her car.

"Hey, missus!" The shout came from behind her. She turned to see a tall, gangly young man ambling towards her over the sodden ground. He was about twenty years old, and his pale complexion was spangled with pimples. When he grinned, he revealed jagged, uneven teeth with a multitude of gaps and discolourations. Oddly enough, he was wearing a suit of the type her late grandfather had worn in the early 1960s, with a white shirt and a narrow tie.

"Yes? What is it?"

"Who's you?" he asked.

June flashed her badge at him. "Constable June Carbage. And you are?"

"Sure, I'm Luke. You knows me." He grinned again, somewhat idiotically, and gestured towards the hole in the ground. "Dat's something, innit? Wonder who put that baby in the ground."

Her senses prickled. He could very well be a harmless idiot, some Kildevil Cove boy who'd been deprived of oxygen at birth and who was, as the local idiom had it, "a bit simple."

"Luke who?" June asked. He reminded her of a girl she'd gone to high school with in Brownsdale, just up the shore. What was her name again…? Alice. Alice Barrett. The popular girls had shunned her for hcr tomboyish ways and hcr love of sports, and she spent the bulk of her free time in the library, reading, or running laps around the softball field.

"Luke Barrett," he replied.

"Unless you have a good reason for being here," June said, "I'd advise you to move away from the area."

He ignored this advice and came closer. He was incredibly tall, towering over June with little regard for the notion of personal space. "I knows you," he said.

June stepped back. "Please leave the area."

"My aunt is buried over that way." He turned and gestured at a lilac tree. Judging by its size and twisted branches, it was very old. "That tree over there. No flowers on 'un yet, but come June there will be."

"Your aunt is buried over there?" June looked in the direction he indicated. "But the graveyard's over by the church, sure. Why'd they bury her here?"

"No, bhoy," he protested. "The new graveyard is over by the church. My aunt died before I was born, and she's over there. Look, I'll show ye." He started off, then stopped when he realised June wasn't following. "I'm not going to do nothing to ye," he said and held out his hand. "Come on. I shows ye."

She refused the offer of his hand but moved to walk alongside him. "Why are you all dressed up?" she asked. "I don't see too many around here in a suit and tie on a weekday."

"I works up to Green's," he replied, referencing the local funeral home. "We're burying poor old Uncle Dicky Button later on today."

"So you're out roaming around here."

"Just stretching me legs, missus. Nothing for you to worry about." He gestured with his chin at the lilac tree. "Over here." When they reached it, he pointed to a slight depression in the ground. "See, this used to be the old Apostolic graveyard. But when the church burned down, they moved everybody to the new one."

June could just make out an old cement foundation, half-buried by an overgrowth of last year's weeds. "Yes, that's right," she said. "The old church was right here." She had a vague memory of being taken to Easter Sunday services there with Kevin when they were both very young. "When did your aunt die?"

"Long time ago."

Well, that is a lot of help. "And they didn't move her to the new graveyard?"

"Guess not." He shrugged. "I s'pose they must have overlooked some of them." He glanced at his watch, a surprisingly expensive-looking model with a gold face. "I got to go."

"Well, thank you," June said. "Er… thanks."

"Luke," he reminded her. "Luke Barrett."

She returned to her car, tugging off her muddy boots and dumping them in the trunk before putting on her usual Converse sneakers. Her partner, Amy, often joked that if a worldwide cataclysm occurred, June could always live out of her car, and it was somewhat true. She believed in being prepared, and the trunk held extra shoes, a change of clothes, a small overnight bag with clean underwear and personal necessities, and twenty bottles of spring water. Her mobile phone rang as she was tying her sneakers. It was Danny.

"What's on the go?" she asked.

"I was just about to ask you the same thing," he said. "How's the work going?"

"I've just been talking to a fella named Luke Barrett. Says he works at Green's. According to him—" June broke off to lace up her sneakers. "According to him, Tommy Power's land used to be the old Apostolic cemetery." She rummaged in the trunk for a bottle of water, remembered she'd forgotten to replace her stash after she drank the last one. "When the church burned down, they dug everybody up and relocated them."

"So you need to take a gander at the church records, in that case," Danny said. June barely suppressed a groan. "I know," he said, replying to what she hadn't said. "I know you don't want to talk to them, but this is important. If that baby was buried years ago, fine and good. They'll probably have a record of who she was and the cause of death. Case closed. But if not, the death could be more recent, and we might have a case of infanticide."

She huffed out a sigh, blew her bangs off her forehead. The day was warmer than was usual, and she was thirsty. "I'll go there now."

"You might not get anything useful out of the church," Danny warned her. "They weren't always circumspect when it came to keeping records, especially years ago."

"Job's comforter," she said sourly. "I think you're enjoying this, sir."

"Let me know how you get on," he said and disconnected. June sat on the tailgate of her SUV, her feet dangling, and took a few deep breaths. The absolute last place on earth she wanted to go was anywhere near that goddamn church. Maybe she'd ask them for a cold drink of water. Weren't they obligated to give it? "Inasmuch as ye have done it unto the least of these" and so on. She pushed off the tailgate and stood up. There used to be a well on this land, if she remembered correctly. On Sunday afternoons, when morning services were over, she and Kevin would go and look down it. Some local people still got their water there; supposedly it was cold and very sweet.

A tiny segment of memory tickled at the back of her brain. There was something about the well… what was it? Being at the well on a hot summer Sunday, her white knee socks making her legs itch, Kevin dressed in a suit and tie… someone else was there, calling out to the two of them, "Take me. I wants to see it. I wants to see it too." A third child, different from her and Kevin. "No," she murmured aloud, "no, stop. I don't want this." But it rose up in her consciousness like a poisoned tide, a series of images flashing against her inner eye. Kevin a young teenager, roused suddenly from sleep and standing at the end of their upstairs hallway in his pyjamas. Someone was crying, pleading. There seemed to be a lot of noise for so late in the night, and then her father came out of the farthest bedroom, carrying something in his arms. She rejected the image but too late; she knew what it was. Kevin turned in her memory and stared at her, his eyes and mouth looking like three black holes in his face. "He killed her."

There were certain blank spaces in her memory where her parents were concerned. As far as she knew, their father had deserted the family when June and Kevin were about thirteen. Their mother said he'd gone away somewhere, but the explanation didn't ring true. And there was a third child at the well with them; she was almost certain of it. No. It wasn't really a memory, just her brain manufacturing endless "what if" scenarios.

She closed the hatchback and got into the car, hesitated before starting it. Her mobile phone was still in her other hand, and she stared at it for a moment like she didn't know what it was. When next she saw him, she would ask Kevin if the memory of the old well meant anything to him.

Lately her brother had been an enigma to her. Rumour around the station—perhaps started by Marilyn, who was friendly with Karen and her dad—was that he'd broken his engagement with Karen and was seeing someone else. But who? He'd mentioned nothing to her. He seemed moody and disconnected, his mind elsewhere, and he still couldn't remember anything about the time he'd gone missing. Supposedly it was all a blank.

When June arrived at the parsonage, she sat in the car for a full fifteen minutes, scrolling through old text messages on her phone. The pastor's car was in the driveway, so she assumed he was home, doing whatever it was men like him did behind the sanctity of closed doors. June had only met him once. His name was Aaron Prine; he was young, a transplant from Alberta and a strict traditionalist who held to the church's belief that women should obey their men. He allowed his own wife scant freedom, as far as June could tell. She'd only ever seen her once, kneeling in a small patch of flowers in the front yard, her eyes downcast and her hair covered by a scarf.

But the pastor's wife was nowhere in evidence now. June got out of the car and went up the trio of rough concrete steps to the door. She rapped on it and waited. The pastor's wife (everyone called her Sister Olivia) had planted pansies in a little pot beside the door. They seemed to be growing well.

"Good morning," June said as the door opened a mere crack and a woman's face peered out. "I'm Constable Carbage," she said, showing her badge. "I wonder if I might have a word with your husband."

Olivia nodded wordlessly, then opened the door and stood aside so June could enter. She gestured to a closed door at the other end of the small living room.

"In there?" June asked. Another silent nod. "Thank you."

The pastor was sitting at a desk with his back to the door, hunched over a pile of papers and a large copy of the Bible. He glanced over his shoulder as June came in. "Oh," he said, and stood up. "Good morning. What can I do for the police this morning?" He was tall, dark-haired, blue-eyed, and clean-cut. He looked like a Mormon missionary, one of those polite, well-spoken young men who now and then appeared in Kildevil Cove, riding their bicycles door to door and handing out leaflets.

"I'd like to have a look at your church records if I may." She made it sound like a request, but it really wasn't. If he refused her access, she'd simply come back with a warrant to search the premises, and who knew what she'd find then.

"Are you saved?" he asked.

June resisted the urge to roll her eyes. "I need to see the records dating back to at least"—she did a quick mental calculation—"the 1920s. If you could locate those for me, I can be on my way."

"What's it for?" he asked. He looked her up and down covertly, his gaze flickering on her mouth, her eyes, her uniform.

"It's in aid of an ongoing investigation," June said.

He started back towards his desk, reaching for the phone. "Perhaps I should talk to your commanding officer."

"Pastor Prine, that won't be necessary. I have his authorisation to examine the records." They all did this, these little tinpot dictators, tried to get over her time, fob her off with excuses, insinuate or say outright that she wasn't fit for the job. She'd been a police officer for twelve years, and it was getting a bit old. "Please fetch them for me."

He replaced the receiver in its cradle. June sensed movement behind her and turned to see Sister Olivia, wiping her hands on her apron. "Aaron, the lady asked you nicely."

Oh, June thought. Well, then. She watched as his gaze shifted from her to his wife and then back again. He blinked, cleared his throat. "Of course."

She waited while he rifled through an old-fashioned steamer trunk in one corner of his study. A strange place to keep important records, but the church was small and couldn't have enjoyed much in the way of financial support from its parishioners, so maybe this was all he could afford. He came up with three ledgers, their pages yellowed at the edges and swollen with age and moisture. "These are all I have: 1922 through to 1957."

It was an odd interval of time, but she wasn't about to look the proverbial gift horse up the wrong end.

"That's perfect," June said. "May I have your permission to remove them from the premises?"

"Of course." He glanced at his wife, who nodded approvingly. "Just as long as you bring them back."

"I will." She tucked the ledgers under her arm and turned to go. "Thank you," she said, turning back to face him.

"You know, the Lord accepts all of us freely, no matter what we've done."

"I will get these back to you at the earliest possible convenience." She offered him a tight smile and all but ran to the front door and down the steps to the safety of her car. She laid the ledgers on the front seat and started the car, eager to be away.

"Disobedient, that's all she is. Nothing worse than a disobedient female." June shook her head as if to shake the memory away, but her father's voice persisted. "You spares the rod and you spoils the child. Get me belt. Go on, get it!"

And Danny Quirke had wondered why Kevin had nightmares.

THE YELLOW April sunlight lay about the corners of the living room and pooled on the gleaming hardwood floors and the tall built-in bookcases that lined three of the four walls. The day was warm, and so two of the french windows were open to the garden beyond, a small green space overflowing with flowering shrubs, lilac trees, and a little wrought-iron bench under a towering maple.

"Good of you to come here," the man said, glancing up from where he'd been idly picking at a loose thread in his worn chinos. "I suppose we could have met elsewhere, but the hospital don't seem like such a good idea for this sort of thing." His brown eyes were cold, and the expression on his face was weary, like a man who'd ranged far and wide over the world for a very long time, looking for something that could never be found and probably didn't exist. He sighed, left the thread alone. "But I want you to understand this is the last time, and I do mean the very last time." There was significant stress on the word "very." "I know that don't usually mean sweet fuck-all to fellas like you."

"You have my word." It was the first time he'd spoken, the older man. He was sitting in a straight-backed chair next to the french windows, gazing out at the garden like a figure in an impressionist painting. He was dressed modestly in dark trousers and a white dress shirt under a navy-blue cardigan sweater. His hands were clean, the fingernails manicured. He wore the kind of small round glasses that had been in vogue back in the 1930s. They made him look like Heinrich Himmler. He liked to collect antiques, so it followed that the glasses might in fact be genuine. He was anything but.

"You got just as much to lose as I do," the younger man said. For half an hour he'd been sitting on a brown leather couch next to the fireplace, unmoving except for his busy hands, which fretted and picked at things: his trousers, the arm of the sofa, the laces of his brown boots. "I could turn you in."

"Could you? And tell them what?" The older man's thin-lipped mouth turned up in an approximation of a smile.

"That you're not what you say you are. That you're a fraud, a fake." He tilted his head to one side and regarded the older man. "Oh, I don't know... maybe you've been diddling little kiddies in your spare time."

The older man threw back his head and laughed uproariously. "I don't think so," he said. "As far as anyone else is concerned, you're my patient, and my records on your case make it clear you suffer from delusions. It would be your word against mine, and who do you think they would believe, hm? Certainly not you. You're mine, bought and paid for." A sudden gust of wind raised the net curtain, almost flinging it into his face, and he batted at it impatiently. "Nobody knows I'm here except my receptionist in St. John's, and as far as she's concerned, I'm just seeing a patient. I've parked my car down on the beach, out of any local busybody's line of sight." He consulted his watch with a brisk flick of his wrist. "Let's get this over with. I haven't got all day." He stood up and held out his hand imperiously. "Come on. Hand it over."

The younger man sighed and got up from the sofa. "You're the boss," he said. He came forward, extending a thick envelope towards the older man. In the center of the room, a sudden change came over him, and his face twisted as he erupted in a sudden spasm of violent coughing. "Can you—"

"Oh, what the hell is it now?"

"Can you get me a—" He struggled to draw breath, whooping noisily, one hand at his throat. "—glass of water? Just in the—in the kitchen. Right there."

He was ready the moment the older man turned, and he rushed towards him on silent feet, plunging the knife blade deep into the back of his neck, just below the skull. It was over in an instant. The dying man was able to complete a half turn before his shredded cerebellum shut his body down once and for all. He fell onto his back on the floor, his head bouncing with the impact. The younger man bent and picked up the envelope of money, tucked it into the hip pocket of his trousers. He regarded the dead man for a moment, his head to one side.

"Own me, do you? Am I still yours now, bought and paid for?" He leaned over, his voice pitched low even though there was no one to hear: "Yeah, that's what he thought too."

He went back to the couch and dragged out the long roll of thick polyethylene he'd purchased the week before. Positioning it to one side of the corpse, he kicked it so it unrolled, then bent and dragged the man's body onto it.

"You don't fucking own me," he muttered. He'd have to wait until it was dark to do the rest, and then he'd haul the corpse out into the shed, or maybe the garage, where there was room to work. By the time morning came, it would be all over, and it would be as if the older man had never existed. "Gonna put you where you'll never be found."

He went to the liquor cabinet and took out a bottle of Jack Daniel's, grinning as he cracked the seal. Still time to have a few drinks before he got started on the night's work. Maybe one or two. Hell, maybe two or three. He fetched down a heavy-bottomed crystal glass, splashed a healthy measure of whisky into it, and sucked it back.

CHAPTER SEVEN

FORD MADDOX was standing some distance away, shouting into his mobile phone, when Danny arrived, but the litany of curse words was easily discernible even at a distance. A bewildered group of construction workers had gathered around an unfinished concrete piling and were conversing quietly amongst themselves.

"Who found it?" Danny asked as he approached. It was midafternoon, the time of day when he'd normally be settling into his paperwork with a cup of tea at his elbow, but a phone call from Kevin Carbage had put paid to that idea.

"You'd better come and have a look, sir." Carbage had sounded almost apologetic. "It's pretty nasty."

He nodded at Danny's approach. "Young fella over there," he said, in answer to Danny's question. He indicated a redhead whose round wire-rimmed glasses were at odds with his hard hat and safety vest. He didn't look like a construction labourer—more like a site inspector or an architect.

"All right," Danny said. "I'll be wanting to talk to him." He sighed and pulled a pair of nitrile gloves out of his back pocket. "Might as well get on with it."

He followed Kevin to the foot of the new bridge span, picking his way through overturned plastic buckets and piles of loose gravel and crushed stone. The wind had changed during the night, and the air was warm and charged with the acrid smell of curing concrete. Danny crouched to examine the piling, wary of the protruding strands of steel rebar.

"Well, that's not something ye see every day." Embedded in the cement was a human hand. It had been neatly severed at the wrist and was almost the same flat grey as the surrounding concrete. There was a tiny tattoo at the base of the thumb, a small bird with a forked tail that might have been a swallow.

"Cement's newly poured too," Kevin said. "Probably the night before."

"You know about cement." Danny looked up at him.

"I do, sir." Kevin seemed overly proud of this fact. "It takes about thirty days to cure completely, so even if it looks set, it's still mushy." He leaned closer and eyed the pillar. "And whoever did it never used enough aggregate—pebbles, sand, that sort of thing. Must have been in a hurry."

"Aggregate," Danny commented dryly. "Thank you, Constable."

"You gonna do something about this?" One of the construction workers, a fat, swarthy man in his late fifties, shouldered his way through the crowd towards Danny. "Only we got work we needs to get done here. Every minute we stands here farting around, we're losing money."

"Who are you?" Danny asked.

"Onslow Button." He glared at Danny as if the question had insulted him.

"Do you know anything about this?" Danny asked. "Maybe it was you who poured the concrete last night?"

"No, sir. Nothing to do with me." Button backed away and rejoined his fellows as they muttered amongst themselves.

"Nobody saw anything," Carbage said. "Then again, they never do."

Danny straightened up. "Is there more?"

"Sergeant Riley has several constables searching right now. We'll know soon enough if there is."

Danny thought he detected a hint of approval in Carbage's voice but opted not to comment on it. This was quite the turnaround from Carbage and Riley's first meeting, on Tommy Power's land. "Bag that hand and get it to Regan Lampe in Carbonear," Danny instructed.

He went to where Ford Maddox had just pocketed his mobile phone. "What's on the go?" Danny asked.

Ford looked like he wanted to cry. "Are you serious right now? I gotta stop work while your boys strip-mine this whole goddamn area? You wanna take a guess how much this is costing me? Danny, I can't afford this! I am up to my fucking eyes in debt."

"Ford, I'm sorry." Danny genuinely felt for him, but it couldn't be helped. "This is a crime scene now."

Ford turned and walked a few steps away, paced in a circle, came back. "I am already three weeks behind with this project," he said in a pleading tone. "Is there anything I can do to… I dunno, speed up the process?"

"I'm sorry," Danny repeated. "I have to shut you down."

"Shut me down?" Ford was incredulous. "Jesus H. Christ, for how long?"

"I'll know more once the investigation is complete." Danny put a hand on Ford's shoulder, but the other man shrugged him off.

"Goddammit, I am haemorrhaging money here!" Ford replied. "This is—" He broke off.

"Tell your men to pack up their personal belongings and leave," Danny said. "This worksite is closed." He watched as Ford stalked off, furious, nearly colliding with Cillian Riley.

"Our boyo's not happy," Riley observed as he drew near.

"Can't say I blame him," Danny said. "From the way he tells it, this project is operating at a serious loss." Ford would be hard pressed to make a profit on it now.

"One of the constables found some other body parts in the woods nearby," Riley said. "A hand, a foot, a male torso, and a head." The gruesome inventory was at odds with Riley's appearance—in jeans and an open-necked henley shirt, the warm breeze ruffling his dark curls. Danny felt a sudden twinge of lust, suppressed it. He was with Tadhg now. He loved Tadhg.

"Christ," Danny moaned. "Tell me they haven't moved anything."

"Told 'em I'd break their heads if they did," Riley said, smiling.

He and Danny left the building site and followed a narrow footpath into the woods. "Right here, sir." Riley indicated a blue tarpaulin. "I tossed this on to keep them dry."

"Good man."

Danny seized a corner of the covering and drew it off, bent to examine what the constables had found. The torso was most definitely male, with a thick coating of grey hair over the abdomen and pectorals and heavily muscled shoulders at odds with the man's apparent age. The hand bore a ring with the Memorial University crest. An educated corpse, then. The most promising find, the head, was unfortunately also the least likely to be useful for identification purposes. The face had been bashed in brutally and most of the teeth were shattered.

"Where's the rest of him?" Danny wondered.

"We did a thorough search of the area," Riley replied. "This is all there is."

It wasn't particularly easy to dismember a human body. It was a messy job, requiring a lot of space and a significant amount of strength. Whoever had done this had obviously had the time, tools, and privacy. For a moment, Danny entertained a fleeting mental image of Regan Lampe, clad head-to-toe in a Tyvek suit and wielding a chainsaw. But that was ridiculous. He well knew Lampe could be vicious, had even been on the receiving end of that viciousness himself, but she would have hardly sawed some man into pieces. Her predatory nature was of a more personal type, as keenly focused as a laser and designed to inflict the maximum emotional damage.

"I'll take care of it," Danny said, effectively dismissing Riley. "Thank you, Sergeant." He took out his mobile phone and dialled Regan Lampe. "I'm sending you some body parts," he told her when she picked up. "Two hands, a foot, a torso, and a messed-up head."

"Whose?" she asked.

"No idea yet," Danny said. "I'm hoping we have the fingerprints on file. Can you print the hands for me?"

"Jesus Christ, do I have to?" she snapped. "I'm up to my eyeballs here, Dan. You don't know what it's like. There's a ten-car pile-up on the Heart's Content barrens. Four dead. Guess where they're going? Here."

"Ten cars?" he asked. It didn't make sense. It was a perfectly lovely day, and the roads were dry and clear. "What the hell happened?"

"I don't have all the details yet. You want fingerprints, you'll have to do them yourself."

"I'm sorry," he said, chastened. "I didn't know." There was no answer. She had hung up.

He went to find a constable to take charge of the remains and instructed him to bring a portable fingerprint kit. When he got back to the construction site, most of the workers had gone, but Ford Maddox was deep in conversation with Kevin Carbage. Something about their respective postures struck Danny as odd. They were standing close together, each leaning towards the other, and the tension between them was almost a living, breathing entity. As Danny watched, Ford put out a hand and stroked Carbage's arm. It was a shockingly intimate gesture, and suddenly Danny understood: Ford Maddox and Kevin Carbage…

… were lovers.

Just then, the young man Danny had seen earlier drove up in a pickup truck, jumped out, and came charging towards Ford, fists clenched and face beet-red with fury.

"This is all your fault!" he roared. "Goddammit, you did this!"

"I had nothing to do with it!" Ford shouted. The young man swung at him, narrowly missing Carbage, who stepped back just in time. His fist connected with Ford's jaw and sent him stumbling backwards.

"Hey!" Danny shouted. "Stop it!" He ran and caught the young man as he was about to swing a second time, neatly pinioned his arms, and got him down on the ground, a knee in his back. He took the set of handcuffs Carbage passed him and snapped them on, then yanked the young man to his feet. "You're under arrest," he said. "What's your name?"

"His name's Craig," Ford said. "Craig Maddox. He's my son."

FORD PACED the length of the interview room, hands behind his back, his cup of coffee untouched. Danny had assured him he wasn't under arrest, that they were simply having a friendly chat and Danny wanted to ask him some questions. Ford had countered with a request for coffee, so Danny pointed him in the direction of the kitchen and asked Ford to bring him a cup of tea while he was at it.

The heat exchanger whirred in counterpoint to Ford's agitated stride, and one of the fluorescents in the ceiling blinked on and off. Danny waited, his own tea on the table in front of him. He had brought printouts of the crime-scene photos with him, the carved-up parts and pieces of the man they'd found in the cement pillar at Ford's worksite. He intended to show them to Ford when the time was right.

"I told you I had a son," Ford said.

"Yes," Danny replied.

"He's been working with me."

"So I see." Danny sipped his tea. It was lovely and strong and still hot enough to be enjoyable. "I was under the impression you were estranged." He indicated Ford's empty chair. "Why don't you sit down? You're making me nervous."

Ford sat down, turned his coffee cup in a slow circle. "He sees Dr. Fahey. He's been having some problems. His mother and me, we didn't get along real great when he was young. All them fights, yelling...." He gazed at Danny, his eyes full of an unnamed sorrow. "I guess we fucked him up good."

"How long has he been working on your site?" Danny asked.

"About two weeks," Ford replied. "I hired him on as a labourer when he showed up here. He's been looking for work, had nowhere to live."

"He discovered the hand. On *your* worksite."

"Sweet Jesus, do you think *I* put it there?" Ford exploded, leaping out of his chair. "You think I killed somebody and chopped them up? Like what happened to me in Afghanistan turned me into some kind of monster?" He sucked in a breath and let it out. "I dunno what they told you—"

Danny lifted his cup to his lips and drank some tea, trying to appear unperturbed. "No one told me anything." He laid the cup on the table and turned it so the handle was facing Ford. "What happened to you in Afghanistan?" he asked quietly.

"Ambush," Ford said. "I don't wanna talk about it."

But Danny already knew. He'd found himself with a spare hour one evening and spent it sorting through the internet, looking for Ford. He discovered that Ford had been a U.S. Marine, deployed to Afghanistan, and was amongst a group who had taken heavy fire near Kandahar during an ambush by Taliban fighters. Ford had been badly wounded, one of his knees shattered nearly beyond repair, and had spent months recovering in a military hospital.

"It took me a long time to get where I am in my career," Ford said. "I worked my ass off in college, graduated with a perfect GPA. You'd think that'd be good enough, but no sir, there was some places wouldn't hire me once they found out I'd been deployed afterwards. I had to go to South America to get work, and even then it didn't pay shit. Believe me when I say I ain't interested in jeopardising the life I made for myself."

Ford leaned against the wall and regarded Danny. A shaft of afternoon sunshine, coming through the window, illuminated the strands of grey in his hair. He was still fit and muscular, a man in his prime, but his true age showed in the gnarled muscles of his forearms, the skin on his hands.

"It was absolute hell over there," Ford went on. He shifted, driving his hands into the pockets of his jeans. "Even worse than all the shit that happened to me when I was a kid. I seen guys blown into little bitty pieces, scattered all over hell's half acre. You never think there's so much blood in a human body until you see it lyin' on the ground. You think I'd want to see that again? Jesus, you really don't know me at all."

"Okay," Danny replied evenly, "so I don't really know you. Is there something else you're not telling me?"

Ford gazed at Danny for a long time, teeth worrying his lower lip. His eyes shifted to the window, then back again. "I might know who he is, your dead man," he said. "That tattoo on the thumb—I seen it before. On Fahey."

Danny stared at him. "Fahey had that same tattoo? Are you sure? A small swallow on the base of the thumb?" He flipped open the folder of crime-scene photos he'd brought and rifled through them until he found a picture of the hand. He held it up. "Like that?"

Ford took a couple of steps towards Danny and leaned in, peering at photo. "Yeah, maybe."

"Either it is or it isn't," Danny snapped.

"Goddammit, I don't know. I guess it could be." Ford retreated back to his position against the wall.

"Fahey was seeing your son, too, wasn't he?"

"Yeah."

The admission fell into the space between them like a dropped rock. "And you didn't think it was necessary to tell me this?" Danny said.

Ford drew himself up, eyes narrowed. "I didn't think it was any of your goddamn business," he snapped.

"What was he like as a doctor? Did you feel that he was helping you?" Danny leaned back in his chair. "Was he a good psychiatrist?"

Ford looked away for a moment. "Well, he did what he did and that was that." He turned to look at Danny, eyes burning with anger. "I guess that was supposed to be good enough."

"What was supposed to be good enough? What did he do?" Danny got the distinct feeling there was something sinister at the back of this that Ford was reluctant to reveal.

"He liked using lots of herbs, plants, stuff like that." Ford picked at a loose thread on his shirt button, probably to avoid Danny's gaze. "I'd go to his office or he'd come over to my place, and he'd put this stuff in a cup." He made a motion like someone pouring something into a container. "It does something. Makes you remember things."

"It sounds fairly unsettling."

Ford raised his head. "It was," he said. "It was goddamn unsettling, and a whole lot of other things, but by God it gets you right down to the root, you know? Right where you"—his hands clenched—"where you fucking *live*." He rubbed a hand over his face. "First time, I thought I was losing my fucking mind. Started seein' all kinds of things. He gets things out of you that you got no intention of saying. Private things. Secrets."

"Why don't you come over and sit down?" Danny gestured at the empty chair on the other side of the table.

Ford did as Danny asked, pulling out the chair and dropping into it like someone landing from a height. "I been under a lot of pressure lately," he confided. "Me 'n' Craig, well, we ain't never been on the best of terms. He blames me for his momma leaving. He ain't wrong." He sighed. "And this bridge project, man, it is bleeding me dry."

Danny sat forward in the chair. "You're losing money on it?"

"This, that, loads of other things." Ford shrugged, his gaze sliding away. "Look, do we gotta get into this now?"

"I'm just looking for information," Danny said mildly, but the muscles at the back of his neck and between his shoulder blades were knotted with tension. "Dr. Fahey's in private practice, so I imagine he was charging you a fair bit to see him. Must have been tough on ye, what with everything else."

Ford's eyes narrowed. "If you are trying to establish a motive, Danny, I'd advise you to give that shit up right now." His voice was a low growl. "I am only answering your questions because we are friends. Any other guy would be hollering for a lawyer about now. I don't know anything about how he got in that pillar or who put him there. I will sign a sworn affidavit to that effect."

"We don't need to go that far. I'm still your friend," Danny said. "Surely to God ye knows that much." Still, he couldn't quite dismiss the feeling of disquiet that rippled through him. "We'd like to have a sample of your DNA on file," he said casually. "Just so we can rule you out."

Ford's eyes widened. He gazed at Danny for a moment, then nodded. "Sure," he said. "Whatever blows your wig back. You want me to piss in a cup or something?"

Danny shook his head, picked up the phone to call Bobbi. "One of the forensic techs will swab the inside of your cheek. … Yeah, Bobbi? I'm

sending Mr. Maddox to you to get his cheek swabbed. Right. Thanks."
He laid the receiver back in the cradle. "Bobbi will meet you in the lab.
Third door on the right when you go out."

Ford turned to leave. Just as he reached the door Danny asked,
"What's on the go with you and Kevin Carbage?"

Ford's back stiffened, but he didn't turn around. "We were...
seeing each other." He moved to face Danny. "He ain't been too keen
on it, on account of that religion of his. That Pentecostal shit gets inside
your head."

"I'm sorry," Danny said. He meant it.

"Yeah," Ford replied wearily, "me too."

The door swished shut behind him.

DANNY TOOK his tea and went to the second interview room down
the hall, where June was trying to coax information out of a surly Craig
Maddox.

"I got nothing to do with my father," he said as Danny entered.

"He gave you a job," June pointed out. Danny nodded at the
running tape machine and gestured that he'd be observing from across
the room.

Craig shrugged but said nothing.

"For the benefit of the tape," June said dryly, "the subject shrugged."

Danny suppressed a grin.

"You found the body part in question," June continued, "in a
concrete piling."

"Don't make me guilty, though, does it?" Maddox replied, his
voice heavy with contempt. "That the best you got? You can't hold me
on that. I know my rights."

The last word echoed strangely in the room, and Danny startled,
his head jerking up. The small window in the far wall had fogged over,
yet it wasn't raining outside. He felt prickly and uncomfortable in his
clothes.

"Did you kill Dr. Fahey?" June asked.

He scoffed. "Like I'd tell you if I did."

June jumped on this. "So you're admitting it."

"I ain't telling you shit." He grinned. "You married?"

June ignored the question. "Maybe he deserved it." She observed him carefully. "Maybe Dr. Fahey, if he even was a real doctor, crossed a line. You aren't the first person to complain about his methods." She tapped the file folder. "We have independent witness accounts of his aberrant behaviour with patients."

"This is bullshit." But some of his initial swagger was gone. He looked down at the table, picked at some invisible spot on its surface. "Ain't nobody can do nothing to me I don't want."

"What did he do to you, Craig?" She reached across, laid her palm flat on the table in front of him. "You can tell me, and it never needs to leave this room." June opened the file folder in front of her and paged through the contents slowly. "We've obtained your medical records." Danny blinked, surprised, but didn't interrupt. "It says here that Dr. Fahey was treating you for anxiety disorder. Now, Craig, you're an educated man." She shuffled the papers. "You've been to university. Civil engineering, wasn't it?"

Craig stared at her, seemingly taking her measure. "Yeah."

"You graduated top of your class, took all the prizes." June closed the folder and rested her hands on it. "A really fantastic career ahead of you, isn't that right?"

"I didn't do   "

"But Fahey really fucked you over," she interrupted. "Didn't he?" She was leaning close to him now, gazing into his eyes. "You went to him in good faith, because he said that he could help you, but he didn't, did he?"

Craig Maddox said nothing, merely held her gaze. Danny wondered which one of them would flinch first. Something told him it wouldn't be June.

"He didn't help you, Craig. He took your money, and he did nothing." June sat back, folding her arms across her chest. It pushed her breasts up and out. Maybe it was deliberate? "It's not fair what he did to you." She drew a long breath and let it out slowly. "Gosh, it's hot in here."

It wasn't, but Danny was sweating. He tugged at the front of his shirt, holding it away from his body. The room was cool, pleasant, but he looked like he was in a sauna. June undid the top two buttons of her blouse, then pressed the backs of her hands to her cheeks.

"I didn't kill Fahey," Craig persisted. "And nothing you do is gonna make me say I did." His gaze travelled to her cleavage and lingered there.

"Okay," June said, "let's suppose for a moment that you didn't kill him." Craig started to say something, but she waved her hand for silence. "Let's pretend that you had nothing to do with Dr. Fahey ending up in that cement pillar."

"I had nothing to do with it!" Craig's face flushed. "Goddammit, how many times do I have to tell you?"

Ease back, June, Danny thought. Push him too hard and he'll be shouting for a lawyer.

"I'm sorry." June touched her mouth, licked her lips. "No, you're right. You didn't kill him." She looked at him directly. "I believe you."

A passing cloud cast a pall of gloom over the scene. Danny was dizzy, faintly nauseated. When he touched his fingers to his forehead, they came away wet. He was aware of June looking at him curiously, wondering, and he shook his head. *I'm all right.*

"I'm thirsty," Craig complained. "Can't I get a drink of water or something?"

"We'll get you a drink in a minute," June told him. "I'm wondering...."

"What?"

June flicked open the file folder again and shuffled the papers around. "It says you've been seeing Dr. Fahey for...."

"Eight months."

"Right." She tapped a sheet of paper with her fingernail. "Yes, that's right, eight months. Hmm...."

"What is it?" Craig leaned forward, trying to see what June was looking at. "What's it say there?"

"You were reportedly seeing him, as I said, for anxiety, but it also says there were some underlying substance abuse issues." She glanced up sharply. "Or maybe these records are wrong. I suppose...." She looked at Danny. "We could request an update from Dr. Fahey's office, but it might take some time." June bit her bottom lip, pretending confusion. "Since you're a suspect, we would have to keep you here at least overnight."

Craig stared at her. "You can't do that."

"I'm afraid we can," Danny interjected. His voice seemed to be coming from a long ways off, somewhere outside of him. Everything in the room—the table and chairs, the window, June, Craig Maddox—all looked incredibly tiny. He squeezed his eyes shut. He was going to be sick.

"Craig," June began, one eye on Danny, "I know you're a good man." She gestured at him. "You're educated, you've got a career. You have every reason to want to live your life."

"I didn't kill him."

"No, I'm not talking about that now." June stood up and moved her chair around to Craig's side of the table, set it down and then sat in it. They were no more than a handspan apart. "Craig, we have statements from at least two witnesses placing you at Dr. Fahey's house the night before he was killed."

We have no idea when he was killed, Danny thought. Regan would supply that information in the autopsy report. But he understood June's tactic.

"Dr. Fahey saw patients in his home," June continued. "And you were his last appointment that day." She leaned down to look into his face. "What did he say to you?"

Craig turned aside. "They're lyin'. I wasn't there, and I ain't got nothing to say."

The churning in Danny's stomach had increased to a roar. In a moment, perhaps before he could make it out of the room, he was going to vomit. He pushed himself away from the wall. "Suspend the interview, Carbage."

June looked up in surprise. "Sir?"

"Suspend it," he repeated. His mouth was filling with saliva.

"Interview suspended at—"

That was all he heard. He only just made the men's toilets in time, flinging himself into a stall and falling to his knees. It came in a rush, blood-hot and burning like acid, the convulsive contractions bending him in half, crushing his abdominal muscles. He retched, the violence of it cracking his jaw joints, spreading his mouth wide open, until nothing came up but bright green bile. Then he slumped back onto his heels on the floor, his cheek against the wall. Maybe he was dying.

"Sir?" Kevin Carbage leaned in and placed a hand on his shoulder. "Are you all right?"

"Nope." Danny shook his head, then reached to trip the flush handle. A vise tightened around his head, the pain increasing until his vision faded to a hard, throbbing blur full of strange lights. "I'm sick," he heard himself say. He tried to stand and couldn't, his legs weak and rubbery. "I need to go home."

"Come on." Kevin's hands in his armpits, Kevin lifting him to his feet. "Lean on me, sir. I'll take you home."

KEVIN CARBAGE parked and helped Danny into his house. "Are ye sure there's nothing I can get you, sir?" Danny was pale and sweaty, and he looked horrible, his complexion almost green. If Kevin didn't know better, he'd have sworn Danny was seasick. "Maybe I should take you to the hospital in Old Perlican."

"No, thank you, Constable." Danny indicated the couch. "Just help me to lie down. I'll be all right."

Kevin got him to the sofa and bent to untie his shoes. Danny was shivering, his entire body racked with violent shudders. It reminded him of the time both he and June'd had influenza, when they were young teenagers, the same racking shivers and cold sweats. "Sir, I think you're really sick, and I'm concerned. Is there anyone I can call?"

Danny lay back on the couch, and Kevin covered him with the heavy tartan blanket that was draped across the arm, tucked it in around him.

"Tadhg Heaney," Danny murmured. "No, don't call him. Don't.... I'll be fine." Danny's voice faded to a murmur as Kevin moved into the kitchen. He got a glass down from the cupboard and filled it with cold water from the tap, brought it through to Danny.

"Sir, I think you should try and drink some of this."

"Don't want it." Danny jackknifed into a sitting position. "I'm going to throw up," he said calmly. "Get the bin from the bathroom over there." Kevin held the plastic bucket for him while he retched violently, veins standing out on his forehead. "Fuck," he breathed, clutching his abdomen. "Constable.... Jesus, I'm sorry. You shouldn't have to—"

A fresh wave of vomiting racked him, this one more vicious than the last. Kevin waited it out, then went to the bathroom to get a cold cloth to bathe Danny's face. He found a clean washcloth on a shelf over the sink and ran it under the tap. Danny was sitting on the edge of the couch when he returned.

"Do you want to do it yourself?" Kevin asked.

"I should," Danny said. He reached to take the cloth from Kevin, but his hand hovered in space, fingers opening and closing like someone picking imaginary flowers. "There is a cloth, right?"

"Let me." It was a strange situation, and it should have felt awkward or embarrassing, but it didn't. Danny needed him, and Kevin was here; it was that simple. He ran the cold cloth over Danny's cheeks and forehead, wiped his lips. "Is that better?"

"Yes." Danny smiled at him, reached out and laid a hand on Kevin's shoulder. "You're a good man, Constable."

"Thank you, sir." Kevin went to flush the contents of the bathroom bin down the toilet, then set the bin in the bathtub and ran some hot water into it. When he came back to the living room, Danny was lying on his side, one arm under his head. He was awake, gazing at Kevin with a placid smile.

"I don't know if I should leave you alone," Kevin said. Danny gave no indication of having heard him. "I think I'll stay until your friend arrives. Can I call him on your phone? I haven't got his number."

Danny, still smiling, reached into his back pocket and took out his phone, handing it across to Kevin. When he scrolled through the contacts, Tadhg Heaney's name was first. He waited, listening to the ringing on the other end, praying that Heaney would pick up, but it went to voicemail. Kevin waited for the beep, but a recorded voice informed him that the mailbox belonging to Mr. Heaney was full. *Fuck.*

"I'm sorry, sir," Kevin said, "but his voicemail is full. Is there another number you want me to try?"

"It's okay," Danny murmured. He gestured vaguely at the coffee table. "Y'can put it there. Best kind, ye are so. Best kind."

Kevin did as Danny asked, putting the phone within Danny's reach. "I don't like leaving you here on your own," he said. "What if something happens?" His own mobile phone rang. June calling. She sounded like she was at the end of her tether.

"You'd better get back here," she said. "All hell is breaking loose, and I can't deal with it on my own."

"What do you mean?" Kevin asked. "What hell?"

"Jimmy Carroll took a swing at Boyd French in Violet Button's shop after Boyd said something to him. Boyd's brother Ches decided he was going to join in, so Jimmy's uncle Bruce did too. We brought 'em all in, but they won't give it up. It's a proper friggin' donnybrook here, it is so."

Kevin disconnected and put his phone back into his pocket. Danny had turned so he was lying on his back, gazing up at the ceiling. "Sir?" He laid a hand on Danny's chest. "I have to go. Are you going to be all right here by yourself?"

Danny caught hold of his hand and held on, squeezing the fingers. "You got to be who you are, Kevin. You knows that, don't ye? If something is meant to be, let it alone. Don't be all the time kicking against it. You can't fight fate." The last four words were uttered with a peculiar emphasis, almost like Danny was talking to someone else, someone who wasn't present at that moment.

"Of course, sir." Kevin tugged his hand away. "I've got to go. Will you be all right?"

"I will," Danny assured him. His pupils were enormous. Whatever was wrong with him, it wasn't sickness; Danny was behaving like someone who'd been drugged. He smiled beatifically at Kevin and closed his eyes. Hopefully he'd sleep until Tadhg Heaney—or someone—could get there.

"Kevin." Danny's eyes snapped open, and he grabbed a handful of Kevin's jacket and held on. "Fahey's bank. Check his accounts." He blinked rapidly, like there was something in his eyes. "Payments. Big amounts of money. Look for large amounts…." He sighed and fell asleep.

Kevin gently extricated his jacket from Danny's grip. "You sleep, sir." He patted Danny's shoulder. "That's the best thing for ye now."

REGAN LAMPE reached to adjust the high-powered light above her table and leaned over the tiny corpse. She hated doing an autopsy on a child, and this was far worse. She laid one gloved hand on the tiny head as her scalpel sliced along the midline, opening the body. The skin was like paper, and even given the mummification processes engendered by the acidic nature of the bog, the body wasn't all that well preserved. She was wary of pressing too hard, not knowing how much pressure the fragile corpse could stand before collapsing. The body of the baby, a little girl, had been in cold storage for several days before she could get to it, and the delicate, papery flesh had hardened. It felt a little like cutting into a chilled piece of fruit.

Her own child had been a girl. They'd brought the baby to her, let her hold it, before taking it away to the morgue. It was tiny but completely perfect, and she'd uncovered the little body, counting the fingers and toes, touching the umbilical stump, that stark remainder of the cord that never needed cutting because Regan's baby had been born dead. Eight months into her unexpected pregnancy, the fetus had stopped moving, and she knew instinctively that something was very wrong. Even then, she didn't consult her doctor right away, opting to wait and see if the baby would revive on its own.

She was in her final year of medical school at the time; any one of her fellow students could have completed an ultrasound, but Regan didn't ask them. This was too private and too personal a thing to trust to someone she hardly knew. She didn't even tell the baby's father, but somehow he found out and showed up in the delivery room, still half-drunk from the night before and clutching an extravagant bouquet of supermarket flowers. "You should have told me" was what he said. "I didn't know."

But that was him all over: dissolute, invested in his own pleasure, a spoiled rich-man's son.

She examined each of the internal organs, weighing the liver and the heart, the lungs and the intestines, all of which were shrunk with age and desiccated. The organs showed no evidence of disease, but when she had first raised the child's head, she found a length of dark red cord knotted around the throat. Not a natural death, in that case, but murder. Danny would be glad to hear she'd found something. She had no ready access to the kind of technology that would allow her to give an accurate date of death, but judging by the condition of the internal organs, she guessed the child had been dead for at least fifty years, and probably more.

She replaced the organs inside the body cavity and sewed the corpse back up. The dark red cord she slipped into a plastic evidence bag, which she sealed and signed with her initials and the date. That would go immediately to Bobbi Lambert, who'd examine it for trace evidence, but Regan had her doubts they'd find anything. The body had been in the bog so long that whatever organic material had been deposited on the cord was gone, and anything they did find would be of doubtful provenance and thus useless to the inquiry.

IT WAS very cold, and Danny couldn't stop shivering. Someone had left the door open, and the wind was coming through the house, blowing the curtains out, lifting up the rugs. The fire in the woodstove had gone out, and it was freezing. What time was it, late or early? He sat up and glanced around, but nothing in the room seemed familiar. He didn't know where he was or how he'd come to be here in this place.

"I should go home." He stood and started for the door, but the room seemed impossibly large, so big that he could never reach the end of it. And then he was outside, all alone, gazing through a darkness so impenetrable he might have been at the bottom of a well. The wind pushed at his back like a thousand invisible hands, and she was there, a little girl.

"Well go on, then." Her voice seemed to come from inside his head. "We all know what you've done, Danny boy."

A hundred metres below, the booming waves curled and leapt, waiting to drag him down, and there was nothing he could do. He was going to be down there in a minute; the wind was pushing him, and he was powerless to affect anything. One step forward, surely no more than two, and he was done—for good this time.

"Ye might as well."

No, this was nonsense. There was no voice inside his head. He was sleepwalking. It had been a feature of his childhood. For years he'd awaken elsewhere in the house, sitting on the sofa in the living room or at the kitchen table.

Wake up, Danny. Ye've dreamt yourself into a fair conundrum this time.

"You want me to kill myself, but I won't." His voice seemed to come from somewhere deep inside him. "You don't frighten me."

"Don't I?" A figure materialised in front of him, a young man in a Royal Newfoundland Constabulary uniform. "It's all your fault, Danny. Sure, you knows yourself." His blond hair was matted with blood, sticking to one side of his head, and the eye on that side was gone. *In the country of the blind, the one-eyed man is king.* "Remember what happened, now.

Don't forget. If you forgets, I'll have to come back and remind ye." He grinned, and the expression slowly morphed into a monstrous gurn, the corners of his mouth lifting impossibly towards his ears. "You don't even know my name."

"I didn't do this." His heartbeat accelerated, pounding in his chest like a trapped animal. "You know I didn't do this. You did this to yourself."

The young man's name was Leon Brazil. He'd joined up the same time as Danny. Sometimes they had a beer together after their shift ended, down at the old Cabot Club on the east end of Water Street… yes, down by the docks it was, the dirty end of town, where all the losers and layabouts congregated, pounding on the bar for drink, shouting and bawling. He and Leon Brazil had been sent to a domestic in the centre of town, a house on Empire Avenue that was a well-known hangout for druggies and drunks. When they arrived, just after two in the morning, the entire place was lit up like a church, and the old missus, somebody's mother or grandmother or aunt, stood out on the doorstep in nothing but her nightgown, with a shotgun.

"I'll blow the arse off anyone tries to take it!" she shouted. "Don't think I won't!" They persuaded her to go inside, where a dozen or more people were sitting around the kitchen table in front of an enormous mountain of drug paraphernalia.

"Bhoys, ye knows this is illegal," Danny had said. "I'm gonna have to take yez in."

A huge young man, easily two metres tall and as broad as the side of a house, stood up. His face was criss-crossed with knife scars, and the corner of one eye was decorated with a teardrop tattoo. "You're not taking me nowhere. If yez got any brains atall, you'll git."

"Ye minds what happened that night, don't ye?" The spectre of Leon wavered and swayed in front of him, like one of Scrooge's Christmas ghosts. Someone was laughing in the darkness behind him, an invisible presence. "It's all your fault I got this." He indicated the chunk missing from his skull.

"You did that to yourself," Danny repeated. "I know you did. Lord Christ, my son, 'twas me what found ye."

Their attempted arrest had gone badly. A little girl had come out from the hallway and gotten caught in the crossfire and killed. By the time backup arrived, the situation had deteriorated into a shoot-out, with

Danny and Leon forced to take cover behind an abandoned vehicle. The bullet that killed the child had come from Leon's gun. He shot himself to death a week later. Danny, arriving to pick him up for work, had found him sitting in his living room, a shotgun between his knees. He didn't even bother looking for a pulse.

I should have asked. I should have asked him afterwards if he was okay.

Once the stand-off ended, they had both returned to the station to write their separate reports, clock out, and go home. Danny had assumed Leon was all right, that he would go home and sleep, and in the morning, or in a day or two, he would be himself again.

Danny sank down on his haunches and put his head between his knees. His gorge rose, and he turned to the side, his empty stomach heaving painfully until he was forced to press his fists into the muscles to make the spasms stop. He spat out some bile, wiped his mouth on his sleeve, and stood.

"We all know what you did, Danny boy." The little girl in yellow reappeared out of the darkness. "Ye might as well jump off." She waved her hand expansively at the roiling North Atlantic. "End everybody's misery... and your own."

"No." Maybe it was the lapsed Catholic in him, but he would never take his own life. He was too afraid of hellfire for that, the eternal damnation that awaited those who would throw God's gift back in his face. The logical, intellectual part of him knew there was no such thing as an actual, physical hell, but some deeper self feared it as a fact.

He moved towards the sagging barbed-wire fence that marked the cliff edge, made himself look down. The water was imbued with a strange silvery light, a bolus of illumination that surged and writhed, a living thing heaving itself inshore with a horrible inevitability. He closed his eyes, pressed his fingers against his lids until pale shapes formed and revolved against the blackness. When he looked again, the beach below him was alive with thousands of tiny fish, all flipping and moving, casting themselves ashore to die.

The spawning capelin surged towards him, and his nostrils were full of the smell of them. He turned aside to retch, expelling nothing, and the pain of his contracting muscles drove him to his knees. There was a boy on the cliffs. Llewellyn Single was standing a stone's throw away, dipping a line into the foaming sea, pulling up fish and dropping them into a plastic bucket at his feet.

Oh God, no. He was prepared, if necessary, to bargain with Llew's ghost, to explain how he and Tadhg had tried to help him, had tried to save him, but the water was too deep, and they weren't quick enough. Tadhg had never been a strong swimmer, and the freezing North Atlantic proved too much for them. They had seen him swept away.

We should have tried harder to save you.

The spectral Llewellyn ignored him and continued to fish, depositing his catch into the bucket with a machine-like regularity. Danny forced himself to turn away, leaving the dead boy behind.

I can't help you anymore. I couldn't help you then. The realisation that this was indeed the truth weighed on him like a blanket made of heavy stones. *If this is a dream, I want to wake up now.*

His eyes snapped open. He was standing at the end of his drive, too close to the cliff edge for comfort. The wind howled and shrieked around him, driving the icy rain into his face, wetting his clothes. Sleepwalking. Had to be that.

He turned and made his way back to his house and shut the door behind him. In a moment a fit of shivering seized him, and the cold poured down his body like he'd been plunged into an icy bath. He pulled his sweater off and dropped it on the floor, then unbuckled his belt, letting his trousers fall, and taking his slow time, he went upstairs and ran the shower hot. The illuminated numbers on the clock radio by his bed said it was 4:23 a.m. Maybe twelve hours had elapsed from the time he'd left the station until now.

Danny stood under the hot water for a long time, letting it run over him, warming him, and then he shut off the shower and wrapped himself in his thick terrycloth bathrobe, a gift from Alison some years before. During their courtship, she'd often complained that he didn't have "proper undressing attire," and he'd laughed at her, but he was glad of the robe now. He went downstairs and boiled the kettle, brewed a strong pot of tea, and decanted a little whisky into his waiting cup.

He wouldn't go back to sleep, not now. He'd stay awake, waiting for the sun to rise, and then he'd dress and eat something, go into his office and get a start on some paperwork. There was always admin waiting to be done. He very much wanted to talk to his sister, Sandra. What time was it in Portugal? He checked the internet; it was a little after eight in the morning. Perhaps Sandra would be awake. He sat down at his computer and logged on to the chat program they both used.

Are u awake?

She replied almost immediately. *Insomnia again?*

He smiled. *Something like that. How's the weather?*

A cartoon sunflower popped up on the screen and morphed into a smiling cat. *Three hundred days of sun a year, Danny boy. You should try it.*

He laughed out loud, wishing she were closer. *I'd burn to a crisp.*

But seriously, Sandra said, *why are you awake this early? Just coming off night shift?*

He hesitated, his hands hovering over the keys, unsure how to frame the question.

Danny? Are you still there?

Something really weird happened. He reached for his cup and took a long gulp of the whisky-laced tea, savouring the spreading warmth.

Weird like what?

The furnace cut in, and he startled at the sudden sound. *Do you remember when I used to sleepwalk?*

You're sleepwalking again?

That's just it, he thought; *I don't know.*

Maybe. He recounted getting sick at work, then waking up to find himself outdoors and recalling nothing of the interim. *I don't remember how I got home from work. I don't remember any of it.*

The cursor flashed; then a series of bubbles appeared to indicate she was typing. *I think you should see a doctor. This doesn't sound like you at all, Dan.*

But do you think it's sleepwalking, or something else?

It could be.

Not very reassuring, but then it was hardly Sandra's fault. She wasn't a doctor.

How's Mr. Melanoma? he asked, referring to her live-in boyfriend, an Australian businessman and avid suntan fanatic she'd met during her first year in Portugal.

His name is Malcolm, and he's fine. How's Tadhg?

He's.... He hesitated, then typed, *He sends his love.*

Best get back to him, then. Love you. Xxxooo

The chat window disappeared, and he reached to shut the lid of the laptop.

His tea had cooled, so he topped it up from the pot, then sat down at the kitchen table again. From the window he could see across the harbour to where the lights of New Melbourne glimmered in the early-morning darkness, underneath a thin fingernail slice of moon that hovered just above the hills. It wouldn't be daylight for a while, and there was comfort in sitting here alone in his kitchen with only his thoughts for company. Tadhg would almost certainly still be sleeping, and Lily too. Most of Kildevil Cove was still asleep, although he could see an occasional light come on in the houses across the water. Old fishermen, probably, used to getting up early and unable to break the habit after so many years.

Tommy Power would have been amongst them once. The fact that his killer was still out there irked Danny. They ought to be doing more—he ought to be doing more—to find whoever had so cruelly slaughtered the harmless old man. And Deborah Harris, her body still lying unclaimed in Regan Lampe's mortuary cooler, what would become of her? Dead in a bog after gouging out her own eye. Tommy Power, propped up against a tree in the forest, his throat slit from ear to ear. Was there any connection between the two?

You're the detective. Figure it out.

The sudden whirring of his mobile phone jolted Danny into the present. He reached for it where it lay on the kitchen table and looked at the screen: Ford Maddox.

"Ford. Kind of early for you."

"Yeah." Ford sounded groggy, like he'd only just been roused from slumber. "Didn't know if I'd get you or not. How are you feeling?"

Ford had been with Danny just before he'd taken ill the day before. It was only natural that he'd call to check up on him. "I'm… I'm fine now," Danny said. "Must have been something I ate." He knew it wasn't. "Nice of you to call and check up on me, though."

"Uh-huh. Sure." There was a period of silence, then the sound of rustling at the other end of the phone. What the hell was Ford up to? "Listen, Danny, I need to know when I can start work again." He laughed, but there was no humour in it. "I am losing money like you would not believe. I don't know how much longer I can keep this up.

They're gonna sue me from hell to breakfast if I can't get my guys back in there working. You feel me?"

"I'm sorry," Danny said. "It's out of my hands."

"Well whose hands is it in, goddammit?"

"Chief Inspector Moira Fraser oversees the crime scene. You'll have to speak to her," Danny said. He could well imagine Moira's reaction when Ford called her. She'd eat him for lunch, but that wasn't Danny's problem.

"How are you doing, Danny?" Ford's voice was soft, deceptively gentle. "I'm sorry you were sick. Did Kevin see you home all right?"

"Kevin?"

"Oh yeah, he brought you home after your... little episode. He was pretty upset about it too. Said you were out of your goddamn mind."

A cold fist of anger massaged the lining of Danny's stomach. "I very much doubt he said that." He searched his memory, could find nothing of the previous day but random images, disjointed and incoherent—riding in a vehicle, examining the fabric of his sofa, standing outdoors in the lashing rain. None of it made sense.

"I did not kill that man," Ford said. "I did not chop him up with a chainsaw, or whatever it was, and I did not place his dismembered body parts in that concrete pillar. You believe me, don't you?"

"Of course I believe you," Danny replied, "but it isn't up to me."

"I can bring pressure to bear," Ford said. "I don't want to, but believe me, Danny, I will if I have to."

"Is that a threat?"

"Nothing of the kind," Ford replied, and his voice was light and easy. "I'm just sayin'."

Danny hit the disconnect button and put the phone face down on the table. The whisky had spread its warmth throughout his limbs, and a pleasant fogginess descended over him. He went to lock the front door, then made his way upstairs. He was tired now, the events of the past few hours having taken a toll on him, and he decided bed was the place for him after all. No more unpleasant dreams, he told himself. No more middle-of-the-night weirdness. Just rest.

He called the station and told the constable on night duty that he was sick and wouldn't be in. Any enquiries could go through Kevin Carbage or Cillian Riley. When he hung up, he stripped naked and slid under the duvet, let weariness and whisky take him down into the velvet softness of sleep.

He dreamt someone was singing outside his bedroom window, the first few words of the old song "Danny Boy," and the music turned on itself, twining into the fabric of his dreams like a clinging vine. He woke with a start, certain someone was in his room, but when he raised his head from the pillow, all he could see was darkness overlaid with pale moonlight.

"Hello?" He listened, ears straining to catch the faintest sound, but there was nothing. It was only a dream. Only a dream. There was no one there.

CHAPTER EIGHT

IT WAS midmorning, two days after his strange hallucinatory sickness, when Danny found himself at the site of Ford's new bridge span over the Veterans Memorial Highway. He'd driven there from home to meet with Kevin Carbage to supervise the removal of the yellow police tape before reopening the site to Ford's construction team. The forensic team had done a thorough survey of the site, and Moira was satisfied that there was nothing left to find.

Ford waited a short distance away, pretending to read something on his phone, but Danny knew the American didn't miss a thing. He intended to ask Ford about what had happened the day he'd taken ill at the station. Ford had been with him; they'd been in the interrogation room together. Ford had made a cup of tea for him and coffee for himself. It wasn't beyond possibility that Ford had put something in Danny's cup, a foreign substance, most likely a hallucinogen. But why would Ford do that? What possible motive could he have for wanting Danny stoned and raving?

"What's it like, in your head?" Tadhg had asked him once. "Suspecting everybody of everything? Because that's how you live your life."

It had stung, but it was the truth. In his long career as a police officer, Danny had learned to rule nothing out. The person you least suspected could be as guilty as sin. Close family and friends were capable of betrayal. Someone you held closer than a brother could turn on you. It didn't pay to let your guard down.

"Sir?" Carbage approached, notebook in hand. "Everything's done. Should I go on to the station?"

Danny glanced at Ford, standing nearby, still texting. "Yes. I'll meet you there." Something occurred to him. "Did you manage to get a look at Dr. Fahey's banking information like I asked?"

Kevin's eyes widened. "You remember that, sir? If ye don't mind me saying, you were in a shocking state, sure."

"Well?" Danny persisted.

"Fahey has been receiving large payments for the past two and a half years," Kevin said, leaning close so those around them wouldn't hear. He flipped back through his notebook. "The most recent was $25,000, a week ago. All in all, there was close to $100,000 dollars deposited into his account in the last few months alone."

Holy shit. No matter how you looked at it, that was a fuck-ton of money. Nothing suspicious about that, now, was there? "Didn't win the lottery, did he?"

Carbage shook his head. "Not that I'm aware of, sir. I requested all his bank records, and I've left a printed copy on your desk."

Danny was impressed. "Good man."

A phone call to Fahey's receptionist earlier that morning confirmed that the late doctor had been a very busy fellow, with a large roster of patients, many of whom were in the Kildevil Cove area. If his bank balance was a reflection of his fees, his clients had been paying through their collective noses. Danny asked her if Fahey had been seeing anyone locally within the past few days.

"I'm sorry, Inspector Quirke." She'd been reluctant to divulge any information about Fahey's schedule. "The doctor wouldn't like it. All I can say is he was scheduled to see a patient outside of the city and then spend a few days at his vacation cottage in Heart's Content."

"Perhaps you could tell me what kind of car Dr. Fahey drives, then."

"He has several, but his usual vehicle is a white Mercedes SUV," she said. "If you wish to contact him, I can call his mobile and ask him to—"

"That won't be necessary," Danny said. "I regret to inform you that Dr. Fahey is dead." He'd waited on the other end of the phone while her grief and shock exhausted itself, which took about thirty seconds all told. Obviously the late lamented doctor wasn't especially loved by his staff. When he pressed her a second time, she relented, told him the patient Fahey had planned to see was Ford Maddox, three days before at Ford's home in Kildevil Cove. Funny how Ford hadn't seen fit to mention this to Danny when they'd spoken at the station.

He waited now till Carbage had gone before approaching Ford. "You can resume work as soon as you'd like," he said.

"Thanks," Ford said dryly. He didn't look up from his phone.

"We've formally identified Dr. Fahey as the victim," Danny said. Ford regarded him blandly. "Luckily we had his fingerprints on file. He was pulled over some years ago for drunk driving. They corroborated what you told us about the tattoo on his thumb."

Cillian Riley had run the prints Danny's constable had taken from Fahey's disarticulated limb. Danny had intended to advise Fahey that his patient Deborah Harris was most likely the young woman they'd found in the bog, but Fahey's death had put paid to that intention. Riley's expression when he delivered the news to Danny was apologetic, given that the inquiry into the Deborah Harris case was now down one very important witness. Riley had volunteered to inform Moira Fraser. Locating next of kin might prove difficult, as Fahey was a widower with no children. Danny had put a constable on that search.

"Too bad for him," Ford said sullenly. "But it ain't got nothing to do with me and mine."

"According to his receptionist," Danny said, "he had an appointment with you three days ago."

"I never seen him," Ford said.

"He didn't show up for your appointment?"

"I never seen him," Ford repeated flatly.

Before Danny could pursue it further, his mobile vibrated in his pocket. It was June, calling from the station.

"Sir, we've got another missing persons report just came in. A woman in Winterton says her foster daughter hasn't been seen in a while."

Dammit. He glanced up to see Ford walking away and debated following him with more questions, but missing children had to take precedence.

"Give me the details," Danny said. "I'll look into it."

"She hung around with the Harvesters," June said, "while they were still on Tommy Power's land. She's not turned up at home or school, and her mother's half-cracked worrying about her."

The Harvesters. It always came back to them, Danny thought. Social services had descended on the group living in the Harrises' vacant house and moved them into more appropriate sanitary housing, where they were subject to frequent visits from social workers. The children had all been given physical examinations by a doctor and would be regularly monitored for as long as they remained in Kildevil Cove. Where they went after that—if they went—was someone else's problem.

"The mother's only reporting her missing now?" Danny asked. "She can't have been that worried." Privately he wondered if maybe the foster mother wasn't grateful to be clear of her. Certainly, some foster children were probably delightful, but many came from abusive or otherwise traumatic backgrounds, with the psychic wounds that went along with it. In his long career, he'd often attended domestic situations involving violent minors who thought nothing of torturing the family pets or setting fire to the house.

"Just passing on the information, sir." Her tone was just this side of chiding, but Danny ignored it.

"Right. Thanks, Constable." He rang off.

"Listen here, Danny, you don't think that I—" Ford caught hold of his sleeve. "Because I'm telling you—"

"Did you?" Danny pulled away from Ford. "Maybe he told you a few inconvenient truths about your mental state, and you decided to shut him up."

Ford stiffened. His face closed down, features settling into hard lines of resentment. "You think everybody is a suspect."

"Everybody *is* a suspect," Danny said, "until proven otherwise."

He left Ford where he was, told Carbage he was going to Winterton and to keep an eye on things in his absence.

He wondered how June had made out with the church records. The last time he'd looked in on her, she was hunched over a pile of old ledgers, reading intently, her chin in her cupped hands. "Getting anywhere with that?" he'd asked.

She shook her head at him. "Not so far, but I'm only just dipping into it. Did you know people actually died of toothache back in the old days? Well, it started as toothache. I guess it was some kind of gum infection." She'd pretended to shudder. "And 'senility.' I'm finding a lot of people who died of senility."

"You'll probably find a lot of babies and young children who died shortly after birth," Danny said. "Also stillborn babies. There was a pretty high infant mortality rate even after the Second World War." He'd leaned over her shoulder to take a closer look at the crumbling ledger. "Yeah, see, right here. Alphonsus Hector White, born May 2, 1947; died May 3, 1947."

He'd have to tell her that the baby found buried in the peat wasn't a victim of anything as ordinary as illness or a simple cot death. Regan Lampe's autopsy report had arrived while he was home recuperating, and he'd given it a look that morning before heading out to Ford's worksite. The child's corpse was at least fifty years old, but the cause of death was ligature strangulation. Could this be Tommy's young cousin Marion? But no. Marion Power had been, what? Six or seven years old? And this was an infant, far too young to have wandered into the woods unaided. She'd probably been stolen, but from whom? And why?

DANNY HAD personally never seen so many children in one small space before, and the effect of their constantly moving bodies and the volume of their noise was overwhelming. The house—a ramshackle two-storey badly in need of paint—was perched on a cliff overlooking the small fishing village of Winterton, about ten kilometres south of Kildevil Cove. He'd parked his car on a tiny strip of land perilously close to the roar and froth of the ocean and hoped it wouldn't roll off into the sea.

"Will you have another cup of tea, Inspector? Sure, go on, have one. There's lots left." The children's foster mother was a kind-faced middle-aged woman named Esther, who plied the enormous Brown Betty teapot with an intensity usually seen in those about to go into battle. From the moment Danny had knocked on her door, she'd been offering him food and drink: "Tea or coffee, Inspector? How about a biscuit, Inspector? I got some lovely chocolate digestives into St. John's the other day. Some good they are. Have one, sure."

By the time he finally managed to get his notebook out, she'd pressed two over-brimming cups of good, strong tea on him, two Peek Freans fruit creams, and a selection of chocolates she'd kept hidden from the children since Christmas.

"They loves to eat, poor little buggers. Young Jamie over there"— she indicated a thin boy of about six, with white-blond hair and invisible brows and lashes—"he can eat the leg off the Lamb of God and come back for the sins of the world."

"You said one of the children has gone missing," Danny said. He applied himself dutifully to the tea, wondering if his bladder would last until he made it back to the station. "A girl. Can you give me some details?"

Three boys came parading through the kitchen, dressed in an assortment of costumes ranging from pirates to army men. One of them was wearing a pink tutu. They stood and saluted Danny until he returned it, then ran away hooting something he couldn't make out.

"Elena. She's eight, I think."

"You think?" Danny winced as a child in another room began screaming vigorously. "You don't know?"

"With the crowd I got running around here?" She gestured at the kitchen, a flapping motion of her hand that took in the stairs and the front door. "Mind, now."

"How many children are you currently fostering?"

"Let me see…." She counted on her fingers, lips moving silently. "Fourteen. Wait, now… no, that's right, fourteen."

"When did you last see Elena?"

"On the Tuesday, I believe. No. It were Monday. Yes, it would have been. I was just after putting the youngsters on the school bus. The bus stops down to the end of the drive here, you know, ten to eight every morning just like clockwork."

"Do the children all go to the same school?"

"Most of them do."

"So they all go to school and come home together."

"Most of the time."

"And did Elena go to school that day?"

"Elena, now, she goes to a fancy school in St. John's, only just started a few weeks back. Paid for by some charity, because you knows I couldn't afford it. Staying in the dormitory with the other girls through the week. I woke her up and told her to get ready, because Mike Hopkins was going to run her into town in his taxi. She wouldn't come downstairs. I was after calling her till I was black in the face, and she wouldn't come down. When I goes to look on her later, she was gone."

Danny wanted to rail at her for waiting so long to call the police, but he bit his tongue. That would get him nowhere. "Has she done this before?" Danny asked instead. "Refused to go to school or run off?"

"She was always a bit strange in the head, that one, God forgive me." Esther got up from the table and went to flick the kettle on again.

"Older than her years, you could say. She came from Romania in the first place, and you knows their ways aren't our ways."

"What was she wearing when you last saw her?" Danny asked.

"What she's always wearing," Esther told him. "Yellow dress with yellow ribbons in her hair. Sometimes it's in pigtails and sometimes she has it done up in plaits. She likes old-fashioned clothes. If ye seen her in a picture, you'd think she was from way back in the year dot. She won't wear normal clothes like the rest of 'em. Got to be different, that one."

Danny noted all this down. "And how long has she been living with you?"

"About three months altogether." Esther leaned against the kitchen counter and watched the kettle. "She was living with a family in St. John's, but they couldn't handle her."

This piqued his interest. "What do you mean?"

The kettle came to a shrill whistling boil, and Esther reached across to shut it off. "She was bad."

"Bad?" A series of loud thumps sounded from overhead; Danny flinched involuntarily. It was interesting that Esther referred to Elena in the past tense: she *was* bad. Maybe she knew more than she was saying. "In what way?"

Esther went to the foot of the stairs. "Teresita, you give that up!" she shouted. Several more thumps sounded in rapid order, then subsided. She returned to the kitchen. "She runs wild when she's not in school. I can't keep up with her. Oppositional defiant disorder, that's what the psychologist said, but it's a lack of proper discipline if you ask me. They told me she had antisocial tendencies."

"And does she?"

"Oh yes. I'll say she do." Esther brought the kettle over to the table, lifted the lid of the teapot, and filled it to the brim with boiling water. "She's as cute as a fox, that one." Danny smiled inwardly at the colloquialism. "Sly, you know," Esther continued. "Lies about everything. I had to hide the matches and lighters from her. She liked setting stuff on fire. We'd have been all burned to death in our beds. Same with knives and scissors. She got hold of young Jamie one night and said she was going to cut his thing off."

"His thing?" Then it occurred to him. "Oh."

"She's a bad girl, Inspector. I've tried to make a home here for her, but it's no good. She don't listen to nothing. I can't handle her anymore. She's got to go back to social services. I was glad when the school in St. John's agreed to take her. At least she was only here on the weekends, but I can't even deal with her then. She's unmanageable. And she's after taking up with some of them religious nuts down the shore. What do they call theirselves? Helpers?"

"Harvesters," Danny supplied. A wayward child who liked to set fires and who threatened to emasculate a small boy was hardly a good candidate for family living. Add to that Malachy's influence, and no wonder Esther was at her wits' end. "Did she know you intended to send her back?" Danny asked.

"She might have heard me on the phone with the social worker." Esther shook her head. "I never meant for her to overhear."

"Do you think that's why she ran away?"

"Maybe. I don't know." She took the lid off the teapot and reached into it with a large spoon, stirred the contents slowly. It was bad luck to do that. His nan always said if you stirred the tea you were stirring up trouble. "She used to go off on her own a lot. Up in the hills by herself. She said her 'friends' were there. I figured she was just making up stories, the way youngsters do, and there mightn't be anything in it, but I suppose she was talking about that Helper crowd. You never knows, do ye?" She got up and went to a drawer, took out a slip of folded paper, which she handed across to him. "That's who she lived with before she came here. They might be able to tell you more. Let me get you a picture of her." She disappeared into another room, came back with a bulky photo album. "This is pictures of all the youngsters over the years. There's been a lot come through this house, I can tell you."

Danny wasn't sure what to say to this, so he kept quiet while Esther paged through the album, occasionally muttering to herself. A group of small girls came screaming through the kitchen and disappeared up the stairs, their stomping feet sounding exactly like a herd of stampeding caribou. Danny wondered how she stood the constant noise and chaos. He'd have gone absolutely mental.

"Here you are," she said finally, prising up the plastic covering one of the album's pages. "That's her. I took that at Chrystal's birthday last month." She passed the photo across to him. "You can keep that."

"Thank you," Danny said, taking the picture and stowing it safely in his inside coat pocket. "I'll have my people look into her disappearance." He gave her one of his cards. "If you hear from her, please contact me immediately on that number."

A flicker of movement caught the corner of his eye, and he glanced up to see a teenaged girl leaning against the doorframe, watching him. He smiled, but she didn't return the gesture. She was dressed in oversized clothing—a pair of baggy black jeans several years out of style and a large orange hoodie whose sleeves fell down over her hands. Her feet were bare, the toenails painted a chipped and peeling blue.

She accosted Danny in the front porch. "She's not telling you the truth," she said.

"What do you mean?" He buttoned up his coat.

"Elena. She's not what she seems. Mind yourself with her." Her gaze flicked over his shoulder, back to his face again. "You got to watch her."

"Why?" He reached out a hand to touch her sleeve, but she jerked away from him.

"Because," the girl said, her voice barely a whisper, "she's dangerous."

He took Elena's photo out when he got to his car, sat looking it over carefully. The girl in the photo struck him immediately as looking far too worldly-wise for her years. There was a certain knowing in her eyes, and an expression of cunning that didn't belong on a child so young. Her smile was the smile of a woman, not a girl, a sly upturning of the lips that emphasised the broad Slavic planes of her cheeks. Her facial features were mature, the bones sharply cut, and the tilt of her chin seemed to indicate an entirely adult wilfulness. Everything about the face unsettled him.

You're making up stories, he told himself. She's just a little girl. You know better than to theorise in advance of the facts. His mobile buzzed, and he fetched it out. The call was from Tadhg.

"Hello," Danny said. "How's Lily doing?"

"Oh, she's nearly back to her old self again," Tadhg replied. "A bit embarrassed about the whole thing, if ye want the truth of it. Kids are resilient." There was a silence. "Er, Danny, do you think…? Remember what you said about Dr. Fahey? How he was giving her that natural medicine?"

Danny wondered where this was leading. "Yes."

"Do you think... maybe that had something to do with... what happened to her?" This was Tadhg's vague, roundabout way of alluding to Lily's episode of self-harm.

"Regan took a blood sample," Danny told him. "I'll know more once I hear from her."

"Yeah. Yeah, good. She's not taking it now, of course. She must have hove it away, because it's not in the medicine cabinet no more." He paused. "Tis a queer business, now I'm thinking about it. I can't believe Fahey was doing anything to hurt his patients. He had a great reputation."

Danny sighed. Whatever Tadhg might have thought after Lily's incident, he was back to defending his original choice of a doctor for her, and Danny had no ammunition to fight back with. He didn't *want* there to have been something harmful in Lily's medicine, but he hoped Regan's tests would settle the question once and for all. At least with Fahey dead there was no chance he could do any more harm.

"Busy boy these days, aren't ye?" Tadhg asked, and there was a note of reproach in it. "I'm beginning to forget what ye looks like, sure."

"Are you saying you miss me?" Danny grinned.

"I always miss ye," Tadhg confessed. "How about coming over for the weekend? I just got the house plans back from the architect if you wants to see them."

"House plans?"

"For your grandfather's land, bhoy." Tadhg's laughter filled his ear, warming him. "Jesus, ye're so stun as me arse sometimes."

"I'm not coming over if you keep insulting me." Danny tried to inject a note of hurt into his voice and failed. "I got nothing to say to ye."

"Come over for supper on Friday and stay the weekend," Tadhg urged. "I'll make it worth your while."

Danny was reminded of the myriad ways in which Tadhg could potentially make it worth his while, and it gave him a pleasant tingle. "Okay," he said, and, "I love you."

"I love you too. Now go and do your job."

"I'll see you tomorrow," Danny promised and rang off.

His phone buzzed almost immediately with an incoming text message. Thinking it was Tadhg, he tapped the screen to open it—and wished he hadn't. The only thing on the screen was a photograph, a close-up of a human eye, obliterated by some unspecified injury and hanging by its optic nerve. "Jesus." He swiped the message into the trash and made a mental note to contact his service provider to have his mobile number changed.

HE WAS able to track down the girl's previous foster parents, a university professor and his wife, after many missteps and dead ends. During a phone call, the father confirmed everything Esther had told him. Yes, Elena had been adopted from a Romanian orphanage under somewhat suspicious circumstances. What sorts of circumstances, Danny wanted to know. "Are you saying the adoption was illegal?"

"Nothing like that, nothing like that." The professor sounded nervous, but Danny couldn't figure out why. The girl was nothing to do with them anymore. "It was all done through the proper channels, as far as we knew. My wife and I applied to foster Elena with a view to eventually adopting her, but it didn't work out."

"What didn't work out?" Danny asked.

"We decided not to go through with it."

There was a long silence. Danny felt his patience fraying around the edges. "I can have the records unsealed," he warned, "and it will tell me everything I want to know. However, I'd rather get that information from you." He'd already requested all pertinent documentation from social services—specifically, the caseworker who'd handled Elena's placement with the Divers—but he didn't tell Dr. Diver this. People were wont to open up and volunteer information if you kept them in the dark.

"Fine," the man huffed. "Good God, you'd think we were living in some kind of communist-bloc police state." He drew a long breath, exhaling audibly. It reminded Danny of a relaxation class he'd once gone to during a police conference in the States. A very tall, very thin woman with short grey hair had made them lie down on yoga mats while she projected images of the Milky Way galaxy on the ceiling. "Feel yourself merging with the universe," she'd said. "Breathe and become one with all that is." He'd done as she'd instructed but got nothing for his trouble but a backache from lying on a thin yoga mat on a concrete floor.

"We found it extremely difficult to get much information about Elena," the professor said. "Even the orphanage had very little. I'm positive the birth certificate they showed us was forged. I wanted to call a halt to the whole thing, but my wife was adamant. We'd been trying for a child for years, and she had her heart set on a Romanian orphan."

Danny wondered how a Romanian orphan was any different from a Newfoundland orphan. Maybe the willingness to go all that distance to adopt a child conferred some kind of elevated status on the adoptive parents, or maybe a homegrown orphan wasn't good enough.

"So you went to Romania to adopt Elena. I assume you brought her back here with you."

"Correct. She came to our home in St. John's. At first, everything was fine. She's a beautiful child. Have you seen her?"

"I have." The knowingness in the girl's eyes, the seductive smile. Even thinking about her chilled him. "She's a very unusual girl."

"She's a little viper," Diver spat. "Vicious. She tried to kill my wife. We were going to press charges."

"Did you?"

"No. We ultimately decided not to. There was no point."

"Because she's a minor?"

Diver laughed humourlessly. Danny wished he could see the professor's face, but Diver had refused an in-person interview, insisting that a phone call was all Danny was going to get.

"Is she? Have you seen her, Inspector? Have you looked into her gaze? She only appears to be a child. There is nothing childlike about her cunning, or her malice. She put drain cleaner in my wife's coffee, did you know that? Drain cleaner. It was lucky Louise only took a single mouthful. As it was, she spent three weeks recovering in hospital. That was the final straw. Elena had been… wilful, destructive, evil. We gave her a hamster as a pet. Do you know what she did?"

"You don't need to recount the event, Dr. Diver." Danny wasn't interested in hearing it. Animal cruelty in particular, above all other crimes, enraged and disgusted him. "So you decided not to adopt Elena.

You and your wife had her placed elsewhere after she proved to be a violent child."

"She's not a child," Diver reiterated. "Believe me when I tell you, sir. That... creature might be a lot of things, but she is not a child."

IT WAS a lot nicer here than back in that horrible old bag's house. At least here she could do as she pleased, think what she wanted, speak or not speak. The horrible old bag was forever trying to get her to "Take part, Elena. Go and play with the other children, let them get to know you." As if she wanted to get to know those dimwits, whores' offspring, and idiots from a polluted gene pool who'd run a mile for the promise of chocolate and an hour sitting in front of the television set. She was never allowed to have any fun, at least not the kind of fun she wanted to have.

The last specimen she'd pulled from the herd, that cute young copper, turned out to be queer, which was a bit of a disappointment, and she hadn't come across any suitable candidates since. It was exhausting, going from foster home to foster home, hoping that the next place she went would welcome her, but no one ever did. Each foster mother told her to call them "Mam" or "Mother" or even "Mamma," but that wasn't possible.

If she'd ever had a mother, she knew nothing of her. The woman might as well have been a fantasy, a creature culled from the imagination. Her earliest recollections were of lying in a dirty alley between two buildings, one which was very quiet and the other very noisy, especially at night. Later she would learn that one building was a convent and the other was a brothel, but she could never work out how the two managed to coexist so closely together. The country, many people said, had gone to hell in recent years. As far as she could tell, it had mostly always been that way.

She had no mother that she could remember, and she had no father. When the brothel was bombed by anarchists early one morning, she found herself wandering in unfamiliar streets, alone again, always alone. A kindly nurse had found her and taken her to the orphanage, dressed her in children's clothing, given her a different name. Someone would come and adopt her. She would be taken to another country, perhaps America or Canada, the United Kingdom. She was so very pretty someone was bound to want her. But for a long time no one came, and she began to despair and to plot ways of escaping from the orphanage, where the other children screamed and cried incessantly and there was never enough food for everyone.

The Divers had seemed a dream come true for her. Mrs. Diver especially, with her expensively coiffed hair and her shiny porcelain teeth, had fallen in love and demanded to take Elena home with them then and there. Her husband hadn't been quite as certain as his wife. Perhaps he saw something in her too-knowing gaze that unsettled him. She had that effect on men. They saw past the little-girl façade, the pretty party dresses, and the ribbons in her hair. They knew she was anything but innocent. The wife, on the other hand, was besotted.

"She's absolutely perfect," she told her husband. "Please, let's not wait. Let's take her home right now. We can finalise the adoption later." Elena had marveled at the view from the window of the airplane taking her to their far-off island. She'd never been in a plane before. She'd never been anywhere before. It was incredible to soar so high above the clouds, to see the land below her, flattened and obscure, like the folded maps in the schoolteacher's office when she was a small girl.

The dream hadn't gone the way she'd planned. She'd hoped to get Dr. Diver all to herself, to work her charms on him until his wife was out of the picture. No hope of that. He was desperately in love with Mrs. Diver, even though the woman was venal and silly, existing in a dream world she'd invented for herself, a land that existed only in her imagination. Elena tried to get rid of her, arranging little accidents for her: an unplanned trip on the stairs, getting locked in the freezing-cold attic of their Victorian house, finding drain cleaner in her morning coffee instead of the sugar she'd asked for.

The damned woman was indestructible. She spent three weeks in hospital recovering from chemical burns, and then she was back in the house and Elena was out, taken away in the social worker's car late one evening, all her meagre belongings packed in her tiny suitcase. She was going to a new home, they said, somewhere she could live with other children her own age. Elena had smiled secretly at this. As if this were even possible. The social worker, like most others of her type, was profoundly stupid, seeing only what she wanted to see and ignoring evidence to the contrary. Moving to the countryside was the most ridiculous nonsense, a grave misstep, Elena thought.

Until she met the Harvesters.

They were fervently devout, and they travelled as the Roma often did, moving from place to place in groups, depending on the kindness of those they met to provide their basic needs. They gathered in the public squares of the towns they visited and sang, and read the Scriptures aloud, passing a plate around for monetary contributions. They interested her, so she often sought them out, hanging around the fringes of their group whenever she could free herself from the foster home in Winterton.

She didn't believe in their Jesus, but that didn't really matter. The itinerant nature of their existence could be of benefit to her. Were she to travel with them, she could choose a new playmate from the towns and villages they visited. There were plenty of people upon whom she might work her curious appeal, and when she was done with them—they almost never lasted as long as she might have liked—she could discard them somewhere out of the way. When the bodies were found—if the bodies were found—she would be long gone, safely out of range and blameless.

So she watched and waited and planned to join them when they moved on. But Malachy's group didn't seem interested in moving along soon enough to suit Elena, and then the police stuck their noses in, ruining everything. That was where she'd first seen the head copper poking around the body of the girl they found in the bog, stupid bitch that she was. That copper was a sharp one; she could tell. She'd have to keep a careful eye on him.

Some Harvesters didn't follow the path the others did, though. They saw no need to wander, and once they reached Kildevil Cove, they were content to set down roots, establish a community deep in the forest and away from the rest. Elena liked them better. Although they didn't travel, the place they lived was much better than Malachy's squalid camp. They had a quaint cottage at the end of a lane leading off the main road in Kildevil Cove, surrounded by thick woods, the trees so close together as to be nearly impenetrable. A small brook running behind the house provided water, but there was also an ancient well, its slightly brackish water tasting of iron.

These Harvesters didn't agree with Malachy's ways or his ideas about things like God and holiness. They were believers, yes—in the Holy Trinity, the communion of saints, the forgiveness of sins, and the life everlasting—but these Harvesters held it was better to take themselves out of the world, to be separate, but to make themselves pleasing to God by embracing all aspects of his creation. So they danced and played, drank the strong drink they brewed themselves, hunted, ate the animals they killed, and coupled enthusiastically whenever the mood was upon them, with whoever seemed amenable to the idea. After so many years of being stuck in the orphanage and then in foster homes, Elena had found others more like herself.

She especially liked being so deep in the forest that even sunlight didn't penetrate. She could make herself as still and small as a wild animal, watching. She'd seen the old man there, wandering lost in the woods. He was the best playmate she'd found so far. He'd even left a gift for her, a souvenir, and now and then she'd take it from its hiding place and open it, run her fingertip along the blade, and smell the mingled scents of blood and steel.

That's what *she* was, blood and steel. That's all she was. Just that, and nothing more.

DANNY'S PHONE conversation with Dr. Diver had left him craving something sweet, so he left word with Marilyn that he was going to Strange Brew, a newly opened coffee shop, to pick up pastries for their afternoon coffee break. It never hurt to ply one's colleagues with refined carbohydrates.

The pleasant weather had held, so he decided to walk the short distance. Strange Brew had begun as a summer project for some graduate students from Memorial's MBA program and quickly established itself as the go-to place for exotic coffees and decadent pastries. It was rumoured around Kildevil Cove that some local bigwig was a silent partner and the primary investor, but this was unconfirmed. The shop occupied an empty storefront that had once belonged to a local boat-tour operator, and the youngsters running it kept everything ticking over like the proverbial well-oiled apparatus.

"Morning, Inspector Quirke!" Jennice, one of the baristas, greeted him as he came in. "Lovely day out there."

"It is so," Danny agreed. He ordered a flat white for himself and picked out a selection of pastries to take back with him.

"I seen someone finally moved that car that was parked down the beach," Jennice said. "Queer place to leave a fancy car like that."

"Car?" Danny watched as she spooned espresso into a filter and pressed it down. "What car was this?"

"Someone"—she raised her voice to be heard above the machine—"left a car parked down the beach." She turned to take pastries out of the display case and slot them into a box. "A Mercedes. Now that's what ye calls 'all the bells and whistles.'" She packed the lid of the box down tight.

"What colour was this Mercedes?" Danny asked.

"Uhm… light-coloured, I think." She poured milk into a steaming jug and plunged the steam wand in for a couple of short bursts. "Yes, white," she said. "It was definitely white. A white Mercedes SUV. But like I said, it's gone now."

Danny paid for the box of pastries and his coffee and thanked the barista. He'd just stepped outside the door when his phone pinged with a text message. It was Riley.

Some kids called in a car fire on an old woods road in Grates Cove.

Well, if that wasn't a coincidence to end all coincidences. *Mercedes SUV, was it?*

Yes.

Get a cordon around it and don't let anyone else near. I'm on my way.

Danny called Ford Maddox. The line rang half a dozen times and went to voicemail. "Ford, this is Danny. We need to talk. Call me as soon as you get this."

His mobile rang as soon as he'd hung up, but it was Kevin Carbage. "Sir, we've got a VIN from the car. Do you want me to run it?"

"Yes."

"Just putting it in now," Kevin said. "It's registered to Dr. James Fahey."

"Thank you, Kevin. I figured as much." Danny closed out the connection and tried Ford again. This time he picked up. "I've been looking for you."

"Danny, Jesus. I'm so sorry." Ford sighed. "I've just been so busy I ain't hardly had time to sleep, what with everything going on at the job site. You know how it is."

"Why did you lie to me about James Fahey being at your house the day before he was found?"

There was a long pause. "What? I can't hardly hear you. Did you go under a bridge or something?"

Danny swore a long stream of profanity at him. "Dr. Fahey was at your house the day before his body was found. I think you'd better come into the station right now."

"Goddammit, I can't!" Ford snapped. "I am just run ragged. I've been back and forth to the job site several times today already, trying to get the rest of the concrete footings poured."

"We found Fahey's burned-out car. Someone reported it parked down on the beach near your house until recently." He waited, but there was only silence. "I know he was there, Ford. I told you his receptionist confirmed it."

"I can't help what somebody else said." There was a note of cunning in Ford's voice now. "And I ain't got to say anything without a lawyer present."

"Ford, I'm your friend—"

"Bye, Danny." The connection dropped. He redialled immediately but got only a busy signal.

"Fuck."

Danny resumed his walk back to the station. On the way, he called Tadhg. "I need to ask you a question about concrete," he said.

"Right," Tadhg said. "What about concrete?"

"When you pour concrete, say for footings, like bridge footings, do you have to keep going back and forth to check it?"

"Absolutely not. The mixer truck comes and dumps it into the forms and that's usually it," Tadhg said. "Why?"

"So if somebody poured concrete, there wouldn't be any reason to keep checking it."

"None whatsoever."

The suspicion Danny had been nursing since speaking to Ford grew. He'd had this feeling before. He hated this feeling. "I was afraid of that."

"Ye're not making any sense," Tadhg said. "What's this about concrete? Are you planning on doing away with me?"

"I was just talking to Ford," Danny told him. "I've been trying to get hold of him, but he keeps ducking me. When I asked why, he gave me some bullshit story about having to go back and forth to the job site because he was having concrete poured."

Tadhg scoffed. "I don't know what kind of concrete he's pouring. It's not a friggin' Christmas cake. Not like ye got to sit around and babysit it. Sure, it sets up all on its own."

"That's what I thought," Danny said. "Okay. I'll talk to you later."

"Are ye still coming over tomorrow night or what?" Tadhg asked. There was a note of pleading in his voice that made Danny smile.

"I will try my very best," Danny said.

"Doesn't sound promising."

"I love you." Danny hoped this would soothe Tadhg a little.

"Mmm. Don't know if I believes ye," Tadhg replied in a mock-hurt tone. "Bye."

Once back at the station, Danny dropped off the pastries, returned to his office, and got on the phone to Moira, but the call went straight to voicemail. He took a sip of his disappointingly cool coffee and then tried her office number. A young-sounding female constable answered and told him Moira had gone to St. John's for meetings and wouldn't be back until Monday morning. "Is there anything I can do, sir?"

He needed a warrant to search Ford's house for Fahey's DNA, but that wasn't going to happen without Moira. Until he got the go-ahead from her, his hands were tied. It was all fine and good to suspect Ford of murdering Fahey, but unless Danny had actual, tangible proof, it remained a suspicion and nothing more. He couldn't exactly go charging in there and arrest Ford on a hunch.

"No," he said, "but thank you. I'll keep trying her mobile." He closed the connection, dropped his forehead against the desk, and groaned out loud. Moira's absence had bought Ford more time. How much more depended on whether or not Danny was able to get hold of her.

Of course.... No. He banished the thought the instant it appeared. Moira would kill him stone dead if he dared go over her head on this. She'd made it clear to him from the very beginning that formalities like warrants and resources and the like were to go through her, and if they didn't, there'd be hell to pay. He could approach a judge about a warrant on his own, he supposed, but when Moira found out—and she would, no bloody fear of that—she'd have his guts for garters.

Then again…. He could show up at Ford's house while Ford was out. Maybe the door would be unlocked. He'd have to wear gloves, of course, and make sure not to leave any trace behind.

No, that wouldn't work, either. Once Bobbi Lambert got in there with her forensics techs, they'd find traces of him all over the place. Any place you entered, you left something of yourself behind and took with you evidence of whoever else had been there. So that idea was a non-starter.

Maybe he could send someone else in, someone who had reason to go to Ford's house? But the only person friendly with Ford besides Danny was Kevin, and he couldn't ask Kevin to go in there and swab for DNA—not to mention it wouldn't be admissible in court. Kevin could only seize something if it was in plain sight, and that didn't include DNA. Besides, Ford could argue that of course Fahey's DNA was in his house, because Fahey had come there to see him. By itself, it proved nothing. Still, there could be some other evidence at Ford's place.

He hated this feeling, knowing that Ford was likely complicit in Fahey's death but unable to do anything about it. While he was waiting to get hold of Moira, Ford could pick up and go wherever he liked, and there was nothing to stop him. He could quite literally get away with murder. About the only thing Danny could do right now was bring Ford in for questioning, and he knew how that was going to go. Ford would refuse to speak to him without a lawyer present, and the lawyer would insist they either charge Ford or let him go, and….

Yeah. It was a vicious circle.

Danny left the station for his car and followed the lane back to the main road. He dialled Moira as he drove, but the call went to voicemail again. Where the hell was she? What sort of meeting required you to be out of touch for hours at a time? And her all over him when he didn't contact her immediately with updates. How could he do that if she was not to be found?

He was still fuming about it when he arrived at Grates Cove nearly an hour later. The wreck of Dr. Fahey's Mercedes sat at the end of a woods road on the outskirts of the village. Kevin Carbage and Cillian Riley were waiting for him.

"This is what's left of it, sir," Kevin said as Danny approached. "Didn't burn all the way down, but as far as the insurance is concerned, it's most likely a write-off."

"Too bad," Riley said. "Nice vehicle."

Danny walked around the entire car, noting that the damage seemed to be confined to the front half of the vehicle. The bonnet was a charred wreck, and the tires had been completely destroyed, as had the front seat, which meant the fire had most likely started there.

"Probably used gasoline," he said, gesturing at the driver's side, "and dropped a match." Danny was no arson expert, but this seemed to make sense. The ground around the front half of the vehicle was burned, the grass singed close to the body of the car. "It's a wonder it didn't explode. Who called it in?"

Riley lifted his chin in the direction of three children playing a short distance away, two boys and a girl. They were about ten or twelve years old, mature enough to know what they'd seen and to remember it. "I asked them if they saw anyone, but the car was on fire when they got here."

"Right. Okay. Let's arrange to get this towed." Danny glanced at the sky, heavily laden now with thickening cloud. "It's supposed to rain later, and I don't want to lose whatever trace evidence might be there."

"There's a bloke just down the road," Riley said, pulling out his mobile phone. "I'll ring him now."

"I don't understand it," Kevin said. "Why would someone torch a car out in the open like this?"

Danny shrugged. "They probably think of this area as deserted, just empty space on the edge of a small fishing village. Who's going to notice?"

Kevin scoffed. "In a place like this? Everybody. And they didn't even remove the licence plates or the VIN."

"He was probably panicking," Danny said.

"Who, sir?" Kevin frowned. "You said 'he.'"

"I meant they," Danny backpedalled. "Whoever did this. They were probably panicking, wanting to get rid of it as soon as possible and get out of here."

Quite possibly they'd meant it to look like the car had been stolen and torched, as was so often the case, but car theft in the Kildevil Cove area was virtually unknown. Ford, who'd lived away for so many years, might have forgotten this, so abandoning the vehicle in a deserted area and setting it alight seemed the most reasonable thing to do.

Riley disconnected his call and came to where they were. "Be here in five minutes, sir. Where shall I tell him to take it?"

The tiny Kildevil Cove station had neither the space nor the facilities to store it properly. "Have him take it to the impound yard at the RCMP detachment in Harbour Grace. I'll call ahead and let them know it's evidence." Whether he could trace it back to Ford—or anybody— remained to be seen. He'd get the forensic techs to go over it. Fingerprints or DNA from the vehicle might not be definitive but would certainly be useful.

THE COMPLEXITIES of the case and the events of the previous few days had taken their toll on Danny. By the time he arrived on Eigus Friday evening, he felt defeated and worn down, exhausted to his very soul. Tadhg met him at the door and enfolded him in a hug before Danny had even taken off his coat, holding him close until Danny's ragged breathing slowed.

"You're all in, aren't ye?" Tadhg asked. He released Danny and stepped back, reaching to take Danny's coat as he slipped it off. "Come on in," he said, "and have a glass of something to put you right."

Danny followed him through to the immense glass-walled living room, where a fire had been laid to offset the weather. A driving rain with a touch of sleet in it had started while Danny was crossing from Portugal Cove, and he was glad to get in to the warm. He sank into the squashy cushions of the big leather couch and allowed himself a sigh of relief.

"It's good to see you," he said. The smell of something warm and full of tomatoes and olives and garlic drifted to him from the kitchen. "You're cooking?"

"I am," Tadhg said. "Ratatouille right now, but there'll be stone-baked pizza later. The dough is rising in the pantry as we speak."

Danny canted a look at him. "You made pizza dough? Kneaded it and everything?"

Tadhg flexed his fingers. "You'd be amazed what I can do with these hands, bhoy."

He poured two fingers of Macallan into a heavy-bottomed glass and passed it to Danny. "Here. Get that down ye." He poured one for himself and came to sit beside him. "My poor man," he said, "I think ye needs some looking after."

Danny tossed back his Scotch and went into Tadhg's arms. They were quiet together for a long time; then Danny asked, "Where's Lily?"

"Gone to spend the weekend with Gemma." Tadhg leaned forward and laid his glass on the coffee table. "So it's just you and me, my dear."

"She's not coming home at all?"

"Nope. You're in my clutches now," Tadhg said, "so you'd better get used to it." Danny sank into silence again, and he must have been quiet for too long, because Tadhg sounded concerned when he asked, "What is it?"

Danny raised his head to look at him. "Sorry?"

"What is it you're chewing over in your mind? I'm thinking it's something pretty serious, considering." He smoothed Danny's cheek with the backs of his fingers. "Do ye want to tell me about it?"

Danny sighed, and something loosened deep inside him. "I can't see my way clear," he said. His voice sounded tired and raspy to his own ears. "This case is kicking my arse, Tadhg. I don't know what the hell I'm doing. It feels like I'm just going round and round in circles, with no letup." Despite his discomfort with the idea of discussing details of his work with Tadhg, he unloaded his fears about recent events: the young woman in the bog with her eye gouged out, the nuisance Harvesters and the dead baby buried in the field, Tommy Power's murder, the reappearance of Ford Maddox. "It's too much. If this were a crime novel, I'd ask the author to back the fuck off about now."

"Do you think they're connected?" Tadhg asked.

"I don't know!" Danny almost shouted. "Jesus Christ, is there any reason why they would be?" He felt Tadhg stiffen, and regretted his outburst immediately. "I'm sorry."

"What you are is tired," Tadhg said. "You're tired and worn out, and ye've got far too much on your plate right now." He lifted Danny's chin and kissed him, a caress that started out gentle and quickly grew heated. "I know what you need," he murmured, standing up and reaching out a hand. "Come on."

"What about your ratatouille?" Danny asked. "And your hand-kneaded dough?"

"Right now, I don't care if the bloody stuff meets me coming in the door." Tadhg tugged at his hand, drawing Danny to his feet. "Bedroom, immediately if not sooner."

DANNY MUST have slept, for when he woke the light was gone from the room and Tadhg was bending over him, smiling. "Hungry?" he asked. He sat on the side of the bed and drew a hand down Danny's cheek. "Supper's ready."

"How did I…?" He was clean and dressed in his boxer briefs and one of Tadhg's expensive French T-shirts.

"You were beat, my love." He kissed the corner of Danny's mouth. "I gave ye a wash and dressed you, let you sleep for a bit. Did you a world of good, it did so."

Danny stretched luxuriously, feeling more than a little decadent in Tadhg's big soft bed. "You do me a world of good," he said. "I loves the bones of ye, I do so."

"Come downstairs and have something to eat," Tadhg urged. "We'll put the hockey game on after, if ye like."

They ate Tadhg's ratatouille over tender steamed rice, followed by slices of pizza and washed down with Iceberg lager from Quidi Vidi Brewery. Danny ate until his stomach bulged like a too-tight drum, then accepted a second bottle of beer to take with him into the living room. The late April night settled in around the huge floor-to-ceiling windows. It had begun to rain profusely, drops hammering at the glass. Tadhg sat against the arm of the couch and pulled Danny close, his back resting against Tadhg's chest, snuggled in Tadhg's embrace.

"Ye should know I loves ye," Tadhg said.

"Do ye now?" Danny clasped Tadhg's hand, intertwining their fingers. "Are you sure? I figured you only invited me here for dinner and a shag."

"Do I have to feed ye to get a shag?" Tadhg asked.

"No, but it helps."

The hockey game was between Danny's favourite team, the Toronto Maple Leafs, and Tadhg's, the Montreal Canadiens. It wasn't going well for the Leafs, and when Montreal scored on an empty net, Danny groaned aloud.

"That's just sad," Tadhg observed. "Jesus, bhoys"—he spoke to the TV set—"give it up for a bad job."

"None of that, now," Danny said. "Give 'em a chance, sure."

Tadhg scoffed. "A chance to lose." He clasped his arms a little tighter around Danny's middle. "We should get married," he said.

This assertion shocked Danny so much he almost dropped his beer. "What?"

"You heard me." He paused. "Unless… you think it's a bad idea."

A throb of pure love lanced through Danny's chest, a physical sensation so poignantly real it made him shudder. He reached to set his beer on the coffee table and levered himself into a sitting position.

"I think it's a great idea," he said. He searched Tadhg's face for some sign it had been a joke and didn't find one. Tadhg was as sober as a judge. "Are ye sure?"

Tadhg laughed gently. "Will you marry me?" he asked.

Danny had to blink back sudden tears. "Ye know I will."

"Good," Tadhg whispered, overcome with emotion. "I don't take rejection all that well." He clasped Danny in his embrace and kissed him.

FORD MADDOX had been drinking since about half past four Friday afternoon. It was now well after eight and he was not exactly drunk. He was not exactly sober either. The flask of Jack he'd consumed sat uneasily on top of the gas station ham-and-cheese sandwich he'd had for lunch. He'd barely managed to choke it down.

For a long time afterwards, after the thing was done and he was left alone with… it, he'd fought against the impulse to throw himself off the nearest cliff or get his old Marine Corps knife and open his veins. He knew exactly how to do it. He'd seen it done before. A prisoner, an errant Al Qaeda member who'd gotten separated from his buddies, found himself alone with Ford and several other Americans. Nobody intended to hurt him. They weren't like those monsters you saw in those shady videos leaked to the news media, torturing prisoners and forcing them to kneel naked on bare concrete for hours. They gave him food and water, confined him in the Humvee awaiting transport, and everything was fine, except Ford came back to check on him and—

They'd even searched the bastard. He must have hidden the knife up his asshole somewhere. He'd slit his wrists lengthwise, not across, and there was so much blood, so fast, like it was filling up the vehicle, and wasn't that just an image Ford saw too often in his nightmares. That was the weird thing, too, because those guys, they didn't believe in suicide. Completely abhorred it because it was against their religion or something.

There wasn't too much blood this time, when Ford dragged the body out to the garage and took care of it. He'd kept his mind on the task at hand, like his CO always said to do. *Keep your goddamned head down and your motherfucking thoughts where they ought to be.* When he was done, he'd cleaned everything up with some old rags he found in the furnace room. That was it.

It was silent in his rented house, a converted saltbox halfway up Buckler's Hill in Kildevil Cove. He didn't own a television set and seldom listened to any of the local radio stations, which featured too much country-and-western music and too many call-in shows for his liking. Lately he'd been drinking more than was good for him, hitting the booze as soon as he got in from work, sometimes even first thing in the morning, whenever he needed a little eye-opener. He knew the dangerous road he was travelling; he'd been on it before, many times. He knew where it led, and he understood that before too long he'd end up as he had so often before: tethered to a bed in four-point restraints in the psych ward of some local hospital. He didn't want to go there again, but there didn't seem to be any way to stop it.

The bad memories were back, too, stronger than ever. Almost as soon as he dropped off to sleep, he was there again, in Afghanistan, the desert wind blowing hard in his face, the ever-present dust getting in his eyes and ears, his nose and mouth. The goddamn stuff went everywhere. Allied with this was a vague sense memory of his stepfather, sitting at the side of his bed, sliding a hand beneath the covers, pretending they were just having a friendly chat.

"You were having a bad dream, Ford. I came in to see if you were all right."

"I wasn't dreaming."

"Yes, you were. Don't you remember? You were calling out for me."

He'd trained himself to lie as still as a dying animal, barely breathing while his stepfather put his hands on him and did things. He imagined he was a nightbird, sitting up in the branches of the big old sycamore out back where the tire swing was, the one he never used. That was something else his stepfather didn't understand about him, why he didn't play like other boys did. Every night he'd come and put his hands on Ford, sitting by the bed. Later, as Ford got older, his stepfather would lie beside him on top of the covers and rub himself, and Ford would stay real still and quiet his breathing until he wasn't anywhere in that room. Until he wasn't anywhere at all.

He'd been calling Kevin Carbage's number, but Kevin never picked up. He left a flurry of voicemail messages, begging Kevin to get in touch, but his efforts went unanswered. Ford couldn't understand what he'd done wrong that Kevin wouldn't answer his calls, didn't want him anymore. Hadn't they gotten past all that religion bullshit yet? Why was Kevin so terrified of his God that he'd deny himself the solace of a satisfying adult relationship? Ford was so hot for him, wanted Kevin like he hadn't wanted anyone for years, and they were both free and over twenty-one, so what was the problem? Why couldn't Kevin give in to his desires and enjoy what they could have together? Ford wanted to be with him, wanted what they'd had that night in the cabin, during the blizzard, but Kevin kept pushing him away. He always had some excuse: he was busy or he'd gotten held up at work.

"You don't have to put too fine a point on it," Ford had said the last time they'd spoken. He'd run into Kevin at the supermarket in Carbonear when he was picking up some groceries. "You're giving me the brush-off."

"I'm not...." Kevin denied the accusation, but his eyes slid away from Ford's. "Work has been going mad lately. I'm there till after midnight most nights."

Ford had no way of knowing if this was true or not; he suspected it was a lie, and this disappointed him. Kevin was kind and decent. There was an essential goodness in him that Ford had noticed immediately. It reminded him of Joey, a young Navajo who'd been in Ford's squad over in Afghanistan. Joey was like that, and maybe that's why Ford was so hung up on Kevin. He reminded Ford of Joey. Good, kind Joey, who'd give a guy his blanket or his last cigarette. Good, kind Joey, who'd kept him warm on many a freezing Afghan night, curled around him, sharing his body heat. Good Joey—kind, sweet Joey—who'd gotten blown up in Helmand Province and who was now nothing more than a memory.

"We sure showed them." Ford toasted Joey with his raised glass, his voice echoing in the empty house. "We showed them sumbitches a thing or two." The sudden press of tears against the backs of his eyes surprised him. "We showed them, goddammit."

The doorbell rang, and he started, nearly spilling the last of his Jack. "Somebody's here," he said aloud. He laid his glass down on the floor and listened carefully. Maybe it was Jehovah's Witnesses, or somebody like that, and they'd go away if he ignored them—but the doorbell rang again, and he got unsteadily to his feet, supporting himself with a hand against the wall as he went to answer it. The old-fashioned wooden slab door was badly fitted, and it warped in wet weather, so he had to yank it hard to get it open. Kevin Carbage stood on his doorstep, his clothes streaming wet.

"I need to talk to you," Kevin said.

"What do you want to say?" Ford asked. Maybe it was the booze, or maybe it was bad memories, but his heart was flipping crazy somersaults in his chest.

"Only this," Kevin replied. He stepped into the front porch, crowding Ford back against the wall, reaching to clasp his face and kiss him hard.

KEVIN LAY on his side, gazing at Ford's profile in the wan yellow light spilling in from the upstairs hallway. "I love you," he said.

It went through Ford like a spear. For a moment he said nothing, staring at the water-stained ceiling and wondering what he could say that wouldn't sound so much like betrayal.

"That was great, baby." He forced his facial muscles into the semblance of a smile. "Real nice."

He got up and went into the bathroom, ran the water in the shower. He knew he should go back into the bedroom, say something to Kevin, but he was at a loss. What could he say? *Don't ever love me.* Yeah, that was about right. He stepped under the shower, wincing as the too-hot spray struck his tender skin. He took his time washing, spinning it out as long as he possibly could, until the water ran cold and he was forced to get out. He wrapped a towel around his waist and went into the bedroom. Kevin was fully dressed, sitting on the bed.

"I'm sorry," Kevin said. "I shouldn't have said it."

Ford could find nothing to say to this, so he merely stood gazing at him, taking in the sweetness of his expression, the kiss-bruised lips, his rumpled hair. Just looking at Kevin gave him an ache in his chest.

"My father killed my younger sister," Kevin said.

Ford jumped as if he'd been struck. "What?"

"When June and I were thirteen." He swallowed, the muscles of his throat rippling. "She had cerebral palsy, really bad. I guess he just lost his patience with her."

"Jesus Christ," Ford breathed. "Was he nuts or something?"

"Yeah." Kevin nodded. "You know, I'm pretty sure he was." He stood up. "I won't bother you anymore." He was up and out the bedroom door before Ford could even twitch a muscle.

"Kevin, wait. Don't go."

But it was too late. He heard the front door slam. Kevin was gone.

"YOU JUST had to open your great big mouth." Kevin could hear his father's voice in his head—caustic, horrible, berating him again. "Couldn't keep your trap shut."

He knew better than to make a declaration of love in the throes of passion, but he couldn't help himself. It was the truth. It was exactly how he felt, but now he'd ruined everything by saying it.

In shamefaced silence, Kevin crept down the stairs like a thief. He didn't dare look back, knowing that Ford was watching him leave. He couldn't bear to see the scorn on the other man's face. It opened a black hole inside of him, an expanding pool of shame that threatened to devour him. The rain had stopped now, and the air smelled fresh, washed clean. He crossed the lawn at a fast clip that was not quite running, past the old root cellar half-sunk into the ground, and the garden shed. At the bottom of the garden, he reached over the top of the fence to open the little gate that let onto the drive, where Ford's huge pickup truck sat, gleaming with new rain, next to the garage.

The light was longer in the evenings now, and that was probably the only reason he noticed it. At first he assumed it was just a trick of the shadow, a darker patch underneath the garage, where the corner post raised it off the ground. His policeman's instinct urged him to take a second look, and he did. It was a scrap of cloth, soaked with someone's blood. He rummaged in his coat pocket for one of the plastic evidence bags he always carried with him and flapped it open with one hand. Reversing the bag so that the outside faced the cloth, he deftly picked it up, then sealed the bag around it. He didn't want to contemplate where it had come from or why it was there. He took out his phone and called Danny.

"Sir, I've found something I think you might be interested in." He told Danny what it was and where he'd found it, listened while Danny reacted and gave instruction, then asked, "Do you think it was him that did it, sir?"

Danny's reply was carefully noncommittal. "That remains to be seen."

"I'll get it to Bobbi for testing."

Kevin was badly shaken, but he knew he was doing the right thing. Whatever was found on the cloth would either convict Ford or exonerate him. There was no middle ground, no easy out.

DANNY WOKE early Saturday morning and slipped out of bed quietly, leaving Tadhg to sleep. Kevin's phone call had come as he was drifting off the night before and offered him a tiny sliver of hope in the midst of a case that was, as he'd told Tadhg, kicking his arse. The bloody cloth might not mean anything at all, and Danny knew better than to pin all his hopes on any one piece of evidence, but depending on what Bobbi Lambert's people found, it might add substance to the case against Ford.

He made coffee for himself in the kitchen, then retrieved Tommy's letters from his holdall and went through to the dining room with them. The problem of the dead baby nagged at him. If Regan Lampe was correct (of course she was), then trying to identify the body was pointless. So far June had found nothing in the church records to indicate the baby had been given a Christian burial. She was a little girl someone had stolen and killed, for reasons that were likely lost to history. Frustratingly, there was little chance he or anyone else in his department would ever discover the truth about her.

He arranged the letters chronologically, as he'd done before, laying aside the ones he'd already read. Marilyn's declaration that Tommy was the seventh son of a seventh son came back to him, and he wondered about the other items he'd found in the wooden box. If memory served, the length of knotted cord was a witch's ladder, used to place curses and spells. But what about the strip of oddly-coloured leather, coiled about itself? What might it have been used for? He'd never seen anything like it, and even his furtive Google searches the night before (after Tadhg had fallen asleep) had yielded nothing. "Long strip of leather," "continuous leather strip," "curled leather," and "thin yellow leather strip" showed links to crafting sites. "Secret leather" took him to a lingerie company, and "personal leather strip" brought up bondage groups. Something about the piece nagged at him, and he felt he should know what it was… or that he had known and had forgotten it.

He paged through the envelopes, flicking back through the letters he'd already read. He came across the phrase that had given him pause the first time he'd read it: "On the first day of the full moon, take a length of common cord—"

Regan had found a knotted cord around the dead baby's neck. And Marilyn had said that Tommy—as a seventh son of a seventh son—had the power to heal or to kill. Surely Tommy was just a harmless old eccentric who wouldn't hurt a fly? The Tommy Danny remembered was loud, often drunk, and full of bluster, a braggart who always seemed to know where the best fishing grounds were, where to find the thickest stands of birch for firewood, and his creel was always full of the fattest trout. None of this implied supernatural abilities. Certainly he was odd, but that was his right, and there were plenty of odd folk around. His essential strangeness didn't make him evil.

… take a length of common cord….

Danny's mobile phone rang, and he picked it up, hoping it was Moira. Unknown Number. Oh fuck, he thought, not this again. He'd meant to get in touch with his service provider and have the number changed and unlisted so that only people who knew him could call him. Supposedly that would put an end to the crank calls and disgusting text messages he'd been getting. But he'd been so busy, he hadn't yet had the chance. He'd checked the call records for his current number to see if he could determine where the calls were coming from, but to no avail. The only thing that told him was that each call or text message had come from a different unknown number.

"Hello?"

"Oh, Danny boy, the pipes, the pipes are calling…," a female voice sang, before lapsing into silence. "But youuuu don't liiiiiisten…, do you, Danny boy?"

He stabbed at the screen to end the call, then got up and went into the kitchen to refill his coffee cup. Tadhg was there, dressed in his favourite comfortable lounge pants and a long-sleeved T-shirt. Danny went to him and hugged him.

"Good morning," Tadhg said, leaning in to kiss him. "Up putting the birds on the wires, were ye?" He drew back and took down a bag of artisanal coffee beans, then dumped a quantity into the hopper of his expensive grind-and-brew machine.

"I've been getting crank calls." Danny held up his phone in a warding gesture. "I should change the number."

"Are you serious?" Tadhg took the phone from him and tapped the screen, scrolling through the messages. "Jesus, Danny. This is fucking sick."

"Yeah, it's a bit mental." He tried to sound nonchalant, but he wasn't feeling it. People who made abusive phone calls rarely stopped there. All too often the behaviour escalated to physical confrontation and violence.

"It's criminal harassment," Tadhg said. "I hope you're going to report it to that Moira woman."

"I ran a check myself." Danny laid the phone down on the countertop. "The calls came from public phones, but there's no way of knowing who made them." He shook his head. "Whoever it is, they're trying to get to me. Knock me for a loop." He tried to smile, but his facial muscles felt frozen. "Anyway, I've been looking over some letters."

He watched as Tadhg reached across to fill a small glass jug with water, which he then poured into the coffee machine's reservoir. He liked watching Tadhg, enjoyed the way the early morning light illuminated his silvery hair and struck sparks in his dark green eyes. Had he always been this handsome? Or had Danny only begun to notice since he'd been in love with him?

"I assume these letters are work related," Tadhg said, slanting a coy look at him, "or else ye've got a younger boyfriend who likes to send ye mash notes."

"No mash notes," Danny said. "Yeah, it's work related." He shook his head. "It's a Saturday. I shouldn't even be doing this now." *Take a length of common cord.* It had to be a coincidence, and a hell of a big one at that. Tommy couldn't possibly kill a child for no good reason, and surely to God the witch's ladder was related to some village superstition. ... *take a length of common cord....*

"But I know you," Tadhg said, "and all this is acting on your mind. Never mind the bloody phone calls." He gazed past Danny's shoulder to the dining room table. "That what you were working on when I got up?"

"Yeah. They're some old correspondence I found in Tommy Power's house. As far as I can tell, they're from a relative of his in Boston."

"Recent letters?" Tadhg asked.

"No. These date back to the 1950s, so chances are the relative he was writing to is dead." Danny nodded towards the table. "Come and have a look."

They sat at the table, and he handed Tadhg some of the letters he'd already examined while the coffee maker hissed and burbled, doing its magical work. Danny told him about the witch's ladder he'd found amongst Tommy's belongings, and Regan Lampe's discovery of the cord around the baby girl's neck.

"Jesus," Tadhg exclaimed when Danny had finished filling him in. "That's witchcraft, sure. Don't know of anybody around here who's into that." He slid the letters back across the table to Danny. "Did ye find anything else?"

"I didn't bring it with me, but there was this weird strip of leather."

"Strip of leather?" The coffee maker finished decanting its bounty, and Tadhg got up to fetch a mug down from the cupboard. "What, you mean like a belt?" He lifted the carafe off the stand and poured coffee for himself, then reached to top up Danny's cup.

"No, not a belt." Danny spooned sugar into his coffee. "No buckle. Just this weird—" He traced a vaguely circular shape in the air with his free hand. "—strip of leather, continuous."

Tadhg stared at him. "You get a picture of this thing?"

"It's on my phone." Danny went into the dining room and retrieved his phone from the table. He flicked through the various photographs until he came to the one he wanted, showed it to Tadhg. "That. Never seen anything like it in my life."

Tadhg took the phone from his hand, his gaze fixed intently on the picture. He laid his coffee cup down and enlarged the photo, glanced up at Danny. "You don't know what this is?"

"Not a clue."

"Well, I might be wrong." This was Tadhg being modest. "It looks like a spancel."

Danny blinked at him. "What the hell is a spancel?"

"Otherwise known as a spancel of death." Tadhg handed back the phone. "It's a strip of skin cut from the corpse of a dead man. Preferably a soldier, but way back when, you'd often get one made from an executed criminal."

"That's—"

"Disgusting," Tadhg put in. "Yes, I know. I've seen pictures of them with partial tattoos and whatnot."

"You really are a font of esoteric knowledge," Danny said. "How in the name of God did you know what it was?" He narrowed his eyes. "Haven't been dabbling in the dark arts, have ye?"

"Girl I knew in university was into the occult," Tadhg told him. "She knew all about it. Spells, charms, hexes. Claimed she put a hex on me when I wouldn't go out with her, but nothing ever happened as far as I know." He shrugged. "Some women are right into that sort of thing."

"And some men, obviously," Danny mused.

Tadhg turned to get bread and eggs out of the refrigerator before switching on the electric griddle set into the huge Wolf range. Nothing but the best in Tadhg's kitchen.

"French toast?"

"Sure." Danny pulled out one of Tadhg's fancy oak barstools and sat at the counter. "So why would Tommy Power, of all people, have something like that?"

"Well, you saw the letters yourself," Tadhg said. "This aunt or great-aunt, whoever she was, must have been giving him instruction by mail. "'The occult in ten easy lessons,' or whatever."

"But not here," Danny persisted. "Lord Jesus, bhoy, this is rural Newfoundland. Hardly a hotbed of Satanic activity."

Tadhg broke four eggs into a glass bowl, added cream and nutmeg, and began whipping the mixture into a froth.

"Not Satanic," he corrected. "That's an entirely different thing. That girl I knew, she called herself a witch, but she didn't worship the devil. She said most witches don't even believe in the devil. That's a Christian concept."

Danny watched as Tadhg poured the egg mixture into a shallow dish and dropped slices of white bread into it. "Do you?" Danny asked.

"Do I what?" Tadhg turned to the fridge and took out a stick of butter, peeled the foil back from one end, and applied it to the now-hot griddle.

"Believe in the devil."

Tadhg fixed him with a look. "I believe there's evil in the world," he said, "but it's the evil men do, not this imaginary devil with horns in his head." He picked a slice of egg-soaked bread out of the dish and dropped it onto the griddle. It sizzled violently, bubbling around the edges.

"What about hell?" Danny asked.

"Of our own making," Tadhg replied. "Why this sudden interest in the spiritual and esoteric?" He leaned over and kissed Danny gently. "Something on your mind?"

"Not really, no."

But this wasn't entirely true. Danny had seen plenty of evil in his time, ranging from banal to truly diabolical. People had an innate capacity for wickedness that had nothing to do with some mythological demon figure done up in red tights and carrying a pitchfork. An anthropology professor of his at university had put it thus: humans were primates, and primates were by nature aggressive and territorial. Danny felt that summed it up quite neatly. Maybe in a few million years, humans might evolve beyond their more egregious impulses, but part of him doubted it.

"What is it, then?" Tadhg flipped the slices of french toast neatly.

"Where would Tommy Power get a spancel?"

They watched the griddle together for a moment or two in silence. Then Tadhg got two plates down from the cupboard. "God only knows," he said. "Could have been kicking around in the family."

"D'ye think he was using it to try and make something happen?" Danny asked. "The letters make reference to 'the missing.' Tommy's cousin Marion got lost in the woods when she was young."

"Was she ever found?"

"No, not to my knowledge. So what if Tommy had all this stuff to try and make Marion come back again?" Danny tried to imagine Tommy sitting in the centre of a chalked pentagram, surrounded by lit candles, and couldn't. "Is that too nutty?"

Tadhg laughed. "It's not nutty at all, bhoy. People does some queer stuff." He served up breakfast. "Here. Get that down ye."

They chatted while they ate Tadhg's excellent french toast; then Danny cleared away the kitchen and stacked everything in the dishwasher. Tadhg had to make some business calls, so he locked himself away in his study, leaving Danny alone with Tommy's letters.

> *My dearest Thomas,*
> *By now you will have made the appropriate provisions to return the missing, and that is well. You must do exactly as I have indicated and do not, I beg you, veer from the course you have set yourself. It should be a matter of mere moments before all life is extinguished, and you must then lay the corpse in the southwest corner of the graveyard, appropriately swaddled. Do not fear discovery. The spancel will protect you.*

So maybe Tadhg was right, and the spancel had been in the Power family for a while. Where the hell did you get something like that? Tommy's earliest ancestor had come from Ireland in the early eighteenth century and purchased a parcel of what he'd been told was farmland but later turned out to be useless bog. Unable to support the young wife he'd brought from County Mayo, he'd gone to sea, as had every one of his descendants. Tommy's grandfather Eustace had even worked for a time on the Great Lakes, piloting cargo boats back and forth across various continental waterways. Had he met someone who'd given him the grotesque strip of human leather?

Highly unlikely. It strained credulity to think the spancel had come to Tommy via the stolid male side of his family, which meant his mother or grandmother or some other female relative had acquired it from God knows where and kept it. As Tadhg had said, people kept queer things. Danny's paternal grandmother had a set of Victorian mourning jewelry that fascinated him as a child—until he learned it was made from the hair of a corpse.

The letter continued:

> *You will recover her, I have no doubt, and welcome her back into the family fold. I wish you every success in this endeavour.*
> *Yours,*
> *Aunt Ditti*

Danny opened his laptop and did a search for "Marion Power, 1954," not expecting to find anything at all. He was shocked when it returned several dozen hits, some recent re-explorations of the case and some contemporary news stories. According to this, Marion had gone into the woods with her older cousin Tommy late one afternoon in October 1954. Tommy had promised he'd take her picking lingonberries—what locally were called partridgeberries—after lessons. The berries were particularly delicious in the autumn, once the frost had touched them, and Tommy had promised Marion they'd gather enough to make a Sunday pudding. What happened next was all too predictable. Walking deep into the forest, they'd come across a brook swollen with the recent rains and impossible for nine-year-old Marion to cross. Tommy told her to go on home, that he'd pick plenty of berries and meet her at her mother's house as soon as he was done. Marion obeyed, but somewhere between the berry grounds and home, she'd disappeared. A search was mobilised, but no trace of Marion was ever found.

"I blames myself," Tommy was quoted as saying. "I should have never left her. It's all my fault what happened to her. I blames myself."

Danny shuffled all of Tommy's old letters into their envelopes and put the lot back into his briefcase. His phone pinged, and he turned it over to look at it. A Google alert.

The term donepezil *appears in five documents you have recently viewed.*

Right. It was one of the drugs he'd found when he initially searched Tommy Power's house. He'd set an alert for it but obviously forgot to check and see if the search machine had uncovered anything of note.

Donepezil, sold under the trade name Aricept, is a medication used to treat Alzheimer's disease.

Tommy Power had Alzheimer's disease.

CHAPTER NINE

KEVIN CARBAGE turned the key, hoping for once his too-reliable Kia would refuse to start and he'd have to walk to the shop, an option he didn't relish, and on a Sunday, no less, when he should have been at church. He'd spent the entire weekend thinking over the events of Friday night. Yes, he deserved to be punished. He deserved to have no car and to go hungry and be without. He shouldn't have betrayed himself, betrayed his faith, by doing what he did. Being with Ford was great—no, better than great. Astonishing and beautiful and fuck, life-changing.

But it was still a mistake. He shouldn't have done it. He'd been doing so well, staying away from Ford, keeping himself pure. He'd even gone back to church a time or two, attending one of the Tuesday night prayer meetings and volunteering to teach Sunday school the next week. He needed to suppress his unclean desires; he knew this. And now he'd gone and undid all the good by doing… that. With Ford.

Ford, who didn't believe in anything. Ford, who'd been to war and who had seen and done awful things, who'd probably killed men. Ford, who most definitely had blood on his hands.

He started his car and snapped his seat belt on. It was very late, and he couldn't remember the last time he'd eaten something, or even drunk a cup of tea. Probably not a bad idea to go to the mini-mart and pick up the essentials, like milk and bread. He yearned for a slice of his nan's homemade loaf, but she'd been gone for years. He and June were all that were left of the Carbage family in Kildevil Cove. His parents were both dead, Nan and Pop were gone….

Gone. So many people were gone. If he truly believed the doctrine of his religion, he'd have eternity in Heaven to look forward to, where he'd be reunited with his lost loved ones, but Kevin didn't know if he believed that anymore. In the past several weeks, he'd seen more dead bodies than all the rest of his life put together. He'd never forget the photographs the forensics officers had taken of Tommy Power, propped against the bole of a fir tree, his throat slit ear-to-ear in an unholy, bloody grin.

Who could have possibly wanted Tommy dead? He never did anything to anyone. As long as Kevin had known him, the old man had been a recluse, keeping to his home and seldom venturing out unless it was to the spring in the woods for water. Had Tommy stumbled across someone who took issue with him being where he was? Was he in possession of dangerous knowledge that he couldn't be allowed to know? Cutting a man's throat was a sure-fire way to shut him up for good.

He pulled into Cy's Mini-Mart, a small convenience store located on Kildevil Cove's main road, and turned off his car. Cy was behind the cash register, counting scratch-off lottery tickets and noting something in a small book at his elbow. There appeared to be no one else in the shop. Kevin went inside, nodded a greeting, headed to the back of the store where the dairy coolers were, and took out a two-litre carton of milk. He always bought full fat, and June was forever nagging him about it, telling him his cholesterol would be off the charts if he didn't give it up. Kevin had noticed June showed no indication of giving up her favourite premium ice cream, which smacked of hypocrisy. His sister could be a mass of contradictions. He took the carton of milk to the front and laid it down on the counter while he went to the baked goods aisle, looking for bread.

A sudden flicker of movement to the left caught his peripheral vision, and he turned, but there was no one there. His gaze went to the convex mirror mounted in the far corner of the shop. Azariah Harris, holding a small baby and looking at a display of automobile air fresheners. His back was to Kevin, but the mirror was mounted at such an angle that Kevin could clearly see him in profile. It was definitely him. Not wanting to alert him, Kevin left his milk where it was and slipped outside to call Danny. The phone rang several times before Danny finally picked up.

"Kevin?" He sounded like he'd been woken out of a sound sleep. "What's on the go?"

"Azariah Harris," Kevin told him. "Cy's Mini-Mart. He's here with a baby." He kept a close eye on Harris, who was lingering near the checkout counter, chatting with Cy. "What do you want me to do?" He couldn't very well arrest the man. As far as they knew, Azariah had done nothing more than disappear along with the rest of his family. That was hardly a crime.

"Bring him in for questioning," Danny said. "Find out what he knows." He sounded excited now, his voice growing louder. "That son of a bitch knows something. We need to find out what it is."

"What about the baby?" For a hilarious moment, Kevin wondered if Danny expected him to question the baby too.

"One of the constables can look after it."

"Of course, sir."

"Bring him in and question him," Danny said. "You've been in this from the beginning, so you know this case as well as anybody."

Kevin hesitated. Part of him was gratified that Danny trusted him enough to conduct an interrogation, but the other part wondered if he knew what he was doing. He'd grilled people before, in his time with the RCMP. There was nothing mysterious about sequestering a suspect in an interview room and asking him the same questions over and over until the truth came to light. But this was important. Danny suspected Azariah Harris in connection with Deborah Harris's disappearance. Kevin couldn't afford to fuck this up.

"Yes, sir," he said finally.

"You can handle it, Constable," Danny reassured him. "If you need me, call."

"Will do, sir." He rang off.

Kevin watched as Azariah Harris handed Cy some money and accepted a plastic carrier bag from him in return. The baby had begun to cry, and he jiggled it in his arms, with no success. Kevin idly wondered what the appeal was. He'd never understood the allure of being tethered to a squalling larval version of oneself for months and years on end. He waited until Harris stepped out onto the parking lot before brandishing his badge.

"Azariah Harris?"

Harris's face closed down, his expression becoming dark and surly. "Who the fuck are you?"

"I'd like you to come to the station with me to answer a few questions," Kevin said.

"I never done nothing." Harris started for his car, a beat-up Nissan that was more rust than metal, and reached for the driver's side door. "You got nothing on me."

"I just want to ask you some questions," Kevin repeated. "I can place you under arrest if that's what you want, but I'd prefer it if you came along quietly." He nodded at the infant. "We have someone at the station who can look after the little one while you and I talk."

"I said I never done nothing. This is about her, isn't it? That fucking whore."

"Please," Kevin said. He indicated his own car, parked nearby. "The sooner you come with me, the sooner we can get this over with."

"Sure," Harris said and slouched after Kevin.

Kevin opened the passenger side door, wishing he'd driven a patrol car. At least that would give him the option of securing Harris in the back seat. "Get in," he said.

"Whatever you like, Constable."

Harris laid the baby on the seat and fussed with him a bit. He hesitated, his hand on the doorframe. Then he dropped his plastic carrier bag and bolted away into the night.

CILLIAN RILEY felt out of place at the new station. He'd agreed to join when Moira Fraser asked him because he knew Danny would be there, and he'd banked on Danny's dalliance with Tadhg Heaney being over. That hadn't happened. Danny and Tadhg, as far as anyone could see, were sound, if the time Danny spent visiting Lord Mucky-muck's private island was any indication. That, added to the fact it was a cold and drizzly Monday morning, put Riley in a bad mood.

Danny had placed Riley in charge of the Tommy Power murder investigation, which he supposed was a sop of sorts. Danny must have known why Riley agreed to the secondment to the Kildevil Cove station and offered him the Power case so he wouldn't feel bad. Riley had applied himself and his constables to the case with all due care and consideration, but there were pitifully few leads. All of the blood found at the scene was Tommy's. There were no signs of a struggle. The ground around the tree where the body was found had been disturbed, but the mixture of loose earth and spruce needles yielded nothing in the way of footprints.

Danny had been making himself scarce of late and was often away from the office on some pretext or other. Moira Fraser had told Riley that Danny usually worked his own lines of enquiry, and not to take it personally.

"He's a lone wolf," Fraser said. "It's just the way he is. He gets wind of something and he runs with it. Don't get your back up about it."

Everyone at the Kildevil Cove station seemed to regard Danny as a kind of detective savant, a man whose hunches and gut feelings often turned out to be right. He was smart—Riley had to give him that—but not much of a team player, and he had a tendency to concentrate his energies on areas that didn't seem to warrant further investigation. Right now Danny was trying to track down the origins of a dead baby some religious nuts had found. Riley's first task in Kildevil Cove had been questioning that Harvesters gang about the find, but as far as he could see, the dead baby had absolutely nothing to do with the cases they were supposed to be working on.

"Sarge?"

Riley looked up as Bobbi Lambert appeared beside his desk. "Yes?"

"Present for ye." She handed over a plastic-wrapped parcel.

Riley took the package and squeezed it. "What is it?"

"Tommy Power's clothes. We're finished with them, and the poor old bugger didn't have any family, so…." Lambert trailed off, looking uncomfortable. "They said you'd know what to do with 'em."

"Okay. Were there any trace findings?" he asked.

Lambert shrugged. "Some fibres, but it's all inconclusive at this stage. They might have been on him when he went into the woods, or he might have picked them up somewhere else. There's no real way to know." She offered Riley a sympathetic smile. "Sorry, Sarge."

Tommy Power's clothes, the ones he'd been wearing when he died, would be placed in storage indefinitely. If and when new technologies were developed that would allow for deeper examination of the results, then the clothes would be unearthed and examined, the cold case of Tommy Power's death reopened. It wouldn't do Tommy much good—he'd still be dead—but at least there would be some sort of closure.

"Thanks, Bobbi. I appreciate it."

"Seen His Lordship around this morning?" she asked. "I looked in his office, but he's not there."

"Inspector Quirke? Haven't seen him," Riley told her. "You can try his phone. Is it anything important?"

"Constable Carbage—Kevin—passed on some evidence he found and wanted me to test it for him."

Riley leaned closer to her and smiled. "And?"

She burst into laughter. "None of your business, bhoy. Ye got some bloody cheek, you do."

"I won't tell a soul."

"No, that you won't. Because it don't concern ye." She turned and headed off in the direction of the break room, changed her mind, and came back. "I can tell ye, though, that we found DNA in the Mercedes. Ford Maddox and Dr. Fahey. Whoever burned the car used gasoline as an accelerant."

"Oh," Riley said, pressing a hand to his chest, teasing her, "so I am worthy of your consideration after all."

"Ye're the light of my existence," she said, "you are so." She gave him a wave and headed down the corridor to her lab.

Something occurred to him, one of those little tics of recognition that he'd learned to pay heed to over the course of his career. On impulse, he picked up the phone and called the medical examiner. He'd quickly learned that Regan Lampe could be prickly and off-putting, with an enormous chip on her shoulder, so he tended to avoid her unless it was necessary.

She answered on the first ring. "Dr. Lampe."

"It's Cillian Riley. I'm calling about Tommy Power's autopsy."

She sighed audibly. "What about it?" Looked like she was going to be as friendly and accommodating as usual, then.

"The results." He pulled up the case file on his computer and scrolled through it. "Did you perform the post-mortem?"

"Of course I did."

"The post-mortem says he died of exsanguination and haemorrhagic shock," Riley said.

"Yes," she confirmed, her tone frosty, "the gaping wound in his throat was responsible after all. Imagine that."

Riley yearned to tell her where to go but bit his lip instead. "You didn't notice anything in particular about the wound?" he asked. "Hesitation marks, tailing abrasions?"

"I noticed it was in his throat, Sergeant," she snapped and hung up on him.

His fist clenched around the receiver, and he forced himself to replace it in the cradle very slowly and gently. He took a few deep breaths, then let it go, turned to the autopsy file open on his computer. There were several good-quality photos of the throat wound that killed Tommy Power—a gaping laceration like a gory second mouth. There were multiple smaller, shallower cuts at what Riley suspected was the point of origin, under the lobe of the left ear. The main cut, the one that killed him according to Dr. Lampe, sliced downwards across his throat, ending about five centimetres above his collarbone. Riley scrolled through the document until he came to the list of items found at the scene: fir and spruce needles, some of which had insinuated themselves into the deceased's clothing, a half-smoked cigarette, and a two-centimetre-long piece of yellow ribbon, polyester, readily available in any shop carrying such items. That was it. There was no weapon. The presence of hesitation marks suggested something he had suspected anyway, though the missing weapon was a problem.

He picked up the phone again and called Danny. "Riley, sir," he said, when Danny answered. "I want to see Tommy Power's medical records."

There was a prolonged silence on the other end; then Danny asked, "Why?"

"I have a hunch." He didn't want to go further into it than that. If his supposition proved to be wrong, he would look like a fool.

"Is it to do with the case, or are you just curious?"

That hurt. Riley reached for his cup of rapidly-cooling tea and swallowed some, throat muscles working hard to get it down. "What do you think?" he asked, surly now. "Sir," he added, as an afterthought.

"Cillian, I didn't mean—"

"It's all right, sir," Riley retorted. Danny's use of his Christian name was an attempt to mollify him. He could be a manipulative bastard, Inspector Quirke. "No offence taken. By the way, Bobbi Lambert is looking for you, something to do with evidence Kevin Carbage handed in."

"Thank you," Danny said, sounding chastened. "About the other— I'll see what I can do."

"Thanks." Riley hung up before Danny could say anything else. He was behaving childishly, he knew, but fuck Danny anyway. He went to the break room and dumped his cold tea down the sink, set the kettle to boiling for a new one.

Kevin Carbage wandered in, looking like he'd been dragged backwards through a knothole. Riley said good morning to him, but Carbage shook his head as if to say it might be morning but it was anything but good.

"That bad?" Riley asked. He fetched down a second cup from the cupboard and dropped a teabag in, waited till the kettle flicked off, then filled both of them. "Here." He pushed the steaming mug towards Kevin. "Get that down you. Cuppa tea will do you the world of good."

"Wish it were that simple," Carbage replied. He went to the fridge and took out a carton of milk, brought it over to the countertop. "Lately it feels like every goddamn day is Monday." He attempted a smile, but the muscles of his face seemed frozen with what Riley recognised as grief. He'd seen that expression on his own face often enough.

"Everything all right?" Riley added milk to his own tea and took a sip. "You've got a gob on you like a wet week."

"Nngh," Kevin replied, around the rim of his cup.

"Any sign of young Harris yet?" Riley asked.

Kevin shook his head. "Almost had him last night, but the fucker took off into the woods. We've been to Old Perlican and back with a fine-toothed comb, but there's no sign of him." He uttered a half-hearted laugh. "It's all bad enough, but he left his little fella on the passenger seat of my car last night."

"He never did!" Riley was shocked and didn't know whether to laugh or not at the absurdity of it. "He left the baby in your car?"

"Sure, you knows he did." Kevin took a long drink of his tea. It seemed to be doing him some good. "I had to bring him down to June's until social services could show up. She didn't thank me for that, let me tell you."

Maybe Carbage had made the mistake of thinking of all women as inherently maternal, Riley thought. "Where's the baby now?"

"Social services in Harbour Grace," Kevin replied through a yawn. "Poor little bugger." He patted Riley's shoulder as thanks for the tea and wandered back out of the break room.

Riley's phone rang as he arrived back at his desk. It was Danny again. "I managed to get you in to view Tommy's records. They won't allow us to take anything out of the clinic, so you can forget that. Whatever you want to see, you'll have to look at it there. Okay?" A beat. "I'm sorry I couldn't be of more help, Sergeant."

"No, it's great, sir." Riley was briefly ashamed of how he'd spoken to Danny earlier. "Thank you. I'll let you know if I find anything worthwhile."

THE SMALL medical clinic in Winterton was decorated in early-seventies kitsch: moulded wooden chairs with gleaming chrome legs and reproduction prints of big-eyed children in Edwardian dress. A handful of people waited patiently in the silence, their hands in their laps, while a plastic clock in the shape of an owl with moving eyes tick-tocked out the passing moments. Riley crossed to the reception window and came face to face with a stout woman in her late fifties, her hair dyed an unappealing bright red. She picked savagely at a computer keyboard with both forefingers, as if it had furnished her an insult.

He flashed his badge. "Sergeant Cillian Riley."

"Good for you," she replied, without looking up.

"I requested the medical records of one of your patients. I'm here to see the file."

"Is that right?" She raised her head, looked him up and down, and went back to her work. He could tell his authority as a police officer meant absolutely nothing to her.

"I can see how busy you are," he began, "and I appreciate you taking the time to see me. I'm sorry to be such a pain in the arse." He leaned on the desk and allowed his Geordie accent to deepen and broaden. "Lovely lass like you, working her fingers to t'bone. S'not right. Bet you've not even had a break."

The hands stilled on the keyboard, and she raised her head slowly to look at him. "Sure, you're not from here."

"Not originally," he replied, "but I'm here now." He grinned. "What've ye got to do to get a cuppa round 'ere, eh?"

"Tommy Power, wasn't it?" The suspicion was slowly fading from her eyes, but she still didn't trust him. Not yet.

"That's right. My boss rang earlier. Said there was a lovely lass at t'desk what could 'elp me, like." He gazed into her eyes. "Guess he were talkin' 'bout you."

"What's your boss's name?"

Riley told her.

"Oh, him." She snorted, an unpleasant noise from anyone, but from a woman of her age and bearing, it sounded like something uttered in a barnyard. "I knows all about him."

Riley didn't ask what it was she knew. She got up from her chair and opened the side door, beckoned him into the office.

"Thank you so much," he said. "I can't tell ye what it means t'me."

"Come through to the back," she instructed. "I'll put the kettle on."

"Cheers," Riley answered, and, "you're a star." He followed her pointing finger to a series of shelves set against a back wall, each filled with row upon row of colour-coded file folders.

"Power." She pulled a step stool over to the farthest shelf and hoisted herself up onto it. "P.... Power.... Tommy. Sure, he's dead, bhoy. What do ye crowd want with his file?"

"It's to aid in an ongoing investigation," Riley replied primly.

"Here we are." She pulled a thick file out and climbed back down. "Tommy Power."

Riley took it and thanked her. "Is there anywhere I could go to look at this in private?" he asked.

"You can go in the break room," she said. "Only me uses it. Doctor Fung, now, I've never seen him eat. I don't think he's even human, to tell you the truth. I've put the kettle on for ye. There's bags and cups in the cupboard over the sink. Help yourself." She directed him towards a door marked Private. "I'll leave you to it."

Riley pushed the door open to find himself in a small cubicle with a table and one chair, a microwave oven, and the aforementioned kettle. He flipped open Tommy's file and took out his phone. Some coppers still made notes by hand, but Riley found that time-consuming and unnecessary in this day and age. He skimmed through quickly, taking a photo of each page in turn, emailing them to himself. Tommy's medical history was about what he'd have expected for a man of his years and personal habits. As a solitary old-age pensioner who smoked and drank heavily and whose diet was loaded with unhealthy processed food, he had all the usual complaints. High blood pressure, narrowing of the arteries, incipient cirrhosis of the liver—all of which could be controlled with medication. Riley was three pages in before he saw something that surprised him.

Tommy Power was in the early stages of Alzheimer's disease when he died.

Riley closed the folder and sat back. Someone with Alzheimer's could absolutely wander off into the woods and get lost. It didn't account for the cut throat, though. He stood up and went back to the file room to put the folder back on the shelf. His gaze automatically travelled to various names in the rest of the row. P: Power, Price, Pryor.... Q: Quinn, Quinton, Quirke....

Quirke.

He hesitated, his hand hovering over the spine of the folder. He shouldn't even touch it. It had nothing to do with him; it was none of his business. Everybody went to the doctor, even Danny, and since Fung was the only doctor between Carbonear and Old Perlican, it made sense that Danny would go to him. The folder was in his hand before he knew it, and he was crouched over it, flipping it open. He glanced over his shoulder, worried that the receptionist might come back and catch him in the act, but he could hear her talking to someone on the phone. He was safe, at least for a little while.

Danny had apparently been seeing Fung since he was a very small boy. There was a long list of the usual childhood ailments: colds, bronchitis, chicken pox, strep throat. He'd broken a bone in his foot playing ice hockey when he was fifteen and was treated for concussion at eighteen after a fall from the roof of the Heaney family home. There was a curious note appended to the medical report: *RHnull blood type, same as birth mother.* Birth mother? Danny was adopted? Riley shrugged. So Danny was adopted. No big deal there. More than likely Danny knew, and it had nothing to do with anything, not really.

After Danny reached age eighteen, the file was empty, presumably because Danny had left Kildevil Cove to begin his education. He would have been seeing a doctor elsewhere during those years. Riley was just about to close the folder and return it to the shelf when he noticed an official-looking letterhead from a Doctor Elias Balto. Balto was a St. John's psychiatrist who maintained a practice on Waterford Bridge

Road in the city's historic district. Riley had come across the name before while working in St John's. The letter—Riley merely skimmed it before taking a quick snap with his phone—detailed a two-week stay in the provincial psychiatric hospital for a court-ordered assessment. Deiniol Quirke—Inspector Deiniol Quirke—had done a stint in the loony bin.

DANNY'S MOBILE rang the very moment he set foot on the doorstep of the police station. He thumbed the little green circle to accept the call with one hand and pulled open the door with the other. "Quirke."

"Good." Regan Lampe's voice crackled through the speaker. "I ran some tests on that bottle you gave me. I also got the results back from the young Heaney girl's blood tests."

"Oh?" Danny nodded a hello to the desk sergeant as he went down the corridor towards his office, stepping neatly around a couple of phone-company technicians whose bent backs indicated work of some importance near June Carbage's empty desk.

"I can't often say I'm surprised where you're concerned," she continued, "but this takes the cake."

"Really?" He reached his desk and shrugged out of his coat, hung it on the coat tree by the wall. A stack of pink message slips was tucked beneath his phone, and the African violet Lily had given him for his office needed watering.

"She had ayahuasca in her system," she said.

Danny thought he remembered seeing something like that in the report on Deborah Harris—something he couldn't even pronounce. "It's aya-what?"

"Ayahuasca. It's traditionally used by South American shamans to… fuck, I don't know, conjure the devil or something. The concoction he was giving her was full of it."

Danny sat down in his chair. "South America. Are you sure?"

She muttered something in Inuktitut. "Yes, I am sure. That's not the worst of it. This ayahuasca, it causes powerful hallucinations that can seem very real, and a proper dosage titration has never been established. Unless you know exactly what you're doing, you can fuck somebody up really badly with this stuff."

He thought back to the night Tadhg had sent a helicopter to bring Regan to Eigus. Lily had sliced open her arm, claiming there was something in it that she'd been trying to extract. A cold fist of anger massaged the lining of his stomach. "So he was... what the *hell* did Dr. Fahey think he was doing?"

She laughed mirthlessly. "Fucked if I know," she said. "He had some other things in there, too: dandelions, catnip, and *Datura*. You know, jimson weed."

"Also poisonous, I'm guessing." Poor Lily. How long had she been taking this lunatic's potions?

"Very. Can mimic the effects of strychnine. To his credit, it was a small amount, but it probably didn't help what she was going through with the ayahuasca." She sounded concerned and almost... civil. "Will you let Mr. Heaney know?"

"Of course."

"Oh, and thank him for the bracelet," she added. "He apparently thinks diamonds really are a girl's best friend."

She ended the call before he could question this last. A bracelet? Tadhg had sent her a diamond bracelet? It was like Tadhg to make grand gestures, but still. He'd never given Danny a diamond bracelet.

June Carbage appeared in the door, bearing two cups of tea. She laid one down on his desk and leaned against the wall. "So," she said.

Danny raised an eyebrow. "So?"

"Kevin got him." She sipped at her tea. "Just now."

"Azariah Harris?"

"The same. Found him in the woods up behind Buckler's Hill." She was grinning. "You'll never guess how."

Danny couldn't guess.

"According to his story, he tripped over an exposed tree root and fell onto the jagged stump of an old spruce. Impaled him right through the upper arm"—she indicated where on her own arm, her cup of tea wavering dangerously as she did so—"but he managed to call for help on his mobile phone. Kevin's just now collected him and is taking him to hospital in Carbonear. He'll be back soon enough for questioning."

Christ, Harris had led them a merry chase; that was bloody well sure. Danny was glad Kevin had managed to catch up with him. "You and Kevin want to do the interview?" he asked. It was only fair, and he knew Kevin was more than capable.

"Love to," she said, turning to go. "Enjoy your tea," she added.

"Thank you."

Danny phoned Tadhg as soon as June left, but the call went to voicemail. Tadhg was in Kildevil Cove, supervising the laying of the foundations at Danny's grandfather's old property now that the frost had gone out of the ground. He left a message telling Tadhg to call him at once; it was important. He'd barely hung up when his phone rang. It was Tadhg.

"Regan Lampe said your Dr. Fahey was giving Lily a dangerous South American herb, ayahuasca, mixed with jimson weed." Danny tried to keep a note of reproach out of his voice and failed. Tadhg had to have known Fahey couldn't be trusted. The man was a charlatan and a quack, for Christ's sake.

"What?" Tadhg sounded almost ridiculously incredulous. "Are you.... Jesus, are you sure?"

"Yes, I'm sure," Danny retorted. "Regan said she couldn't believe it."

"That's—" Tadhg broke off as someone in the background called his name. "Can we meet up? I'm at your grandfather's place. I'd rather not discuss this over the phone."

"Fine," Danny said. "I'll be there in five minutes." He gulped the cup of tea June had brought him and took his coat from the hanger. This was just like Tadhg. He was forever going off half-cocked, doing stupid shit and hoping it would come out all right. He was a habitual gambler, willing to roll the dice no matter the odds.

Tadhg's company pickup truck was sitting to one side of the old garage when Danny arrived. He pulled up beside it, parked, and went through the gate to where his grandparents' house had once stood. It was still a shock to arrive at the place where he'd spent his childhood and find nothing but an absence where the house had been. It had burned to the ground the previous autumn, the victim of arson by a disgruntled employee of Tadhg's late father. For his entire life the white biscuit-box dwelling had presided over an expansive green space, planted round with fir, spruce, and shrub roses that in the summertime released a heavenly fragrance. On the hill behind the house were pin cherry trees and wild blueberries, the fruit as large as the top of a thumb, bursting on the palate with a taste sweet as wine. The old stable stood where it always had, untouched by the fire but fallen into disrepair now, the doors sagging on their hinges, the exterior missing entire rows of its ancient wooden shingles.

He found Tadhg there, standing in the midst of a group of construction labourers wearing hats and work boots. They were gathered around a makeshift table crafted out of two sawhorses and a couple of planks. A set of draughtsman's drawings had been spread out upon the surface, and Tadhg was explaining some aspect of the build.

"These walls have got to be perfectly plumb," he said, "and make sure the footings are sunk to the appropriate depth."

"Tadhg." Danny's voice seemed to break into their midst like a klaxon. "Could I speak to you, if ye don't mind?"

The group around Tadhg all raised their heads in unison and gazed curiously at Danny.

"Sure...." Tadhg rolled up the drawings briskly. "Why don't ye crowd go down and start digging for the footings," he said, addressing the labourers, "and I'll be along now the once." He waited until they'd gone before addressing Danny. "Poison, you said."

"Tadhg, what the Jesus were you thinking?" Danny asked loudly—he didn't really give a fuck who heard him. He was too upset on Lily's behalf to hide his anger, although part of him knew this was the worst possible approach to take with Tadhg. "She could have done serious harm to herself that day in the bathroom. Christ almighty, she did do serious harm! Did ye even check to see if this Fahey character was credible?"

Tadhg's eyes narrowed. "Now hold on a second. Of course I checked. D'ye think I'm a fool? She's my daughter. Jesus, Danny."

"Did you bother to ask what was in the bottles he was giving her?"

"I asked him!" Tadhg shouted. "I told ye that. He said it was dandelion, ginger, that sort of thing. He gave me a goddamn list, for fuck's sake." He stared hard at Danny. "You think I'm an unfit parent."

"I didn't say that." Danny struggled, backpedalling furiously. "Look, all I'm saying—"

"No." Tadhg interrupted him. "You don't think I'm fit to raise Lily."

Danny sighed. This was going so very, very wrong. "By taking her to that quack, you exposed her to danger. You don't ever put a child in harm's way. You should know that."

"So I deliberately put her in danger, is that it?" Tadhg's expression was incredulous. "Is that what you mean?"

Danny's mouth opened and closed. He half turned, wondering if he should just leave now, forestalling any further damage. It would be all too easy to say something horribly hurtful, something he would regret deep down later on. On the other hand, maybe he ought to tell Tadhg what he really felt, make him see that his cavalier attitude about so many things was hurting the people he cared about.

"I think," Danny said finally, "that sometimes you don't do your due diligence. I think you hurt Lily by sending her to that quack, when any parent—"

"You are not a parent!" Tadhg roared. "You haven't got a fucking clue what you're talking about."

"Ye don't have to be," Danny said, "to know right from wrong. That's always been your trouble, Tadhg. Ye're never quite sure, but ye're always willing to do what ye think ye can get away with."

The second after he'd said it, he knew he'd gone too far. A palpable chill descended like the dropping of an invisible veil, settling around them both. But it was the truth, Danny thought, as if this were any sort of defence, as if he hadn't just lobbed a hand grenade into the guts of their relationship.

The lines of Tadhg's face hardened, a bleakness creeping into his features. He reached into his pocket and withdrew a small green box. "Guess I won't be needing this after all," he said, and turned to go.

"Tadhg."

"Never mind, Danny," Tadhg called from the doorway, "you've made yourself perfectly clear." He closed his fist around the little box and left without another word.

"SHE JUST went." Azariah Harris was surprisingly talkative, sitting at the table in the interview room, sipping a cup of tea with obvious enjoyment. The wound in his arm didn't seem to be giving him much trouble, but that might have been a result of the local anaesthetic the emergency room doctor had injected. Kevin guessed it would hurt like hell as soon as that wore off. "Mother was telling her to feed the little fella, but she wouldn't. She just got up and went. That's a sin, that is. He's still on the breast, sure."

"Did she say where she was going?" Kevin asked. He was bone-tired, his clothing muddy and dishevelled from his long trek through the forest looking for Harris. He was in no mood to be lenient or even civil.

"She cursed on Mother." Harris said this in a tone of awed wonder, as if he couldn't imagine anyone swearing at his sainted mother. "Not fit, she's not."

"Did she say where she was going?" Kevin repeated.

"What's that got to do with it?" Harris blinked at him, turned and did the same to June. "I just told you what she said. What's that got to do with anything?"

"Just answer the question, Mr. Harris," June said.

"I wasn't there. I was off cutting wood. She told Mother she was going out. That's all she said. Just… going out."

"Why didn't you report your wife as missing?" Kevin asked.

"She was after taking off before. She always come back. I figured she'd come back this time too, sure." Azariah drained the last of his tea, then looked pointedly into the cup. "Don't suppose there's another one where this came from, is there?"

"No," June replied shortly. She shot an exasperated look at her brother. "Mr. Harris, you mentioned that your baby son was still breastfeeding. Wouldn't you need to look for your wife so she could feed the baby? Surely an infant of his age can only go so long between feedings."

"Me mother was helping out," Harris replied, and there was something evasive about it.

"What do you mean she was helping out?" Kevin asked.

"Er… looking after 'un. Makin' sure he wasn't hungry."

June blinked in surprise. "Surely he's not on solid food yet?"

"No, she was helpin' 'un."

Kevin rubbed the back of his neck, fighting back the anger that was surging in him like a storm tide. "How was she helping him?"

Silence. Azariah looked at Kevin, then away. June huffed out a frustrated breath while the tape machine hissed gently.

"How was she helping him?" Kevin asked. His hands curled into fists.

"She used to let 'un suckle from her."

June looked at Kevin and mouthed "…the fuck?"

"But your mother is well past the age of being able to lactate," June said after a moment.

"She got some pills from Deborah's doctor," Azariah said. "To make 'er milk come in, like."

June leapt at the recorder and stopped the tape, then gestured to Kevin. He followed her out into the corridor and shut the door to the interview room behind him.

"He's a fucking piece of work," June said. "His mother? Taking pills to lactate? Christ!"

Kevin was shocked and disgusted in equal measure. "Do you think he's telling the truth?"

June rolled her eyes. "I think he's telling something."

"Can you really get pills to do that?"

"Maybe. I don't know. Some women can still produce milk well into menopause… maybe his mother isn't as old as she seems?"

"Fuck," Kevin breathed. "I suppose we've got nothing to charge him with."

"Nope," June confirmed. "Gonna have to let the fucker go, I guess."

"All right."

He opened the interview room door and ushered his sister in, closed it behind them. June started the tape rolling again. "So, Mr. Harris… just to clue things up here… when your wife went out that day, you didn't go after her because you say she'd run off before and she always came back."

"Yeah, but I didn't want her to come back, to tell you the truth." He gazed at them both with guileless eyes. "Sometimes the Lord makes his will known through the actions of men. If it was the Lord's will for her to go, then she should go."

"Where did you think she would go?" June asked.

"Back where she come from."

June raised her eyebrows. "Back to St. John's."

"Yep."

"And because it was the Lord's will that she ran away, you decided to let her go," Kevin said.

"It was the Lord's will." Harris stood up, his injured arm held protectively against his chest. "Where's my little fella?"

"He's in the care of social services." June took a business card from her pocket and handed it across to him. "Contact the number on the card and someone there will help you."

Harris took the card from her and put it in his pocket.

"Mr. Harris, aren't you even a little curious about where your wife is?" June asked, eyes narrowed.

He shook his head. "No."

"Interview terminated," Kevin said and stopped the tape. "You're free to go," he told Harris.

June opened the door and waited till Harris had gone through it. She closed the door and leaned on it. "What a fucking arsehole!" She gazed at Kevin. "Does he even know his wife is dead?"

Danny arrived at the connecting door just then, swiping his access card to let him into the secure part of the building. He saw June and Kevin standing by the wall and came over. "Well?"

"Swears up and down he's innocent," Kevin said. "Nothing to charge him with, so we have to let him go."

"Christ," Danny breathed. He pinched the skin between his eyebrows. "I want him under surveillance. That bastard knows more than he's letting on." He looked at Kevin. "Follow him when he leaves. Find out where he goes. Let me know the minute he does something unexpected. And Carbage?"

"Sir?"

"Don't lose him this time."

KEVIN CARBAGE watched from the window as Azariah Harris got into his rattletrap car and started it up. The ancient Nissan was rusted around the fenders and spackled here and there with Polybond. He slipped outside and into his own car to follow Harris at a discreet distance, hoping the younger man wouldn't bother looking in the rearview mirror or, if he did, would discount Kevin's presence as mere coincidence. Kevin had already lost him once; it wouldn't do to lose him again. Danny would probably sack him on the spot. But Azariah gave no indication he even noticed Kevin behind him as he passed through the main part of Kildevil Cove and climbed Buckler's Hill to the south side. He turned onto a narrow gravel road and drove into the woods for perhaps five minutes until the lane terminated at a white bungalow that seemed oddly familiar.

Had Kevin ever been here before? Unlikely. Yet the house presented itself so powerfully in his memory. Perhaps he'd visited when he was a child, with June or his mother? Looking at it now, he felt as if he could walk inside and know precisely where everything was, every room and corner, every door and window.

Kevin parked near the main drag and got out to follow Harris on foot, keeping himself well behind the other man. Azariah knocked once on the door of the house and then opened it, letting himself inside. He was obviously known to the occupants, who greeted him by name. Kevin took up a position underneath the front windows, which were open to allow the April breeze in.

"Ye didn't have to do that to her," he heard Azariah say.

"We did nothing to her," someone—a young man, judging by his voice—said. "She came here with the little maid, and we gave her a drop to drink and sent her on her way. Whatever happened after that, it had nothing to do with us."

"The cops are after asking me questions about Deb. You told me you'd take care of it," Azariah said. "You said you'd send her back where she come from and there'd be no more to it than that. I told yez she wasn't fit. Now she's gone, and nobody knows where she is."

"Questions about Deb?" This was a different voice, an older woman, someone Kevin couldn't place. He knew just about everyone in Kildevil Cove, so this had to be an incomer, perhaps one of Malachy's bunch. The Harvesters seemed to attract a ragtag all and sundry.

"Questions about Deb," Azariah said. "You said you'd take her out of the picture because she wasn't fit. That's all."

"That's not my fault, my son." There was a long period of silence, and Kevin flattened himself against the wall, half expecting someone to come charging out of the house to catch him listening.

"I paid you good money to do what needed to be done," Azariah said, "and you fucked it up."

Kevin took out his mobile phone and called the station. June answered. "Get me some backup," he said. "I'm about to arrest Azariah Harris for the murder of his wife." He disconnected and put the phone away just as Azariah reappeared at the top of the stairs. As soon as he saw Kevin, he leapt down the front steps and took off into the woods, but Kevin caught up with him easily, tackled him to the ground, and cuffed him very neatly.

"You said you knew nothing about it," he panted as he hauled Azariah to his feet. "You lying bastard."

CHAPTER TEN

AZARIAH HARRIS was seriously pissed off. He was being held in a small interview room at the police station until Inspector Quirke decided what to do with him. Inspector Quirke had already decided that Az had killed his wife. Now he would try to get Az to confess to it, even though Az was innocent and had nothing to confess to.

He had wanted the help of fellow believers, holy women and men who would lay hands on Deborah, anoint her with oil of spikenard, and chase the evil out of her. That was the only reason he went to the Harvesters in the first place, because he knew of their beliefs and their steadfast righteousness, knew they understood the nature of the demons Deborah had inside of her. He never meant to hurt her.

But they weren't the same kind of Harvesters he remembered from years ago, when he and his parents had travelled to Grand Falls every summer to attend special revival meetings. Back then, the sect had been more rigid, more rigorous in their beliefs and practices. There was no such thing as dancing and drinking, embracing the morals of the world and giving oneself over to the pleasures of the flesh. His parents had been dismayed when his mother's sister, Aunt Milse, had decided to leave the Apostolic faith and join them, but it was Aunt Milse who helped Azariah the most by helping Deborah. Someone had to help Deborah.

It was all Deborah's fault to begin with. His marriage to her had been a bad deal from the start, ever since he met her on a chilly St. John's street corner, trying to wave down a taxi. He recognised her for what she was but foolishly believed he could redeem her, a low and common woman. He paid for a hotel room at the Delta, put her up for the night, and when she went down on her knees in front of him and unzipped his fly, he allowed it, even though he knew that intimate congress with her would place the stain of fornication on him.

He'd expected Kevin Carbage and his sister would eventually come and question him, but they hadn't bothered to make an appearance. That other one, Quirke, had come by and looked in at him, saying nothing. Maybe he intended asking all the questions. Azariah didn't much care for that idea. Danny Quirke was a hard-looking man, the kind of cop who'd start by pecking at you with his questions, but before long he'd be pounding you like a pile-driver. It was all bad enough, but him being a queer made the entire situation that much worse. Suppose he tried something? He was the head of all the cops here and could probably make Az do anything he wanted. Would anybody hear him if he shouted for help? Maybe they were all queers. He wasn't safe. The scriptures said for one man to lie with another as with a woman was an abomination. Azariah shouldn't even be talking to a man like him.

The door opened and Danny Quirke was there. He stepped in, and the door fell shut behind him. "So." His eyes were a dark blue that looked almost black in the dim light. His blondish-brown hair was going grey at the temples and the front. "Turns out you weren't telling the whole truth, Mr. Harris." Danny sat down on the chair next to his. Azariah moved away, stood up and went over by the door.

"Don't be at me," he said. His voice trembled more than he would have liked. Quirke would think he was scared. Azariah wasn't scared of him. A true servant of the Lord had nothing to be afraid of. He could take up serpents with his bare hands and not be harmed. He could drink poison and he wouldn't die.

"I'm not doing anything to you," Quirke remarked. He reached across and pressed a button on the tape recorder that sat at one end of the table. "Come back and sit down."

"I knows what your kind is like," Azariah told him. "I'm washed in the blood of the Lamb. Nothing you can do to me."

Quirke ignored this. "Sit down." He waited until Azariah had taken the seat across from him. "Mr. Harris, you were observed discussing your wife with certain other parties. These other parties have independently confirmed that you contacted them and asked them to—and I quote—'take care of' your wife. What exactly were you asking them to do?"

"I never done nothing," Az said. Danny Quirke's blue eyes gazed at him, through him, boring a hole in him. He knew at once that he couldn't hide anything from this man.

A long silence stretched between them, and Azariah's injured arm throbbed painfully. He shifted his eyes away from Quirke's incisive gaze, watched some dust motes twirling in the still air.

"Take care of her how?" Danny persisted.

"I don't remember saying that." Maybe if he kept stalling long enough, he could wear Quirke down. "I never said that."

"Take care of her how?" Quirke's tone was infinitely patient. His posture said he could do this all day. There was a knock at the door; he got up to answer it. Carbage's sister—she was a queer too—handed in a cup of tea and a wrapped sandwich.

"Thought Mr. Harris might be hungry," she said by way of explanation. Danny handed the food across the table to him.

"You've been here for four hours," Danny said. "Now, I need you to start talking or I'm going to assume you're guilty and keep you here indefinitely."

A jagged shard of fear went through Azariah's gut, and he stared at Danny, trying to judge whether he was telling the truth. "Can you do that?" He reached out for the tea, drew it close so he could examine it. It smelled all right. It looked like ordinary tea. "What's in this?" he asked.

"Tea," Danny replied.

"Did you put drugs in it?" He'd read somewhere that queers would drug you so they could rape you and make you like them.

"There's tea in it," Danny repeated. "Milk and one sugar."

"You're not going to poison me?"

Danny's eyebrows rose. "Why would I want to poison you?" he asked.

Azariah unwrapped the sandwich and smelled it: turkey with mayonnaise, on white bread. His favourite. He took a bite, chewed and swallowed. It tasted good.

"Who were the people you went to see?" Danny asked. Azariah concentrated on eating the sandwich and sipping his tea. "Answer me."

"Am I supposed to have a lawyer present?"

"That is your right if you want one," Danny told him. "Do you want one?"

"The social service crowd took my little fella," Azariah said. He felt the loss of the baby as a palpable ache. Maybe he would never get the boy back now. Social services would place him with another family, or in foster care. Azariah might never see his son again. The idea of it felt like being punched.

"Do you want a lawyer?" Danny asked again.

"No." He finished the remainder of the sandwich in three bites and crumpled up the wrapper. He could have eaten another one like it, he was that hungry.

"Who were the people you went to see?"

"They were our people, some of 'em," Azariah said. "They used to be with Malachy and them, but they don't go with him no more, so."

"They aren't part of Malachy's church?"

"No. They likes to stay where they're to. They got their own ways, better than Malachy's crowd."

"So what did you want from them?" Danny asked. "What were you expecting?"

Azariah thought about what he wanted to say. If he said the wrong thing, gave the wrong answer to a question, this queer cop would put him away for years. "They were going to lay hands on her," he said finally, "anoint her with oil like it says in the scriptures and send her back where she come from."

"Send her back how?" He made a lot of notes on the yellow pad in front of him, this cop, his pen scratching noisily, like a chicken rooting around in the dirt.

"With prayer." It was useless, trying to explain it to an unbeliever. "We'd pray over her and the demons would leave her. And my Aunt Milse would give her a little drink to ease her down."

"A drink of what?" The pen went on scratching, and the cop's blue eyes bored into him.

"Aunt Milse makes it. She got a name on it. She makes a batch up every winter, puts it down into the cellar." What was it called? He struggled to remember. "Switchel."

"Switchel," Danny commented, "is what my grandfather used to call weak tea. Is that what it is?"

"Yes, tea and other things. She'd put it down the cellar until it was ready."

"Fermented, you mean." He made another note on the pad. "So it's alcohol."

What did it have to do with anything? "I s'pose, bhoy."

"Your aunt gave her alcohol. That's all. Just a drink of this… switchel."

"Yes." He wished Danny would shut up and leave him alone.

"Did you pay them any money?"

Azariah nodded.

"For the benefit of the tape," Danny said, "the suspect nodded in the affirmative." He leaned his elbows on the table. "How much?"

"Two hundred."

"Dollars?" Danny asked sharply.

"Yes."

Danny swore under his breath. Amazing how easily unbelievers took the Lord's name in vain. "To get rid of your wife."

"Not to hurt her!" Fear surged up into Azariah's chest and throat. For a moment he thought he might vomit the sandwich he'd eaten. "I just told them to send the demon back to hell, the demon that was in her. That's all."

"Your wife, Deborah Harris, was found in a bog," Danny said. He spoke slowly and carefully, as if weighing each word before he uttered it. "Deceased, with one of her eyes gouged out."

"No." Az's knees started to tremble, and a violent shaking worked its way up into his belly and chest. Invisible hands clasped around his throat. "She's not. She's gone back to town, sure. I knows she is."

"Azariah Harris, you will be charged with conspiracy to commit murder—"

"Deb's not dead. Sure, she can't be dead. Nobody did nothing to her." He stood up, nearly overturning the table in his haste. "She was alive when I saw her. We had a row, then she went out. She just went. I never did anything to her!"

Danny Quirke opened the door, spoke quietly to someone outside, and then two constables appeared, each taking hold of Azariah to lead him from the room. This wasn't really happening. None of this was really happening. He was dreaming it.

"The joy of the Lord is my strength," he murmured. "The joy of the Lord is my strength."

They led him down the hall to a cell, a heavy metal door painted blue that opened once and clanged shut behind him.

CILLIAN RILEY switched the lights on one by one as he passed through his rented house on his way to the kitchen. The daylight was a lot longer in the evenings now, but the air after sundown was cold, and there was still frost in the early mornings. He longed for a real spring, an English spring, rather than the cold, wet misery of this northern island. He reached to turn the kettle on for another cup of tea.

It was just after eight in the evening, and he'd spent the past two hours reading and rereading Tommy Power's file, comparing it with the Deborah Harris case and trying to find similarities. So far, the only thing that stood out was the fact that both were found in the same general area. Tommy's throat had been cut and Deborah had gouged out her own eye with her fingernails, probably a result of the ayahuasca concoction that quack Dr. Fahey had given her.

He ought to call Danny and share his suspicions about Tommy: that it wasn't murder, but suicide. Deborah Harris too. Being treated with Dr. Fahey's dubious concoction, she had probably clawed her own eye out in the throes of horrific hallucinations—especially if she'd been exposed to alcohol. Would it be premature to tell Danny what he thought? Or should he wait until he had something more concrete, something proven beyond the shadow of a doubt?

He could have gone to Danny's office any time and spoken to him in confidence, but he didn't think he could bear being close to Danny right now. Not within touching distance, certainly. He saw Danny every day, but whatever chance he might have had with Danny was gone. In its place there was an uncomfortable tension, arising whenever they spoke more than a handful of words to each other. Danny was always there, either in his actual field of vision or in his thoughts and daydreams.

He gazed out the kitchen window into the dark, impenetrable woods beyond the confines of his rented yard. Nothing here truly belonged to him. The house had come completely furnished, even down to the bathroom towels and the dishes in the kitchen. The car he used was borrowed from the constabulary. He owned nothing but the clothes on his back. He'd failed to make friends at the station, through no fault of his own; he'd made overtures, but most of the other officers seemed to regard him as an exotic curiosity and avoided him. He was desperately lonely.

His phone was in his hand before he ever realised what he was doing, and he was dialling Danny's number. He held the instrument to his ear, hoping it went to voicemail so he could leave a nice, tidy message and have done with it.

"Deiniol Quirke." No such luck.

"It's Riley, sir. I've been looking over Tommy's case, and I have a theory."

"You do." Danny's voice was harsh and brittle. Maybe he'd had a hard day. Maybe he was pissed off that Riley was calling him after hours instead of waiting till they were both back at work.

"Sorry, sir." Riley swallowed hard, his chest and throat tight with tension. "I… shouldn't have bothered you. It can wait."

"No, Riley." A slow intake of breath on Danny's end of the phone. "Please. I'm interested to hear what you've got."

"Are you sure?"

"Absolutely."

"Right, then." He told Danny what he thought about Tommy's death, adding what he found in Tommy's medical records, that he'd been diagnosed with Alzheimer's disease. "Sir, don't you think he could have killed himself? If you look at the post-mortem photos, there's hesitation marks on his neck. You wouldn't get that if someone else had done it, would you? I mean, unless we've got some experienced serial killer running about. There's no defensive wounds on his hands either. It looks like suicide to me."

"But there was no note," Danny replied. He spoke slowly and quietly, as if he were considering Riley's words. "He'd have left a note, surely."

"For whom, sir? He'd no dependents, no one close to him. Kevin Carbage said Tommy had been a recluse these past few years. According to his medical file, he'd been informed about the Alzheimer's disease. So he must have known what was coming for him, and maybe he just decided to opt out."

"So what happened to the weapon?" Danny asked. "He used something to cut his throat. Where is it?" A long pause, then, "Are you at home?"

"Yes, sir."

"Feel up to hashing this out?"

Riley, surprised, blurted, "Now?"

"You have plans." Danny sounded disappointed, or maybe that was Riley's imagination.

"No, now is perfect. I'm just"—he glanced towards the kettle, now boiling merrily—"I'll put the kettle on, will I?"

"See you in a bit," Danny said, and the call disconnected.

Riley went upstairs, stripped off the rumpled sweats he was wearing, reapplied deodorant to his armpits, and put on a fresh shirt and a clean pair of jeans. He rubbed at the stubble on his cheeks and chin, briefly considered shaving, then dismissed the idea. No point in seeming too eager. He went into the bathroom, brushed his teeth and rinsed with mouthwash, ran a comb through his short, curly hair.

"You'll do nicely, lad," he said to his reflection in the mirror. He undid another shirt button and went back downstairs. Through the small glass window in the door he could see Danny on the doorstep, hand raised to knock. Riley opened the door. "Nice evening, sir." It was a stupid thing to say, considering the near-solid sheet of rain streaming off the eaves of the house. "Er... come in to the warm. I've just put the kettle on." He ushered Danny into the foyer and closed the door behind him. "I suppose we should have waited for a break in the weather."

"Sergeant, if you wait for a break in the weather around here, you'll never go anywhere," Danny replied, shrugging out of his waterproof and handing it to Riley. "Can you put that somewhere to dry?"

Riley hung it on a peg in the porch, next to one of the radiators. "Come through," he said. "Kitchen's the warmest spot in the place." He followed Danny in, pulled out a chair at the table for him. "Teabag good enough, or do you want a proper brew?"

Danny grinned. "I wouldn't say no to a good strong brew in the pot," he said. "I never take time for it anymore, and Tadhg's partial to coffee."

Salvo number one, Riley thought. Not five minutes in the door and Danny had to go and mention that wanker. Maybe it was preventative, to disabuse Riley of any notion this was a hook-up.

"Pot it is, then," Riley said with forced cheerfulness. He fetched it down from the cupboard and laid it on the counter, brought out the pound of Yorkshire Gold he'd found at the Dominion supermarket in Carbonear. When the kettle boiled again, he poured water into the pot and swished it around, dumped it into the sink. This allowed him to ignore Danny's presence at his kitchen table, to hopefully quell the flutter of nerves in his belly and the undeniable pull of desire he felt whenever Danny was around. He spooned loose tea leaves into the pot with hands that shook, doused them with boiling water.

"You've been busy," Danny said as Riley turned around. He'd taken off his heavy jumper to reveal a T-shirt in a deep teal colour that accentuated the blue of his eyes. It clung to his strong shoulders and his biceps in a way that was almost obscene.

"Yes, sir. I'd just about signed off on Tommy's case, but the marks on his neck... it wouldn't leave me alone." He moved to the table and reached into the file Danny was looking at, drew out the pertinent photographs. "You can see it really clearly in this picture." He laid the photo in front of Danny, indicated the close-up view of Tommy's neck with a fingertip. "He made a couple of attempts before he worked up the nerve."

"Hang on for a minute." Danny caught hold of Riley's hand and pulled it out of the way so he could take a closer look at the photo. "But couldn't those be scratches?" he asked, fingers still curled around Riley's wrist. "He might have come into contact with branches or tripped and fell. He was an old man."

"He was," Riley agreed. "But I'll bet he knew these woods better than anybody. Every dip in the trail, every exposed root—he knew where it was. A man like that, he knows his way around, knows right where he's putting his feet. If he was impaired in some way—drugs or drink, say—I could see it. But the autopsy found nothing out of the ordinary in his stomach, and the toxicology came back clean."

He pulled his hand out of Danny's grasp slowly and went to search for the strainer in the jumble of his kitchen drawers. The heat of Danny's fingers had burned itself into his skin like a brand. He was grateful for the small task of pouring tea, of getting the milk out of the fridge and the biscuit tin from atop it. He wanted nothing more than to pull Danny up out of his chair, push him back against the wall and kiss him over and over, until Danny understood that Tadhg fucking Heaney could never give him what Cillian Riley could. What would Danny do? Probably arrest him for assaulting a superior officer, Riley thought, suppressing a smile. Still, it might be worth doing, if only to see Danny that way, all kiss-swollen lips and rumpled hair.

"Here you are, sir." He poured the tea carefully through the strainer and laid a cup down in front of Danny, along with the milk jug. "No sugar, if I remember correctly?"

"You do indeed," Danny replied, smiling. He splashed some milk into the cup, declined Riley's offer of a biscuit. "So you don't think Tommy Power was murdered."

"No, sir, I don't." Riley helped himself to a chocolate-covered digestive from the tin, the heat of his hand making the chocolate melt over his index and middle fingers. He stuck them in his mouth to suck them clean, watched as the pupils of Danny's eyes blew wide open. *Like that, do you?* "I firmly believe those are hesitation marks on his throat. What happened to the weapon afterwards, I don't know. My guess is someone found it and took it away. Maybe he had time to fling it from him before blood loss caused him to pass out." Riley picked up his tea and sipped it, gazing at Danny over the rim of the cup. "Thirty seconds to a minute until unconsciousness, so he could have flung the knife or whatever it was into the woods, if he'd the presence of mind to do so." He picked the rest of the photographs out of the file folder and fanned them on the table so both he and Danny could see them. "There's nothing to suggest any other person was present when he died. No other footprints were found at the site."

"They could have been obscured by the falling snow," Danny interjected.

"True," Riley agreed, "but Tommy's own footprints were still visible under the initial layer of snowfall. So it wasn't snowing when he sat down under that tree. We picked up several clear boot prints from the ground. Spruce and fir needles aren't an ideal surface to get prints off of, but Bobbi and her team managed it."

"She's very good at what she does," Danny commented. He turned his gaze on Riley. "You are too."

"Thank you, sir." *You know what else I'm good at, don't you?* Maybe Danny had forgotten their one-time tryst in a St. John's hotel, but Riley would never forget it.

"Tommy was a recluse," Danny said, "and used to looking after himself. He wouldn't have wanted to be a burden on anybody. I found a bottle of Aricept in his house. It's prescribed for Alzheimer's disease. He may well have committed suicide rather than allow dementia to take him down." He nodded. "I suppose we should be grateful he wasn't being treated by Dr. Fahey. Did you read Deborah Harris's post-mortem report?"

Riley had. "*Amanita muscaria*? Ayahuasca? What in the hell did he think he was doing?" He shook his head. "He was using them as guinea pigs is my guess. The *Amanita*'s bad enough, but ayahuasca can be deadly if you mix it with alcohol. No wonder he ended up carved like a Sunday roast."

"You've done your research." Danny grinned. "So let's say Tommy Power did kill himself. Where does that leave us?"

"Death by suicide," Riley said. "Or death by misadventure… death by bad luck?"

"Not having a weapon still bothers me," Danny said. "There's got to be a weapon. His throat didn't cut itself." He pulled the photographs towards him, stacked them and shuffled them like cards. "It doesn't sit well with me, the idea that it's just a suicide. It feels like there should be more to it. Maybe he did kill himself, but I still feel like he had help."

"You mean encouragement?"

"Exactly. Tommy often went into the woods to get water from the spring. Nobody found his water bucket," Danny said, "so maybe this wasn't a trip to get water."

"Or maybe he lost the bucket somewhere on the way," Riley said, his mind running over the presumed details of Tommy's last walk in the woods. No water bucket, but no weapon either. "Sir, do you think someone gave him the weapon?"

"And he used it to kill himself?" Danny considered this for a moment, then shook his head. "It's too far-fetched. I don't see it."

"It's almost as odd as Deborah Harris." Riley got up to retrieve the teapot and the strainer. "She'd a row with her husband and left. Next thing she ends up dead in a bog. What happened in between?"

"Azariah Harris claims he paid some of the Harvesters to drive the demons out of her." Danny's mouth twisted. "What a load of superstitious rubbish that is. God only knows what the Harrises put her through." He got up from the table and handed his cup to Riley. "Thanks for the tea, Sergeant."

"You're not going already?" Too late he realised the panic evident in his voice as he gestured stupidly at the teapot. "There's still half a pot left. Did you have supper? I could make us something."

"I've eaten," Danny said gently, "but thank you." He started towards the front porch, reaching to retrieve his raincoat from the peg. "Can you put your thoughts about Tommy in a report for me? I'd like to have something for the file before I close the case." He reached for the latch, but Riley positioned himself between Danny and the door.

"You never gave us a chance," he blurted. He was standing close enough to see the fine needles of silver stubble on Danny's jaw, the subtle quiver of his throat as he swallowed. "I could be good for you. You don't know me. You've never—"

"Cillian." Danny laid his palm against Riley's cheek. "You are an incredible man. You deserve someone who's available to you, and that's not me."

Riley closed his eyes so he wouldn't have to see the overwhelming compassion—no, pity—in Danny's gaze. Danny's other hand joined the first, both palms cupping Riley's face between them, and then Danny was kissing him, and Riley gave himself to the kiss, opened his mouth to the press of Danny's tongue between his parted lips. He held Danny back against the still-closed door, and they went on kissing, the space between their bodies shrinking until they were clasped together, belly touching belly, chest touching chest.

He opened his eyes then, blinked himself into the reality that Danny had left immediately after his last utterance and Riley was entirely alone, with the cold rain blowing in through the open door while he stared dumbly, devastated, at the empty driveway.

THE SPRING winds had been battering the island of Eigus nonstop for some hours when Tadhg let himself into his house and shut the door behind him. He'd spent the entire day supervising the digging for the foundations of the new holiday cottages at Danny's grandfather's old homestead in Kildevil Cove in the driving rain, and he was cold, hungry, bad-tempered, and soaked to the skin. The argument with Danny hadn't helped matters, he thought sourly. He intended to sink into a hot bath with a glass of Glenfiddich and forget everything for an hour or so. It was a school day, so Lily was in St. John's and wouldn't be home until the weekend. He toed off his shoes and left his wet coat in a heap in the front porch, not caring where it landed. The coat was lamb leather, bought on impulse one weekend in Montreal and hardly suitable for a construction site, but he wanted to keep up appearances, dress like the boss once in a while.

As he mounted the stairs, the faint strains of technopop reached his ears. He tapped on the door of Lily's room and looked in.

"Hi, Dad." She was sitting in her pyjamas, propped up on a mound of pillows, a box of tissues at her side. She appeared to be doing some homework on her laptop—at least Tadhg hoped it was homework.

"Thought you were away at school," he remarked. He wasn't that surprised to see her. Yesterday she'd phoned from her dorm to say she felt a bit feverish, and if it developed into anything, she'd come home. Her neuroblastoma had gone into remission, but Tadhg knew cancer liked to come back, so he tended to overreact to even the slightest sniffle. Her recent episode of self-injury had alarmed and disturbed him, and he often wondered if she was truly all right. What went on in her head? What sorts of things did she think about, talk about with her friends, that she didn't tell him?

"My nose turned into a snot factory, so Mrs. Walsh said I'd better go home." Mrs. Walsh was the school nurse. "I'm going to skype the rest of my classes."

"Oh, the wonders of the twenty-first century," Tadhg said. "Make sure it's schoolwork you're doing on that thing."

"I will. By the way, you look like shite," she observed.

"Thank you," he said dryly. "I'm going to sit in the bath for a bit. You okay on your own?"

"I'm not a baby."

He went closer and kissed the top of her head. "Ye're always my baby, and don't forget it."

He went and started the bath running in the big tub, threw in a couple handfuls of Epsom salts, and laid out a clean pair of flannel lounging pants and a T-shirt, along with a fluffy towel of fine cotton, one of a set he'd found in an Istanbul souk during a business trip. He fetched a bottle of Glenfiddich and a heavy-bottomed tumbler of Waterford crystal out of the liquor cabinet in his bedroom and carried these into the bathroom. He stripped and sank into the water with an audible groan. It had been a shit day, and he was glad to be shot of it. A drink and a long soak would do him good. He was hungry, but that could wait, and maybe he'd make something for himself and Lily later. He ran through a mental list of the pantry's contents, putting together a tentative menu. Too bad Danny's workload didn't allow for an unscheduled night on Eigus. Tadhg could have used the company—and the comfort.

True, they'd had a pretty nasty quarrel about the harm Dr. Fahey had done Lily, and for a while Tadhg had been furious with Danny. Problem was, when he'd cooled down enough to think it through, he had to admit to himself that Danny was right. Not about everything, of course. Tadhg was a good father. But he was impulsive at times and quick to think that the more money he spent, the best answer he was bound to get to any problem.

He and Danny'd had some ugly fights before, and they likely would again. Couple of stubborn men, both set in their ways. But there was enough love between them to make up for it. Tadhg needed Danny in his life, and he believed Danny needed him as well. So they'd fight and they'd love and it would all come right in the end.

He soaked for an hour, sipping his Scotch and enjoying the Miles Davis playlist on Spotify. When his fingers and toes were sufficiently prune-like, he dragged himself out and towelled off vigorously, dressed in his clean clothes, and put the bottle of Glenfiddich back in his liquor cabinet. He passed by Lily's door on his way downstairs and looked in on her, but all he could see was a heap of duvet decorated with used Kleenex tissues. He went into the kitchen, intending to put his empty glass in the sink for handwashing later. Even he knew you didn't put Waterford crystal in the dishwasher.

Tadhg was reaching across the worktop when a slight noise caught his ear, and he turned to see a small girl, perhaps eight or nine years old, standing near the fridge. She was dressed all in yellow—an old-fashioned yellow party dress, with yellow ribbons tied around her sopping pigtails and water streaming from her clothes. At first glance she looked innocent, a child entirely, except for the mature knowing in her eyes, a wisdom beyond her years that said she was anything but.

"He thinks you're safe," she said.

"What?" Tadhg blinked at her. "Who are you? He who?"

"Your policeman pal." Her face twisted into a grotesque parody of a smile. "Your *lover*…. Your sodomite."

"How'd you get in here?" Tadhg asked. Her words and attitude were beginning to alarm him, for all she looked like a child. He glanced behind him. His phone was on the countertop, just out of reach.

"Don't touch that," the girl said. Again, the hideous twisting of her lips, a smile like a ruined skull.

"I asked how you got in here," Tadhg repeated, inching towards the worktop. There was a panic button mounted near the cutlery drawer. He'd had it installed, along with the alarm system, when the house was built, for Lily's safety when she was home alone. Initially, it triggered the alarm inside the house and alerted members of Tadhg's staff via their smartphones. If it wasn't deactivated within thirty seconds by punching in a code, it then rang through to the main constabulary station in St. John's. "This is an island," Tadhg added, playing for time. She'd have had to have arrived there by boat.

"That moronic Mexican who brought your girl over didn't notice I'd stowed away. I've been attending the same school as Lily. Did she tell you? An exchange student from Romania."

"You're-you're that girl." He'd seen her image on TV and on the internet, a missing foster child whom the police were very eager to locate. "What do you want here? Do you want money? I'll give you some. My wallet is in the other room. Just let me go get it."

"No." She laughed scornfully. "I don't want your money."

"Then what do you want?"

"To teach your Inspector Quirke a lesson," she said.

"Then you should probably take that up with him." He was moving closer to the panic button. It was within reach now. If he could distract her long enough to slip in behind the counter, he would set it off.

"He's a lot harder to get through to than you might imagine," she replied. "And not inclined to listen. I've sent him several messages, but he keeps ignoring me." She stamped her feet on the floor so hard the dishes in the cupboards rattled. "He keeps ignoring me. And I won't have it!" She smiled sadly. "So you see my dilemma."

Tadhg was repulsed by her, by the adult sentiments coming from her childish mouth. She was dressed as a child, but her speech and diction, the way she moved, all were most definitely adult.

"I think you had better leave," he said, "or I'll call the police and have you arrested for trespassing."

"Trespassing?" A brittle grunt of laughter, and that dreadful gurning of her facial muscles. "That's hardly a criminal offence at all." Her hand dipped into the pocket of her dress and came out holding a small paring knife with a yellow handle. Tadhg's mother had had one just like it, a postwar relic dating back to at least the early 1950s. "Might as well make it a really good one."

And she was on him, so fast Tadhg hardly saw her move. She leapt for his head, knocking him to the floor, slashing at him with the tiny blade, inflicting deep cuts that burned like fire.

"You should have told him to stay away!" she screamed. "To mind his business and not interfere. But oh no, he had to keep on picking at it and picking at it."

Tadhg tried to roll away, to shake her off, but she clung to him like a monkey, stabbing and slashing wherever she could reach until the floor beneath him was wet with his blood.

"Dad?"

He turned to see his daughter—oh God, *Lily*—standing by the worktop. She'd obviously heard the commotion and come downstairs.

"Lily, no!" He struggled to sit up, to throw off the tiny demon straddling his chest, and succeeded for the fraction of a second necessary. "Go to your room," he gasped, "lock the door. Call Danny. Tell him—"

The girl's blade sliced deep into his upper arm, and blood sprayed up like a fountain, pumping hard with every beat of his heart. This was bad. The thought was so ridiculous that he laughed out loud. He was bleeding to death on his kitchen floor. Oh, this was one for the books. There was a pause, and he heard a shriek. Then something heavy hit the kitchen floor and rolled under the table. He saw a soapstone Inuit sculpture of a polar bear caught in midstride. The girl was gone now, and Lily was in her place. She tore a dish towel off the rack and ripped it into strips, knotted a tourniquet around his arm, torqueing it tight with a wooden spoon from the cutlery drawer.

"Where is she?" he asked. He'd lost a lot of blood already, knew it because he was seeing spots in front of his eyes.

"Dad, stay with me." Lily crouched in front of him, holding his face between her palms. "Don't pass out. I've already called Danny. The air ambulance is on its way. Dad, please…. Dad?"

The world faded to black, and he was gone.

CHAPTER ELEVEN

THE WAITING room was crowded, even at this hour of the night, and smelled unpleasantly of antiseptic. Danny had spent far too much time in hospitals over the course of his career, and although he recognised them as necessary, he didn't care for them. He glanced at Lily sitting next to him, dressed in what looked like a pair of footie pyjamas fashioned to look like a unicorn.

"What's going to happen to her?" she asked him. "That little girl?"

Danny drew a slow breath, wondering how much of the story he should reveal. "The doctor said her injuries are minor, probably a slight concussion. Good move, knocking her out with that Inuit sculpture."

"I just wanted to get her away from Dad." Lily grimaced. "She was cutting him to bits, Danny. There was so much blood. It was horrible."

"Your dad is going to be fine," Danny said. "The Inuit sculpture, I'm not so sure about." He glanced up as a hawk-faced young man in green scrubs appeared in the doorway, then stood to greet him. "Doctor."

A cold light flickered in the doctor's dark blue eyes as he extended a hand for Danny to shake. When he spoke, his voice was gruff, rather brusque, as if he were impatient to be about his business. "The stab wound severed his brachial artery, but we were able to repair it. Keep him away from sharp objects." Then he was gone.

"Short and sweet," Lily remarked, "but he *is* a total snack."

"He's a what?" Danny asked.

"A snack." She gazed at him as if he'd just landed from another planet. "He's good-looking."

"And much too old for you."

"Oh my *God*." She rolled her eyes. "You sound like Dad."

Danny was about to reply when his mobile phone rang. He took it out of his pocket and looked at it but didn't recognise the number. This again. "Deiniol Quirke."

"It is you. Thank God," a woman's voice said. "We've been trying to reach you. We only just got back in the country."

"I'm sorry, who is this?" Danny glanced at Lily, who raised an inquisitive eyebrow.

"I'm Bridget Coyle," the woman explained, "Deborah Coyle's mother."

Danny stood up and walked away from Lily, wanting a measure of privacy for this. "Mrs. Coyle, I am so sorry for your loss."

"Thank you. My husband and I have been in Australia. He's been working as a lecturer at the University of Melbourne for the past eight months. We've had no news from home, and we assumed Deborah...." Her voice broke. The sound of her weeping sliced into Danny like a blade. "We assumed she was happy in her married life."

"You have my deepest sympathies." Danny had to stop talking as tears began to prick at the backs of his eyes. He took several deep breaths to compose himself.

"Where is my daughter? I would like to take her home and... bury her. She deserves that much."

"She... she is in care of a local physician," he told her. He couldn't bring himself to say "in the morgue at Carbonear hospital." "I'll see to it that her body is released to you as soon as possible."

"She had a baby, didn't she? A little boy. That is... we heard she'd had a boy."

Danny wondered how out of touch someone could be to not realise their own daughter had given birth, but maybe it wasn't for him to judge. His own family was far from perfect. "Yes, a boy. He is safe in the care of social services."

"Inspector Quirke, have you found the person who killed her?"

It was the question he'd been dreading. "The case is still open, and we are currently working on several promising leads. I'm afraid I can't tell you more than that at present." He looked up to see Lily beckoning him. The angry-looking young doctor had returned. "Mrs. Coyle, I'm afraid I have to cut this short, but I will be in touch. You have my word on that." He listened as she thanked him, then disconnected the call.

"You can see him if you want to," the doctor said, his gaze darting from Danny to Lily and back again. "Five minutes. He's only just coming out of the anaesthetic, so he might not make much sense."

Danny and Lily filed into the curtained-off portion of the hospital's surgical recovery room where Tadhg lay, eyes closed and one arm encased in a long white dressing. Danny's stomach clenched at the sight of him, so pale and still.

"Ye've got to stop doing this," Danny said affably, to avoid dissolving into tears. "It's getting so I spend more time in hospitals than I do anywhere else."

"Dad… I'm glad you're okay," Lily said, rushing to his side. She embraced him gently, mindful of his injury. "I love you."

"I love you too," he replied, kissing her hair. A gentle squeeze and he released her. "Listen now, my love," he said. "Can I have a word alone with Danny?" He waited until she left, then said, "You remember that day in your grandfather's old stable? When we had the fight?"

Danny remembered it all too well. "Tadhg, you don't need to talk about that now—"

"Shut yer gob." He nodded in the direction of the small bedside table, where his clothes sat bundled into a plastic bag. "In the pocket of my pants. I've been carrying the damned thing ever since."

Danny winced at the sight of the bloody clothes. He probably shouldn't disturb the evidence, but it wasn't like they didn't have Tadhg's attacker dead to rights. He reached carefully into one pocket of Tadhg's lounging pants, found nothing, and then moved to the other. He came up with a small green box. "Should I open it, or is something inside going to bite me?"

"I'm going to bite you," Tadhg said sleepily, "if you don't bring it here. For Christ's sake, Danny, before these damned drugs pull me under again."

Danny did as he was told.

"Now open it," Tadhg instructed. Inside, lying on a bed of deep emerald velvet, were two Claddagh rings. "You should marry me." Tadhg looked from the rings to Danny. "I think we've waited long enough." He smiled. "What d'you think about eloping? Maybe go to Scotland…." He trailed off, appearing to doze for a second, then woke again abruptly. "Say yes, will ye? For fuck's sake, I'll be asleep in a minute."

Danny leaned over and kissed him gently, mindful of his arm. "Yes," he murmured.

A shadow fell over them from the doorway. The cranky doctor was back. "I said five minutes, goddammit." He came to where they were, his gaze fell on the rings, and he smiled. It was a brief flicker of emotion on an otherwise impassive face, and it transformed his features. Lily was right, Danny thought. He was indeed a "snack." "Congratulations," he said with something approaching warmth, then, "now get the hell out of here before I throw you out myself."

"Go home," Tadhg said, "and I'll meet you there in a day or two, all right?"

"You're kicking me out as well?"

"Go back to Kildevil Cove." Tadhg smiled faintly, half-asleep. "You're needed."

DANNY HAD thrown himself into work as soon as he'd left Tadhg's hospital room. It was now Thursday, the middle of the week, and he'd set himself the task of reviewing the files for all the recent cases, just in case he or some other member of the team had overlooked anything. He was satisfied that Tommy Power had killed himself, albeit there was no weapon found at the scene. Dr. Fahey's murder was still unsolved, but it was looking more and more like Ford Maddox might be responsible.

He'd read through Regan Lampe's autopsy report once already, but he went through it again, alert for inconsistencies or things he hadn't noticed on the previous read. Lampe had included a number of photographs, and Danny examined these carefully, making copious notes of anything that attracted his attention. Whoever had killed and then dismembered Fahey had done so in a chillingly expert fashion, taking the body apart at the joints by severing the ligaments. The smaller joints had been cut using a very sharp knife, while the larger joints—the hips and shoulders, the head—had been done with a chainsaw.

Lampe had noted the knife was probably a hunting knife, in which case the number of suspects equalled the entire male population of Kildevil Cove and surrounding areas. Danny allowed himself a few choice swear words at this. Every able-bodied man with a moose or caribou licence owned a similar knife and carried it on his person. Even the local fishermen kept filleting knives sharp enough to slice through skin and muscle easily. Good fucking luck tracking down the killer on that piece of evidence.

He paged through the rest of the photos, stopped at a picture of Fahey's skull. Regan Lampe had shaved it, looking for any head wounds that might have proven fatal. At the very back of Fahey's head, where his skull met his neck, was a vivid puncture wound about five centimetres wide. The edges were sharply defined, with purple-shading-to-black bruising. In the margin of the photo, Lampe had noted *perimortem stab wound to C1 vertebra cause of death.*

Dead bodies didn't bruise or bleed. Whoever had killed Fahey had knifed him in the back of the skull. It would have been nearly instant, and something close to silent, with very little blood—a precise killing. A military-style execution.

"I did not chop him up, with a chainsaw or whatever it was." Ford had said that to Danny on the phone. He knew Fahey had been cut up with a chainsaw, and Danny had missed it. He'd missed it. Maybe that's why Ford had given him the hallucinogenic tea, to distract him and stop him from prying further into his affairs.

His phone chimed with an incoming text message. He tapped through to the appropriate app and read it. It was from Bobbi Lambert.

Blood and DNA on rag found at Maddox property belongs to Dr. Fahey. Smaller amount present belongs to Maddox.

Danny clicked out of the messaging app and dialled Moira's mobile. She picked up after a single ring, listening in silence as Danny told her what he suspected.

"Are you sure?" she asked.

"Almost. It makes about as much sense as anything I've so far considered. We haven't pinned down the motive yet, though I have my suspicions. But we have enough forensic evidence to build a solid case." Moira was silent, so Danny asked "Do you want me to arrest him now?"

"Danny, he's your friend," she said. "I don't know—"

Danny interrupted her. "He is my friend. All the more reason I should do it."

DANNY DREW level with the white rail fence in front of Ford's rented house and shut off his car. He sat for a while, staring at his hands on the steering wheel, listening to the ticking of the radiator as it cooled. It had been raining earlier, but now the sun had come out, and the air was full of the smell of warm earth. Maybe they'd have a real spring this year. Stranger things had happened.

He took the keys from the ignition and got out of the car. He didn't want to go into the house, do what he must, say the things he had to say. Yet it wasn't the first time he'd had to arrest someone he knew and liked, someone he'd once cared about a good deal.

Ford's pickup truck was in the driveway, which meant he had to be about the premises somewhere. It was odd for him not to be at the construction site in the middle of the day, but there could be any number of reasons why he'd returned home. Best to check it out.

Danny went up the seashell-covered walkway to the neat front door, which was painted light turquoise, and knocked. There was very little wind, and he could hear the rustling of a small animal in one of the nearby trees—a bird or a squirrel, perhaps. He waited, listening intently, then knocked again.

"Ford, it's Danny. Can you open the door? We need to talk." He leaned against the front porch railing and felt the press of his handcuffs in the pouch at his side. He hoped he wouldn't have to use them, trusting that Ford would come along quietly, let Danny do what he needed to do with a minimum of fuss. How would he even begin to phrase such a request? "I have reason to believe you killed Dr. Fahey, and I need you to come with me to the station." Would Ford resist, still insisting he was innocent like he'd done that day in the interview room?

"You think I killed somebody and chopped them up?" he'd said. "Jesus, you really don't know me at all."

But there was no answer to Danny's hail, so he fished out his mobile phone and dialled Ford's number. A recorded message advised him that the number was no longer in service.

"Ford?" Danny hammered on the door. "Can you come out?"

A small black-and-white junco hopped down onto the railing next to his hand and regarded him with one shiny black eye. "Do you know if he's in there?" Danny asked. The bird twittered at him before disappearing into the air, gone in the blink of an eye.

Danny reached for the door handle and pushed. It gave easily, creaking open with a homey chuckling sound. He stepped into the front hall cautiously, called out for Ford again, but there was no answer. The front hall was perhaps a five-foot-square space with an empty boot tray resting against the wall under an electric heater and a closet rail that held nothing besides a row of unused wire hangers. The hall opened onto a set of wooden stairs on the right, going up to the second floor, and a small sitting room at the left. He moved into the sitting room and looked around. A pair of brown leather sofas faced each other across a low coffee table made of glass and reclaimed driftwood. There was no sign that anyone had been there recently, given the coating of dust on the coffee table's glass top—or maybe Ford just wasn't big on housekeeping.

Danny left the sitting room and followed a short hallway into the kitchen at the back of the house. It was furnished with a vintage chrome set, the tabletop and chairs the same turquoise hue as the front door. An old-fashioned Enterprise wood-and-oil stove had been refurbished with top-of-the-line gas burners, and a shiny stainless-steel fridge stood next to the back door. Danny couldn't say for certain what Ford was paying in rent, but it had to be a lot. This place was fitted out like a five-star hotel.

He left the kitchen and went upstairs, treading slowly, not wanting to startle Ford if he was somewhere in the house. "Ford?" He mounted the top landing and looked around, feeling like a cop in an American TV drama, wondering if he should have a gun shoved down the back of his trousers.

There was no sound, but Danny checked the rooms anyway. The master bedroom was empty, the duvet thrown back, the pillows tossed about the way they would have been if someone had slept there the night before, but the room was otherwise undisturbed. He went along the hallway and peered into the bathroom, a spare bedroom, and a third, smaller room apparently used for storage, but Ford was nowhere to be seen.

Danny began to get an uneasy feeling, the same kind of feeling he'd had on the Clontarf sea wall in Dublin the year before. He went downstairs quickly, wanting to be out of the house that felt somehow haunted to him, leaving by the back door. Directly across the lawn was a large outbuilding, the sort of thing that doubled as a storage shed and a garage, with double doors opening onto the south-facing portion of the property. The doors were open now.

He had taken no more than three steps inside before he saw Ford—hanging from a beam in the centre of the room.

"Fuck." Danny went to him and clasped him around the knees, forcing slack into the rope, but it was no use. Ford Maddox had been dead a long time. "Jesus, Ford. Why?" He stumbled backwards, desperate for light and air, found the doorway and went through it. "Fuck," he said again, his voice cracking as sorrow tightened into a fist around his throat. "Fuck, fuck, fuck." He fumbled for his mobile phone and dialled the station. June Carbage answered. "Get Old Perlican hospital to send an ambulance," he told her. "Ford Maddox hung himself."

"God love him," she said, "the poor soul. I'll get right on it, sir."

"I'm at his house," Danny said. "I'll want the forensics team here. And whatever you do, keep Kevin away. I don't want him finding out by accident. I'll... tell him myself."

He waited for them by the front gate. The ambulance arrived first, followed by Cillian Riley in a patrol car. He got out and came to where Danny was.

"Forensics are on their way, sir. Where...?"

Danny nodded towards the garage. "In there."

Riley went inside, followed by Bobbi Lambert and a second forensics tech, both dressed in white Tyvek suits and face masks. They paused in the doorway to slip protective covers over their shoes. They were professionals, people who had presided over many tragic scenes and who were proficient at controlling their emotions, so seeing Ford Maddox hanging from a ceiling beam wouldn't affect them very much. They didn't know him the way Danny did, had no history with the man. He was never a friend to them the way he had been to Danny and also to Tadhg.

Tadhg. Danny would have to tell him. But the worst would be telling Kevin Carbage. If Kevin and Ford were romantically involved, as Danny suspected, this would be one hell of a blow. He'd have to keep Kevin away from the scene until he could find a quiet place and time to speak to him. The last thing he wanted was Kevin here while forensics worked the scene, gathering their evidence—although it seemed pretty clear that Ford's death was indeed a suicide.

Ford had been a troubled man. His war experiences had doubtless damaged him in ways that weren't readily apparent, and there was what Ford had told Danny about his abuse at the hands of his stepfather. But taking his own life now? From everything that Danny could see, Ford was doing well enough. He owned a business, was trying to reconnect with his estranged son. Nor did Ford seem like the kind of man who would be afraid of a prison term. Of course when he sought help for his problems, he'd ended up with Dr. Fahey, and God only knew what sorts of poison he'd been pumping into Ford's body and his mind. Had Fahey's prescription driven Ford to this? Or were there other things going on that Danny didn't know about? Maybe Ford's demons had finally proven too much to overcome.

"Sir." Riley appeared at Danny's elbow, holding a photograph. "Forensics found this near the b—near Mr. Maddox. They've already lifted fingerprints." He held it out. "I think it's… him and his son."

His chest was collapsing; in a minute Danny would cry. He took the photograph and nodded his thanks at Riley, not trusting himself to speak. He would look at it later.

"Oh fuck," Riley said. "Christ, no." He was looking at something behind Danny, and it obviously bothered him. He bolted forward, arms waving. "Get him out of here!"

Danny turned as a second patrol car pulled up. "This place is getting crowded," he murmured to no one in particular. What was Riley shouting about?

"Get him out of here," Riley said again, as the driver's side door of the car opened and a man got out. "Constable, you cannot be here. That's an order. Get back in the car and leave immediately."

Kevin Carbage…. Riley was shouting at Kevin Carbage, who came running up to Danny, face flushed and wet, his mouth open in a silent howl of anguish.

"Is he in there?" he demanded. He tried to move past Danny, who caught and held him. "If he's in there, I wants to see him."

"You don't need to go in there," Danny said. "He's not in the house, Kevin." He tightened his grip on the younger man's upper arms. "Do you hear me? He is not in the house."

"It came over the radio," Kevin said. He wasn't looking at Danny, but beyond him, past his shoulder to where he knew his lover was. "Suicide, male, fifty years old. I knew who it was. I knew it was him, I did." He struggled against Danny's grip. "For God's sake, I want to see him. You have to let me see him!"

"Kevin, he's gone," Danny said quietly, and then he did cry.

HE KNEW she was coming, so June didn't bother knocking more than once. Her brother had left the door open for her. She stepped inside the porch and slipped off her shoes, hung her rain jacket on a peg to dry. It was a lovely evening if you liked this sort of weather: warm, drizzly, no wind. Her mother had always called it "soft" weather, and it was typical for May, which rarely tended towards extremes. Sometimes it even snowed in May, but it was always a gentle snow that fell in silence onto soft ground. It was a good evening to do this sort of thing.

"Kevin?" June went into the kitchen and laid down the bottle of whiskey she'd brought with her. They needed something strong for this, and tea just wasn't going to do it. "Are you here?" She glanced up as the stairs creaked and saw him descending, his face drawn and pale, eyes shadowed underneath with grief that sat on him like a cloak of steel. She went to him and hugged him tight, like she used to do when they were young and he'd awakened from a nightmare. "My poor darling," she murmured. "Ye've been through the mill, haven't ye?"

"What time is it?" he asked. "I was asleep. Didn't even hear ye come in."

"Just after nine," June told him, "like we agreed." She stepped back, releasing him. "You know, there'll be a funeral. If you want, we could—"

"I'm not going." He pushed past her and went into the kitchen, opened the cupboard door to take down two drinking glasses. "There's no point."

"Why?" She moved to sit at the table and cracked the seal on the bottle of Jameson's. "You loved him. I know you did, Kevin." She took the glasses from him and poured in a hefty four fingers each. "I saw the two of you together. I saw the way you looked at him."

He drained the drink in one go, held the glass out for another. "Doesn't matter now, does it?" His features were twisted with a pain he stubbornly refused to relinquish, even to her. "I don't want to talk about him."

June sighed. "Fine. Have it your own way. Then how about we talk about her?" She got up from the table and went to fetch her purse from the porch. "Danny had me looking back through the records for Tommy Power's family, so I decided to do a little digging on my own." She pulled out a large brown envelope and laid it down in front of him. "Went back to Mam and Dad's old place. She had a bunch of pictures kept in the upstairs bedroom. I figured you might want to see."

In truth there wasn't much left; their father had destroyed whatever photographic evidence he'd been able to get his hands on. The handful of pictures June had found were the scant remains that had escaped his notice, precious mementos their mother had hidden from him. She took them out of the envelope and fanned them out on the table.

"See?" she told Kevin. "That's me and you and Mam at New Melbourne Beach. That was a good day. She was happy that day."

Their mother sat with her back to the camera, wearing a dark bathing suit, her long hair loose around her shoulders. Kevin, twelve years old, was to the right of her, perched atop an outcropping of rock, arms hugging his knees, eyes squinted shut against the brightness. June was turned towards the camera, gesturing with her arms spread wide.

"And there's Sherry. Mam put her right down by the water. She loved the feel of it."

A chubby little girl about six or seven years old sat with her feet in the water. Her face was turned towards the camera, mouth open and smiling, eyes crinkling with mirth.

"She was an old soul," Kevin said. He reached to touch the photo with one finger, a fleeting gesture like a caress. "It wasn't right, what Dad did."

"He's still alive out there somewhere." June reached for another of the photos, pushed it towards him. This one showed a middle-aged man in a striped bathrobe, holding a baby in the crook of his arm and staring into the camera with an attitude of resentment. "He did that to her, and then he left. Do you remember?"

Kevin squeezed his eyes shut and shook his head. "I try not to."

"You still have the nightmares, though." She reached across and laid her hand on top of his. "I know you must, because I do too."

Their sister, Sherry, had been what their mother called a change-of-life surprise, conceived when she supposedly was no longer able to bear children.

"He never wanted her," Kevin said. "Said it was all Mam's fault, that she did it on purpose." When Sherry was born with a catastrophic brain injury, he'd blamed their mother. "Like he had nothing to do with it. Fucking bastard. And she in pain all the time."

"He got angry," June said. The room was very quiet, the sound of the kitchen clock suddenly as loud as hammer blows. "Mam couldn't get her to stop crying."

Kevin got up from the table and went to the sink. He stood there in silence, arms hanging loosely at his sides. *He's lost a lot of weight*, June thought, looking at him. His clothes hung on him like rags. She knew Kevin, knew that he wouldn't have been taking proper care of himself, was likely not eating and probably hadn't slept well in a while. He'd had enough on his mind before, and now, with Ford's death, he would likely get even worse.

"I went and talked to Mam the other day," he said, his voice shaking. "Brought up a few flowers and laid on her grave. It's real nice where she's to, up there in the corner, next to Nan and Pop."

June went to him and wrapped her arms around him from behind, laying her cheek against his back. His body shuddered with the force of the emotion he was trying to suppress, and she wished for once her brother would just give in to his feelings. "Oh, Kev."

They would both remember that night for the rest of their lives. Images of their father's brutality, of Sherry's broken body, would inform their nightmares as well as their waking hours. Maybe, June reflected, it was why they'd both become police officers. She could see them as young teenagers: Kevin barely awake and standing in the upstairs hallway in his rumpled pyjamas and herself in a cotton nightgown, rubbing sleep out of her eyes. She'd awakened because someone was screaming, crying, begging with the only voice she had....

"WHAT IN the name of Jesus is she trying to say? Can't you even talk? What? What are ye saying?" Their father, mocking Sherry, and her mother pleading for him to stop. "Please, Harve, don't be at that now." Him roaring with rage then, and the sound of his enormous fists hitting something soft and yielding until all cries fled into a final silence.

"She's not crying anymore," Kevin said. "D'ye think she's after going to sleep?"

Yes, of course that was it. Their sister was sleeping. Easier to imagine it that way. Sherry had cried herself to sleep, and maybe now her pain would ease and they could all rest. But June couldn't make herself go back to bed, knew she would not be able to sleep. Something was very wrong. Sherry's cries had stopped too suddenly, cut off in the middle of a pained exhalation that sounded for all the world like the death throes of a dying animal.

"I don't think she's gone to sleep, Kevin. I think there's something wrong with her."

That night seemed to stretch into infinity, the long predawn hours endless while she and Kevin waited, huddled together at the top of the stairs.

"Someone should call an ambulance," Kevin whispered. "Someone needs to call an ambulance."

But neither June nor her brother could move. Their father was down there in the kitchen, raging and breaking things, their mother nowhere to be seen, and what had he done with Sherry? After a while their father came out of the smallest bedroom, pushing past them and down the stairs, carrying a shrouded bundle.

"Where are ye going?" Their mother, hysterical with grief, threw herself at him and grappled with the pile of blankets in his arms. "Ye can't just…. She's got to have a proper burial! For the love of God."

No God, no love or otherwise. He'd gone out into the night with their sister in his arms and they both knew then what their father, in his rage, had done.

"I WISH we knew where she was buried," Kevin said. He pulled away and went to sit at the table. "Do ye think we could find her if we looked, the two of us? There's got to be some way to find out. She has to be somewhere here in Kildevil Cove, or nearby. He couldn't have just… dumped her off somewhere like garbage."

"I don't know, Kevin." June reached for the Jameson's and refilled both their glasses. "In a perfect world, we'd find her body and bring her home for a proper burial but…." She shrugged. "The only person who knows what really happened is Dad, and God knows where he's to."

"I bet I could find him," Kevin said. He turned the heavy glass tumbler in both hands, gazing down into the amber liquid. "Maybe I'll go looking for him. Find out where he's to, the fucker, and bring him back." He sipped the whiskey, brooding.

Outside, the soft May drizzle thickened to rain that slapped against the windows, beating an agitated tattoo. June should try to talk him out of it, tell him it was a bad idea, that there was no point in chasing down old ghosts. But part of her wanted to know. Their father knew where Sherry's body was. He was guilty of her murder and should be made to pay.

"D'ye think that's possible?" she asked. "Where would you even start to look for him? Lord God, Kevin, he could be anywhere."

"There's nothing here for me." He raised anguished eyes to her. "I got to do something. Ford's gone and left me, and there's not a fucking thing I can do about it."

June nodded. She reached out and shuffled the pile of photos together like playing cards. "Do you want to keep these?"

"You hang on to them until I gets back," he said.

"What are ye going to tell Danny?"

"I'll take a leave of absence. I got a lot of holidays built up from before we came to work here. I can take some time away."

June clasped his forearm and squeezed. "Promise me ye won't do nothing stupid."

He slanted a sly look at her, managed a watery grin. "I'd be lying to ye."

SHE WAS born Elena Ionesçu in Sighişoara twenty-four years before—to a Hungarian prostitute whose name she never knew—and abandoned before she turned five. A nurse had found her in an alley after anarchists had bombed a nearby building and brought her to an orphanage. It was a grim place, but Elena had found she had a knack for surviving. Nevertheless, she was determined to find a better life for herself, and to that end, she set about learning as much as she could.

Schooling was difficult for orphans. Four years of elementary school was followed by high school only for those who passed the proper exams, and most of the orphans never had the chance. That didn't stop Elena from breaking into high school classes after hours to plunder journals and newspapers in English that were used in language classes. English was the language she wanted to learn because the English-speaking world—America, Canada, the UK—seemed like the best places to live. She was good at mimicry as well, and she would shadow the tourists who visited the pretty parts of town and listen to them talk.

When she was seventeen, her chance finally came. A Canadian couple came to the orphanage looking for a child to adopt. The couple assumed she was a child of nine because of her diminutive size—the official diagnosis of dwarfism had never been recorded by the orphanage. The administrator and several of the board members felt it would lessen her chances of adoption, and so they kept her age a secret from anyone who showed an interest in her. "You are little," one of the workers told her, "so you can pretend to be a child, and no one will know the difference." It was a useful fiction.

Adopting a Romanian child takes time, and Elena had to be patient. She persuaded the staff to let her stay at the orphanage after she came of age by threatening to tell the authorities how they lied about her age. But the Canadian couple was as determined as she was, and eventually they took her home to Newfoundland.

It was wonderful at first, and Elena had plans to make it even better. They bought her pretty clothes, mostly yellow at her insistence, and treated her like a little doll. She had to go to school, which was terribly boring, and the other kids didn't like her. Kids sometimes saw through her disguise, but she didn't care what they thought, and they didn't bother her because they were all afraid of her.

Convinced Elena needed "counselling" because of her "traumatic early childhood," Professor Diver and his wife arranged for her to see a psychiatrist, a Dr. Fahey....

"Dr. Fahey?" Danny asked, interrupting her story for the first time. "The same Dr. Fahey who was found dismembered?"

"Yes. Him." She shifted in her chair. The late afternoon sun was shining in her eyes, and the handcuffs were too tight on her wrists, binding her to the table. Her clothing had been taken for forensic examination, and the white coverall suit she wore was much too large for her. She had resisted her arrest—violently—and a Chinese doctor had come from somewhere up the shore to administer a mild sedative. It made her groggy, as if she were swimming through mud, and made it hard to keep her eyes open and answer the questions the police were asking her. There were two of them in the room with her: the head cop, Danny, and a dark-haired woman with pretty eyes. The man asked most of the questions, but sometimes the woman spoke as well when she wanted Elena to clarify a certain point or provide more information.

"When I left the Divers," Elena went on—they didn't need to know about the drain cleaner—"and they brought me to Esther, I didn't see the doctor anymore."

"Why did you run away from Esther's home?" the pretty woman asked.

Elena shrugged. "Esther was an old bag, and all those other kids were screaming brats. None of them could possibly understand what I needed to live my life."

"What did you need?"

Elena gazed at her. The sun coming through the window lit up a halo around her head, like a holy picture. "I don't know," she answered truthfully. "I hope eventually I will find it out. I only know I have never had it."

"What was your relationship with Dr. Fahey?" Danny asked. She wondered why he kept talking about him.

"He was my doctor. He gave me medicine so I wouldn't feel so angry."

"What else?"

She struggled to remember. "He liked me to sit with him, on his lap."

The man and the woman exchanged a look. The woman glanced at Elena and then away.

"Did he hurt you?"

"It didn't hurt," Elena said. "Not after the first time, anyway." After the first time, she let him do whatever he wanted with her in exchange for more and better drugs. Drugs to help her forget, to blur the line between reality and fantasy until her memories of the orphanage might have been something she dreamt once, long ago. He had an idea what was wrong with her, he'd said, and he could fix it if she'd only grant him permission—permission and access to her body.

The dark-haired woman—June, her name was June; Elena remembered now—noted something down on a sheet of paper. "What about Tommy Power?" she asked. When Elena pretended not to know who this was, she added, "The old man we found in the woods with his throat cut. Was that your doing?" She opened a file folder on the desk in front of her and flipped through some papers, chose one and turned it so Elena could see it. It showed a picture of a small paring knife with a bright yellow handle. "This is the knife you used to attack Tadhg Heaney. Is it yours?"

"No. I took it from that old man." She remembered him particularly well. He was half insane, and he smelled bad, was prey to strange fits that made him walk in circles and cry for his mother. In Romania he would have been put away, but here they allowed such a creature to walk the streets unhindered. It had been a laugh, leading him into the woods, farther and farther from where he started, pretending to be a lost child and crying so pitifully. She was good at crying to get what she wanted, could well up with tears and weep so convincingly, all at a moment's notice.

If the tears didn't work, she'd taught herself to tremble like she was ill, shuddering violently all over, and that usually did the trick. The old man fell for it at once, trailing after her for many kilometres, stumbling through thick undergrowth and across treacherous bogs in her wake until she'd quite exhausted him. When it started to snow, she'd led him round in circles until he fell to his knees and begged her for rest.

She liked the old man. He reminded her of Piotr back home, who was also something of a simpleton, him and his retarded dog. Behind his back the others in the village threw stones at him, but Piotr never complained, merely turned and made the sign of the cross. As if they wanted a blessing from someone like him. It had been such good fun.

"Took it after you killed him," Danny said. Elena decided she liked Danny, even if he had gotten in her way. Everything he said had a ring of truth to it. He spoke whatever he was thinking in a forthright manner.

"I didn't kill him." She smiled, remembering. "He was wandering in the woods, and I decided to have a little fun with him."

"*Fun* with him?" June seemed outraged by this. "What sort of fun?"

"Oh, I led him a long way from home. We had a merry dance, the old man and I." It pleased her to recall it. He was such a slobbering old fool. "He killed himself, cut his throat, but I wanted the knife for my own. I told him if he was going to do it, he had best hurry up and get it over with, and he did." She flexed her fingers. The cuffs were making her hands numb. She clasped her fingers together, as if in prayer. The sun coming through the windows was warm now on her face. It felt like spring. It wasn't so bad, being here, although she wished they would take the handcuffs off. Why wouldn't they? "I kept the knife. It's such a pretty knife, don't you think? I liked the yellow handle."

The dark-haired woman reclaimed the picture of the knife, put it back into her folder. Elena asked politely if they had any further questions for her.

"I think that's everything—" June started to say, but she was interrupted by Danny.

"What about Deborah Harris?" He fixed her with his bright blue eyes. Such beautiful eyes! Why would such beautiful eyes be wasted on a man? "Deborah Coyle was her maiden name. Were you involved in her death?"

Elena pretended to think about it for a long moment, opening her mouth as if to say something, then closing it again. She regarded the surface of the table in front of her, its top made to look like wood, and the thin layer of dust recently deposited on it from the to-and-fro passage of files and paper. They had gone to a lot of trouble to establish her guilt, and perhaps she'd already told them far more than they needed to know, but it was immensely satisfying. She liked Kildevil Cove. She'd had a very good time here. She'd be sorry to leave it.

"I don't know who that is," she said finally. "I'm sorry. I don't know that name." She gazed at them, deliberately emptying her face of all expression. "I hope you liked my presents, though, the yellow ribbons? Sometimes people do that, don't they? Tie a yellow ribbon somewhere it can be seen, to invite the lost or missing to return."

"Is that what you were doing?" Danny asked. "Inviting the missing to return?"

She slid her gaze away, focused on the window high up in the wall. A patch of bright blue sky was visible amidst a bank of darkness. There was always weather, yes, but there was brightness too, and hope. "Sometimes it's an invitation to leave and never return."

If he wondered what she meant by that, he wasn't asking. No doubt he thought her yellow ribbons held some exotic clue to this entire situation, but he was wrong. They were just ribbons. Yellow was her favourite colour.

"Elena Ionesçu," Danny said. "I am charging you with aiding and abetting a suicide in the death of Thomas Power and the attempted murder of Tadhg Heaney. You will be remanded in custody at Harbour Grace until your trial." Danny reached across and shut off the tape recorder, then got up and opened the door. Two police constables came in to escort Elena out. One of them was the younger sandy-haired man she'd brought to the Harvesters' cottage that night when she'd found him, the night he'd been fornicating with the American in a vehicle. Disgusting. The American, she'd heard, had killed himself. No doubt that was why the young policeman looked the way he did. She smiled at him as she went by. She wanted him to know God would eventually forgive him for his sins.

God eventually forgave everyone. Even her.

"DO YOU think she killed Deborah?" June asked Danny, once Elena had left the room. She looked shaken by the things Elena had revealed in the interview.

"Sergeant Riley seems to think Dr. Fahey's medicine killed Deborah." He told June about Riley's theory—that Deborah's judgement was impaired the day she wandered into the forest after the fight with Azariah. She'd stumbled upon a sect of Harvesters who'd given her alcohol to drink. The alcohol, coupled with her chronic ayahuasca and *Amanita* poisoning, had likely induced hallucinations. She'd gouged her own eye out and died of exposure, much too far from home.

"We'll have to let Azariah go," Danny said. He shook his head. "What a fucking mess."

"But what about the conspiracy charges?" June asked. She paused at the door to the break room. "D'ye fancy a brew?"

"God, yes," Danny said. "I'd murder for one. You making it?"

"I will, yes." She moved to push the door open. "Milk, no sugar?"

"Thanks, June." Danny grinned at her. "Next time I'll make one for you."

"You will, then." She winked at him. "I'll bring it down to your office."

"There's no way in God's green earth we'll be able to prove conspiracy against Azariah. Any defence lawyer will rip it to shreds in court. Best not to waste the taxpayers' money on a trial."

"I feel sorry for Deborah," June said. "Getting hooked up with someone like him. I mean…." She glanced around to see if they were indeed alone. "Kevin and I were brought up religious. Really religious. Hard-core Pentecostal with all the nutty trimmings. It… does things to your mind. Azariah seems cut from the same cloth. And her coming from town, marrying someone like him?" She shook her head, her dark hair swirling about her face like feathers. "It's a damn sin what she went through."

"You sound like you're speaking from personal experience," Danny said.

"I am, sir." Her face clouded. "I am." She nodded to him and went into the break room.

Danny didn't usually lock his office door, seeing as how their station was comprised of himself, Kevin and June, Cillian Riley, a couple of other constables, and the forensics officers. There was simply no need, because he knew everyone who worked with him and trusted them implicitly. Whatever he left on his desk tended to remain undisturbed, so he was surprised to see a bouquet of out-of-season sunflowers—his favourite flower—lying next to a bottle of Loch Lomond. The small card attached to the flowers read, *Always remember that I love you—Tadhg.*

He reached for his phone and dialled Tadhg's mobile. "Are you looking to score points?" he teased when Tadhg answered.

"Don't know what you're talking about," Tadhg countered, laughing. "Are you high or something?"

"Thank you," Danny said. "I really appreciate it."

"Figured you could use it, after the week you've had," Tadhg said. "The work on the building site is going well, by the way, and thanks for asking."

Danny laughed. It felt good, after everything. "You're a saucy bugger today, aren't you?"

"Come by the site after work," Tadhg said, "and see what we're after doing with the place. I could even spend the night with ye, if ye're so inclined." He paused. "You're still going to marry me, aren't ye?"

"I might," Danny said teasingly, "and I might not. Ye'll have to wait and find out."

Tadhg made an irritated noise. "Good thing I loves ye," he said.

"I loves you too. Bye now." Danny disconnected, still smiling. He glanced up, and his gaze fell on Kevin Carbage, standing by the door, his hand raised to knock. "Oh."

"I wonder if you'd consider signing this, sir." Kevin stepped inside, a sheet of paper in his hand. "It's a leave of absence request." His face was expressionless, but Danny was reasonably sure he'd heard every word of his phone conversation.

"Kevin, we should talk." He stood and tried to usher the younger man into his office, but Kevin stayed where he was.

"I don't believe there's anything to talk about, sir."

The man you loved is dead. There's plenty to talk about.

"Could you just sign this, sir? That would be the best thing." Kevin held the form towards him. "If you're too busy, I can ask Chief Inspector Fraser if she'll do it."

"I'll do it." Danny reached out and took the sheet from him. He glanced over it before signing his name at the bottom. "How long do you think you'll be gone, Kevin?"

"Not sure, sir. Three months, probably. I haven't thought that far ahead." He couldn't or wouldn't look Danny in the eye.

"Going to be hard to get along without you around here."

"I have a signed doctor's note if that helps."

Danny sighed. "Ye're not going to give me an inch, are ye?" He handed back the form. "Kevin, will you…? If you need to talk, I'm here. That's off the record, by the way. Just friends, is all."

"Thank you, sir. I'll clean out my desk." And he was gone.

Danny watched him go, wondering if he'd done enough for Kevin during his time with them. Maybe the constable would never come back, and that would be a shame. Danny had barely gotten to know him. Surely there was something he could say or do to ease Kevin's burden.

"Sir?" Cillian Riley appeared in the doorway. "I've just been talking to Regan Lampe—Dr. Lampe. She's completed the autopsy on Mr. Maddox. They found high levels of *Amanita* and ayahuasca in his blood. She thinks he'd been dosing himself with it after he killed Fahey."

It made sense…. Maybe it was Ford's way of coping with a horrific situation. But in the end, it wasn't enough.

"I see," Danny said.

"He'd some of it done up in teabags," Riley said. "Must have been taking it on the daily, like."

"Teabags?" Ford had given him tea that day Danny brought him in for questioning. Danny had suspected Ford had put something in the tea. Now he knew what it was. Hell of a thing to do to a friend.

"Yes, sir."

"Thanks, Cillian. I owe you a beer."

"No worries." Riley laid a file folder down on Danny's desk. "I just wanted to give you the highlights. The complete report's in here. He'd been paying Fahey thousands of dollars for some time now—more than Fahey's fees for his other patients. I couldn't find any reason for it. We may never know." He laid a small envelope down beside the folder. "We recovered this from the house. It's got your name on it."

Danny waited until Riley had gone before picking it up. There was nothing written on it besides his name on the front. The envelope was wrinkled at the corners and still bore traces of the black fingerprint powder Bobbi Lambert's forensics team had used in Ford's house. Was this Ford's suicide note? Was it a confession?

Riley's report on Fahey's death indicated the killing was a silent, military-style execution, a single knife thrust to the back of the head that made mincemeat of the brain's medulla oblongata, shutting the brain and body down. Ford had been a U.S. Marine, with a Marine's knowledge of killing and a Ka-Bar combat knife that Riley's team had found in his bedside drawer. Lambert had tested it for blood, but the results were inconclusive. Ford had probably scrubbed it with bleach, the surest way of destroying blood evidence. Someone who knew how to kill might also know how to cover it up.

Maybe, as Danny had suspected, Fahey had been blackmailing Ford; all the evidence pointed that way. Likely that's why Ford had killed him. Psychiatrists encouraged their patients to tell them everything, even things they'd never want to see the light of day. The ethical ones kept it to themselves, but Fahey clearly hadn't been within shouting distance of ethical.

Danny opened the envelope, drew out the single piece of paper, and read the message.

I'm Sorry.

That was all it said. It told him everything at once… and absolutely nothing.

CHAPTER TWELVE

SHE COULD have done this over the phone and saved herself the journey. She could have put the bracelet in the mail, except that would have been wildly irresponsible. The thing was worth several thousand dollars. An astonishing waste of money, really, when she'd never had any intention of wearing it. He should have known better.

She found him bent over a set of draughtsman's drawings in the old stable on the hill. He was exactly as he'd been all those years ago, except his once-dark hair had mellowed to a glossy silver, and instead of a fancy leather jacket and designer trousers, he was wearing jeans and a flannel work shirt, his hard hat resting nearby on a bench. He was exactly as he'd been, and he was completely different. She wished they'd been able to have a quiet word the night she showed up to tend to his daughter on Eigus. That might have allowed her to put some things to rest.

"Tadhg."

He glanced up, looked surprised to see her. "Regan. I'd no idea you were coming. It's good to see y—"

She cut him off, taking the bracelet out of her purse and handing it across to him. "I wanted to give this back to you. It's lovely, but I couldn't possibly keep it. It wouldn't be right."

He took it, holding it in his hand and looking at it. "There are absolutely no strings attached. You know that. I just wanted to say thank you."

She nodded. "And now you've said it." She turned to go.

"And I wanted to say I'm sorry for what happened with—" He swallowed, throat muscles rippling. "—with our baby." He was still standing by the bench, hadn't moved an inch towards her, which piqued her a little bit. After all these years, she'd have thought he might have some feeling left for her, but obviously she was wrong. "I didn't forget," he continued. "Don't ever think I did."

"It was my fault as much as yours. I didn't bother to tell you about the baby. By the time you knew, it was too late." She shrugged. "Couldn't be helped." She heard the note of bitterness underneath her words and hated herself for it. "Neither of us would have made a good parent, Tadhg. Not back then. It wasn't meant to be." And him showing up to the hospital then, stinking of the drink, clutching a ragged bouquet of flowers he'd probably bought at a service station on the highway, pretending love and humility.

"My God, why ever didn't ye tell me? I'm pure gutted I am, you knows I am."

How could he have been gutted by the loss of their stillborn child when he hadn't even known of her existence? She, Regan, had known better than to tell him. Tadhg Heaney wasn't the kind of man to make a lifetime commitment, not to her or anyone. She wondered if Danny Quirke knew what he was letting himself in for, throwing in his lot with this one.

"I'd like us to be friends," he said. He put the bracelet in the pocket of his jeans.

"I don't think so." She tucked her purse underneath her arm. "I don't need friends like you."

"I've changed, you know," he said. "I'm not like that anymore. I'm not."

Regan turned on her heels and went—out the door, down the hill, past the burned spot on the ground where the old house had stood and the remnants of Eleazar Quirke's front gate, into her car, and away.

AS PROMISED, Danny stopped by his grandfather's land to view Tadhg's progress. Tadhg seemed a little distracted at first, but he soon rallied and talked enthusiastically about the work. Later that same evening, Danny and Tadhg had a quiet dinner together at Danny's house. Lily had recovered from her spring cold and was spending the night with her friend Gemma, who had a new golden retriever puppy. "Her name's Snap, Dad, and she's so friggin' smart. Can we get one?"

"I'll see," Tadhg had told her. "Mind out, I'm not makin' no promises." Danny knew he'd already arranged with a breeder on the

Southern Shore to purchase a pup for Lily. The new addition to their household would be an unexpected present.

"Hard to imagine new life and rebirth in the midst of all this," Danny observed, sitting back in his chair. Tadhg had cooked scallops in a white wine sauce with rice pilaf, but Danny had barely done justice to the delicious meal.

"I know, my love." Tadhg reached across with the wine bottle and refilled Danny's glass. "For a small place, there's a hell of a lot going on, most of it not good." He topped up his own wine and pushed his plate away. "Is it horrible to say I'm not surprised about Ford?"

Danny glanced at him sharply. "Why do you say that?"

"D'ye remember how he was at university?" Tadhg swirled the wine in his glass. The amber liquid caught the light of the candles they'd placed on the table and reflected it around the room in a rippling kaleidoscope pattern. "There was this... sadness about him." He paused for a moment, considering. "Lily's friends say so-and-so has a 'resting bitch face.' I think it means they look angry even when they aren't." He gazed at Danny across the table. "Ford always had resting sad face. Even when he seemed to be happy, I always got the feeling that he wasn't... that he couldn't possibly be."

"Clinical depression?" Danny asked. It was an illness he knew all too well, his own personal *bête noire*, his nemesis. He'd once spent time in the Waterford Hospital, before his psychiatrist got the dosage right on his medication.

"More than that," Tadhg replied. "I always thought of him as self-destructive. You know, most dealers don't sample their own product, but Ford, he never met a drug he didn't like. He was heavy into the psychedelics for a while."

"What, recently?"

"I ran into him last year down on George Street. He was fucking wasted," Tadhg said. He finished the last of his wine and stood up. "It's still sad, though." He nodded at Danny's plate. "You hardly touched your dinner."

"It was really good," Danny said, "but I haven't got any appetite. Sorry." He reached up and touched Tadhg's bicep. "How's the arm feeling? Still sore?"

"Not too bad. That saucy young bugger did an excellent job of stitching me up. Seems to be healing nicely." Tadhg reached down to take Danny's plate. "Bath?"

"God love ye," Danny replied. He wandered into the kitchen and watched Tadhg scrape the leftovers into the bin under the kitchen sink.

Tadhg slotted their two plates into the dishwasher and straightened up. He came to where Danny was and wrapped his arms around him. "Don't you ever do anything like that to me." He stepped back and tilted Danny's face up, two fingers under his chin. "Promise."

"Promise," Danny whispered. "That goes double for you."

"Cross me heart and hope to not die," Tadhg said. "Now, let's get that tub filled."

Danny went upstairs and undressed while Tadhg started the bath going in the big Jacuzzi. How on earth the reno team had managed to muscle a two-person Jacuzzi onto the second floor of a traditional saltbox house was beyond him, but he was glad of it. He was even more glad when he went into the bathroom and saw the thing brimming over with bubbles and Tadhg waiting in the hot water with a bottle of Glenfiddich and two glasses.

"Come here," Tadhg said, "I loves ye."

Danny sank into the tub, moving to sit with his back against Tadhg's chest. Tadhg deftly poured two fingers of whisky into a glass and offered it. "Thanks," Danny said. He took a sip, savouring the warm burn it made on the way down. "I needed this."

"Me too," Tadhg said. "Ye've been so busy lately I never see ye." He leaned down and placed his lips against Danny's bare shoulder. "Dan, you've got to let go of it." He laid his glass on the small shelf beside the tub and wrapped his arms around Danny's waist. "Ye're torturing yourself. I know you are. I can practically feel your brain churning away at it."

"We knew him," Danny said. "You and me, Tadhg. He was somebody we knew." Like his friend Leon Brazil, who'd shot himself after an armed confrontation gone wrong, and Danny the one who found him. Suicide didn't end the pain, Danny thought. It just passed it on to someone else.

"Did ye look at it?" Tadhg asked. "The picture young handsome gave you"—Tadhg had taken to calling Cillian Riley 'young handsome'— "the one Ford left."

"It's in my coat pocket." He hadn't forgotten it. On the contrary. Given the opportunity, he'd leave it there for good. "I suppose I should look at it."

"No rush." Tadhg's arm tightened around his waist. "Look at it when you're ready."

"It still won't tell me for sure why he did it."

They were silent for a few moments; then Tadhg said, "He was seeing Dr. Fahey, wasn't he?"

"Yeah, he was. Him and his son, and a lot of other people." Connections swirled in Danny's head, but he was too tired to make sense of them all. "You know, I think Fahey is at the centre of a lot of what's been going on around here. Deborah Coyle was seeing him. Ford and his son were seeing him, even the girl—woman—who attacked you." He turned to look at Tadhg. "Why did Ford kill him, though? What did he know that Ford couldn't live with him knowing? To stab somebody in the back of the head like that, it's... so personal."

Tadhg caressed Danny's cheek with the backs of his knuckles. "I don't know, love. Try and not think about it for right now, hm? Ye've got to learn to leave work at the office, Danny. Ye're a bugger for taking everything on your own shoulders." He started to say something else but obviously thought better of it.

"He was my friend," Danny said and felt tears welling up again. He didn't fight it, but gave in to it, let himself cry in Tadhg's arms while the water cooled around them both. Later, when his grief had burned itself out, Tadhg took him to bed and laid him down, made love to him gently, until he could sleep.

J.S. COOK was born and raised on the rugged, wind-swept island of Newfoundland in the North Atlantic Ocean. Her earliest published work was "The Magic Elf," printed in the local newspaper when she was eight years old. This incited an unquenchable thirst for literary notoriety that resulted in novels ranging from literary and historical to steampunk to moody atmospheric crime. The inspiration for her crime fiction often comes from real cases both modern and historical. To aid her research and ensure forensic accuracy, she designs and conducts her own experiments.

J.S. Cook holds a BA (Honours), an MA, and a B.Ed., all from Memorial University. She teaches English and Communications at the College of the North Atlantic. Along with her husband, Paul, and their 'dogter,' Lola, she divides her time between St. John's and Corner Brook, Newfoundland. Many of her books are set in Newfoundland and are written in a powerfully descriptive style that borrows heavily from the Newfoundland landscape, geography, and weather.

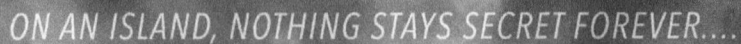

ON AN ISLAND, NOTHING STAYS SECRET FOREVER....

DARK WATER

A KILDEVIL COVE MURDER MYSTERY

J.S. COOK

A Kildevil Cove Murder Mystery

They say trouble comes in threes. Detective Danny Quirke is already mourning his wife and mired in an internal investigation that will likely spell the end of his career. Now he must return to the Newfoundland fishing village of his youth to bury his abusive grandfather. At least his three are up. Right?

Then the bones of local boy Llewellyn Single, drowned thirty years before, wash up on the beach, and secrets Danny thought were buried forever rise violently to the surface. Only two people know what really happened: Danny Quirke and his former best friend, millionaire Tadhg Heaney.

Danny and Tadhg have been bitter enemies for years. But when Danny is accused of Llewellyn's murder, he needs Tadhg's help exposing the truth—before those who believe he is responsible get their revenge.

After all, on an island, nothing stays secret forever....

www.dsppublications.com

J.S. COOK

BECAUSE YOU
DESPISE ME

When Feldwebel Horst Stussel is murdered in Jake Plenty's Moroccan brothel, local police chief Nicolas Renard suspects Jake's involvement in the crime. Renard has loved Jake since their service in the Legion Etrangère during the Great War, but in this era of concentration camps, gas chambers, and the infamous pink triangle, his love for the American dare not speak its name.

When sadistic Nazi officer Major Danzig, a fanatic who excels at the arts of torture and interrogation, comes to Maarif, it isn't because of the Feldwebel. He is in search of Christophe Picard, Resistance leader and Jake's former lover. Danzig will stop at nothing to uncover Picard's whereabouts, to find him and destroy him, and in so doing, strike a fatal blow against everything Picard stands for.

With an Allied invasion of North Africa mere days away, Jake and Renard must combine their wits, cunning, and courage to help Picard escape to America and freedom. In the midst of war and struggle, the two men are drawn into the fight of the century—and each other's arms.

www.dsppublications.com

For more
great fiction
from

DSP PUBLICATIONS

visit us online.
WWW.DSPPUBLICATIONS.COM